The PHOENIX

The crowd turned as a slim woman slid through the store's rear wall. She wore a jet-black battle-suit, running as a seamless piece of armor from the boots on her feet to a shiny, featureless helmet encasing her head. The intruder carried no weapons but exuded menace and grace. The unknown newcomer stalked through the crowd, headed for the Kid.

"Do I know you?" he said. "I don't believe I'd head-mailed you an access key, athletic, sexy stranger?"

She tapped the side of her expressionless helmet. "My key is in here."

Horrified and helpless, Kid Omega tried to wake up, to abandon his construct for the physical plane, but found his psyche stuck fast and unable to move, as if trapped like a fly in amber. He was unable to return to his body or stop the mysterious woman standing with him on the psionic plane from reaching out to grab his throat.

More X-Men Adventure

MARVEL SCHOOL OF X

THE PHOENIX CHASE

NEIL KLEID

ACONYTE

FOR MARVEL PUBLISHING

VP Production & Special Projects: Jeff Youngquist
Editor, Special Projects: Sarah Singer
Manager, Licensed Publishing: Jeremy West
VP, Licensed Publishing: Sven Larsen
SVP Print, Sales & Marketing: David Gabriel
Editor in Chief: C B Cebulski

First published by Aconyte Books in 2023

ISBN 978 1 83908 208 5

Ebook ISBN 978 1 83908 209 2

Cover art by Christina Myrvold

Distributed in North America by Simon & Schuster Inc, New York, USA
Printed in the United States of America
9 8 7 6 5 4 3 2 1

ACONYTE BOOKS

An imprint of Asmodee Entertainment Ltd

Mercury House, Shipstones Business Centre

North Gate, Nottingham NG7 7FN, UK

aconytebooks.com // twitter.com/aconytebooks

This one's for Stan, Jack, Arnold, Don, Neal, Grant, Frank and especially Dave

PROLOGUE

[HEROES COURT | CENTRAL METROCENTER | NEW D'BARI | SPACE]

Powerful hands dragged the hero across the square.

He struggled in their armored, contracting grip. His own battle-suit fractured against the broken pavement as thousands of D'Bari stared at him from parapets, shrinking in fear from the sweeping, impassive gaze of the hero's tormentors.

There were five of them, dressed in intimidating, gleaming uniforms, narrow helmets hiding their faces from view. They carried no weapons and made little noise. One of the invaders – larger than the rest – lifted the D'Bari hero by an arm, hauling him bodily and scraping his once-pristine armor against the ground. The servomotors in the hero's jet boots shattered as the other four assailants followed them across the court.

Above loomed an unfamiliar warship. Massive, it bristled with cannons and blocked out the midday sun. The attack had been swift and devastating. Central MetroCenter now lay in ruins, hundreds of lifeless D'Bari strewn around the plaza like broken toys, exterminated during the invaders' initial volley.

Defiant, the hero tried one more escape, augmenting the radius of his armor's shields in an effort to throw off his captors. A shuddering pulse vibrated outward from the shattered battle-suit… but had very little effect. The mammoth being that towed him to the center of the square stopped and looked down, taking note of the pitiful creature struggling in its grip. The invader's chest hitched, as if it had laughed. The hero's suit was far too damaged – the carapace broken, its shields too weak – to prove a threat. All the D'Bari had accomplished was further harm to the rubble beneath his feet.

The hero exhaled, breath rattling against his chest. He fell limp. His gargantuan captor silently resumed its task, carrying its beaten charge out to the great Starhammer Monument waiting at the center of Heroes Court.

The other four invaders met them at the monument – a beautifully carved, stoic representation depicting the D'Bari hero in native stone. Eyes to the horizon, the monument's central figure lifted an arm in triumph, grasping an impressively carved broadsword by the base of its sculpted blade. The imposing Starhammer's other hand, clasped in a fist, was thrust out in warning to any who might threaten those the hero would deign to protect. But the five obsidian raiders paid it no heed. Working in tandem, they strapped their prey to the monument's leg, releasing the hero to let him slump forward, his crippled boots scrabbling for purchase along steps that encircled the statue's base.

One of the raiders – male and tall, green D'Bari blood staining his otherwise polished, expressionless helmet – leaned down to grab the hero's throat. The raider spoke quickly, a greasy, sibilant voice querying the battered captive. The D'Bari hero understood both the question and, of course, the language. Most did who inhabited this galactic sector. The translation discs within his demolished Starhammer armor would hardly be necessary. Still, he would not provide the satisfaction of an easy answer.

The interrogator's clawed fingers constricted. The hero choked.

"Where?" asked the raider again. "Where did you battle the–?" This last word was one the hero didn't recognize. The word was oily and unfamiliar to his ears, uncommon and unaccustomed to the being's mother tongue. The weakened Starhammer armor struggled to provide a more recognizable translation, the result of which widened the hero's eyes in astonishment.

"Where?" the interrogator asked for a third time, tightening his grip. "Where did you last face it, D'Bari? Your cosmic aura – your psychic imprint – called from across a tapestry of stars. You have battled our prey, you retain its stink... the scent. Tell us now where it is. Where did you last see an Egg?"

The hero coughed as he laughed through the pain. He closed his dry, swollen eyes. Yes, he remembered. The memory was ever-dear, the reason he'd finally achieved contentment and purpose on this peaceful little world, among those he'd saved from extinction – his people, these last of the D'Bari... those who would resurrect the world they'd lost. Yes, he knew the entity these monsters sought, a demon itself. A blight upon the cosmos. And he, the hero of New D'Bari, the first – nearly last – and best of his kind, had obliterated it from the universe.

"Egg? I faced no... no mere Egg. But I did ensure its death," the hero sputtered through a mouthful of fluid, sprung from some ruptured organ deep inside his gut. "It no longer exists," he announced to his tormentors with glee, taking solace in the fact that no being residing here or across the cosmos would again suffer their target's malicious whims.

The interrogator loosened his grip and beckoned to a second raider, a slim woman who shouldered through her fellows, coming to a stop at the hero's feet.

He laughed, trying to stand as the new arrival presumably stared into his eyes.

"You are too late, my friends. What you seek, the behemoth you hunt... I killed it! Me, yes... the Starhammer – Vuk, greatest of all D'Bari, hero to all." His boots scraped against the crumbling stairs, voice straining to be heard by those gathered and listening, gazing down at their savior in Heroes Court.

"I tracked the devil and battled its host, wiping the threat from existence. I am an avenger! A protector! Victorious, I gathered the remains of my people – all whom the monster had not snuffed away – and brought them here to New D'Bari to continue our lives, finally in peace." Vuk spat a glob of verdant paste from bruised lips and labored to gesture, to indicate the thousands of openmouthed D'Bari watching their beaten champion with hopeful sorrow.

"Our world... our days... we spend them now in celebration, in joyous remembrance of those decimated by the Great Devourer. The very being I destroyed in righteous vengeanc–"

"The D'Bari is lying."

Vuk froze. The woman stepped back to join her compatriots, nodding to the other four in quiet confirmation.

"Lying? How dare you!" Vuk bristled at the matter-of-fact accusation. "I was there, interloper. You were not! By my word as Starhammer, I promise you this: I pursued the ravenous beast to–"

"To Earth, yes." She finished his sentence, revealing their destination. "Vuk's memory is cloudy, but the imprint does not lie. They clashed upon the astral plane, but only a host was found, like on the other worlds. As suspected. Not an Egg itself... as I had assured you when first insisting on this ridiculous distraction. There is no other Egg. And though Vuk faced it, he was hardly triumphant. He was fooled and would be little use to our purpose."

The five invaders turned away, circling in conversation beyond the monument's steps. Vuk tried to stand again, but his feet were bleeding, and shards of metal – flaking from the broken armor – dug into his legs.

"Flark it all," the male raider snarled, oily voice doing nothing to betray his impassive, hidden face. "Fine, you were right. So, now what?"

"To Earth, as I mentioned. I had already foreseen our next steps and our optimal target."

"Him? We'll never get near him. That one has a keen eye."

The woman laughed. "Amusing. But no, we'll need an emissary of a type. Someone to approach him. Thankfully, I have–"

"Hey." Vuk endeavored to regain their attention. The five assailants seemed to have dismissed him as either a threat or prize, visibly ignoring the hero as they contemplated among themselves. "I know what you seek, and I am telling you – I killed the Phoenix!"

Five helmets silently gazed down upon the indignant, embattled D'Bari hero lying at the base of his own monument.

After a moment, each of them laughed, a collection of rattling cackles that pierced Vuk's soul.

"You deceive yourself, D'Bari," the female raider pronounced, sweeping an ebon gauntlet out to indicate the astonished crowd, "as you do your people. Yes, you met consuming flame in battle, but were gulled by its host. The entity cannot be killed."

Vuk's jaw hung agape, staring at the pompous raider. "You... you are trying to mislead me. To tarnish my reputation and turn these people against their hero—"

"To what purpose? You are beaten. We already own your truth."

"The Phoenix is dead!"

The raider shook her head. "Only a vessel. And your victory against even that one was no more than a cruel mirage."

Vuk slumped upon the steps. "No... but I... she... the mutant died at my hands..."

The woman bent her knees, hunkering to Vuk's level.

"Eventually. But not at your hands. She was a legend. But even legends are no more than a memory. Her remaining bloodline – that of her genetic code – was foolishly extinguished. But that which the code hosted... the glorious entity that made her a threat... endures, as always."

Vuk stared into the raider's glossy helm, seeking eyes behind the armor but only finding his own discouraged, hopeless reflection.

"If I could not destroy the Phoenix, with all the power of the D'Bari and years of planning at my disposal, then the five of you don't stand a chance."

His enemy laughed again, an unctuous, grating chuckle. "Destroy it? Oh, D'Bari. We Remaining have no intention of witnessing the destruction of the Phoenix. In fact, we will soon celebrate its glorious rebirth."

The raider got to her feet and rejoined her fellows.

"Come," she said to the others. "As discussed, we shall find what we require on Terra."

They turned to leave. Lost, drowning in his failures, Vuk allowed a scream to emerge from his strained, anguished throat.

"You said the host is dead! Jean Grey is dead. You will not find a Phoenix Egg on Earth!"

The raider turned back to the vanquished hero – and by the tone of her voice, a horrified Vuk imagined a dangerous smile and salacious wink beneath the polished mask. "No, we won't. Yes, the Grey line has been eradicated. That particular host will be of little help.

"Thankfully, she is hardly the last."

CHAPTER ONE

[QUENTIN | THE OMEGA SHOP | THE PSIONIC PLANE | EARTH]

Thirty teenagers grooved and danced in a cavernous pink store.

A diverse playlist – a healthy mix of synth-pop, heavy metal, and hip-hop – echoed throughout the space, rhythms nearly as varied as the kids circulating and chatting inside the temperate, coral, vibrating chamber.

There were T-shirts for sale by the walls. Blank and black, they were carefully folded and stacked upon six-foot tables hovering above the floor, artfully dotted around the hip, attractive pop-up shop. Logos and slogans blurred and reappeared upon the shirts to the delight of the browsing clientele, many of whom (after a quick, contactless exchange of funds) slapped a hand upon a particular design only to find it reflected on an identical blank shirt that had magically appeared upon their own chest. Like the shirts, murals morphed along the walls, randomly displaying a mix of motifs, revolutionary imagery, and irreverent cartoons. No refreshments could be found, nor was there a single door or window. Smiling, laughing shoppers – a wide range of genders and body types, some boring, drab, and humanoid and others sporting more unusual, specific, and wondrous mutations – instantaneously vanished and arrived through no marked egress, curious to explore the shop and happy to mingle with friends, lovers, strangers, and colleagues.

At the center of this bustling pink whirlwind of both commerce and entertainment sat a smirking, gangling teenager in a low-slung hover chair that hid one of his legs from view. The other leg was draped over the top of the chair (bare, peeking out from stylish gabardine shorts, the foot encased in a black sock and shocking pink shoe), where an array of viewports and dials hung before him, spread out and arranged for easy access. From here, the teen could survey his work and manipulate controls from which he might regulate the music, temperature, shirt or wall designs, and also restrict or provide access to the shop itself.

The teenager smiled through pouty lips and adjusted his glasses – a pair of sparkly pink shades, matching his short, single strip of fuchsia-colored hair. He toggled a dial, rotating the walls like spinning music. A previously displayed violent cartoon was suddenly replaced by a salmon-tinged tableau upon which heroes of the mutant community were led into battle by the pop-up's owner, creator, and key instigator: the kid in the chair, one curiously named Quintavius Quirinius "Quentin" Quire, known to a few cherished friends and many (many!) more key detractors by his preferred sobriquet, Kid Omega.

Quentin was a mutant, as were those patronizing his shop. Each of them possessed the "X-Gene"– a genetic trait that at puberty provided its bearer either superhuman powers, cosmetic deformities, or both. Often referred to by the Latin Homo sapiens superior – or simply Homo superior – mutants were considered the next stage in human evolution, despite the fact that the majority of them were hounded, persecuted, and feared by their intolerant, non-powered human cousins. Some mutants could fly or manipulate energy types. Some possessed great strength, speed and agility, the ability to lift objects or perceive thoughts using the force of their mind. Those were the lucky few. Others, unfortunately, exhibited abnormal physical qualities, most of which would be considered grotesque by human and mutant alike. Mutation was a coin toss: one side could lead to fantastic abilities and the envy of peers, while the other potentially led to shame, revulsion, and an innate desire to hide from the world.

Kid Omega, thankfully, gravitated to both kinds of mutants. He himself possessed a growing array of marvelous talents but also knew what shame and revulsion felt like inside, having grappled with self-loathing early in – and then sporadically throughout – his brief but evolving career. As a result, the few the Kid actually thought of as friends were a mix of mutants deemed by society (both humanity and mutantkind) as both beautiful and ugly. Despite often having terrible opinions too big to fit inside his constantly flapping mouth, he treated those dear to him with fierce, albeit sarcastic, loyalty.

It was difficult for the Kid to make friends. He wasn't what one might call "likable," and to some he was downright irritating. His personal history had been riddled with missteps – several considered criminal to a conservative society – and Quentin had always struggled with the value of forming connections and making friends... or at the very least, doing what he could to not drive people away. He didn't have a lot of admirers or pals, but those he did (the ones he found he was able to tolerate) were some of his favorite mutants. And here in his impossible, pink, psionic pop-up shop – a store he'd built entirely in his own head – surrounded by all kinds of mutants both fashionable and hapless, Quentin Quire's closest friends were oft put on a level that befit his own: that of Omega.

As an Omega-level mutant, Quentin possessed a power of which the upper limit could not be registered. The strut in his walk and gleam in his eyes reminded folks that there were only a handful of Omega-level talents on the planet. For the Kid, whose abilities were as varied and awesome as his T-shirts, his Omega gift was telepathy – the ability to read another's thoughts. Sure, Homo sapiens superior could manifest several mutations, but only one could really be classified as an Omega gift. But because he never settled for less than the best, with the help of teachers (many reluctant) and using his swole, underestimated intelligence, the Kid had managed to spin that ability into a catalog of useful psychic tools.

Kid Omega (a name he'd adopted to call attention to the aforementioned vaunted level) had also learned to harness telekinesis, the power to move objects via non-physical means, paving the way for personal levitation and flight. He could shape his telepathy into a deadly construct, able to attack others with the power of his mind. And most recently, thanks to the tutelage of an equally impressive instructor, Quentin had learned to expand that talent: he could now build psychokinetic spaces into which the minds of others might enter, moving about it as if in a physical location… like his psionic store, the Omega Shop, in which he and his friends were currently gathered.

The ability was new and still difficult to maintain (even now, the edges of the room wobbled, and he had to mentally push himself to keep the structure intact). No one in the shop was physically present; they were all mentally projected into the Kid's carefully curated space, gaining access via individualized telepathic verification codes. The effort to maintain the construct and keep tabs on multiple, specific psychic patterns was causing Quentin strain… but the minor headache would be worth it in the end. Even now, like always, Kid Omega had a plan.

Twisting some dials, he lowered the music and rotated the various messages displayed upon his guests' intangible shirts. Each of his handcrafted hot takes vanished from their chests, and a single maxim reappeared: KID OMEGA WAS RIGHT, emblazoned beneath a smirking headshot of Quentin himself. Everyone laughed. It was a clever take on a familiar message, the words "was right" usually preceded by a popular Homo superior revolutionary, some of whom stood at the helm of notable mutant schools, two of which were home to the teens in attendance, including the Kid.

The Jean Grey School for Higher Learning was a school for squares and narcs. Located on a posh bougie Westchester estate, it was headed by Wolverine, an irritating Canadian with claws and unbreakable bones. Also? Wolverine was old. Like, really old. So old that… forget Gen X; Wolvie was Gen A. Then there was the Charles Xavier School for Mutants, colloquially known as the Xavier Institute. Chuck Xavier was mutantkind's original dreamer, a kindly professor-type who'd died hoping mutants and humans would one day coexist. His namesake school boasted several headmasters, most prominently Charley's first and favorite student, codenamed Cyclops (Also? He was Charley's accidental murderer. But more on that later, maybe.) Along with some others, Cyclops steered the ship that was the Institute, located in a Canadian hole in the ground (What was the fascination with Canada in mutant circles? Frankly, the Kid preferred LA), a former military installation, a far cry from a snazzy, tastefully kept mansion in Upstate New York.

And now, if Kid Omega had his way, there would be a third mutant school.

"Welcome, discerning students!" He scrambled atop his hover chair – patterned after one used by Charles Xavier, but with an omega symbol psychically "spray-painted" across its salmon-tinged chassis – spreading both arms to indicate the gathered teens.

"Tickle me – Dare I say it? Yes, I dare! – pink to see so many of you here for our inaugural day of class. And so fashionably dressed, to boot!" Laughing, Quentin indicated their shirts and his slogan, just as one shimmered into existence upon his chest.

"Oh, did I say 'class'? Yes, you heard right, true believers," he announced to the hooting kids. "And while Kid Omega epitomizes class, my amused friends, I meant the word as in 'lessons.' Coursework! The syllabus of tomorrow, eager beavers, in what you and I shall lovingly and non-ironically refer to as 'school, sweet school.'"

"What's this about, Quire?" jeered Julian Keller, aka Hellion. The cocky mutant had an arm slung around one of the Stepford Cuckoos: Celeste, sister to one of Quire's close friends. "You promised us fun and freedom. What's this about lessons?"

"I'm glad you asked." The Kid spun another dial, a physical representation to others of what to him was purely a mental muscle. The walls changed again, and now displayed a pink diorama of five mutants in quaint, old-fashioned spandex costumes. The quintet smiled next to a severe looking bald man in a suit and tie, the latter seated in a quaint, manual wheelchair. Several in the crowd cheered... for many in attendance, these were the original mutant heroes. Professor Charles Xavier and his first five X-Men. The OGs, the original team, well before the franchise had expanded and X-squads littered the globe.

He pointed a finger at the nostalgic tableau. "You know what they say, mi compadres: those who forget history are doomed to repeat it, yes? And there, depicted on the walls as the cringe fashion disasters that they were, is displayed our history, yours and mine. Behold, the first school! Charley Xavier's Fancy School for Gifted Not-Mutant Lads and Ladies. No, not a single X-Gene to be found in upper-crust New York, am I right?" The teenagers chuckled, nodding their heads to acknowledge the obvious sarcasm.

"I am wrong!" Kid Omega slammed a fist down on his chair and spun another dial. Thirty to forty additional mutants sprang into existence along the wall, dressed in splashy uniforms loaded with pouches, pockets, powers, and attitude, crowding in behind Xavier and the five originals, obscuring the mansion in the background.

"Mutants on the lawn! Mutants in the foyer! Freaking mutants in the bathtub, basement, and an aircraft hangar cleverly hidden beneath a retractable basketball court! Mutants, mutants everywhere – but not as far as the regular folk can ever know." Smirking, Kid Omega put an index finger to his lips. "Shhhh. Be vewy quiet, wabbits. No mutants here, Ossifers. No, not here in – gasp! – the Hudson Valley!"

Laughter rippled throughout the shop. The Kid had their attention, and loath to lose the opportunity, he pounced.

"Well, at least they added some diversity along the way. But I digress with my woke leanings. Regardless! The first mutant school, yes? A fine idea, though far too secretive and subjugated for Kid Omega's taste... as well as that of my intelligent, early-adopter besties. Over the years, Charles Xavier welcomed all kinds of mutants through his doors: young, old, evil, British. Mutants from many different walks of life..."

Quentin spun a final dial, and the X-Men disappeared, apart from two, facing off against each other with malice in their eyes: a hairy man in a tank top, brandishing razor-sharp claws and curling his lip at a slim, stoic brunette across the way, a pair of ruby-red cheaters covering the second mutant's eyes.

"...though some of them never really could get along. And so," Quentin continued, swiping the walls clean with a wave of his hand, "what was once one became two."

He snapped his fingers, and the clawed, hairy mutant – Logan, aka the Wolverine – appeared on the left wall, standing before Xavier's mansion, a handful of students (some of them patrons in the Omega Shop) gathered behind him. The slim, bespectacled man – Scott Summers, also known as Cyclops – graced the opposite wall, standing by a snow-covered hill, accompanied by a select number of disciples, several of whom were in attendance below.

"The Jean Grey School. The Xavier Institute. Each with their own ridiculous ideology and never the twain shall meet. Except now" – grinning, the Kid plunked himself down on the edge of his hover chair, gesturing to those gathered in attendance – "because here you stand, students from both schools, now enrolled in this third, magnificent, inevitable iteration of Charley Xavier's military boardinghouse for secret lovelorn mutants. Welcome, my friends – finally – to Kid Omega's School for Mutants Without Borders! I hope you survive the experience. I know I will."

The amused teenagers kept smiling, but the laughter and catcalling settled down to a skeptical buzz. Quentin slid off his chair and joined them on the floor, listening to the kids' whispers. He could hear everything, as they were all inside his head, in a solid, psionic construct held together exclusively by the power of his mind.

"C'mon, Quire," one of them asked, "what are you talking about?"

"Yeah," replied Shark Girl, a girl boasting... well... a massive shark's head. "Professors Logan and Summers aren't gonna go for this. Do they even know what you're doing?"

"Who cares?" He shrugged both shoulders and snapped his fingers. Blindfolds sprang into existence on the wall, obscuring the eyes of both Cyclops and Wolverine.

"Did either of them 'go for it' when they started up their respective schools? Do either of those headcases have actual teaching licenses? C'mon, kids. Why should you and I spend our lives hiding in plush mansions or filthy boltholes, pretending to tame our powers and go along to get along, hoping the world outside doesn't remember that we terrifying mutants actually exist? They know – trust me! So, why hide it? Heck, if we're going to be hated-slash-feared anyway, why not do it out and proud, in public amongst the regular type folk?

"Look," he continued, spreading his hands and wiping the walls to their original pink. Kid Omega's shirt – all of the shirts – faded to black, the letters MWB appearing across the upper left breast. "I'm not playing the fool or villain, OK? This isn't a scam or bit, and I believe it needs to happen sooner rather than later. I've seen the future, and the future of mutantkind isn't victimhood. It isn't us hiding in a basement somewhere in the frozen north, or sticking our collective heads in the sand like mutant ostriches. Ostrichi? Ostrich aside, the future of our people is all of us together, united in harmony without labels – no more 'heroes of the atom' or 'evil mutants' – cooperating as a nation, thriving alongside humanity as Xavier intended.

"We've devoted our lives – some reluctantly, I'll admit – to the dream of coexistence. A few have pursued it in a slightly more aggressive manner than others, sure. But I'm telling you: it's gonna happen. No, humans and mutants will never be happy neighbors, sharing cups of sugar and laughs over a fence in the suburbs. But we will coexist." He had their complete attention, teenage heads nodding, slowly absorbing his every word.

"So, why wait? If the end result is détente and peaceful coexistence… why hide? We should be able to live, laugh, and learn anywhere we want."

He held out the corners of his shirt.

"Kid Omega's Mutants Without Borders; MWB for short. We'll meet anywhere, live anywhere, train anywhere. Look around." He gestured to the store. "I can bring us together here in my head." He tapped a patch of skin next to his mohawk. "And we can travel the globe, actually seeing it, not masked behind palatable disguises or cloaked by holograms… no."

Frowning, he waved a hand, and their shirts went blank. "We live how we are. Where we like, with whom we like, recruiting others to do the same. We'll learn and train together. Stand together publicly as mutants. Many of us are already spread around the world. Some in New York, some in Japan, Kenya, Scotland, you name it. And some of us – my aforementioned early adopters, the original Mutants Without Borders – are with me now…"

The Kid clapped his hands, and the walls and floor faded away. The collected mutants started, gasping at the sudden visual shift, adjusting for balance as they braced for a fall. But no one did. They held their ground, psionic imprints held aloft by the power of Kid Omega's mind. The shop had turned invisible, and they all looked down into a posh hotel suite with a view of downtown Toronto.

"…here in Canada."

Five mutant teens sat below, lounging around a suite on the physical plane with heads lolled and mouths agape. Comatose on tasteful chairs and sofas, the mutants boasted various shapes, genders, and sizes. One, a bulky, see-through pink automaton with a visible skeleton, was spread out on a couch next to a serene, attractive Nigerian girl. A brain in a jar, several hypodermic needles studding its glassine surface, hovered next to a slack-jawed, shaggy-haired kid with a ridiculous goatee, awkwardly lounging in a rolling desk chair. Finally, settled on a plush armchair by the window, primly sat a pretty blonde in a white, summery dress.

Across the room on the bed, Quentin's physical form sat propped against a multitude of impractical cushions, straining to maintain the integrity of his now invisible pop-up shop and the thirty or so psychic signatures gaping from above. Kid Omega's psionic self saluted his glorious body and smiled at his five best friends. It was crazy to think that he, Quentin, even had best friends. But there they were, and at the very least he was happy they believed in him. He turned to his guests and waved a hand, as if suggesting they inspect the scene as well.

"See? Glob, Oya, No-Girl, Hijack, and Phoebe Cuckoo. My early adopters, the MWB's original quintet, as Cyclops, Jean Grey, and the others were to Xavier. There they are… well, their bodies anyway." Quentin winked, gesturing to the psionic manifestations of his five pals smiling at him from the back of the shop. "And there I am, swain as ever, protecting us even as I use Omega-level swagger to" – he snapped his fingers, and the floor and walls returned, obscuring the hotel suite below – "keep the party going."

The Kid turned to friends and enemies old and new, potential students every one.

"You see? We can be together in person or check in remotely. My school is fully contactless, the lesson wherever it happens to be that day."

Many of the teens were now nodding in agreement, incrementally buying into the plan. The Kid was just getting started, frothing at the mouth and building up a head of steam. His voice rose, as did his body. He floated back to the hover chair, mentally raising the music. A steady, pulsing beat thrummed in time to his charismatic diatribe: Kid Omega was orating to the addictive rhythm.

"So join me! Become a Mutant Without Borders. You all know what's good – that Kid Omega is right." The crowd cheered, and he slapped a new slogan on their shirts: WE DON'T NEED NO (OTHER) EDUCATION. "None of us have to listen to sad mutant has-beens telling us how, in the old days, they walked through twenty feet of snow to fight a

Sentinel and liked it! Who cares about the old days? These are the new days! So why not now? Why not here? Let's chart our own destinies, because that destiny is coming, my Q-Men, and it is–"

"Staggeringly pathetic."

Confused, the crowd turned as a slim woman slid through the store's rear wall. She wore a jet-black battle-suit, running as a seamless piece of armor from the boots on her feet to a shiny, featureless helmet encasing her head. The intruder carried no weapons but exuded menace and grace. Her voice, oily and amused, betrayed a slight, unusual accent hinting at its rough, intimidating edges. The unknown newcomer stalked through the crowd, headed for the Kid.

"Do I know you?" he said. "I don't believe I'd head-mailed you an access key, athletic, sexy stranger?"

She tapped the side of her expressionless helmet. "My key is in here, host."

"Host," Kid Omega mused. "I've been called worse. But what're you–"

A shriek pierced the air. He swiveled, and Oya – Idie Okonkwo, the Nigerian mutant with the ability to manipulate temperature – clutched her head and disappeared. A second later, Hijack – David Bond, goateed master of mechanical vehicles – followed her lead. At a loss, the Kid dropped the pop-up's walls again, and was horrified to look down and find his Canadian hotel suite breached by four additional strangers in obsidian armor. Kid Omega's teenage audience began to vanish, winking out in an effort to escape whatever madness was about to happen.

But for the MWB – the mutants who'd been caught unaware

below – it was too late. Horrified and helpless, Kid Omega watched as his friends' comatose bodies were subdued by the quartet of mysterious assailants, their psionic selves dissolving from the Omega Shop into thin air. The Kid tried to wake up, to abandon his construct for the physical plane, but found his psyche stuck fast and unable to move, as if trapped like a fly in amber. He was unable to return to his body or stop the mysterious woman standing with him on the psionic plane from reaching out to grab his throat.

Kid Omega managed a croak as her fingers constricted. "Wh- how d- did you–?"

"I have been playing the minder game longer than you have, host. Long enough to know that you do not possess the location or knowledge of an Egg. Though you know one who might. One inaccessible – and treasured – to me and mine. One you equally revere and mistrust."

"Egg…?" Baffled and angry, Kid Omega struggled. The woman's grip – both mental and physical – was too strong for him to break. "What does… have to do… with poultry products? H- how are you doing this…?"

"Come now, Quentin Quire, who once touched the rapturous face of the Devourer, it that hath ravaged and blessed hundreds of worlds. You, who have stood inside the White Hot Room. We both know that you are too smart to act the fool."

Her helmet tipped, indicating the suite below, where her intimidating companions – dressed like a science-fiction death squad – were busy shackling his friends and grouping them in the center of the room. The silent invaders gave the Kid's physical body a wide berth. Again, he tried returning to it – to escape the psychic plane and deliver unto his unwelcome guests a world of pain. But the Kid was trapped fast, pinned and immobile, by the amused telepath in gleaming black armor. His body remained where he'd left it, propped upon the comfortable bed.

"Your friends, however, possess no such reliance in your ability to keep your... what is the Earther word I perceive within your mind? Yes. Retain your 'cool.' However, should you wish these others to retain their continued health – and their lives – then you will answer my questions and provide what I desire."

Quentin wheezed through gritted teeth. "Hurt them... I swear... I'll hurt you!"

Kid Omega didn't have many friends. Those he did, he wanted to keep alive at all costs.

The woman laughed, amused by Quentin's impotent bravado. By her attitude, she clearly saw Kid Omega as a minor threat. He wouldn't do her the disservice of believing the same. If this stranger could keep him on a chain while knocking out Phoebe Cuckoo, a powerful telepath in her own right, this stranger and her friends were not to be underestimated.

"I am sure you will try," she replied. "Take heart. We have no desire to hurt you, Quentin Quire. Not as a former host or potential asset. All we need is for you to relay a message. Then my friends and I – we, The Remaining – will take your friends away, out among the endless stars for safekeeping until our request and quarry are delivered."

The Kid strained against her grasp, thrashing to be free, cursing at his captor. Chuckling, the ebon-suited telepath reached up and turned one of his psionic dials, muting Quentin's outraged profanities.

"None of that," she said. "Your friends will join us to provide assurances that both the message and Egg will be dispatched intact. No harm will come to these enhanced Earthers, I vow, unless you refuse. We would convey this message ourselves, but the predestined recipient is not an easy being to contact, nor would he or those with whom he surrounds himself allow we Remaining the liberties we have taken with you, a lesser and weaker host. In the end, we have foreseen that your required intervention will ultimately result in our mission's foreseen success."

Kid Omega seethed behind the mental gag. His chest expanded and retracted with heavy, indignant breathing. The woman leaned close, releasing pressure from around his throat.

"So, do you concede, host? Will you relay our demands?"

He found his voice returned. "Yes," the Kid choked, staring daggers into the polished mask. "What's the frakking message?"

Purring, the telepath leaned forward and whispered it in his ear.

CHAPTER TWO

[QUENTIN | THE NEW CHARLES XAVIER SCHOOL FOR MUTANTS | CANADA | EARTH]

"Summers must deliver a Phoenix Egg to The Remaining."

Kid Omega slumped in a battered metal chair. He numbly stared at his fingers, all his fury and invective having drained away on the journey from Toronto.

These Remaining – whoever they were – had left him on the hotel bed, frozen in abject submission. The Kid had counted an hour after they'd beamed away before finally regaining the use of his mind, mouth, and limbs. He didn't know if his attackers were humans, mutants, aliens, or robots. His primary assailant had mentioned taking the MWB "out among the stars," so he was leaning toward aliens. All he knew for certain was that they were powerful enough to catch an Omega-level telepath unaware, restrain five mutants, and vanish from the planet.

That the woman in black had managed to pierce his construct hadn't surprised Kid Omega. He was still learning to maintain its structural integrity, thanks to the help of Emma Frost, one of the Xavier School's instructors. The fact that the walls to his psionic shop had broken wasn't problematic. He would shore them up and build better, work harder, learn to keep the store intact.

First, though, he had to rescue his Mutants Without Borders. He had to save his friends.

And that meant, unfortunately, that Quentin had to reluctantly travel back to the frozen northwest – to the Xavier School – and deliver the message to Scott Summers, aka Cyclops. Normally, Kid Omega would have refused to play errand boy and would track the rude alien enigma and her armored himbo boy-toys himself. But today, though he was loath to admit it, the Kid had to swallow his pride and seek out Cyclops. Because, frankly, he was having trouble locating The Remaining on his own.

At first, his mental impotence was due to the frantic, angry aftermath of what happened in Canada – having been unable to move, speak, or think as the minutes ticked away. But once the Kid had finally, blissfully escaped his unwelcome state of forced immobility, not even his most focused mental scan... his most desperate, uneven efforts to telepathically locate Phoebe, Glob, and the others had been fruitful. He was still learning to send his mind that wide, and he'd been unable to find them anywhere on Earth – not a breath, not a whisper, not a stray thought. And if Kid Omega couldn't find them, that probably meant they were off-planet... or they were dead.

And he couldn't bear to let his heart even consider the latter.

"Tell it to me again." Scott Summers leaned forward on a battered chair of his own, glaring at Quentin through a form-fitting black mask, two bands of ruby-red quartz crossing over his eyes, both of which held his force beams at bay. He waited quietly, moving not a muscle, gazing at the Kid as if he expected a prompt reply.

Cyclops was like that: a pompous authoritarian and a stickler for doing what he believed to be right while ensuring those around him did the same. Unfortunately for Kid Omega – a mutant who'd rebelled against authority since his freshman year at Xavier's Original – that often put him at odds with Summers' supercilious wonk agenda.

Sure, the last few years saw Cyclops set aside a straight-edge teacher's pet attitude to embrace a platform upon which he aggressively advocated for mutants to take their place in the public eye: as saviors, educators, across social media, and as architects of a future where Homo sapiens superior stood next to humans astride a global stage. Faced with two schools cultivating dissimilar teachings, Quentin naturally gravitated toward Cyclops' new proactive and revolutionary approach rather than remain mired in history lessons taught by the stodgy, old-party-line, ostriches in the sand at the Jean Grey School.

OK… to be fair, he'd been asked to leave the Grey School, and Cyclops – probably worried about what havoc the Kid might wreak out in a vulnerable human world, operating sans restrictions – had corralled him into forced education under strict tutelage at the New Xavier School. Thus began a cat-and-mouse game between the immovable rule-maker and the unstoppable rule-breaker.

Since that moment, most of Kid Omega's acts of oppositional defiance had been harmless – except for one incident wherein he'd pierced the time-space continuum (but it all worked out in the end, so the less said about it the better). Still, he and

Cyclops could not get along. Quentin envisioned himself to be a glamorous salmon, swimming upstream against a conformist agenda while skirting the line between "evil" and "revolutionary." Summers, meanwhile, was the honest-to-Charles first-ever X-Man, co-headmaster of the Xavier School, known and hated by half of humanity, super-humanity, and mutantkind... while lionized and celebrated by the other.

But more relevant to the day's concerns, Cyclops was the former lover to and then host of a vengeful cosmic firebird known as the Phoenix. Only a handful of earthly mutants had hosted or even touched an aspect of the Phoenix's ancient, unlimited cosmic power. The Kid had, of course, been one. Jean Grey – Cyclops' deceased wife, a powerful telepath after whom they'd named a school – was another. Even worse, Jean's entire genetic line – parents, cousins, even the dog! – had been murdered by the Shi'ar, a different set of alien bird-people who'd vowed to make sure that no one on Earth would wield the Phoenix Force ever again. The only Grey that the Shi'ar left alive had been Rachel Grey, Scott and Jean's daughter.

But if Quentin had to lay Vegas odds on the reason for ol' Scotty's intense curiosity here, it probably had to do with the fact that good ol' Professor Summers and four other mutants had split aspects of the Phoenix Force between them, vowing to make Earth a better place (they did, for a while) for humans (kinda) and mutants alike. Eventually, the "Phoenix Five" had turned upon one another and aw-shucks Cyclops ended up as sole possessor of the Phoenix Force... which he used to accidentally eviscerate Charles Xavier – Teacher! Mentor! Father figure! – right before the X-Men managed to finally oust the Phoenix from Scott's body.

So, yeah. The history was super messy. But that's kind of why Kid Omega had returned to the Xavier School. He came north to tell Scott Summers, mutant messiah, that the Kid needed help to find the deadly force that killed Cyclops' mentor – oh! and caused the death of his wife – so he, Quentin, could use it to ransom back his BFFs... y'know, the ones he'd irresponsibly lost to five unknown aliens who could be anywhere in the galaxy by now.

Whoever they were.

Piece of cake.

"Quire? Tell me again?"

Kid Omega looked up. Cyclops was staring at him.

"You didn't see where these beings went? How they left the planet? A ship, a translight jump gate or some type of long-range teleport? Any discernible markings on their armor?"

"No." The Kid shook his head. "By the time I could move or control my thoughts, I was... well, let's say... OK, I was blindingly vengeful and didn't think things through. This telepath, she was jamming me. If you know what I can accomplish with my brain – and I know you do – that means we're talking about someone with capabilities beyond Omega-level. By the time I shook off her mental shackles and did a global scan, I couldn't even locate a psychic afterimage. Whoever that telepath might've been, she even scrubbed the psionic plane. She was thorough and had foresight. She was... is good."

"Good enough to corral an irresponsible child, perhaps," sniffed blonde, statuesque Emma Frost, towering over Scott, her stoic former boyfriend, like a terrible work of art in dark, impractical leather and lace.

"This mysterious telepath might be able to hide her tracks

for now," Emma continued, "but she'll find herself wanting in any regard when facing those more practiced in these matters. Others lacking in, shall we say" – she sneered at Kid Omega, a smile curling the corner of her cold, ruby lips – "a certain mental elegancy."

Quentin winked through his psionic spectacles. "I'll give you this much, Emma–"

"That's 'Ms Frost,' you impudent enfant terrible…"

"You've got that telepath's icy affectation down to the last imperious bon mot. I wonder: where was your psychic self earlier today? Hiding behind glossy black armor?"

"…you dare accuse me?" Emma stalked past her ruby-eyed ex-beau, nostrils flaring as she approached Kid Omega's chair. Quentin stood to meet her with bright, shiny teeth.

"Dare I do! J'accuse!"

"That's enough!" Scott stepped between them, holding out both his palms. The telepaths glared at one another, the tension so thick that Cyclops could have split it with a force beam. Emma turned and sniffed, returning to her original position. The Kid remained where he was.

"Listen," Scott continued, "we don't have time to fight amongst ourselves. Every second we waste is a second these Remaining gain to hide in a universe so large it's too staggering to fathom. Quentin." Summers turned again to Kid Omega, trying to wrest any final bit of information from his most difficult student. "Are you absolutely sure that this was it? Do you have any more information to go on? Just the Phoenix Egg and my name, nothing else? Not even a handoff location, a requested drop point, anything like that?"

"No. Four armored enigmas, admittedly semi-powerful,

partnered with one smarmy snack of a telepath. I mean, isn't the Phoenix Egg enough? Also, since when does the Phoenix come in egg form? Can it be scrambled? Poached? Had over easy... no, wait. Don't answer that last one. Too much innuendo."

Scott paced the room as he answered. "Though essentially immortal, the Phoenix Force – aspects anyway – can be harmed. And it can be destroyed... as we learned with Jean. Usually, that's only possible when the entity is bonded to a mortal host, as it had been when..."

"When it possessed you."

Cyclops pursed his lips and didn't acknowledge the Kid's statement. Shaking his head, the headmaster continued, "In those rare instances, the shattered aspect is always reborn inside a living cosmic egg. It grows and matures, waiting for someone to release the Force within. Once hatched, the Phoenix can bond with a new host, free to menace the cosmos once again."

"Which would be disastrous," deadpanned cold, beautiful, snobby Emma.

Every mutant in the room chewed on that. The Phoenix was one of the universe's oldest and most primal forces. The nexus of all psionic energy, it represented both creation and destruction, worshipped by many life forms but feared by countless more. The ravenous entity's cruel and cataclysmic judgment burned away parts of existence – and worlds – it believed no longer belonged, that no longer helped to evolve the tapestry of eternity.

Scott ignored Emma, Quentin, and two additional mutants seated at a table in a darkened corner. The Kid recognized them, of course. So far, the duo had listened in silence, seemingly content to let the others deliberate. Before he could address their presence, however, Cyclops wheeled, pointing his mutant moneymaker in Quentin's direction.

"Did these Remaining say why they wanted me specifically, Quire? Or the Egg? Do we know if they're hoping to use it, destroy it…?"

The Kid shook his head. "It didn't sound like they meant it harm. The telepath… she talked about the Phoenix like, I dunno, she was in awe of it. In love, maybe. She said The Remaining didn't want to hurt any potential hosts. Me. This guy. I was the host she meant."

Cyclops finally stopped pacing and turned to face the two silent mutants.

"Awe? That could mean worship, right? Or it may mean they possess a healthy relationship with their own sense of fear. A race that might feel threatened…?"

"Scott." One of the mutants leaned forward in her chair, straight blonde hair spilling into the light. "We'd know if it were–"

Cyclops ignored her. "Not for certain, Illyana. It might be those blasted Shi'ar again, especially after what they did to Jean's family. What they might have done to Rachel."

"Scott."

"Quentin said that one of The Remaining was a telepath. The Shi'ar Imperium has employed telepaths as members of its elite Imperial Guard. One of them is named Oracle, but there are others. Any of them could have been this woman. You don't know, Magik!"

"No, I don't," the blonde mutant agreed. Slim and short, she stood and made her way around the table. Her voice, lightly accented, belied the varied locales the speaker might confidently claim to be her home.

Born in the former Soviet Union, near the Siberian Ust-Ordynski Collective, Illyana Nikolaievna Rasputina possessed the ability to teleport herself and others by means of portals she referred to as "stepping discs" – literally using them to step across time and space. After being chosen as one of the "Phoenix Five," the level of Illyana's mutant energies had dangerously increased. A complicated mutant with an unbelievable personal history (even within X-circles), Illyana had long proven herself a valuable ally, fierce protector, and loyal friend.

Magik placed a hand on Cyclops' arm.

"It might be the Shi'ar. It might also be the Skrulls or any number of extraterrestrial or interdimensional species that have long wished us harm or felt the talons of the Phoenix and want to see it annihilated. The X-Men have shaky alliances with every single one of those species. But from what Quentin is telling us" – she shot Kid Omega a threatening look filled with doubt and malice – "assuming he's telling the truth, it sounds like the motives of these Remaining are less destructive and more opportunistic. They want to use the Phoenix, not kill it."

"Perhaps." The second mutant shoved back his chair with a scrape, its weight barely able to support his frame. Colossus – Magik's brother Peter, actually, a second-generation X-Man armored with fancy, shiny armored skin – joined his sister. He looked down at Cyclops, placing both hands on his friend's shoulders; hands that had been known to bend steel and stop juggernauts, but could also perform such delicate acts as painting a watercolor or gently caring for a wounded comrade.

"Scott, tovarisch... I have answered your call, though I hold no position at this or any mutant school. As your former colleague – as an X-Man and friend – I have always perceived you to be a man of measure and tolerance. A strategic leader for whom logic trumps emotion. It has been... an emotional time for many of us." Colossus gestured to the room, indicating the gathered mutants at the Institute, and perhaps the world outside its walls.

"But know this," Peter concluded. "I believe – as I'm sure in your heart, in a place where reason resides, you feel the same – that when it comes to the Phoenix, emotion cannot blind our actions as it has in the past."

Colossus hung his head and closed his eyes. Kid Omega didn't need to be a telepath to know what Peter Rasputin was thinking or that he was trying to block unpleasant memories as were the others in the room. The Rasputins, along with Scott and Emma, had been members of the Phoenix Five. They had drastically changed the planet, but eventually their lust for power had proved their undoing... and what happened after that had, of course, been tragic.

The Kid could taste their fear and concern. He briefly touched their minds, skimming the surface. Each of them was frightened. These four mutants had wielded the power of a merciless cosmic vulture, and it had utterly consumed them, affecting even their genetic mutant gifts. Since Xavier's death, Scott, Emma and the Rasputins had been struggling with unreliable fluctuations to their unique power sets, as had several mutants who'd confronted the Phoenix Five. The Kid's instructors were worried what might happen should they once again face the cosmic entity, undertake this mission, and obtain an Egg – an artifact waiting for someone to break it open, release its power, and be seduced by the creature contained within.

Could they handle it, knowing now what they did? Or would the older mutants again misuse the cosmic energy and allow it to fall into the wrong hands? And after their recent disastrous exposure to the Phoenix Force... were the hands of these four X-Men the wrong hands to begin with?

Kid Omega believed that they were. He'd been sitting quietly for far too long. Raising his hand, he did what he often did, the one thing that always, always got him into trouble: the Kid opened his mouth and began to speak.

"Look, based on my global scan, I believe The Remaining are off-planet. I'm going into space to find a Phoenix Egg," he said. "Give me a ship. I'll rescue my friends."

Magik smiled. Colossus cocked a skeptical eyebrow. Emma laughed.

"Don't be ridiculous," she scoffed. "You're the one who lost them in the first place."

"Bet. Accurate," he replied, turning to face Scott Summers, "but of the five of us, I'm the only dude who's touched the Phoenix without automatically becoming a pompous, murderous psycho rage-cow. Of this group, I alone have faced The Remaining. I can still feel their mental aftertaste. So maybe I think that puts me at the top of the list for this particular rescue mission, before any of you has-been, frightened lot."

Cyclops cut him off, slicing a hand across the air to indicate that the suggestion was ludicrous. "Forget it, Quire. You've already done enough."

"Oh, but I don't think I have. Sure, fam, I've lost five of my students–"

"...your students?"

"–but you gotta admit it was hardly my fault. If any of you

jokes had been there, you'd have seen. Lady Telepath was Omega-level times fifty–"

"Yes," Emma interrupted. "Which is why–"

Quentin ignored her. "Which is why it's not only my responsibility to make things right, but why I'm most equipped to stop her, as the smartest, strongest, sexiest telepath in the room."

"Well, that's all bunk."

"Is it, Emma?" Kid Omega raised a finger to her elegant, symmetrical face. "I know that, like your nose job, right now your powers are less than optimal." He turned, addressing the older, respectable mutants. "The same can be said for any of you Phoenix Five. After your brush with that messy flaming pigeon, all of you are having trouble with your powers."

The four mutants cast embarrassed looks at one another, confirming Kid Omega's accusation with their eyes.

"But I'm not," he gloated. "My powers are growing, and I'm the one with actual experience fighting these Remaining. What I don't have, though, is experience in space, chasing down smarmy alien telepaths in galaxies far away. I also don't have a ship. I mean, I could maybe make a psionic spaceship… but if The Remaining's telepath can break my construct when I'm sleeping in Canada, I'm kinda worried what she'll do when I'm floating through space… that airless, coldest of heartbreakers. So perhaps one of you could help in that department?"

Scott shook his head. "No. I don't trust you, Quire. Not with this mission, or with something so valuable as a Phoenix Egg and mutant lives you may have already lost."

The Kid set his jaw and glared into the ruby-quartz band across Cyclops' eyes.

"And I don't trust you with the Phoenix Force, Glasses. Nobody does. Not after you used it to kill Charles Xavier."

The room fell silent. Kid Omega had definitely gone too far, and he could feel anger and frustration radiating from the instructors... but he also knew that they agreed with the sentiment. Even Cyclops, grappling with his failures while struggling to live up to his responsibilities, knew that the Kid was speaking truth.

"I've got a score to settle with these Remaining, whatever they are," Kid Omega explained. "I want to – no, I need to rescue my friends, what few I actually have. Like you said, Emma. I'm the one who lost them. I should be the one to get them back. And I have a history with the Phoenix, too – I've hosted it, albeit briefly. I can handle that flaming drama queen if and when push comes to mental shove."

"Fine," Scott said after a moment of hesitation. "But you aren't going alone. Like you said, you have no experience in space. Frankly, I want someone with maturity to watch your back. Tomorrow morning, you and I will–"

"No." Magik shook her head. "Though I never believed I'd ever say these words out loud... Quentin is right. It can't be you, Scott. If word got out to the humans that you were after a Phoenix Egg, after what just happened... and plus, you're needed on Earth. You have to be here to protect and guide the students of the Xavier School."

The Kid watched as Cyclops gritted his teeth and silently wrestled with half a dozen counterarguments. Eventually, Scott relented and slowly nodded his head.

"OK. Then I expect one of you...?"

But none of the others stepped forward. Kid Omega could

feel their reluctance to accept the mission, to put themselves in the path of the Phoenix. Broken as each of them were, the vivid pain and memories of their last encounter were probably too sharp and visceral to bear. Emma shuddered and waved a hand, begging off. Colossus simply shook his head, refusing to volunteer.

Magik shrugged. "I'm needed here, same as you. And you can understand our hesitation, Scott. It's... at the moment, our gifts..."

He nodded again. "Yeah, I get it. But we can't send Quentin alone."

Kid Omega scoffed. "Why not? All I need is a–"

"I'll rephrase that: there's no way I'm sending Quentin alone. I want a responsible instructor by his side, someone with experience in this arena. Who knows the landscape."

Emma raised a perfectly sculpted eyebrow. "A teacher from the Jean Grey School? McCoy, perhaps, or Pryde? They must have also lost students–"

"No," said Cyclops. "The Phoenix was part of the reason we split our schools, as was brash Mr Quire here." Quentin grinned, savoring the irony. It was true. Before his kinder, gentler days, Kid Omega had incited an incident at the United Nations – psychically forcing gathered delegates to reveal their delicious secrets on national television – the results of which had instigated a schism between the X-Men. Cyclops glowered and ignored the Kid's satisfied smirk.

"We find an impartial party, someone we can trust. Who I can trust."

Kid Omega raised his hand. "I'd like final approval, if I may."

"Shut up, Quire." Cyclops turned to the other X-Men. "I still think we should contact the Shi'ar Empire, to confirm that this isn't them. At least get alibis from their telepaths."

Colossus grunted. "If it is the Shi'ar, by contacting them we lose the element of surprise… even with telepaths or precognitives on their side, who may already see us coming. And if it is not the Shi'ar, we will have alerted their emperor – a dangerous and powerful ally with vast intergalactic resources – to the fact that someone, a threat perhaps, is seeking the entity his people most fear… hoping to harness its endless, destructive power and use it for… what? No one knows. And the fact that we X-Men have kept this from him and the Shi'ar until now… Will they handle that confession with grace or violence? We do not know that either."

Magik agreed. "That could put the kidnapped students in harm's way. No, I agree with Peter. Let's try to solve this cleanly and quietly. A small team with little disruption to our already shaky peace with the Shi'ar."

"But the fact that this telepath asked for me by name–"

"Scott," Emma interjected, "she must know your mind. How close you are to the Phoenix, and the fact that you cannot – will not – abandon your students or mutants in need. It's clearly a trap, designed for something nefarious."

"She's right." Kid Omega crossed his arms with wicked satisfaction. At the very least, he wouldn't have to deal with uptight Scott Summers second-guessing his every move.

"Shut up, Quire. Fine. If that's everyone's stance, I'll stay here. Quentin will go to make this right, and we'll send along adult supervision versed in the politics and intricacies of the galactic landscape, with resources and connections out among the stars. Someone with honed leadership skills and a person I absolutely trust with this sort of mission… as I've trusted him with my life."

Magik cocked her head to one side. "Who are you thinking?"

Scott smiled. "These Remaining asked a Summers to deliver a Phoenix Egg, right? Well, thankfully, I'm not the only Summers available for the job."

CHAPTER THREE

[ALEX | AVENGERS MANSION | NEW YORK | EARTH]

The airplane vibrated, violently shaking as its rudder burst into flame.

The family of four braced themselves as the plane yawed to one side, pressing each of them hard against the upholstered seats. In the cockpit, one of two adult travelers – a suave, debonair pilot – jerked the control yoke in an attempt to right them, then shouted back to the second adult, struggling to be heard over the roar of the dying engine.

"Do it now! They're right on top of us!"

The second adult, a willowy blonde, leaned back to address two small boys. Her sons gripped their seatbelts with white-knuckled terror. The older boy, dark-haired and pale, shrieked as his mother snapped her fingers. Sternly and calmly, she gazed into their eyes, regulating her breathing as she tried to calm them down.

"Scott. Alex. Boys—"

The plane shuddered again. A massive shadow bore down upon the small aircraft, blocking out the star-dappled Alaskan sky. A volley of fireworks lit up the night, forcing the boys to squint as they screamed. The pilot cursed and twisted the yoke, doing his best to escape pursuit.

"I can't breathe," squalled the older kid. His brother, younger and blond, simply wailed. The smoke was thick, and he worked to undo the belt strapping him to his seat.

"Oh, god," he cried. "Mommy!"

His mother worked quickly to undo both belts. "Boys," she said again, trying to keep her voice even and sure. "You have to unbuckle and come with me."

"I. Can't. Breathe!"

The pilot raised his voice, straining to be heard. "Do what your mother says, Scott, and you do it now!"

She finally released Scott's belt and grabbed a bulky pack from under his seat. Moving fast, wincing as the airplane shuddered for a third time, she pulled the heavy knapsack down over the boy's thin, tense shoulders.

"What is happening…?"

"Scotty," their mom barked, "you hold onto your brother, Alex! Hold on for dear life, do you understand? Don't let go, no matter what!"

Scott stared in horror as their mom unstrapped little Alex from the adjacent seat.

"A… are you coming too…?"

"It's the only parachute. Take it and trust that your dad and I—"

Something nearby burst into flame – the fuselage, perhaps. Whatever it was, the pilot – the boys' father – fell and lost his grip on the controls.

"Oh, god," he cursed. "I can't hold it!"

Alex's mother shoved him into his brother's arms. She secured the parachute around Scott's chest. The plane was awash in orange *and yellow, and she took a moment to stare into the eyes of her frightened sons for the last time, caressing Alex's hair and touching Scott's chin.*

"I love you," she promised them. "I love every part of you."

She hugged them, her hair fanning against their faces. Her tears mingled with their own, and then she took them by the arms and tossed them out the aircraft door.

The Summers brothers fell together, crying in the cold Alaskan sky…

"Alex?"

Startled from the childhood memory, Alex Summers turned from where he stood at the window. Tall and slim, with a cropped shock of sandy hair atop a haggard, unshaven face, he shared only fleeting physical similarities with his more infamous brother, who stood across from him in the Avengers Mansion's ornate, tastefully appointed drawing room. What the Summers men lacked in similar shades of hair or eyes – Scott's obviously hidden behind the ever-present band of ruby-quartz – they shared in stance and posture. The brothers carried the weight of the world on their shoulders, and it showed in their overall demeanor.

It had been decades since that fateful, horrifying night, when they had lost their parents and tumbled out of a burning airplane into an uncertain future. Since that moment, Scott's every step had led him down a winding series of highs and lows. He'd been a hero, leader, criminal, and now both teacher and revolutionary.

Alex, meanwhile, separated from his brother via adoption, had eschewed the spotlight after he was older, when he learned about his mutant powers and had been reunited with Scott.

Tagged with the reluctant codename "Havok" – possessing the ability to absorb ambient cosmic energy, process and return it via channeled waves of destructive plasma – Alex drifted on the outskirts of the life to which Scott had ascribed and married. A geophysicist first, Alex wanted to exist apart from the madness and mayhem that drove his brother. And though he'd briefly been an X-Man, Havok committed only as far as being a part-time member. He chose instead to explore post-graduate studies alongside his at-the-time girlfriend and occasional fiancée, Lorna Dane. But like Scott, Alex couldn't avoid the chaos for long. Eventually, as with all things related to the star-crossed Summers brothers, the mayhem would come knocking.

He'd been to space, where he'd traveled with friends and battled dictators, fought alongside pirates and aliens alike. Alex had loved and lost. The more he'd attempted to discard the dangerous life of a hero, or the responsibilities of a leader – a title to which he'd always felt ill-suited – the more the mantle was thrust into his reluctant arms. And now, standing in a beautifully decorated, storied Fifth Avenue mansion across from Central Park, the responsibilities of a leader had again been placed upon Alex Summers' heavily burdened, black-garbed shoulders.

He was an Avenger now, with all the honor and responsibility the title conveyed, charged to inspire and galvanize a team of human and mutant superheroes as the ultimate embodiment of Charles Xavier's belief that all kinds of people might come together to work in harmony. He'd been personally selected for the job by "Earth's Mightiest Heroes" after the tragic conflict between their two teams, the heartache and strife caused by the actions of his brother and the Phoenix Five. They hoped that by leading a unified squad of their very best – X-Men and Avengers, working together, setting a cooperative example – Alex might finally, once and for all, prove Xavier's dream.

It was only Day Three. Still, so far so good.

"Alex? Is it a yes or no?"

He turned to address the psychic manifestation of his older brother, Scott, mentally projected into the Avengers Mansion from parts unknown. It was like speaking to a hologram, though Alex knew that unlike a hologram, thanks to whichever skilled telepathic mutant had secretly bypassed the mansion's ultra-sensitive security to insert Scott's image into the drawing room, that if he so wished Alex could reach out and physically touch his brother. The wall, festooned with colorful portraits depicting various Avengers teams, was visible through Scott's translucent body. Cyclops crossed his arms, waiting for an answer.

"So, if I've got this straight," Alex said, repeating back the request, "you're asking me to go into space with Quentin Quire, of all people, in order to find a mysterious group of unidentified aliens who could be anywhere in the galaxy by now – if they're still in this galaxy at all – in order to save a group of kidnapped kids."

Smiling, Scott's projection scratched his temple. "Essentially."

"And, because that isn't enough, you want me to bring these aliens – whoever they are and wherever they might be – the Phoenix, of all things."

"An aspect of the Phoenix. An unhatched egg."

Alex chuckled. "You never ask for much, do you?" Sighing, he turned back to the window, splaying both hands against the sill. He stared at the lush greenery of Central Park, stretching into the distance across the busy avenue.

"You know," he began, "I just got started here. The Avengers. I can't pick up and leave."

"I wouldn't ask if it wasn't important."

Alex looked over his shoulder. "I can get them to help, you know. I'm the leader, supposedly. Assemble and all that?"

Scott shook his head. "This has to be quiet. Fast and under the radar. Your team, Alex" – he waved his hand, indicating the mansion and photos, the history – "is anything but. Besides, after everything that's happened, how will the Avengers react when you tell them that I've asked you to find me a Phoenix out among the stars?"

"Fair point. But why me? You can go, or Magik…"

"I've already explained why."

"Wolverine? One of the others?"

This time, Scott was the one who sighed.

"Alex, there's no one else I trust. After the schism between our schools and the incident with the Phoenix Five… Professor Xavier, everything… I don't trust anyone but you."

"But, and at the risk of repeating myself, why? I'm no tracker, barely a leader. I mean, not yet, anyway. We… this Avengers team just faced a group of super-Nazis, and the others did most of the work. There are better options, better teachers and heroes than me. You don't have to ask Wolverine, but there's Storm, Captain America–"

Cyclops cleared his throat. "Though I don't agree with most of what you said, Alex, there's one thing you are that those others are not."

Alex raised an eyebrow. "Anxious?"

"Family."

The word hung between them, as did the intervening years. The sound of a failing engine whined in the back of Alex's brain, growing louder as it was overcome by a child's pitiful sob.

"Scotty," barked Katherine Summers, *"you hold onto your brother, Alex! Hold on for dear life, do you understand? Don't let go, no matter what!"*

"Look, Scott. If this is about Mom..."

"No," Cyclops said, his voice terse. "It's about me, Alex. After the Professor – well, after what happened, I've had a difficult time letting anyone get close to me. Emma, of course–"

"Of course." Alex smirked; Scott ignored him.

"But the others... colleagues and teammates... old friends like Hank and Bobby. Part of me feels, well..."

"Judged."

"Not judged exactly." Scott turned to peruse the wall, the photos of various Avengers teams past and present. "Guilty, I suppose? Worried what might happen if I let anyone get too close again. Would I let them down, or would proximity to Scott Summers put them in harm's way? Jean got hurt."

Alex started to protest. "Yeah, but that wasn't–"

Scott ignored him, moving from picture to picture, his fingers lingering on the image of their blue-furred mutant friend, Hank McCoy, the Beast. "Then there was the Professor, of course. Others, too. Thunderbird. Madelyne. Nathan, my son. Even Rachel."

"What happened to Rachel?" As far as Alex knew, Rachel was an instructor at the Jean Grey School. Something must have happened between father and daughter after the schism between the two institutions.

His back turned to his brother, Scott Summers stopped in front of the last photo, that of the current Avengers lineup – a ragtag group of humans and mutants working to uphold Charles Xavier's dream. Scott rested his fingers on Alex's masked, smiling face.

"Recently got into a tight spot out in space. Rachel and a few others – Dazzler, Lorna–"

Alex's heart skipped a beat. "My Lorna?" Truthfully, he hadn't seen Lorna Dane in some time. Calling her "my Lorna" might have been premature and nostalgic in nature. Still, he wanted to make sure that she was OK.

"They're all fine, don't worry. They saved me, Magneto, a few others. Rachel and I were imprisoned together during the craziness, and though I was happy to see her… afterward… well, let's just say that I gave her distance."

"Scott."

Cyclops held up his palm and faced his brother, forestalling Alex's sympathetic gesture. "Look, I handled it poorly. I was worried about doing the same thing to Rachel as I have to everyone I've ever loved, especially those I've called family. I pushed her away and didn't give her a chance to understand why. Now I'm trying something different. I'm lowering my emotional defenses and opening myself to, well, connection again. I figured I'd start by trying with you."

The Summers men stared at one another, years and tragedies filling the space between them. The last few decades had driven a gap between the siblings, but with no more than a sentiment they were back in that falling, dying aircraft, holding each other for dear life, their mother's tears upon their cheeks for the final time. Since that fateful day, Scott and Alex Summers had spent more time apart than they'd been together. Alex had been adopted from the orphanage that was their home following their mother's death. Scott was left behind. Until recently, Alex had lived a genuinely happy life. Scott's, meanwhile, had been marred by failed purpose, tragic heartbreak, and the ever-present specter of death. But now they had a chance to narrow the gulf. Alex's brother had been humbled and was reaching for a lifeline. This favor he was asking, though both the timing and effort involved might be less than ideal... the trust involved was Scott's way to make amends for a lifetime of absence.

Alex cleared his throat. "So. Scavenger hunt in space, huh?"

"Yeah, it seemed like your wheelhouse." Scott smirked. Before Alex had become an Avenger, he'd spent five years gallivanting through space as a... well, as an interstellar pirate, captaining an infamous crew of galactic freebooters known as the Starjammers.

"Sure, we've got connections up there who may be able to help out."

"I know we do."

"And Quentin Quire? That's a dealbreaker?"

Scott scratched his head and grimaced. "Unfortunately. Look, I know that Quire's the ultimate problem child. But he responds to strong leadership, and to mutants who advocate for other mutants, both of which you've been achieving here."

"Well, I don't know that I'm–"

Scott ignored Alex's self-deprecating stammer. "So, I figure there's a chance you can bond with Quire, and maybe teach him a little bit about responsibility and tact while helping to undo a wrong that he's actually feeling guilty about."

"Bond, huh?"

"If you can get past his Colossus-sized ego." Scott grinned. "Look, do what I couldn't with Rachel. Put aside your pride, be open to connection and intimacy, and maybe allow yourself to learn something along the way. Avoid my mistakes, both with Quentin and, well, also…"

Alex nodded. "Yeah. 'Well, also.'"

He knew what – or who, actually – his brother was thinking about. In order to complete this mission, Alex and Quentin would need allies. Finding a Phoenix Egg and The Remaining would be like hunting needles in a universal haystack. There were few in the galaxy – several galaxies, actually – better suited to that particular task than Alex's old crew aboard the Starjammer. And if he was planning to travel with the Starjammers, that meant Alex would need to work alongside the pirate crew's current captain.

Scott's projection walked across the room and placed a hand on Alex's shoulder.

"It'll be fine. Remember what I said about Rachel and Quire. Try not to push away the ones you love, especially those you can call family. Sure, it'll be awkward to see him again, and I know that you both have issues to resolve. So did we. Once I let myself connect with him, our relationship has never been stronger. So try. For me, OK?"

Alex allowed a tight smile to reach his lips, and he placed a palm on Cyclops' insubstantial hand. "For you, sure. So what now? Should I fly to your location so me and Quire can hail the 'Jammer?"

Scott shook his head. "Like I said, under the radar. Quentin's already aboard the Starjammer. Once you make excuses to your team, we'll get you up there."

"Oh?" Alex looked around the room. "Magik coming? Are we going to teleport aboard using her stepping discs?"

"Illyana's... her power is a bit unpredictable right now, ever since the Phoenix, you know. I don't think we could fool Avengers security to ignore the chaotic nature of her abilities at the moment. But we do have a back-up."

Twenty minutes later, after Havok relayed his impending absence to the Uncanny Avengers under the guise of a family visit, he met Cyclops' mental projection in his living quarters, wearing his costume and ready to go. Moments later, a pink circle fizzled into life in the center of Alex's room, sparking and swirling wider until a lithe, purple figure stepped through. It was a young girl with magenta hair and bright, white pupilless eyes. A diamond-shaped marking sat prominently over her nose and additional marks dotted her brow and cheeks. The young mutant smiled as she hopped through the portal and gave Alex a fierce, happy hug.

"Alex! I haven't seen you in forever!"

"Hello, Blink. Long time."

Clarice Ferguson – a teleporting mutant – stepped away and looked at him, a wide grin dimpling her cheeks and crinkling her blank, white eyes.

"Yeah, it's been a crazy few years. Decades? I dunno. But thankfully, I'm finally enjoying a little bit of peace and normalcy."

"Good for you. I hear you're at the Jean Grey School now?"

She nodded. "Yeah, I kind of go where I'm needed."

"And with Magik on the bench...?"

"Yup. Put me in, coach. Ready to go, Avenger?"

He shrugged and sighed. "C'mon. Stop."

Clarice chuckled and stepped aside with a flourish. Holding

out a palm, she gestured toward the portal, inviting him through.

Alex turned to face his brother. "Wish me luck?"

"You always find your own luck," Scott replied. "Find those kids, too. Bring 'em home safely. And come back safely yourself. Also? Try not to kill Quire along the way, all right? I know that's a tall order."

Scott grinned. Their mother's smile flashed before his eyes, and Alex blinked away the memory. The Summers brothers, putting on brave faces, constantly leaving one another as per usual. Alex waved at Cyclops and nodded to Blink. Then he walked through the portal, traveling light years like a crosswalk as her portal closed behind them.

Havok had left his vanilla-scented, moderately heated Avengers quarters and found himself breathing in the spicy and medicinal pressurized air of a fully converted Shi'ar battle dreadnought. His body felt heavier, and he allowed himself a moment to acclimate to the modified gravity of an interstellar spacecraft, settling onto the unforgiving panels of the ship's steel floor. He was cold. Alex's costume – made of black unstable molecules, responsive to energized matter and adaptable to his physical characteristics – barely protected him from the chill of space lurking outside the Starjammer's walls. The craft itself was shaking, and Alex lost his footing. Looking around, he placed himself near the port guns; the bridge was behind him and a level higher. That's where Havok would find the crew. No one had come to meet him, but by the muffled vibrations and intermittent tremors, he assumed that all hands were probably on deck.

Back in space and under attack. Be it ever so humble, he mused.

Adjusting his pace for the heavier gravity, Alex ran aftward to the rear of the ship, hooking his fingers onto an interior handhold leading up to the forward level. The Starjammer shook, taking heavy fire from an unknown assailant. Klaxons and lights blared inside the corridor as he climbed, bathing the bulkhead, handholds, and his fingers in shades of crimson.

As he clambered up the ladder, voices reached Alex's ears, raised in dissent. The lights were getting sharper, the noises louder. He could hear the squalling sounds of the 'Jammer's particle beams, no doubt deployed against the unidentified foe. Return fire screamed across the ship's port side, raising a fresh set of tremors, threatening to dislodge Alex as he rose.

Finally, his head broke the top of the corridor, and he could make out frenzied activity on the bridge: the traditional sights and sounds of a starship crew under attack. As Havok pulled himself up and into the forward level, screams rose above the volley of cannons and the passing shriek of at least three sublight torpedoes.

"–hands off those guns, kid!"

"Let me help! I'm trying to–"

"You've helped enough!"

Alex smiled. He recognized both voices. The first, older and gruffer, roughened by decades of vice and trouble, warmed his bones. Deja vu tingled Havok's skin – an aircraft under fire, a frustrated pilot, the sounds of thunder and fear. The years melted, and he was in his brother's arms again. He shook off the memory and walked forward, allowing himself to be seen.

"Let me talk to them," whined the second voice. "We'll never find out if we don't ask."

The older voice roared as their enemy came around.

"You don't just hail a passing Kree cruiser and ask if they've got a Phoenix Egg!"

"How was I supposed to know? I'm never in space! I don't know the protocol!"

"Kid, what you don't know... Alex?" The older voice softened, and the argument died, fading into the stuffy, medicine-scented air trapped within the bridge. Everyone turned as Havok smiled and waved, meekly offering salutations as the Starjammer shivered and its crew clung to their seats.

"Hi, Dad."

CHAPTER FOUR

[ALEX | THE STARJAMMER | THE PAMA SYSTEM | KREE SPACE]

"This is Major Christopher Summers, United States Air Force! I'm in command of the HMSS Starjammer, and the three of you are surrounded!"

Corsair winked at Alex and turned around, giving the helm his full attention. Heart beating fast, Alex scrambled into a jump seat alongside Quentin Quire, who'd been summarily banished to his chair. Quire, wearing a ridiculously impractical ensemble of shorts and T-shirt, crossed his arms and sulked as the Starjammers tried to undo the damage he'd caused.

Ch'od, the 'Jammer's emerald-hued Saurid navigator, squeezed his nine-foot reptilian bulk next to battle command, charting a route away from the circling Kree warbirds. Nearby, the physician Sikorsky – a Chr'yllite, resembling a small, gray insectile helicopter – coaxed the ship's two hundred terajoule hyperlight engine into responding to their pilot's commands. Manning the guns, both starboard and port, were Raza Longknife – a cyborg marksman, the only Starjammer who actually looked like a pirate – and Mam'selle Hepzibah, a highly attractive feline Mephitisoid, similar in appearance to a humanoid skunk. Hepzibah winked at Alex. Behind her, strapped to the pilot's chair, was her paramour and captain... Christopher Summers, also known as Corsair, a pirate and rogue whose head commanded a thousand bounties.

Alex knew each of them intimately. As the Starjammer's former captain, he'd traveled the stars with Ch'od, Hepzibah, Raza, and Sikorsky, among others, facing down conquerors and working against all odds to protect the galaxy.

And, of course, Corsair was his father.

Major Summers swiveled in the pilot's chair, spitting venom at Quentin.

"You couldn't do this near Ciegrim-7? Or out by Zenn-La, for flark's sake? No, you had to open your loud, pink mouth in the heart of Kree space!"

Quentin tried to protest, but Corsair turned to his son, face creasing into a wide, charismatic smile. "Good to see you, kiddo. How's your brother?"

"Dad!" Alex warned. A warbird came around for another pass at the 'Jammer, and Major Summers swiveled back to the controls, spinning his ship to evade a round of torpedoes.

Quentin rolled his eyes. "Dad? Oh, god. That's right. I forgot. That makes so much sense."

"Zip it, peanut gallery! I got it, I got it... hang on!" Corsair tripped some dials and pushed down on the yoke, sending the ship into a power-dive toward a nearby planetoid. Sikorsky chittered and whined, apologizing to the engines as the forward level shook and both Alex and Quentin held on for dear life. The Starjammers were smiling, one and all. This kind of action was a walk in the park for Corsair's crew. Give us a real challenge, those smiles said, none bigger than their devil-may-care, swashbuckling leader.

Quentin struggled against his straps, gesturing at the Kree. "Let me out there, and I'll give those blue-skinned Top Gun rejects an alien headache they'll never forget!"

Hepzibah, gritting her teeth as she pumped the port guns, growled at the Starjammers' cocky, pink-haired guest. "Psionic shielding! Think first minder the Kree have faced, you are? Sit! Silent! Learn!"

Publicly scolded, Kid Omega sulked, muttering curses aimed at the beautiful Mephitisoid. Next to him, Alex smiled and hung on as the Starjammer leaned into its descent.

The warbirds followed them down, all four starships breaking into the planet's atmosphere. Corsair tugged the controls left and back, putting the 'Jammer into a hairpin turn. The Kree fighters were slow to respond and hurtled past. Corsair grinned, lifted a hand, and cocked an eyebrow. Nearby, Ch'od punched a flashing dial, peered at a list of datapoints scrolling on a screen, and then responded to his captain with a positive thumbs-up.

"Hang on, folks," Corsair warned. "I'm putting this system in our rearview."

Sikorsky, worrying over its diagnostics, offered a chattery little whimper as Christopher Summers placed both hands on the yoke and drove it forward. Ch'od threw a switch, and the engines thrummed louder, vibrating the Shi'ar dreadnought like a concrete mixer. Before them, a translight jump gate shimmered into existence: a wormhole, like Blink's but larger and engineered, connecting two different points of space-time. It spread out like hexagonal tiles against the stars, and the centermost shape yawned wide. Corsair applied pressure, and the Starjammer raced through the gate, exiting Kree space and entering a different galactic sector, leaving the pursuing warbirds behind.

Everyone took a moment to collect themselves as Ch'od scanned their new surroundings for signs of threat. Sikorsky scolded Corsair, warning him that the 'Jammer's engines would hardly be able to endure these kinds of battle shenanigans if they happened with increased regularity. Raza and Hepzibah powered down the guns, each bemoaning the lack of a continued firefight. Quentin immediately unstrapped himself and stalked to the aftward window, still sulking, casting the others withering looks as he glared into space. Extricating himself from his own seat, Alex glanced at the brooding mutant teen.

"You all right?"

Kid Omega sniffed. "What d'you care?" He turned away, staring at an infinite horizon of twinkling stars. "I'll be all right when this Wacky Racer excuse for a starship gets the show on the proverbial road. I'll be all right when cretins start realizing that the Kid knows better, and could have ended that in nanoseconds, and stop telling me – me! The Omega! – to keep quiet and open my eyes. I'll be all right when…"

Rambling, Quentin seemed to note Alex's sympathetic expression, ended his manic diatribe, and moved away. "Forget it, Not-Cyclops. Let's just go, OK? There's a cosmic space buzzard out somewhere in the galaxy, and we're not gonna find it by sitting on our hands, sharing our feelings."

Alex exhaled, realizing that he'd been holding his breath during Quire's jagged little rant.

What's this kid's deal? He wondered. Sure, the X-Men – and mutants, in general – were particularly moody and rebellious, but Quentin out-James Deaned even the worst of the lot. Scott was right; this was going to take work. Alex could be open to connection all he wanted, but so far it looked like the only thing he might learn from Quire would be how to cop a bad attitude.

"Hey, kid." Both mutants turned as Corsair loped forward with a determined swagger.

Havok nervously smiled as his father approached... but his cheeks burned. Something about Corsair brought out an unusual mixture of love, pride, shame, and anger in Alex Summers. Perhaps it was the man's laconic grace or the nerve to travel the galaxy in flamboyant, pirate-meets-astronaut couture, an azure bandanna around his brown, curly locks and a dashing, Errol Flynn mustache above his lazy smile. Or maybe it was that earliest of memories: Chris Summers' barked, impatient orders over the roar of an engine as their mother tossed Alex and Scott from a dying plane. In this case, though, Havok believed it was the fact that the last time he'd seen Corsair, his father had been killed by a third, wayward Summers brother: Gabriel – or Vulcan, as he was infamously known – mad emperor of the Shi'ar Empire, a galactic system encompassing nearly one million worlds, and one that Vulcan had taken by force.

Vengeful and horrified, Havok had replaced Corsair as captain of the Starjammers, partnering with them to dethrone Vulcan by any means necessary. In the end, Gabriel's pride and rage were his own undoing. He led the Shi'ar in an effort to expand their empire and met an end at his enemies' hands. The

Shi'ar had elected a new ruler: Kallark, also known as Gladiator, an invulnerable purple powerhouse with superhuman strength, speed, and stamina … and former captain to the Shi'ar Imperial Guard, a collection of superhuman warriors. Alex had bid farewell to the Starjammers, leaving them without a captain to call their own – though somehow they'd managed to resurrect the original. And in doing so, Alex regained a father for the second time.

Turning from Quentin's bad attitude, Alex rushed to meet Corsair in a deep embrace. Tears flowed down Alex's cheeks as father and son hugged, Havok's heart pounding in his chest. He'd known – through Scott, of course, always through Scott – that Corsair had somehow returned. And sure, he still felt that awkward undercurrent of pride, shame, and anger. But this moment was purely about love. About being reunited with the father he'd thought he lost forever. And Quentin Quire aside, Alex Summers was going to hold tight to the moment for as long as it would last.

As it happened, it didn't last long. The other Starjammers crowded in, jovial and laughing, thrilled to see Alex – their former captain – just as much as was Corsair. Ch'od lightly punched Havok on the shoulder, and both Raza and Hepzibah gave him short, fierce hugs (the latter adding an affectionate, purring kiss on the embarrassed mutant's cheek). Sikorsky chittered and whirled about their heads, beeping happily, and for a moment Havok had forgotten about the trials or tragedies in the Starjammers' shared past, as well as the reason he was here in space. And then, of course, Quentin Quire had to go and open his mouth.

"Sheesh," the Kid said. "Get a room."

Corsair whirled and jabbed a finger at Quentin, a barely diffuse flush receding above his mustache.

"Listen, Pinky. That stunt may have cost us free rein in Kree space and compromised this mission! Those warbirds are probably on the horn to the Shi'ar right now!"

"I don't care, Space Magnum." Quire's blood was up, clearly annoyed at having to continue this conversation. "I want to find the Phoenix and get my friends back. If that makes your commute a tad inconvenient…"

Corsair stepped closer. "Careful, junior. I'm babysitting you as a favor to my son–"

"Hey, Star-Dad? You, your two sons" – this was directed toward Alex – "and your flying junk-heap filled with sci-fi rejects can bite my shiny mutant–"

Alex stepped between them. "OK, that's enough. Neutral corners. Mistakes were made, Quentin. Let's try to learn from them, all right?"

Quire rolled his eyes. "You can suck a Phoenix Egg too, Not-Cyclops. And the name's Kid Omega." The Summers men watched him storm away, headed toward the crew quarters.

Once Kid Omega was gone, Corsair broke into an amused grin and turned to face Alex.

"To be fair, I'm sure the Kree were already flarked at me for some sacred item that Ch'od may or may not have liberated from their throne world, Hala. So maybe I should go apologize to Pink Attitude over there."

Havok shook his head. "No, let it go."

"Copy that, Captain Summers." Corsair placed a hand on his son's shoulder and pulled him in for another hug. "It's great to see you, sport."

Havok awkwardly patted his father on the back and then softly pushed away.

"You too, Dad. I mean, under the circumstances." Instinctively, he snapped a glance at the 'Jammer's cockpit. The captain's seat, specifically.

Corsair followed his gaze. "Been a minute for you, has it? Don't worry. You'll get your star-legs back under you pretty quickly."

"That's not it."

"Ch'od and the lady... I mean, Hepzibah, they tell me you performed like an absolute champ at the helm. You have my thanks for keeping this crew together while I was gone, kiddo. You have my admiration for everything else... what you had to, y'know..."

Corsair trailed off, the sentiment unspoken. Perhaps they wouldn't speak of Vulcan or what Gabriel Summers had done, just like they'd never spoken of Alex's mother even when things had been easy between them.

Vulcan had allied himself with the royal traitor to the Shi'ar Empire's ruling family – Cal'syee Neramani, also known as Deathbird – and a secret order bent on deposing her sister, Lilandra, the Shi'ar empress at the time. The order hoped to place her throne into the hands of D'Ken, Deathbird and Lilandra's insane brother. Vulcan had come to the Shi'ar throne world, Chandilar, to kill D'Ken for murdering Katherine Summers, Alex's mom, years before. Havok's parents had survived that terrible night in Alaska, kidnapped by Shi'ar scouts assessing Earth for vulnerabilities. Christopher had been imprisoned, his pregnant wife made part of D'Ken's harem. In a fit of annoyance, D'Ken had torn baby Gabriel from Katherine's womb, killing her before her husband's eyes. Gabriel was secreted away, incubated, raised to adulthood, and sold into intergalactic slavery. Eventually, the boy made his way to Earth and was recruited as an X-Man – as both of his brothers had been – by Charles Xavier.

Vulcan's first mission alongside a team of unprepared mutants had ended in disaster; most of his squad had lain dying, including Vulcan himself. To spare a distraught Cyclops the anguish of losing a brother, Xavier had mentally altered the memories of the X-Men, erasing the existence of Gabriel and the others, and sent their bodies into space. Vulcan managed to heal and returned to Earth. He tried to kill the X-Men, then renounced his brother and vaulted back toward the stars, determined to take revenge on the Shi'ar Empire himself. But when he learned that a coma-struck D'Ken no longer ruled, Vulcan joined forces with the Secret Order to oust Lilandra and take over. He married Deathbird, healed a grateful D'Ken... and then murdered him when the time was right. Gabriel became Emperor Vulcan, tightening the grip of the Shi'ar Empire across millions of planets.

Oh, and he'd killed Corsair, his own father.

Alex smiled, answering Corsair's unspoken sentiment.

"I know, Dad."

Christopher Summers cocked an eyebrow. "What's with the sudden cold shoulder, then? This about me coming back and not calling? I told Scott that I was going to explain everything to you, the minute–"

"It isn't that."

"What, then? I feel like I messed up again somehow."

"No, it's..." Havok wiped his eyes and glanced at the

'Jammer's forward window and the gleaming stars. Ch'od sat at the helm, piloting calmly through the sector, preparing to plot their next course. Deja vu settled into Alex's belly, and visions of former Starjammers flashed before his eyes. Korvus and Rachel. Lorna and Lilandra. Fighting together, battling a war to avenge his father and regain an empire. They'd been captured by Vulcan and the Shi'ar Imperial Guard. Separated from one another. Tortured. Broken by his own brother, physically and emotionally, piece by terrible piece.

"…it isn't you, Dad. Post-traumatic flashbacks, I suppose. Remembering everything me and the others went through while you were gone."

"Alex—"

"Truthfully, I failed them all. Failed you, too. Nothing I really did made a lick of difference. I didn't stop Vulcan. And while I was imprisoned on Chandilar with the rest of the crew I was supposed to keep safe, jailed and impotent, back on Earth… Scott… he…"

"Hey." Chris placed both hands on his son's shoulders. "You did your best. No captain is perfect, and no one blames you for—"

"I blame me, Dad. And now" – he gestured in the direction Quentin had gone – "now I have all this on my plate. Am I up to it? I'm not a captain anymore. You are. I'm barely a leader. Quire reminds me a lot of Gabriel, you know? One wrong move… one bad decision… I dunno, Dad. Lord only knows what kind of teacher I'll make, as well."

Havok smiled, and this time he clasped his hand to Corsair's shoulder.

"It's all right, Dad. Maybe it's jitters talking or the post-battle yips. Look, either way, I'm happy to see you again. Really."

"Same, kiddo." They hugged once more.

"Hey," Alex remarked, "I'm an Avenger now. In charge of the team, actually."

Corsair grinned. "An Avenger? Hey, that's great. Congratulations."

"You seem ... less than impressed?"

Chris shrugged. "It's a big galaxy, pal. I've partnered with celestial gods and abstract entities. It's hard to get dazzled by a team of Earth cops."

"Speaking of big galaxies ... any clue on where to start?"

"Well," Corsair replied, "I was hoping you'd have an idea – at least, one that doesn't involve shouting 'Anyone know where we can find the Phoenix?' at a passing Kree warbird."

Alex laughed. "OK, so no leads? Either on that or these Remaining?"

His dad shrugged. "Scott didn't give me much to go on other than what you've learned yourself. But we can ask around, turn the usual rocks and see what wriggles. I've got Ch'od and Sikorsky cross-referencing any Phoenix chatter from Spartax to the Anvil. If someone's talking about it, we'll know. Frankly, finding the ol' firebird seems like an easier task than your mysterious telepath, even though any persistent inquiry is bound to raise alarm when it reaches the ears of the Galactic Council."

"Fair enough. Do what you can without getting us murdered. Meanwhile, I may have a few ideas on who to ask, too. And I'll check in with Quentin, to make sure he behaves."

Corsair saluted his son and turned to the helm. "Sounds like I have the easy job. Glad to have you aboard for this one, pal. Looking forward to catching up."

"Same, Dad. Back soon." The sentiment in Havok's reply didn't quite reach his eyes. Truthfully, Alex was happy to see his dad ... but part of him also hoped that he would be too busy chasing the Phoenix, wrangling Kid Omega, and rescuing the other students to have a real moment alone with his father.

I love my dad, he thought. But between our history, absences ... and with everything that's going on with me ... the situation is too awkward for any real conversation. I need to get through this and get home, let our relationship breathe – like I'm doing with Lorna – and then me and Dad can reconnect down the line.

Besides, if Alex was a glutton for punishment and wanted an awkward moment, he only had to look as far as his next conversation.

Havok found Quentin rummaging in the crew quarters, tearing his way through square mesh bins filled with fabric, steel, and leather. The floor was a mess, littered with discarded clothes, cast-off boots, and a number of satin-lined capes that seemed impractical for space travel. Quire ducked his head into a bin and, cursing, tossed it as he frantically dug through the contents.

He'd managed to change his clothing in the short time since Alex had seen him last. Gone were the shorts and sneakers. Kid Omega had swapped his black shirt for a plain white tee, and donned a pair of gray, heavily pocketed cargo pants with complicated knee straps. Chrome bangles encircled his wrists, and he'd abandoned his psionic spectacles for a sensible pair of black, rectangular frames. Compared to Alex's form-fitting uniform and the flamboyant costumes worn by the Starjammers, Quentin's outfit seemed almost plain for space.

"Looking for something?" Alex stepped forward, clasping his hands behind his back.

Kid Omega looked up. "Yeah, actually. Trying to find anything in this floating lemon that'll tie this look together."

"Have you considered a muzzle?"

Kid Omega rolled his eyes and ducked back into the bin.

"Shouldn't you be in New York, pretending to be Captain America's mutant sidekick?"

He's trying to push your buttons, Alex. "No, I'm here to help save your friends, Quentin. Any ideas on how you'd like to start?"

"Kid Omega. And I had an idea, remember? Captain 'stache-and-burn out there shut me down."

"He didn't…" It was like talking to a nine year-old with a law degree. He wouldn't allow himself to be drawn into a debate with Quentin Quire.

"Look, I get that you're tense. Your friends were kidnapped, we have no leads… and trust me, I know what it's like having to admit that you need help."

"I don't need–"

"You do, and that's fine. I'm not Scott. I'm not here to slap your wrist. But I'm also not gonna spare your feelings like Xavier would've done. I want to finish this and get home."

Quire snorted. "Yeah, right. You love it up here on Daddy's spaceship. You miss it. I don't even need to read your mind to see that."

Breathe, breathe, breathe. "Sure, sometimes I do. But tossing out little time bombs to try to hurt me isn't going to distract from the fact that you need help. Time bombs are a different mutant's power, and trust me, she'd be far less help to either of us in this situation. So why don't we iron out our differences and get to work?"

Quentin looked up. His expression cracked, a smirk.

"That was funny, Cyclops-Lite. Who knew one of the Summers brothers had an actual sense of humor?"

"Glad you approve. Can we get to work now, finding your friends?"

"That depends on you and Major Dad out there. If the two of you are going to naysay and micro-manage the Kid–"

"No one is micro-m–"

"–then, I say thee nay." Quentin tossed aside the bin and grabbed another, fishing out a set of Hepzibah's leather boots. "Skunk shoes. Pepe Le P.U. Look, as soon as I pull this outfit together, you can drop me at the nearest intergalactic Piggly Wiggly so I can question the locals. After that, I'll figure out how to hail a space Uber or a passing surfboard, or whatever."

This was ridiculous. They had no strategy, the kidnapped mutants were no closer to being found, and here was this difficult, infuriating hipster monster trying to go lone wolf...

Wait. Something Quire had just said sparked a plan in Havok's brain.

They could absolutely use this. He grabbed Quentin's hand, forcing the Kid to drop Hepzibah's boots.

"Hey! Hands off, grabby..."

"Quentin. You just gave me an idea."

"I did?"

"You did."

"...was it 'space Uber'?"

Alex smiled. "Not exactly. Look. The Remaining are in the wind. We don't know who they are or where to find them. But they do want to be found, right? How else can we bring them the Egg?"

Quentin cocked an eyebrow. "Go on."

"But we don't know how to find an Egg. And we can't go asking half the universe about the Phoenix."

"Maybe you can't. But the Kid–"

Alex interrupted him. "The Kid has to learn that sometimes tact and diplomacy will get him farther than shooting off his mouth and whining his way through a situation. Listen: the galaxy cannot know that two mutants from Earth – one of whom has touched the Phoenix Force, the other who's related to the husband of its favorite host – are out looking for one of its Eggs. Forget the Kree. That'll bring the entire weight of the Shi'ar Empire down around our ears, along with maybe the Skrulls, Badoon, and even the Galadorian Spaceknights to boot. Got it?"

"Galadorian...? You made that up!"

"Quentin," Havok said, ignoring the younger mutant's constant interruptions. "What we can do, though, is travel under the radar and make discreet inquiries of those in the know. We can heavily imply to the galaxy's secret gossip-hounds, those who traffic and deal in information, that someone out there wants a Phoenix Egg for nefarious purposes, and we – the X-Men, known heroes on the side of angels and allied with the political juggernauts that are the Kree and Shi'ar – want to find them... so we can stop them."

Surprisingly, Kid Omega stopped to consider the proposition.

"OK. So, urban super hero 101? Crash a bar, tell the barflies that renowned mutant revolutionary Kid Omega and his plasma-firing X-flunky are out to arrest these dastardly Remaining – and are not after the Phoenix itself, which everyone knows is totes dangerous, and hey maybe y'all should steer clear – and by doing so, some gossipy alien trash will open its big, tentacled mouth to point us in the right direction. And if not…"

"And if not, then at least the Shi'ar or others won't worry that we're after it for the wrong reasons and start looking for The Remaining themselves. The Remaining, in turn, will feel that heat and also hear from said aliens that the X-Men have been asking in all the wrong places, get nervous, and tip their collective hands because they want what they want before the Shi'ar, Kree, or another galactic heavyweight gets involved. Maybe they'll even broadcast a drop point for the Egg… which, perhaps, is where they're holding your friends."

Quentin shook his head.

"Uh-uh. These particular mutant-nappers don't get nervous or tip hands. At least that's not the impression I got from their telepath; she was far too sharp. Like, she could see ten steps ahead of me. It won't work, and probably all it will do is get the Shi'ar to come running sooner than we'd like and maybe get my friends killed. So much for under the radar then, right? But, I gotta admit, Plasma-Firing X-flunky… part of the plan has merit."

"Oh, yeah?" Amused, Havok folded his arms, waiting for Kid Omega to elaborate. "Which part? Bearing in mind that I'd rather our inquiries err on the side of diplomacy and subterfuge, if and where we can, as would my brother. Your headmaster."

Kid Omega grinned and stuck an arm inside another bin.

"I bet he would. Allow me to complete this fabulous ensemble. After that, if you'll have Mustache Lone Star and his large, dinosaur co-pilot find us a local watering hole, I'll show you all what I have in mind."

CHAPTER FIVE

[QUENTIN | THE ROTTEN CORPS TAVERN & DATAPOINT | NEW XANDAR | THE TRANTA SYSTEM]

Knocking aside two Kallusians, Kid Omega smiled, cracked his knuckles, and leapt atop the winding bar that encircled the Rotten Corps Tavern.

He shot his cuffs. The buttery gray leather of the pilfered jacket enveloped the Kid like a hug. Three blank buttons were pinned to his lapels, and he mentally adjusted them to cycle through a handful of slogans, telepathically filtering the messages through a modified psionic application interface calling to the Starjammer's data repositories and translation software. The buttons visually shifted to whatever language the viewer spoke – currently, from smallest to largest, the pins displayed a raised fist on pink, a firebird silhouette on yellow, and the words CELESTIAL BODY INSPECTOR in dark red against white. Stitched to his left sleeve, a red physical patch displayed Kid Omega's personal logo: a black omega symbol above a rotated letter X, displayed on a scarlet field.

Yes, he thought. The jacket, a final addition to his ensemble, not only tied the outfit together, but was properly intimidating and most indubitably badass.

Unfortunately, no one in the tavern could see it. Though he, Havok, Corsair, and Hepzibah had stormed in wearing their usual garish, colorful outfits, Kid Omega was ably projecting psionic disguises atop the costumes, ensuring that everyone else in the bar was actually seeing four beings in black, intimidating armor, gleaming and covered from head to toe, narrow helmets hiding their no-good faces from view. To the patrons of the Rotten Corps, the Kid and his friends were now The Remaining... and as was their story in the three bars they'd previously raided, they were seeking information leading to the capture of a Phoenix Egg. Alex's plan – to pretend they were X-Men, and to lean on that group's wonderful, intergalactic reputation – felt safe and, frankly, heroic. This way – the Kid's way, twisting it enough to stick it in the faces of The Remaining, wherever they might be – felt more satisfying. It felt like something he could get behind... and once he'd altered the plan, the others really had no choice but to follow along. It took little effort on Kid Omega's behalf. Unlike his previous construct, the Omega Shop, he wasn't holding together a physical structure so much as placing visual suggestions into the minds of the barflies. The mutants and Starjammers weren't actually wearing psionic armor over their clothes – the patron's inhabitants were simply seeing what the Kid wanted them to see.

Cackling, he lashed out with his mind, telekinetically hoisting a struggling Pheragot from where the bulky semi-humanoid sat at the bar, nursing a glass of sour Ceigrimite ale. Now the meek, ten-foot pacifist pinwheeled its muscular arms as alien, drink, and chair all went careening toward the back of the tavern.

This was the fourth seedy establishment that Kid Omega, Havok, Corsair, and Hepzibah had invaded. The first had been a Majesdanian taproom, located on a shard of the demolished planet Majesdane's broken moon. After that, the Starjammer had touched down on both Z'nox and Tekton, avoiding the inner Skrull worlds for now. The Kid had wanted to risk it, but Havok continued to suggest that talking about the Phoenix near Skrullos, the Skrull throne world, could bring the weight of the Tarnax System down upon the Starjammer. Instead, they stuck to obscure planets dotting the Andromeda Galaxy, broadcasting their message to the patrons of ramshackle bars and any outpost in which scum gathered information and then ferried it across the galaxy.

"We're after a Phoenix Egg," Kid Omega amplified through speakers built into the black, psionic armor, ignoring the stricken expression only he and the Starjammers could see on Havok's face. "Save yourself time and trouble. Tell us what you know, before things get uglier than that guy over there."

The first time the Kid had trumpeted their intentions, Havok had been taken by surprise, still clinging to the naive hope that – as X-Men – they planned to please-and-thank the mopes that populated the universe's unforgiving frontier. Kid Omega could understand why. The Majesdanians, bioluminescent humanoids and manipulators of solar energy, had been struck dumb by their appearance and the brazen gall of Quentin's announcement, gawking as he levitated himself above their bar, telekinetically smashing bottles that contained the shimmering concoctions enjoyed by locals, the Kid's projected helmet hiding the gleeful expression plastered upon his face. And though their drinks were indeed spectacular, the frightened Majesdanians were little help. They hadn't seen a Phoenix Egg.

The same could be said for the Tektons, primitives whose world skirted the edge of Skrull space, and the Z'nox, interstellar pirates and rivals to the smaller, nimbler Starjammers. Though the reptilian Z'nox, whose world had been attacked by the Shi'ar during Gabriel Summers' reign, coveted the Phoenix Force for their own interests... they still felt the humiliating sting left by Vulcan's assault and wanted to avoid notice by the Shi'ar as they continued to rebuild. Ultimately, the Z'nox wanted nothing to do with the Phoenix, repelling Kid Omega's line of questioning with curses and threats.

Now they were on New Xandar. Here disreputable dives grew like weeds, providing shadowy harbors and convenient hubs for pirates, smugglers, and the galaxy's underworld to share information and acquire work both honest and unscrupulous, depending on the pleasure. It was in places like the Rotten Corps, owned and operated by a sour, shapeshifting Popuppian, that Kid Omega chose to seed rumors that The Remaining were hunting a Phoenix, leaving their intentions open-ended to those who might infer the worst. He knew that Havok didn't approve of the ruse – nor would Alex's by-the-book brother – but truthfully, the Kid didn't care. All he wanted to do was save his friends and get revenge. He needed to shake loose a clue. The only way he knew how to do that was to assume the identity of his enemy, move fast, get loud, and call enough attention to themselves that the true Remaining might finally reveal their hidey-hole and take steps to shut him down. Let the Summers brothers worry about any damage left in Kid Omega's wake.

Havok was a joke, hardly the inspirational figure that was Cyclops. Every team that Alex Summers ever led had been a failure: from X-Factor to the pathetic Starjammers reboot he'd led after Corsair died. So why should Kid Omega listen to him? He was a millstone around the Kid's delicate neck. A burden that Scott Summers had forced him to drag around the galaxy. Here Alex was – a mutant with the patently useful ability to blast destructive waves of plasma into people and objects – and instead he was encouraging his team to employ tact and diplomacy, to stay "under the radar."

Were Alex and Corsair planning to invite the Phoenix to tea, expecting the ravenous parasite to meekly allow itself to be traded for a handful of Earth mutants? Did Havok believe that The Remaining – who really could be anyone or anything under those expressionless black helmets, even Phoenix-eating telepathic vampires! – would play by archaic codes of honor, allowing ten paces before a duel and firing into the air, Hamilton-style, so that the Kid's Aaron Burr might nod and forgive, letting them take both the Egg and his friends for their own amusement?

No. Flark no, to use the galactic parlance.

And honestly, flark the Summers family. Even before Kid Omega had stepped aboard the Starjammer he'd been following the lead of one Summers or another. And though he appreciated the attitude and risk-taking embraced by Corsair's Muppets-Take-Manhattan collection of alien weirdos, the Kid still bristled under any would-be authority trying to make him fall in line. Like he'd explained to Cyclops, the Omega didn't

need anyone's help to mop up his own metaphorical spills. All
he needed was for the supporting cast to provide the resources
and then stand aside and let him do the job. And right now,
"doing the job" meant capturing the attention of these
interstellar yokels.

"Are you listening?" He thundered around the room,
adopting the cold, imperious tones he recalled being used by
The Remaining's vixen of a telepath. The Poppupian owner
climbed atop the bar, flexing its molecules as it shifted its body
into a more menacing configuration, attempting to regain
control of its tavern. But the Kid mentally fused the Poppupian's
atoms into place, limiting the confused proprietor to its current
form as it tried – and failed – to change shape. Smirking and
satisfied, Kid Omega gazed out at the inebriated crowd.

"We're after a Phoenix Egg. There are none on New Xandar,
but one of you vermin must have a delicious lead or filthy
rumor." He paced, clasping both hands behind his back.
"Maybe you've heard about us in passing, frightened whispers
while traveling the galaxy. We are The Remaining. Oh, yes. And
my crew, though witless and subservient they may be" – the
Kid indicated Alex and Corsair, the latter of which rolled his
eyes – "are powerful beings. Cross any of us at your peril, my
friends. In point of fact…"

He waved a hand and a table of patrons rose into the air.
They spun around the room, trying to hold onto their drinks
and constitutions, laughing no longer.

Havok sighed and raised a fist. A series of white concentric
circles radiated out from the center of his chest, oscillating
against his black uniform as the fist began to glow. He opened
his hand, flexing outward, and the circular pattern dove toward

his fingers. He released the building pressure, firing a beam of plasma that – with a rushing whine – obliterated an empty table in the far corner of the bar. Everyone jumped, unsettled by the blast. Kid Omega lowered the spinning aliens, each of which composed its respective, nauseated digestive systems, and after a moment, Havok picked up the ball from the younger, laughing mutant.

"We are only four of The Remaining," said Havok, repeating the fabrications they'd altered after Kid Omega had changed the original plan. "Our collective army contains multitudes. We have dealt with the Phoenix in the past and are intimately familiar with the devastation it has left in its wake and what, if allowed to return, it might do to destabilize the galaxy. When we find it, those who've refused us... their planet will be first to bear its fury. Help us now. Avoid extinction. One of you must know something?"

The Kid interrupted before anyone could answer. "Should any of you scum attempt to lie, know that I am an Omega-level telepath–"

"Hsst," Alex mumbled between his teeth. "Minder."

"What?"

Alex turned his way, patiently explaining, "They may not know what a telepath is. They're called 'minders' out here."

"I don't care," he whispered back, then raised his voice, returning to the crowd. "Know that I can rummage through your heads and rip out the information we need." Kid Omega drummed fingers against his temple. "Or you can save yourselves pain and grief. Spill your guts. Either way, I'm getting what I want."

"All right, cool it," Corsair said as he finally approached the disoriented patrons, hands raised out in a placating gesture. "This is ridiculous, humiliating, and undignified. Let's drop this disguise nonsense, OK? Look, citizens. My comrades mean no harm. The truth is, my name's Corsair, captain of the Starjammers. This is my crew. Perhaps you've heard of our dashing exploits or maybe even hired us in the past. It's imperative we find this Egg because–"

The Kid interrupted, annoyed at having his plans disrupted, bored with dancing around the truth now that everything had been spoiled by Havok's interfering father. Rolling his eyes, he dropped their disguises, revealing their actual uniforms beneath.

"–because we need it to ransom back some kidnapped Earthlings from a group that calls itself 'The Remaining.' Has anyone heard anything about these creeps, or can you point us toward a Phoenix? Time's wasting. I'm about to start raiding memories."

Corsair turned and frowned. "Are you kidding? This is delicate, kid. Earth isn't popular out here. Any one of these beings may be on the line to the Shi'ar Imperial Guard in a nano-second. But maybe we can placate them with cold, hard cash–"

"Hey, Earther scum."

The trio swiveled. An older Xandarian woman, deep into her cups, beckoned them down to the end of the bar. She was half blind and alone, nursing a mug of Kymellian sweetmud, wearing a faded uniform with a dirty sunburst across the chest. The uniform was frayed and filthy, as if she'd lifted it from a corpse. Kid Omega followed Corsair to the Xandarian as Hepzibah covered their backs with a sonic repeater, making sure that no one could take them by surprise. Meanwhile, the tavern resettled and the sympathetic Pheragot helped the Kallusians to their feet as Havok went around, apologizing to the Poppupian and its patrons in an effort to convince them not to betray the mutants' true intentions.

"D'you know something?" Corsair asked, placing a gloved hand on the bar. When he removed it, a flat card was left behind – ten Xandarian units. The woman snatched it up and hid the units away, instructing the bartender to refill her mug.

"You've been paid," Corsair continued. "Now, have you seen a Phoenix Egg?"

She shook her head. "Nah, captain. Lhoran-Khan, your humble servant, has heard tell of one's existence, though. Rumors amid the space-lanes." She smiled as the Poppupian poured the aromatic sweetmud, licking her lips in anticipation.

"The last Nova corpsman and his allies dismantled the Annihilation Wave, scattering Xandar's murderers to the cosmic winds–"

Quentin held up both hands, indicating the need for a time-out.

"Whoa, whoa," he said. "Slow down. The Nova what now? Annihilation Wave sounds like a great name for a rock band, but gimme context, please."

Letting out a perturbed sigh, Corsair humored him.

"Look, Kid. New Xandar is 'new' for a reason, OK? Originally, Xandar was kinda like the center of the universe, and base of operations for the Nova Corps, a peacekeeping force tasked to police the galaxy."

Lhoran-Khan ran a hand down her filthy uniform, attempting to smooth the fabric and the once-proud sunburst stitched upon the chest. Corsair hardly noticed as he went on.

"The Corps' proudest achievement was the Worldmind, a supercomputer that housed the strategies, memories, and data of the Xandarian people. But recently, a destructive armada of interdimensional insects – an Annihilation Wave – swarmed and destroyed their planet, leaving only a single corpsman to protect the Worldmind."

"So, lemme guess," Kid Omega interjected. "He found a planet and started over."

"Him and the dispopulated Xandarians. He slowly restored the Corps… but their numbers are far from optimal. And this new world, though thriving, is hardly the technological marvel that had been the original Xandar."

"Ain't that the way with technological marvels? Man, I miss my iPod. Anyway, what happened to the Wave? Did Neue Corps eventually stop it?"

"Yeah, but only with help from other planets, races, and heroes. Including the Starjammers. To be honest, the enemy's admirals and factions eventually warred with one another, imploding the Wave, each searching for an advantage to use against their former compatriots."

The Kid began to understand. It was what he would have done if given a chance. "And the Phoenix Egg we're trying to find. One of them has one?"

"Nah, Earther youngling," said Lhoran-Khan. "The admirals Deko and Salo… Ravenous, Warlord Smyt, and all the rest of the Wave's generals… none of those cowardly leaders were bold or foolish enough to tame an aspect of the Great Devourer. But another, one of Nova's allies – rumors point to his having gained an Egg to use against the Wave's architects. Against those he'd hated, who stood in the way of his universal domination."

Alex had finally come over. He glanced at Corsair. "This ally. You've spoken to him about the Egg? Verified its existence?"

Lhoran-Khan chortled through her drink. "Me? No. Like I said, rumors. But as your humble vassal, I can tell you who he is and point toward those who might provide verification. Be wary, though," she advised, sucking the pungent sweetmud through a metallic straw.

"Your quarry? Powerful. Cagey. A conqueror, that one. Come, he did, with the Wave, partnered alongside its architects. But he was betrayed, and joined those standing against it. No, captain. Lhoran-Khan would not stand in this being's presence for all the units on Xandar."

Exasperated, Kid Omega moaned. "This is taking forever. Let me scoop the info from her head with a psionic melon baller."

"Quentin!"

The Xandarian smiled. "Peace, child. Lhoran-Khan has not seen the Egg, but others have, some nearby, heroes and potential allies. They can confirm the rumors. Those who also allied themselves with the last Nova corpsman. They who defend the galaxy from vengeful creatures like your target, he who is accursed… the brutal Baluurian monarch – the Living Bomb-Burst!"

CHAPTER SIX

[ALEX | THE UNIVERSAL MARKETS | NEW XANDAR | THE TRANTA SYSTEM]

"Blastaar? Blastaar has a Phoenix Egg?!"

Twenty minutes later, they were striding through Xandar's Universal Markets, elbowing past aliens perusing brightly colored stalls. Havok and Corsair commiserated about this latest news as Hepzibah eyed the crowd for danger and Quentin hustled to keep up.

Alex shook his head in dismay. "Blastaar has an army, Dad. He's incredibly strong and can fire concussive blasts from his hands–"

"So can you, sport."

"And he's a king! I don't care how much Scott believes in me, there's no way we can steal his Egg."

Corsair grinned and threw an arm around his son's shoulders. "Not with that attitude, Alex. C'mon, this way. We have to move."

Huffing for breath, Quentin finally caught up to the Summers men. "I'm sorry, but I'm new to all things cosmic: what exactly is a 'Blastaar'?"

Corsair beckoned through the crowd, putting a finger to his lips. "Quieter, kid. Broadcasting the name of an interdimensional despot isn't the best idea in mixed company, especially after we've already name-dropped the Phoenix."

He thumbed back in the direction of the bar. "Any one of the beings back there – including and especially Lhoran-Khan – could've called the Nova Corps or the Shi'ar by now. I'd like to get our verification and then put distance between us and this planet."

Quentin tapped his temple again. "We can always take it indoors."

"Ha!" Corsair stuck a finger inside his headband, stretching it out so the others could see a mesh of circuitry woven through the inner fabric. "Thanks, kid. Your little psychic costume change may have worked on the tourist trade, but the Starjammers have dealt with too many beings trying to get at secrets hidden inside our skulls. I'm sure you've got the best intentions, but me and the Cat Lady prefer to keep our vaults locked." Nearby, scanning for threats and weapons, Hepzibah grinned and used a claw to reveal the same jamming technology woven into her own green bandanna.

Corsair turned a corner, past a pink Krylorian hawking bins of pungent furry melons. He beckoned for the others to take a right into an alley connecting one end of the market to the other. The quartet moved inside, Hepzibah guarding their rear with her repeater.

"Blastaar's a wild card, Pinky. I don't know what kind of mutant menaces you've been unlucky to tackle on Earth, but like most beings out here, Blastaar's in a league beyond compare. He's from another dimension, see?" Major Summers indiscriminately waved a hand, vaguely gesturing everywhere. "Not another planet. A whole other deadly plane of anti-matter they call 'the Negative Zone.'"

"Came from the Zone, the Annihilation Wave did," Hepzibah informed them, hissing with distaste. "With legions of nasty bugs and creepy-crawlies, and–"

"And Blastaar," Alex interjected, picking up the debrief as they walked. "He ruled a planet in the Zone, but was overthrown by his own people, the Baluurians... kind of like gray, bipedal lions. He's been attacking our universe ever since. At some point he'd hitched his wagon to the Wave's leaders, but they betrayed Blastaar, and he came over to the side of angels out of spite, allying himself with enemies against his own kind."

Quentin grinned. "Sounds like a few mutants I know, but with a stupider name."

"Look who's talking, Quintavius Quirinius Quentin," Alex continued. "Blastaar's no mutant. He's a king and a threat. They call him 'the Living Bomb-Burst' because of the force blasts he can create with his fingers. He can use them to fly or punch holes in battle-class dreadnoughts, so don't try or say anything foolish when we finally meet him."

"Foolish? Me?" Kid Omega adopted an expression of mock-insult.

Corsair chuckled. "You talk a good game, Pinky. But so far 'acting foolish' seems to be your actual mutant power." The Starjammer captain had reached the alley's end, the sounds and sights of vendors and shoppers coming back into view. He nodded to his Mephitisoid first mate and stepped into the market.

"Let's go. It's happy hour. Three rows down and a left, we

should find our guys. They're here every week at this time, like clockwork. Honestly, we might've saved ourselves a lot of time, effort, and exposure if we'd simply asked them in the first place. Alex, I still don't know why you were against it!"

"I had my reasons, Dad. But with our cover blown to hell, I guess they no longer make any sense. C'mon, Quentin." Alex turned to follow his father, but the younger mutant hesitated and hung back, clearly angry and fuming.

"What's the problem? Let's catch up."

"Kid Omega."

"How's that?"

Quentin stood up. "My chosen name – my real name – is Kid Omega. I picked it so that no one would underestimate me. So folks would know that I'm an Omega-level mutant. I hate it when people call me 'Quentin' and when they think I'm stupid."

Alex softened. He'd been so focused on the "find Phoenix/ save kids" part of the mission, that he'd dropped the ball on attempting to bond with Quentin. "Hey, I don't think you're stupid. I didn't mean anything by…"

"I know it's a mouthful, which is why I give folks a pass when they use my sapien name. People assume that 'kid' means 'juvenile,' that I'm not worldly or a mutant to be taken seriously. But remember, I hosted the flarking Phoenix. I can manifest things that would blow your insignificant little Summers brainpan. What, 'Havok,' are you only good at destroying things? At causing 'havoc'?"

"No, of course not. But–"

"But nothing." Kid Omega leaned in. "Stop treating me like an idiot. And tell James T. Jerk out there to stop calling me

'Pinky.' Sure, you both have more space experience than I do, but despite my name I'm not a child. I can handle this Blasturd or whatever – who, by the way, seems to have the same exact stupid power as you do, so I'm not sure why you're shaking in your black skintight skivvies. I'm just as good as you or the Starjammers, if not better."

Alex absorbed the outburst, allowing himself a second before replying. His father and Hepzibah were probably halfway to their destination.

"Fine," he replied, holding up both hands in surrender. "I said I was sorry. But you admitted that both Corsair and I have more off-world experience… and despite best efforts to prove otherwise, you have been acting like a child. This is sensitive work, Kid Omega. Navigating the galaxy, both physically and politically, takes tact, patience, and diplomacy. So far, you've failed to master any of those things."

"I don't have to be tactful. My friends–"

"–are gonna die unless you stop yourself from saying the first thing that comes to your mouth the moment you want to say it." Alex pointed to his own eyes and ears. "Look. Listen. Think before you make a choice. I know this is absolutely not the Kid Omega Way, but I promise if you want to find these kids and stop The Remaining… out here in the galaxy, you catch more flies with honey."

Quentin rolled his eyes and tapped his shirt, which now read I CATCH MORE FLIES WITH DANK MEMES. "I told you, Not-Cyclops. I don't need your help. I don't want your help, your space Dad's help or any folksy proverbs or lessons from the Chuck Xavier's Dummies' Guide for Teaching Wayward Gifted Youngsters."

Kid Omega tapped the lone white circle on Havok's chest. "Take your diplomacy and your advice and shove it up your–"

"OK." Alex swatted away Quentin's finger. "I get it. You've made things perfectly clear. You think that you can do this without my help or the Starjammers'? Fine. But I'll tell you this: it's a big galaxy out there, not to mention the universe beyond. You definitely need our ship, technology, and connections. Without those, you'll never locate Blastaar and through him, a Phoenix Egg. The louder you get, the more risks you take… and sooner or later the Shi'ar or Kree or someone else will come knocking, trying to get the Egg before you do, and maybe endanger your life and the lives of your friends."

"Hey, I wasn't the one who blew up the plan in that bar, Havok. That was your stupid dad. I was sticking to the script."

"The plan you originally changed, but sure. You're right, and I'll mention that to him. But you were there the moment it happened, calling attention to the fact that we're from Earth. That was risky. That may have gotten us and your friends killed." Alex indicated the market, waving an open palm. "Look… I don't like you, and you don't like me. I'm only partnered with you as a favor to my brother. But I did make a promise to him, and we have to work together from now on. Unless you'd like to wander the Xandarian Markets alone, looking for quarry and leads you can't find, light years from a planet that you know and hate?"

Kid Omega crossed his arms and grunted, a mulish expression crossing his face. He shook his head, acknowledging that wasn't what he wanted.

"Great," Alex continued. "Then put aside that Omega-level ego and take my lead once in a while, OK? Tact may not be your strong suit, but the guys that we're heading to meet right now... well, they're no diplomats, I grant, but I promise that the wrong misstep in their company might not only turn this from a still-somewhat-stealthy mission into an incident of galactically public proportions, but also end up with several of us missing a valuable extremity."

"What was that Corsair said? Why didn't we go to these guys in the first place? You said you had reasons."

Alex sighed. "Because as connected as they are, they have a reputation for being trouble magnets. Anytime they walk a galactic tightrope, one of these guys ends up breaking the cord. They're loud and a bit of a disaster, if you have to know. I was trying to stay under the radar, remember? These guys are anything but."

Kid Omega raised an eyebrow. "Who are they? I like them already."

Havok laughed. "C'mon. I'll introduce you."

Five city blocks away, Corsair squatted in a large open-air stall, hoisting metal drinking tins with a group of boisterous salarymen, fresh from a day cataloguing data transfers from across the Tranta System. Corsair's companions lounged against a plethora of cushions wedged into three curving booths, enjoying smoking skewers of grilled tentacles, the discarded spits of which littered the ground. They shouted unintelligible toasts to one another, and Corsair threw a friendly arm around a red-faced, sweating Xandarian.

Seated nearby were three outsiders. The first, a grinning, handsome blond humanoid in a pilot's windbreaker, a stylized sunburst on the breast, rested one hand against a gunslinger's holster on his belt as the other hefted his own metal tin. Next to the blond sat a lithe, beautiful, green-skinned woman with yellow markings around her eyes, barely visible beneath a white hood pulled down over her ears. She wore a form-fitting suit of purple-and-white and brandished the largest sword that Alex and Quentin had ever seen.

Closer to the group, roaring with laughter and spitting out flecks of tentacle meat, sat what appeared to be an Earth raccoon. Beady red eyes squinted as it gnawed, pieces of its snack settling into the bristly brown and white fur covering its four-foot frame. The raccoon grabbed a tankard from the ground and quaffed the contents into its mouth, a viscous fluid dripping around the creature's muzzle and staining its red and cobalt jumpsuit. Two very large, complicated rifles rested at the raccoon's feet. Hepzibah, ignoring her captain and the salarymen, inspected the guns. She appeared to be admiring them, nodding her approval to their small, receptive owner.

"Hey, Summers," the raccoon chortled with a gravelly voice as Alex arrived. "Just couldn't stay away, could ya? I understand," it mock-sympathized, setting aside its drink. "As far as places t'live go, what with the backwards tech and flarknard smell, Earth's one step down from a poisonous H'ylthrian vineyard!"

"C'mon, Rocket," Havok said, settling down next to Hepzibah, "it's not that bad."

The raccoon considered and smiled. "Well, the pizza's all right, I guess. Welcome back to civilization, anyway. Who's the krutackin' fashion plate?"

Alex jerked a thumb toward Quentin. "This is Kid Omega, a future X-Man."

Kid Omega bristled at that. "Hey, I can speak for myself."

"Kid Omega? You call yerself that, but on purpose?" Rocket

leaned forward, squinting at Quentin. "What're ya, some kinda Earther super sidekick?"

"I'm no sidekick, Ranger Rick. So kindly keep my glorious name out of your filthy scavenger piehole."

"OK, but I mean puttin' 'kid' in your name really ain't no way t'strike fear into the guts o' yer enemies. 'Kid Galactus.' 'Kid Thanos.' See? Krutackin' adorable." Rocket turned to the blond humanoid with the holster. "Ranger Rick? That one of your Earther music gods, Quill?"

The blond smiled. "No sir. Pink Mr T there's comparing you to a beloved kids' cartoon raccoon from the nineteen sixties."

Rocket snarled and raised an eyebrow. "What's a 'cartoon'?"

"Look," Corsair interjected, leaning over from the throng of salarymen, "as much as I enjoy a good dose of witty repartee, the clock's ticking, and trouble's coming. You all know my son, right? This is Quent–"

"Kid Omega."

"–yeah, him. Kid, meet Rocket, Gamora" – this to the green woman – "the most dangerous woman in the galaxy. And that handsome half-human pirate is Peter Quill, the legendary Star-Lord. Say hello to the Guardians of the Galaxy."

Kid Omega snorted and laughed. "Seriously?"

Peter Quill lazily unsnapped his holster. "Something funny, 'Kid'?"

"I mean... 'Star-Lord' pretty much speaks for itself."

"You know what else speaks for itself?" Quill remarked. "My one-of-a-kind element gun. Wanna know what lightning feels like from close up? Wipes your smile clean off, Buttons."

"Not as smoothly as a psychic knife. Let's see what's faster: your gun or my brain."

Star-Lord and Rocket put down their tins and stood, the latter raising one of his complicated rifles. Kid Omega moved to meet their advance. Alex stepped between them as the inebriated salarymen dug into another round of spitted tentacles.

"Hey... no one's getting lightninged or knifed," said Havok. "We just want answers, and then we'll be on our way. Then you can get back to your Xandarian ale or whatever. OK?"

The Guardians sneered, and Quill, glaring at Quentin, nodded and returned to his seat.

"OK, fine," said Peter Quill. "We'll stand down for you, Summers. But this ain't ale," he protested, lifting his drink. "It's a protein smoothie made with the finest and sweetest berries in the galaxy, harvested from the Gardener himself, one of the cosmic Elders of the Universe."

Corsair laughed. "Harvested?"

Quill cracked a smile. "OK, fine. Stolen. I mean, he's one of the cosmic Elders of the Universe! He ain't gonna just give up his berries. But they're worth it, Corsair. Try the blue. The blue's fantastic."

"Oh, yeah," Rocket mumbled, taking a healthy drink. "We got those berries, all right."

Kid Omega turned to Havok, crossing his arms in doubt. "Them? Really? These guys are gonna help us find a Phoenix Egg? Captain Smoothie Berries and Space Meeko?"

"Hey," shouted Peter Quill, "don't knock the smoothie till you try it. There's bits of Asgardian apple and Sakaarian bramble-grass in there, too. Good for the eyes. Also, we're not gonna help you find a Phoenix Egg. No way."

Rocket barked in laughter. "Ha! What d'we look like, a

bunch of garkin' dinkwafts? No!" He slammed his tankard on the floor, drops of smoothie splattering everywhere. "We're the krutackin' Guardians of the Galaxy! Even we know that wranglin' a Phoenix Egg is a fool's run."

Quentin sneered. "So you're scared."

"Of course we're scared," Rocket said, pointing a paw at the young, cocky mutant. "And you should be, too, if y'even have the tiniest brain of a Skrullian sch'mag. It's the krutackin' Phoenix we're yakkin' about. If you ain't scared – even a little bit – then there's something seriously wrong with you, Earther!"

"Read the shirt, trash panda." Kid Omega tapped his chest; the words WACCOON SEASON appeared above a cartoon hunter. "Get the reference on your own time, after you've gathered enough nuts and garbage to get you through the long, cold winter."

Rocket snarled again, glaring at Quentin, teeth bared with a claw on his trigger. The stand-off continued for three seconds, maybe five… and then the Guardian smiled, slapped a paw on Quentin's chest, and recovered his overturned drink.

"Ha! Yer OK, kid." He snapped his fingers at the multi-eyed vendor manning the cart. "Smoothie the kid, willya? Me too. A coupla blues! It's on Corsair."

The Starjammer captain started to protest but stopped himself and nodded at both Rocket and Quentin. "Smoothies all around. Now, what's this about not helping to find the Egg, Quill?"

Star-Lord leaned forward, setting aside his drink. "We're not getting near – or involved with – the Phoenix. That wasn't the ask, Summers. You wanted to know whether Blastaar had an Egg and where you might find it, and that we can do. Point the way, like. But I agree with Rocket... nothin' good ever came from poking that particular entity. What you're doing" – Quill pointed at all four of them, mutants and pirates alike – "it's suicide. And though sometimes we Guardians stumble into situations that maybe sorta feel suicidal, we tend to avoid that kinda risky maxiflark so we can, y'know, continue to guard the galaxy."

"Not me," Gamora disagreed in a low husky whisper, the first thing she'd said since Alex and Quentin had arrived. "I'm up for suicidal."

"Even so," Star-Lord concluded, "if I were you, I'd find another way."

Alex shrugged. "There is no other way, Quill. We'd explore it if there were. No one else has seen or heard of an existing Phoenix Egg other than Blastaar's, and nobody knows anything about those who want it. The aliens who kidnapped Kid Omega's friends."

Rocket jerked a thumb at Quentin. "This kid's got friends?"

Kid Omega smiled as he accepted his drink from the vendor. "Right now, trash panda, this smoothie's my only friend."

"Heh. You just wait. The blue's krutackin' amazing."

"OK," Alex said, trying to verify the information they'd come to find. "So you won't help us. That's fine. But can you at least confirm Blastaar does have a Phoenix Egg, and that you don't want to get involved because it's the actual thing?"

"Yes. Yes, I can confirm that Blastaar has an Egg and, Gamora aside, none of us want to go anywhere near it."

"Where did he get it? Does he still have it? Where is it now?"

"Whoa, whoa," Star-Lord replied, raising his hands to defend himself from Alex's verbal assault. "What is this, twenty questions? We don't know where he got it, and we don't wanna know. But if it's up to me," he said, firing a warning glance at Gamora, "I'd ask him to put it back or leave it be. If you people wanna tramp over to the Xanthan Graveyard and check yourself, verify its existence with your own eyes, then that's your own deal. Ask the Living Bomb-Burst how he got his planet-eating parasitical buzzard, see why he wants it and make sure it's still ticking. Yeah, that'll work out for all involved. That what you want, Summers?"

"Yes, Peter. That's what I want."

"Then you're an idiot. And this is gonna blow up in everybody's face."

"I wouldn't be surprised. The Xanthan Graveyard? Is that what you said?"

Quill nodded. "Yeah. I got a tree on our ship who can beam over the last known coordinates." He took a breath and sighed. He looked at an expectant Gamora and then silently screamed. "OK, look. Fine. Are you sure that you don't want our help? I mean, toying with a Phoenix is a monumentally stupid idea, but if it's fate of the galaxy stuff and with kidnapped Earth kids..."

Alex smiled. "Thanks, Quill. I appreciate your position. We could use the hands, but it's probably better if we run lean from here on in."

"Fair enough. But call if you change your mind."

"Thank you."

Star-Lord settled back and lifted his smoothie, raising it to Havok, Kid Omega, Corsair, and the others. The clueless salarymen returned the toast, hoisting their drinks and squealing approval on a deal well closed.

"Don't thank me unless you survive," Quill answered.

"Frankly, I think this is a huge mistake and at least half of you are gonna die. So please, for me? Try to avoid that."

Kid Omega raised his smoothie in Alex's direction. "Don't get murdered. Heck of a send-off. About right for us, though."

Havok nodded and clinked his tin against the Kid's. "Don't get murdered."

The mutants drank their smoothies. Quentin's eyes lit up.

"This… this is delicious."

Quill smiled. "Right? The cosmic Elder berries. I told you."

"It tastes so… blue."

"Yeah, that blue," Star-Lord agreed as he finished his own drink. "It's flarking fantastic."

CHAPTER SEVEN

[QUENTIN | THE STARJAMMER | EN ROUTE TO XANTH | SPACE]

Kid Omega raised an armored hand, lifting it to defend himself from Raza's cutlass.

The pirate swiveled, swinging a short, silver dagger to attack the Kid's right. The blade sparked against Quentin's psionic battle-suit, deflected by his coral carapace as the combatants backed toward neutral corners.

Raza Longknife grinned. His topknot, a fiery mane of crimson sprouting from atop his skull, gaily flipped as he danced away. The cyborg spread both arms, his knives pointing toward the 'Jammer's opposite hulls, and assumed a stance as he nodded approvingly to his opponent.

"Very good. Thou art practiced. Again!"

The Starjammer sprang, whirling like a dervish, slicing and slashing with diagonal thrusts. Kid Omega raised the flat knives housed in the armor's gauntlets. As Raza rained blows, the Kid instinctively used his wrist-blades to weather each strike.

Alex, Ch'od, and Sikorsky watched the action, lounging

and cheering on the wide floor of the 'Jammer's twenty-two-thousand grassy acres of "farmland," a cargo area generally used to store foodstuff, long since converted to conceal smuggled contraband. Havok and the Starjammers followed the exercise as they enjoyed a snack procured from New Xandar: vacuum-sealed jerky, Majesdanian lightblossoms, and bottles of sweet Vodani seawater. Kid Omega wiped sweat from his brow as Raza broke the attack, allowing the mutant a moment to catch his breath.

The pirate laughed, harsh lighting from the ship's interior glinting against his cybernetic eye. "Well done. Thine instructors, from whichever shore they doth hail, should feel pride."

Kid Omega grimaced. His arms throbbed. "I'm mostly self-taught."

The Starjammer raised his cutlass in salute. "A fast study, then. Few there are that hath ably defended themselves from the Twin Fists of Yon-Rogg, a technique culled from the disciplined teachings of the Priests of Pama."

The Kid sniffed and shrugged, allowing his psionic armor to dissolve like a paper raincoat. "Oh, yeah? Is that like using the Pop Shot technique to counterattack your enemies and get a Fortnite Victory Royale?"

Confused, Raza wrinkled his brow.

"Thy strategies require clarity and context, pink one."

"Yeah, I didn't grok your nonsense either, One-Eyed Willie. Hey, Summers... tell me again why I've gotta do this?"

Havok washed a lightblossom down with a slug of Vodani water. The older mutant got to his feet, handing his snacks to a receptive Ch'od, and approached the resting fighters.

"Thanks to the coordinates we received from Quill, the 'Jammer will be at the Xanthan Graveyard in no time at all. Facing down barflies is one thing, Kid Omega. An army of savage Baluurians is quite another. Blastaar isn't going to share smoothies with us, nor will acquiring his Phoenix Egg be an easy task. The Starjammers are hardened fighters, sure, and you've been in a few scraps, but this is different. This is dangerous, and it's best to use what little time we have to prepare and train."

Kid Omega grabbed a bottle of water. "What, by swashbuckling with robot Jack Sparrow over there? C'mon, Not-Cyclops. This isn't Westchester."

"What do you mean?"

Kid Omega waved a hand, indicating the empty hold. "I mean, this is hardly the X-Mansion's secret Danger Room," he said, referencing the underground, multi-purpose training facility the X-Men used to hone their mutant skills against a rotating sequence of holographic scenarios complete with accurate tactile and olfactory feedback. "We're playing at pirates in the belly of a starship, light years from the closest coffee shop, headed to steal a cosmic egg from an interdimensional warlord who may or may not still possess it. These," Quentin said disdainfully, pointing to Raza Longknife's... well, long knives, "are comic book nonsense compared to that. I mean, didn't you ever see The Untouchables?"

Sikorsky rotated and chittered excitedly. They turned its way. Ch'od nodded, listening intently, and then translated the Chr'yllite's statement for the others.

"Sikorsky says, 'Excellent film, QuentinQuireKidOmega. Brian DePalma. 1987. Sean Connery. Don't bring a knife to a gun fight.'"

Kid Omega raised a pink eyebrow. "How...?"

"Even out here," Ch'od answered, "we get the Earther streaming services."

Havok crossed his arms. "What are you saying, Kid? We're not training hard enough?"

Kid Omega shook his head. The fight had taken a lot out of him. Raza was brutal. But the exhaustion didn't eclipse the frustration Quentin now felt toward his inadequate chaperone.

Maybe I shouldn't have campaigned so hard to lose the older Summers brother, the Kid admonished himself. At least with Cyclops, he wouldn't have to suffer fools or continued failures of leadership. Since Kid Omega had left the Earth, he'd endured a half-assed goose chase for information, scuttled a solid plan to gather leads, and horked down the galaxy's best blended drink with a green smokeshow, a filthy raccoon, and a half-human idiot.

Now he found himself crossing swords with a pointy-eared buccaneer to the delight of a tiny cinephile helicopter, an amused crocodile, and the lamest excuse for an instructor that Quentin had ever met.

He was finished taking Havok's lead. At least Scott – the more impressive Summers brother, a tried and tested leader – was someone that Kid Omega could respect. Cyclops had weathered the front lines, served his time steering the ship. The Kid had gathered that diplomacy, though hardly his strong suit, was more important than he'd believed... but he also knew that sometimes you needed to rely on guts and wits, devil take the results. Scott Summers knew that, too. He also knew how to lead a team. Quentin didn't trust Alex to lead them out of a paper bag.

And it was time to make himself heard.

"What I'm saying is, Blastaar won't use a knife, and there's no way he's waiting for me to stick him with the pointy end. The dude's a gun. You said it yourself. 'The Living Bomb-Burst,' with the power to blow ships out of the sky using just his hands."

"Your point being?"

Kid Omega smiled. "Who else do we know with a power like that? That's who I should be dueling. Not Swords McGee over there."

Havok scratched his head, a dubious look on his face. "OK, I get you. But using my abilities on the Starjammer... I could damage something, or accidentally puncture the hull. It isn't safe, and Corsair would have my head."

"Then we'll spar elsewhere. I know a place sans hull, where there's no way you can wound anything other than your pride. You know, after I win."

"Oh, yeah? And how do we get there?"

The Kid tapped his skull. "Click them ruby slippers, Havok. Oz is closer than you think."

"No. No way." Alex raised his hands in protest. "I'm not getting inside your head."

"Why not? And it isn't my head; Emma taught me how to make constructs into which I can upload not only my own psyche but others as well. True, I had a little setback in Canada..."

"You mean when five kids got kidnapped?"

"But I've been practicing, jerk. I'm getting better. Besides, that Remaining witch is MIA, and as far as I know, there are no other telepa– Excuse me, no other 'minders' around with the power to home invade the Kid. We'll be safe. I promise."

Havok seemed skeptical. "I don't know."

Kid Omega held out a hand. "C'mon. You keep asking me to follow your lead, to trust you. Well, trust works both ways. All I want to do is prep for Blastaar. I've got a better chance countering his explodey hands if I train with someone who has similar powers. Sure, I could create a psionic puppet of you or Blastaar inside the construct... but I'd be the one controlling it with my mind, as I do everything within the space. It won't be the same. I need you in there, making spontaneous decisions and moves, ones I have to counter. And the battleground's contained; the only damage you'll do is to my ego."

"That's what I'm worried about. Your ego's damaged enough."

Quentin smiled. "See? The only Summers brother with an actual sense of humor." He turned to Ch'od, Raza, and Sikorsky. "He's doing it. You know you're doing it, Havok."

Alex rolled his eyes. "Fine. Just keep your projections focused on the exercise, OK? I don't want to be exposed to more of your greasy thoughts than absolutely necessary."

"Will do, teach."

"Great. So how do we begin?"

The mutants were suddenly standing inside a large, pink, empty box. The Starjammers were gone. Havok started, disoriented by the visual and spatial shift.

"OK," he said. "Where are we?"

Kid Omega smirked. "Think of it as 'the Omega Room.' It's like the Danger Room, but bound only by the limits of my mind. And as you know, the Kid's mind is limitless. Here, I can adjust the space – what's in it, size or temperature, number of obstacles – simply by thinking."

"Handy. So, now what? Do we just... fight?"

"Well, I thought it'd be helpful to introduce some battle conditions."

"What do you–?"

The walls disappeared, and the Omega Room came to life with sound and color. They now stood on a rocky landscape in the heart of a dangerous asteroid field, debris and planetoids whirling and crashing overhead. Kid Omega encased himself in the psionic armor he'd been wearing to duel Raza, this time with cannons mounted into the wrists. Havok glanced around, and the Kid rose into the air. He strafed the ground around his opponent's feet as pieces of broken, flaming asteroids plummeted from the sky.

"Let's go, teach. You wanted to train? Let's train!"

A determined expression settled upon Havok's face. He wove and ducked for cover behind a nearby boulder. Quentin laughed, and a labyrinth sprang up around them, enclosing both mutants and providing an obstacle to open shots. Kid Omega floated down into the labyrinth and began stalking his prey, carefully turning corners to avoid an ambush. Usually, when he brought another psyche into his constructs, the Kid knew the mind's location and what it was doing at all times; like breathing, the awareness was simply part of him. But now he flipped a mental toggle, turning off that particular function. He wanted to keep himself blind to Havok's whereabouts and actions. This was supposed to be a challenge, and the only way for Kid Omega to stay on his toes and ensure that he was prepared to face Blastaar was to level the playing field.

"Come out, come out, wherever you are!"

He turned another corner and primed his wrist-blasters. Truthfully, toying with Havok was more fun than trading steel with Raza. All of the tension and frustration he'd felt toward Alex over the last few days... all of his annoyance with the Summers men, in general... this was a great way to scratch that itch. And he was particularly proud of how far along he'd come this time when constructing the Omega Room. He had finally been able to introduce realistic color, ensuring that their surroundings seemed authentic, and not a candy-colored replica of an actual environment. Next time, Kid Omega would try to introduce smell and maybe taste, convincing his opponents that they were in the real thing, not a nightmare of his own devising. That would mean he could use his constructs to deploy effective traps.

As he patted himself on the proverbial back, the Kid was suddenly shaken from his reverie, back into the fight. An earsplitting whine echoed over the wall, and a concussive blast demolished an entire section of labyrinth to Quentin's right. He carefully peered through the hole. Havok had abandoned stealth for a direct approach, using his mutant power to fire plasma through the labyrinth. The older mutant held out his hands, balled into fists, as white, concentric circles radiated from the center of his chest.

"Wherever I am is right here, Kid. Why don't you come out now?" Alex called, taunting his opponent. "Blastaar isn't going to play cat-and-mouse, Quentin. He's going to flatten us, like a tornado through a trailer park." Another whine, and a second bolt of plasma took out the wall to Kid Omega's left. "He's got the numbers. He's got an army. What do you have?"

"What do I have?" the Kid repeated. "It's not a knife, right? If the Living Bomb-Burst has an army... I suppose I'll have to recruit one of my own."

Kid Omega floated up out of the labyrinth, and he spread his arms. The rubble from the walls Havok had decimated now began to glow, then vibrate. Smiling, Quentin opened his palms, and the debris morphed and lengthened, growing torsos, bodies, and faces. He winked at Havok, then pointed to his own shirt. The words SAY HELLO TO YOUR LITTLE FRIENDS appeared on the Kid's chest. Below, the rubble turned into people, each wearing familiar faces and costumes ... recognizable mutants, heroes, and villains from Earth. A Cyclops drone, murderous look upon the visible lower half of its face, raised an arm and beckoned the soldiers forward. Kid Omega's psionic drones marched in unison, forming up on Havok.

"Oh, come on," Alex moaned. "No fair."

He blasted plasma into the sky, aiming for Kid Omega. The shots went wide, instead bombarding falling pieces of flaming space rocks, splintering them into smaller chunks that then spread out as they dashed to the ground.

The Kid winked. "Whoever said life was fair, teach?"

Now Havok fired at the drones, deploying his abilities to thin the herd. They kept coming, overwhelming the black-garbed mutant, bolstered by constant reinforcements. Each drone that Alex destroyed was immediately replaced by two more, Kid Omega thinking them into existence as fast as he could to maintain their overwhelming numbers.

Laughing, sweating with both the exertion needed to preserve the Omega Room and also press his attack, the Kid decided that it was finally time to claim his victory... and do it in a way that would not only humiliate Alex but also prove that Kid Omega needed no one but himself to stymie an intergalactic warlord. Flexing a mental muscle, he willed fifty new drones into existence – duplicates of the Starjammers, X-Men, and Avengers – and circled them around his frustrated, would-be instructor, urging their ranks toward Havok's location. As the inexhaustible wave of bodies closed in, Havok lost room to operate, unable to strike the drones without exposing himself to additional sets of clutching, grasping hands. Two of the psionic manifestations – simulacrums of Corsair and Cyclops – pinned Havok's arms while the others hammered his body, pounding his torso like a piece of meat, using fists, claws, hammers, shields, and weapons to tenderize poor Alex Summers.

Serves him right, Quentin mused with glee. Havok goaded me, questioned my abilities.

He'd been underestimated all his life. Him, the Omega. The X-Men only ever saw Quentin Quire as a squirmy menace, an annoyance at best, to be dealt with and then ignored. Others – both mutants and humans – slapped his wrist and spoke to him like a child. Why did he need to be "instructed" by an older mutant? Why did Quentin ever even need to attend a mutant school? Just look what he could do on his own. Blastaar had an army? Big whoop. Kid Omega was an army unto himself. He didn't need Havok. He didn't need anyone. He winked, and three giant Sentinel robots sprang into being, their clunky metal boots settling upon his enemy like crushing pylons. Kid Omega grinned. Perspiration coursed down his spine and skull. The snarky credo upon his chest slowly dissolved, replaced on his T-shirt by the Kid's personal icon: the Omega symbol above a rotated "X," slowly morphing into a death's head skull. Victory was close… he could taste it, both salty and sweet. He couldn't even see Havok within the swarm of punching, biting, gnashing psionic drones, tearing and lashing out on the Omega's behalf...

"Kid!"

Gritting his teeth, he ignored the desperate intrusion. Kid Omega closed his ears to the voice and opened a hand. One of the Sentinels raised its cannons.

"Kid, that's enough!"

The voice again, more determined this time, accompanied by a slight physical tremor. An unseen presence shook him by the shoulders. Havok's muffled screams rose as the drones continued to tear Alex apart...

Something stung the Kid on the cheek, snapping his head back and to the right.

"This is your last warning, kid, before Ch'od dumps you out an airlock!"

It struck again. Both cheeks burned. Kid Omega opened his eyes.

He stood in the Starjammer's cargo area, swaying now on unsteady feet. Corsair, eyes aflame, grasped him by the shoulders. Quentin lifted a hand to his face. His cheeks were hot and raw. He'd been slapped. Nearby, Alex lay huddled and unmoving on the floor, groaning and clutching his skull. Ch'od, Raza, and Sikorsky crouched by his side, the little medical whirlybird chittering as it hovered and checked the mutant's vital signs.

Corsair snapped two fingers in front of Kid Omega's face. "Hey. Hey, wake up."

He shook off the pain and adrenaline, willing himself to regain his composure. Quentin still felt a satisfied tightness in his arms and legs, a pounding in his chest. He'd been consumed by battle lust, ignoring all else but his aggression and the need to win.

Major Summers snapped again, "That's enough, kid. Fight's over."

"I know. I'm... hey, quit snapping."

"You nearly killed him!" Corsair snatched the front of Quentin's shirt, and the younger mutant shoved him off.

"No, I didn't. Trust me. If I'd wanted him dead, he'd be dead."

"You self-absorbed, reckless little–"

Raza stopped Corsair from renewing his attack. Fuming, Chris Summers stalked away in disgust, seeing to his son. "You went too far. I don't care how important this mission is or how integral you are to making it happen... I'm not going to stand there and watch you murder my son."

"Oh, save the drama for the Priests of Pama. Your boy there wanted to train. We trained. I was just listening to teacher. Look, I admit I... I got lost inside myself there for a second. I went too far... I'm sorry, all right?"

"You're a real flarknard. You know that?"

The Kid sadly tugged the lapels of his jacket. "Yeah, I know."

Sikorsky chittered, and Havok, groaning, slowly sat up, supported by Ch'od. The concerned Saurid turned to his captain. "Sikorsky believes Alex will recover. No signs of permanent trauma. Any physical damage sustained has resulted from stress manifested via psychic onslaught. That said, captain, if not for your timely intervention, the boy may have suffered worse at the youngling's hands."

"Why didn't you stop him, then?" Corsair glared at Ch'od and Raza in turn. The latter shrugged a shoulder and scratched his cheek.

"'Twas an exercise, captain. Thy son... the boy... t'were in no real danger."

Alex struggled to his feet. He coughed. "Tell that to my chest. It feels like someone hit me with a planet."

Kid Omega rolled his eyes. "Or a tornado."

"My dad's right. You were reckless. Once you had me pinned, you should've turned off the room and let me up."

"Will Blastaar let us up after we're pinned, Havok? I thought the point was to be the gun, not the knife." The hypocrisy and, frankly, the contradictions were ticking him off. One minute Alex wanted the Kid to step it up, the next he wanted him to back off.

"You said 'army.' Army's what you got."

Havok winced. "Yeah, but you were so busy trying to win, to prove your point, that you forgot this was a training exercise. I'll be fine, Quentin, but your impulsivity – that need to claim victory by any means necessary – blinded you from the fact that you were facing a teacher, not an enemy."

"I told you. Don't call me Quent–"

"Why? You're not a kid. You said it yourself. But today you acted like one. Children have to be reminded who their friends are. Children need to be told the difference between a game and combat and when to stand down after they've snatched victory from a friend. Not you. You know – or should know – when to press, when to stop. When to use tact and when to rush in. But you don't. You always have to be right. You want to be the winner so badly that you don't care who you hurt along the way."

"We were sparring. There are winners and losers."

"But you'd already won. I was down and beaten. Why didn't you let up?"

"I was…" His face felt hot, not from Corsair's slap but because of the interrogation. The way the others were looking at him now, judging him.

"You were angry. Too busy trying to prove to me and the Starjammers – heck, to the universe – that you need no one else but Quentin Quire. Right? That's what you've been saying this entire time, since you first approached my brother."

"I don't need–"

Alex ticked off on his fingers. "You didn't need us to find The Remaining. To find a Phoenix Egg. To escape the warbirds. To travel from bar to bar, planet to planet, and get a lead on Blastaar. You didn't need anyone, right?"

The Kid stood and seethed, hands balled into fists. Havok continued, "Because the great Kid Omega doesn't need anyone but himself. Forget the humans; he doesn't need teachers or colleagues. He doesn't need an escort or anyone to fight his battles. He doesn't even need his friends."

"That's not true. I do need them. That's why–"

"Why you lost them? Maybe it wasn't because of an alien telepath, Quentin. Maybe you lost them because you were foolish, impulsive, and reckless. You were so busy trying to win, to fight your own battles without asking for help. Maybe the Kid was too busy showing off for his friends instead of keeping them safe, and now who knows where they are or if they're even still alive? Congratulations, Quentin. You did what you wanted, when you wanted, without tact, teachers, or partners. Now as a result, you may have lost the only friends you actually had."

The cargo bay fell silent. The Starjammers glanced at one another as Alex got to his feet.

Kid Omega glared at Havok. His cheek flinched, and a muscle jumped in his jaw.

Corsair touched his son's arm. "Alex…"

"That about right, Quentin?"

"Shut up." He said it quietly, nearly to himself.

"Prove me wrong. Show us that you're more Omega than kid. Be a tornado all you like, but Blastaar's no trailer park. He's a general and a king. You've got the power, sure, and the guts. He'll figure out how to deal with both. So, unless you have a plan, I suggest you wipe that arrogant smirk off your face and join us on the bridge."

Havok held out a hand. Kid Omega wanted to slap it. To reach out with his mind and crush the fingers in his psionic grip. He tried breathing, to cool down.

Then he thought about Phoebe Cuckoo and Glob. Ayo, Hijack, and No-Girl. Out in space, somewhere out in the vast, dangerous, unknown galaxy.

Havok extended his fingers, reaching out for Kid Omega's.

"Trust works both ways, remember? We're coming up on Xanth. Let's figure this out together, OK? And let's remember who our friends are, kid. Because right now? Me, Corsair, and the others? We're the only friends you've got."

The Kid's face burned with anger and shame. He glared down at Havok's hand.

Reluctantly, he took it.

For now.

CHAPTER EIGHT

[ALEX | IMPERIAL DUNGEONS | CHANDILAR | THE SHI'AR GALAXY]

Years Ago...

Havok could hear screaming through the walls.

Manacled, arms spread akimbo, he struggled to break free of his chains. He was alone and isolated from the other Starjammers. The cell was sterile and dim, low lights serving a dual purpose – not only to provide the barest of illumination, but to drain all ambient cosmic energy from the room... anything that might fuel Havok's powers.

He was exhausted. Hanging by his arms, knees dragging on the floor, his head was bent low with his eyes shut in a poor attempt to muffle his senses.

But he couldn't drown out the others' screams.

Lorna. Lilandra. Korvus. Ch'od, Raza, and Hepzibah. His family. His team.

He'd failed them all.

Submerged in guilt and regret as he was, doing his best to

block out the anguished cries of his friends and colleagues, no doubt undergoing cruel and brutal beatings he couldn't help but imagine inside his own tortured head, Alex never heard the sound of approaching footsteps.

The door opened, introducing a square of light from the hallway. Someone stepped inside. A guard, perhaps, here to deliver Havok's meager allowance of food – a meal that sometimes never came. He tried looking up, but the bindings forced him into a submissive position, facing the ground. Suffering, frustrated, he waited for the guard to raise him up and force-feed his wanting portion of unpalatable gruel.

But the visitor did not approach.

"Hello, brother."

Havok recognized the voice. He wouldn't answer.

Gabriel Summers, Alex's estranged brother and jailer, began a slow circuit around the paltry cell, pacing as he spoke.

"Enjoying the accommodations? I can't say the same for your friends. The traitors Korvus and Lilandra... your girlfriend, the green-haired, magnetic witch. And, of course, the other Starjammers – our dear, departed father's crew."

"Killer," Alex finally spat, barely getting out the single, accusatory word. Rage fueled him now, not cosmic energy. "You dare mention our father after the way you–"

"Murdered him? Purified his body with cleansing fire? Yes, yes. I admit it, for my sins. And I have no regrets, older brother. Like you, Corsair stood in my way. Unlike you..."

Gabriel – the Shi'ar Majestor, dubbed Emperor Vulcan by his councilors, colleagues, and subjects – took Havok by the chin, lifting it so he might look his brother in the eye.

"Unlike you, Alex, the man was a threat. And he never would

have languished in chains, nor allowed his merry band of space pirates to do the same. No, Daddy dearest had the fire. He had a burning spirit, like me. Like Scott."

Vulcan sniffed and dropped Alex's chin. "I suppose you got your spirit from our mother."

Alex squeezed back tears, clenching his jaw. "You're nothing like us, nothing like him!"

"Really? Corsair was a captain – a leader of men, like me. Like Scott. The three of us have faced trials and terrors… and we have stepped into flames to take what is ours by right. We have led armies and empires, and done so with vengeance, determination, and success."

Gabriel's palm swatted Havok's cheek. "And you, Alex? What of you? You ran from the loss of your parents! Hid from your mutant heritage! You've led a sequence of failed collections of outcasts, misfits, and traitors – including those imprisoned in my dungeons. So, tell me: which of us is a true Summers, hmm? Which of us demonstrably takes after our father or carries Cyclops' blood in his veins? One might question that, were that being an impartial spectator."

"Shut up, Gabriel. I'm going to get out of here and make you eat those words."

"Oho! The Summers fire. Too little too late, I'm afraid."

"Shut up. You're not a Summers. Family is more than just blood. You're a monster. You're not a part of this family."

Vulcan stopped pacing. Havok couldn't see, but by the tone of his voice, he imagined Gabriel's face had lost any trace of charm or bemusement.

"Of that you are right. I was never a part of this family – or any family, for that matter. Torn from my mother's womb and enslaved alongside strangers. Even when I found my dear brother Scott on Earth... instead of coming to my aid, instead of exploring every last option to return me to life – as he did Jean Grey and many others! – he let Charles Xavier jettison my body into space. My dear, deceased father never searched for me–"

"He didn't know you existed! Neither did I!"

"Hardly an excuse! No one cared! Not him, not Scott, and not you. The only ones who ever cared for me were my former colleagues, the X-Men with whom I 'perished' on Earth, and my love. My empress. My burning bride."

"Who... Deathbird?! Gabe, she's using you! Can't you see that she only wants you to take the throne from Lilandra? So she can rule the Shi'ar through you."

This time Vulcan used not an open palm, but a closed fist. Alex's head rocked to the left; the lights got dimmer, intermittently flashing as he nearly blacked out from the force of the blow.

But he didn't scream.

Gabriel hunkered down next to Havok, his breath wafting across Alex's nose.

"You are wrong, little brother. Cal'syee loves me, and I her. She has healed me as no one can, her fire burning alongside mine, our souls intertwined. She is the only family I have ever truly known. The only one who loves and understands me. Together, we will rule this galaxy, raking the talons of the Shi'ar Empire across the stars, stoking its flames into an inferno, a dynasty ablaze and all-consuming as we conquer Hala, Skrullos, Spartax, and Earth!"

Alex spat again. "I'll stop you, Gabriel. Scott and I will never let that happen."

Emperor Vulcan laughed. "Scott? Well, we shall see how his X-Men fare against the power of the Shi'ar Empire, the Superguardians, and my love's devoted cadre of assassins. You... I may use you for bait, Alex, but other than that, you're hardly a concern."

Gabriel stepped to the door. "You were right about one thing. I'm nothing like you. And you, my older brother, are nothing like me. You have no idea of what I'm capable – as you have no idea of what I can accomplish ruling at Deathbird's side. Trust me. One day, after our oldest brother is dead – for I cannot see a day where the two of us will ever coexist – and the reign of Vulcan extends to every border of the known universe, you will appreciate the value in seeing me as family. Because alone in this cell, after spending the next years of your pitiful existence listening to the tortured death cries of the friends and colleagues you've once again let down... you may realize Deathbird and I are the only family you have left."

"I'll see you both in your graves before that happens."

Gabriel clapped as he let himself out. "Bravo, Alex. See? Maybe we were both wrong. Maybe we are more alike than we think."

And with that, Vulcan left Havok to the chains and screams, alone in his cell, imprisoned with guilt and sorrow.

CHAPTER NINE

[ALEX | THE STARJAMMER | THE XANTHAN GRAVEYARD | THE JATSKAN SYSTEM]

Decades ago, Xanth was a vibrant, populous world in a remote corner of the Milky Way galaxy with technological innovation thousands of years more advanced than that of Earth. Uninterested in space exploration, the Xanthans invested resources into their planet's beautiful cities and the marvels that made their lives easier and happier rather than using them to build rockets and starships. Unfortunately, that proved their world's undoing when a runaway asteroid veered toward Xanth, destined to collide with the planet and demolish their civilization. Thanks to a band of heroes from Earth, the Xanthans managed to escape before the world was destroyed.

Now the splintered remains of once-auspicious Xanth – its beautifully terraformed landscapes and once towering cities – floated through the Jatskan system, a roving graveyard of asteroids and technology. Here, within a silent cluster of satellites moving out among the stars, hid Blastaar and his minions and with them, Alex hoped, a Phoenix Egg.

The Starjammer maneuvered out of a jump gate and into the asteroid field, Corsair trying to avoid both making noise and damaging the ship. Alex sat in a jump seat, massaging his chest. His body still ached, sore from the beating he'd taken at Kid Omega's hands. Nearby, the perpetrator of his wounds sat at Operations, poring over a star map with Sikorsky and Hepzibah, familiarizing himself with potential strike zones and ingress routes to the Xanthan Graveyard, provided to them by Peter Quill.

Havok's ribs hurt, as did his head. Quentin hadn't held back; he'd meant to hurt Alex, and if Corsair had been too late... who knows what might have happened? Ultimately, he was glad that Kid Omega would be an asset in their upcoming assault on Blastaar, but he still felt uneasy about the boy's impulsive nature. The Kid had abandoned the script on Majesdane and New Xandar – at all the taverns they'd visited, seeking information. Quentin was a loose cannon. He was a wild card in any given situation. And on this mission, one that required a level of stealth and precision, how could he trust the Kid not to go left when they needed to go right?

"Keep your eyes peeled," said Corsair, carefully steering through the debris. Here and there, shattered technological infrastructure, long decayed and worn by the collision and ensuing years of interstellar migration, jutted up from Xanth's fragmented remains.

"We're looking for a large building," the Starjammer's captain continued, "something the Xanthans called 'Kurrgo's Ring.' Quill and the others, they believe it to be a type of former arena or gladiatorial venue. A place where thousands gathered, maybe more."

Quentin cocked an eyebrow, looking up from the star map and reams of incomplete data.

"I thought these Xanthans were scientists and tech-fiends. What were they doing with a 'gladiatorial venue'?" He flipped through pages, not bothering to wait for an answer.

"Kid Vicious over there has a good point." Corsair snapped a finger in Sikorsky's direction. "Hey, 'Korsky, compile a collation analysis match for datapackets on the Superguardian Stargate network for terms 'ring,' 'Xanth,' 'Kurrgo,' and 'gathering.' If anyone has intelligence on this place, it'll be the Shi'ar." Havok's father returned to the helm, refocusing himself on piloting the ship through the treacherous field of asteroids.

Alex leaned forward, peering out the window as the Starjammer's technician began its task and the ship's all-wave scanners digested each rock, every piece of Xanth's remains, in search of Kurrgo's Ring and Blastaar's location.

"Hey, Dad."

Corsair raised an eyebrow at Alex's furtive whisper. "What's on your mind, sport?"

Havok double-checked that the others had their attention focused elsewhere. "Are we even sure that Blastaar's here? I mean, Quill, Rocket... they aren't exactly known for being reliable. What if there is no Egg?"

"He's here. Have faith, son."

"I have to find those kids. We have to find them."

Corsair looked over his shoulder. "We will, Alex. I'd never let you down."

Alex stared at his father, the interstellar privateer. A flush reddened his cheeks, and the years peeled away. He was a boy again, strapped to a rumbling airplane as it died over the Alaskan tundra.

"Oh god," Alex cried. "Mommy!"

Katherine Summers quickly undid his seat belt.

"Boys," she said. "You have to unbuckle and come with me."

Major Summers raised his voice, straining to be heard over the roar of the sputtering engine. He wouldn't turn. He wouldn't meet his sons in the eye. His attention was focused on the plane, on escaping the advancing alien vessel.

"Do what your mother says," he yelled. "Do it now!"

The boys fell.

Alex shook off the memory, returning to the chilly bridge of the silent starship. His father had turned back to the helm, hands gripping the yoke, piloting through an ocean of stars while evading the pinwheeling shards of a long-obliterated planetoid.

I'd never let you down.

Alex started to answer, but before he could, Sikorsky chittered excitedly, whirling in place as it transferred a datapacket from a connection hub to the forward screen. A series of panels superimposed themselves against the window, sliding against the side to avoid obstructing Corsair's view. Havok and the others watched as a three-dimensional schematic of a squat, heavily armed fortress projected itself into the bridge, rotating slowly to display all angles. Five smaller structures orbited the primary edifice, then spread out to distribute themselves around an abstract sphere… like a ring around a planet.

"Kurrgo's Ring," Ch'od intoned, translating for Sikorsky again. "Not an arena, but a system of military installations placed at key strategic geolocations, circling Xanth of old."

The schematic splintered with a flash, and the various sections of the holographic planet resettled into a mass of asteroids. The five structures – the Ring, its installations cracked and demolished – drifted with them, conjoined to whichever fragment they had been attached. The largest, the focal point of Kurrgo's Ring, had been cracked in two, as if struck by lightning, and the larger half resembled the curved cross section of a tri-level office building, its walls jagged, orbited by debris and floating laboratory equipment. Suddenly, a handful of insubstantial rods extended from the central planetoid upon which the broken structure sat. They were dowels or cable attachments, sunk deep into the surface of each connected satellite, holding together the remnants of the Ring.

Hepzibah pointed to the dominant structure. "There Blastaar should be." She rotated the holographic model. "The command center, see, this is. Look here: a hangar to the left, docking rings to receive and launch. The quarters" – she turned the model – "on the opposite side, an armory at the far end. Stored there, perhaps, our quarry?"

"The Phoenix." The word felt uncomfortable upon Alex's tongue. Heavy, as if it carried baggage. Years of history weighed down the name, none of them pleasant.

Quentin peered closer. "And what's that? We only counted four structures, but there seem to be five." He pointed to an oblique shape at the bottom of the Graveyard. "What's this here?"

"See for yourself."

Corsair banked the Starjammer low, out of the belt, and the bottom of the asteroid field came into view above. They could now see the physical manifestation of what the Kid had been studying: a half-moon structure listing dangerously into a vast chasm bisecting an asteroid, the building reinforced by cables and pylons clamped to the planetoid's face. Rows of identical seats could be identified from this distance, winding around the interior, up until the sudden drop into the gap. A flat empty space yawned away from the lower seats – a stage or an arena, a place for beings to gather and participate in either performance, presentation... or pain.

Corsair smirked as he skimmed the field's edge. "Like I said: 'gladiatorial venue.'"

Kid Omega rolled his eyes. "Save me from the kitschy ridiculousness of outer space."

The Starjammer skirted the Xanthan Graveyard, keeping its distance. Thus far, no living beings had been perceived by the all-wave scanners. There were corpses everywhere, broken bodies scattered across each major satellite – aliens of all shapes and races – bound by the pull of its gravity. From what they could ascertain, the asteroid field was a graveyard not only in name but nature.

Alex locked eyes with his father. "You really think he's here?"

"Trust me, bud. We'll find him."

Skeptical, Alex joined the others as they formulated a strategy. Corsair, Ch'od and Sikorsky would bring the 'Jammer around to the hangar situated on the Graveyard's left side relative to the ship's approach. Piloting one of the two scout crafts, Raza and Hepzibah planned to circumnavigate the field and land on the asteroid closest to the quarters. Once there, both ships would use particle beams to disengage the cables keeping the Ring together, leaving any beings hiding on those asteroids to the mercy of the Graveyard. Should either team encounter resistance – from Blastaar, or launched starcraft – they would retreat to open space, drawing out the enemy, engaging them in battle while the others continued the mission.

"And what about us?" Kid Omega was ready to go. Havok noted irritation in Quentin's voice. Despite their conversation, the kid still believed he could – and should – capture the Egg on his own.

Havok pointed to the bottom of the Graveyard. "We'll take the other scout ship and disconnect the arena."

Quentin shook his head. "Of course we will. I don't understand why we're bothering with the other sections. Why not hit the main structure, cannons blazing?"

"Because, kid," Corsair patiently explained, "if Blastaar has an army distributed across the Ring, quietly removing three out of five hubs – sending those asteroids spinning into a collision or out into space – decreases our chances of a firefight. Whichever soldiers he has stationed on the outer satellites will hopefully be separated from the central planetoid. Ergo, separated from the place we need to be."

"Unless, of course, they have starships of their own to fly them over."

Corsair tapped his temple. "Which is why we're hitting the hangar first. The rest of you see any outlier spacecrafts, give them a particle beam where the stars don't shine."

Once the three sections were detached and set free, the mutants and Starjammers would be free to engage the Ring's central areas: the main structure and the armory, one of which they believed to be the Egg's location... the other where they might presumably find Blastaar.

"And if not?" Quentin asked, his skeptical tone revealing a

healthy amount of doubt. "If Negative Zone Nellie keeps the Egg warm under his pillow, and we just cut the quarters loose so it could float out into space?"

Alex smiled. "You'll appreciate this one, Kid. That's when we improvise."

"Uh huh. And if his entire army is stationed on the central hubs?"

"Make your own army, like you did back in the Omega Shop."

This time, Kid Omega smiled and Havok could tell he was truly happy.

"Well then," Quentin said, "let's go disappoint some space gladiators."

Ten minutes later, the scout crafts disembarked from the Starjammer's forward bay. Havok steered their shuttle into a whirling maelstrom of asteroids, trying his best to keep from crashing. By his side, Kid Omega projected a psionic shell around the ship's native shields, focused on ensuring that no errant fragments collided with the scout craft before they managed to land. To their left, Raza and Hepzibah guided the other shuttle away from the 'Jammer, circling the Xanthan Graveyard, headed toward the quarters on the other side.

Corsair hailed Alex, his cheerful voice crackling from the speakers as the mutants moved into the asteroid field. "Good luck, guys. Watch yourself out there and get back safe."

Havok smiled despite the mocking, sarcastic gagging noise issuing from Quentin in the passenger seat. Alex returned the hail. "You too, Dad."

"Do what your mother says," yelled Major Summers.

The ship died around them. Scott was screaming, Alex crying. Their father never turned around. "Do it now!"

The boys fell.

Blinking, he accelerated, evading a midsized piece of debris. The Starjammer disappeared behind an asteroid. Havok and Kid Omega were on their own.

Alex pointed through the field. "Let's settle there. It's closest to the cable."

The Kid nodded, oddly solemn. Quentin peered out the window with an anxious, expectant look on his face.

"You OK?" Havok asked.

"Peachy. Stop wasting time on my feelings, and let's get this done."

Alex sighed. Tension was getting to everyone. He maneuvered the scout craft toward the adjacent satellite, landed on its surface, and powered up the particle beams.

"OK, I'm going to detach the cable from here."

"Works for me. Let's just do it." The Kid looked out the window and down onto the cracked arena. The two mutants had an excellent view of the terrain. Havok could see skeletons and corpses draped across the bloody, broken seats. Discarded weapons and dismembered body parts littered the flat, dusty floor. There had been a fight here – a game of skill and murder, perchance, but more likely a pitched battle. The chasm yawned at the opposite end, and into it ran the far end of the sturdy cable attachment Alex and Quentin were here to sever. Thankfully, all they needed to do was snap it in the middle. There was no need to disembark or descend onto the eerie, silent planetoid.

Havok activated the cannons and opened fire. A dull whine rocketed from beneath the ship, then released itself into space. Twin beams of light dashed off the taut cable, ricocheting away. He fired again, with no result. While the Starjammer's more formidable particle beams might be up to the task, the smaller and less powerful cannons housed within the scout craft simply could not break the cable.

"Now what?" asked the Kid. "Should we land and detach it from the asteroid itself?"

"Yeah, I think we have to. But we can't land on the Ring's central hub, because our arrival might set off an alarm and notify Blastaar that we're here, so…"

Quentin sighed. "So, we're gonna take one scary step for mutantkind and detach the end that lives in a creepy cave at the edge of the fighting pits."

Alex cocked an eyebrow. "I don't get the reference."

The Kid rose from his seat. "That's because you're the wrong kind of nerd. C'mon, let's go do something stupid."

CHAPTER TEN

Five minutes later, Havok landed their shuttle in the center of the Xanthan arena.

They pulled on flight suits, borrowed from the 'Jammer's leftover stock. Kid Omega wrapped them both in psionic force fields, in case the air wasn't breathable or was toxic or any number of deadly scenarios that might suffocate, asphyxiate, or plain old kill the two mutants. Warily, teacher and student made their way out onto the killing grounds.

This is such a bad idea, thought the Kid. The arena was frighteningly silent; only the shifting sands, kicked aside by their approach and trembling due to the asteroid's gradual orbital rotation, reacted as they passed.

Hey, there. The Kid toed an alien skull with his boot. Whoever its owner, the being once had multiple ocular sockets and a strangely elongated jaw. Glancing around, he noted beings from all kinds of races and species. Humanoid, Skrull, Shi'ar… but not a single Baluurian. Kid Omega had done the barest amount of research on the way from New Xandar, and nowhere in sight could he find the square, leonine skull type that easily identified Blastaar's people.

The Kid sent a telepathic text message into Havok's head.

<<Where's the army, you think?>>

Alex winced. It'd clearly been a while since the man had held a telepathic conversation, and Kid Omega's overture had startled him. After a second, Havok sent back a reply.

[[I'm sure this is part of it. Maybe parts of multiple armies.]]

<<But not a Baluurian in sight. Not our boy Blastaar's army, I gather?>>

[[Maybe. Could be he's got troops holed up on another hub, like we expected, or on the central section. Maybe the gladiatorial games are just for weekends, to entertain the troops. Like going to the movies.]]

Quentin laughed. <<Space drive-in, but with lots more murder.>>

[[C'mon, I don't want to be here any more than you do. Let's get this over with, Kid.]]

They approached the chasm, kicking up dust and bones. The gap swallowed any light the galaxy had to offer. The heavy cable attachment led down into the darkness, sinking at a sharp angle at the edge of the jagged crack. Kid Omega strained to hear, listening for any signs of life. He wanted to get a sense if anything might be hiding in the chasm other than the terminus of the cable. But all was quiet in the vacuum of space.

<<Hey, Havok, if it's all the same to you, I'd rather not go down into the Dark Side cave, all right? Can't we sever this thing from up here and get moving?>>

[[We can try. If we can dislodge it from afar… or shatter this visible section somehow then, yeah, none of us have to see our face on our father's body.]]

<<OK, that flarking reference you got.>>

[[May the Flark be with you, Kid.]]

<<So, any suggestions? I can telekinetically feel around for the end of the cable with my mind, maybe dislodge it. But if there is something else down there, I'm kinda worried about waking it up.>>

[["Something"? What do you know that I don't?]]

<<I don't know. Bad feeling, is all. Look, let's see if we can break this section. I can do a psionic buzzsaw…?>>

[[Not to worry. Can you make me a porthole?]]

Havok held up a fist. The lone white circle around his chest began to oscillate as he absorbed the Graveyard's ambient cosmic energy, birthing a set of concentric circles leading down toward his flexed hand. Kid Omega understood and created an airtight seal around the man's wrist. He siloed a small opening in the psionic shield near Alex's radiating fingers, allowing his companion to expel a solid beam of cosmic plasma, fired directly at the gargantuan cable.

The shot rebounded, vibrating down the length of the cord. Havok had singed the cable, but the blast wasn't enough to split its length. He tried again, the cold white of his blast illuminating their faces. Havok grimaced as he poured on the plasma, doing what he could to snap the line. The cable throbbed, displacing sand and grit as it rocked on the floor. Kid Omega joined in, using his mind to inflict additional stress to the section bearing Havok's assault. It started to give, the metal blackening and curling.

Then… an earsplitting, gut-churning roar. The mutants, pouring on the energy, turned to face the black chasm.

A huge sinuous reptile slithered its way up to the surface. Shockingly purple, covered with scales and spines, it boasted two ravenous mouths, each revealing four rows of sharp, rotating fangs. Tongues spit from the eyeless heads, saliva dripping to the ground where it sputtered and steamed; acidic, no doubt. Like a millipede, the creature scrabbled forward on hundreds of segmented legs, clawing its way out of the hole and across the sand, hurrying toward the astonished mutants.

[[That's your 'bad feeling'? You couldn't read its mind?!]]

Kid Omega shot a psychic meme into Alex's brain: the image of a bored black cat, calmly filing its nails, the words GET OVER IT plastered beneath in large, white letters.

<<Look, I didn't think about it, OK?! My telepathic gut is to shoot first, scan later – not the other way around! Quit whining and finish the job!>>

Havok lifted both hands; the Kid opened a second porthole, and the younger Summers brother redoubled his efforts. The creature was scrambling faster, kicking dirt into the air as it closed the distance.

[[I'll sever the cord! You deal with Fin Fang Freaky!]]

<<How the maxiflark d'you expect me to do that?!>>

Alex winced. [[You're using 'maxiflark' wrong – never mind! Just do to it what you did to me. Summon that psychic army thing!]]

If Quentin Quire could roll his eyes any farther, they'd be staring out the back of his head. <<Hey, just be happy that I'm trying to learn the language! And do you even understand anything? I could only do that inside a psionic construct!

I'm not strong enough yet to create a manifestation of that magnitude in real space!>>

[[OK. Look, I almost have this... can't you take that snake inside your mind, then? Like you did to me?]]

The Kid frowned and glared at the oncoming predator. He reached out, attempting to psychically snag the creature's brain.

<<It isn't working! That thing barely has a mind to begin with. It's all R-Type lizard patterns, and I can't->>

[[What?! It's what?]]

<<I can't bring its mind into mine because it's smaller than yours, if you can believe that!>> Exasperated, Kid Omega broke off the attempt. The beast was nearly on them now. In a few seconds, he and the lizard would be close enough to kiss.

<<Aren't you almost done?>>

[[Nearly. It's giving...]]

The Kid glanced at Havok and turned to measure their distance to the rapidly approaching beast. He needed to buy them time so that Alex could finish snapping the cable.

<<OK, hang in there. I'ma try something.>>

[[What? Wait-!]]

Ignoring Havok's cries, Kid Omega flexed his mind and lifted himself from the ground. The eyeless, salivating creature reared up as the Kid passed overhead, looping around and peppering its reptilian back with dozens of psychic blades. It howled in response to the attack. Quentin had caused it pain. The Kid howled in reply, hooting as he lashed the thing's tail with a psionic lasso.

"Get along, lil' doggie," he shouted to no one in particular, the sound of his voice contained only within the helmet of his spacesuit. Kid Omega pulled, telekinetically soaring over the length of the cable, dragging the scrabbling, frustrated reptile back toward the chasm.

Hundreds of tiny legs dug into the surface of the asteroid. The beast did its best to stay put, to grapple Kid Omega and his mental lariat. Quentin was now in a game of tug-of-war with a deadly, enraged space lizard. <<I'm losing ground, Summers! Now or never!>>

[[It's going... it's going... one more blast–]]

Havok's optimistic reply was interrupted by a sharp, forceful shake and a turbulent shower of rocks and grit. The asteroid shuddered and rotated sharply. Invisible waves of gravimetric force washed over the arena, dislodging both the mutants and their confused reptilian assailant. The planetoid convulsed. The tiniest earthquake further splintered the already broken stadium. Turning while attempting to find his footing, Kid Omega spied a diffuse blast of white-orange light between the rocks and asteroids that comprised the Xanthan Graveyard. The ground beneath his boots felt less steady than before... looser, somehow, and both he and Havok struggled to regain their balance and composure, as did the determined space lizard.

<<What was that?>>

[[Felt like part of the Ring gave way! One of the other teams must have detached their section from the others, which completely threw off our center of gravity.]]

<<OK, that makes sense. I just saw a light show across space. Looks like it came from the direction of the hangar.>>

[[That'd be Corsair. The Starjammer will be heading for the Ring's main hub, so let's finish playing with this giant gecko, demolish the cable, and join them.]]

Havok clenched his fists and sent one last volley, funneling white-hot plasma into the already weakened section of the near-unbreakable cord.

The force of his attack pushed the cable to its breaking point. It gave, metal shattering, and the frayed ends flailed toward opposite corners of the planetoid. The stub still connected to the central Ring serpentined across the dirt and slid over the side, dangling out into space. The bit still anchored to the fissure snapped backward and hit the surprised beast, uprooting its already shaky grasp of the arena floor. The end of the cable slid down into the chasm. The injured lizard clambered forward, using multiple appendages to reassert its hold. It made a last-ditch effort to resume its attack on the mutants, but it was too far away, sliding backward with every advance. The asteroid was now freely floating away from Kurrgo's Ring, headed toward an adjacent asteroid. If Havok and Kid Omega didn't hurry, they would be caught in the collision and smashed to smithereens.

[[Come on! It's done, let's–]]

<<Hold on!>>

Kid Omega reached out with his mind and telekinetically lifted Havok from the sand. Together, the X-Men leapt toward the Starjammer's scout craft. It slid dangerously toward the gap... and the waiting creature. The Kid threw up a psionic wall to block it from snagging the ship as they darted inside, foiling the beast from getting its myriad claws on his posh ensemble or Havok's hide.

Alex slid behind the controls as Kid Omega slammed the door. The shuttle skated wildly toward the crater as the asteroid spun out of control, the breaking of the cable helping to add to its dizzying momentum. They were seconds from impact, two rogue planetoids bearing down onto their own. Sweating, Alex powered up the engine and pulled hard on the yoke, doing what he could to keep them from falling into the dark, hungry chasm. The lizard shrieked and leapt for the shuttle, its claws scraping against the hull.

Exhausted, Quentin snagged the craft with his mind, hoisting it like a crane, jerking it off the ground and away from the spinning, approaching asteroids. Havok shoved the yoke. The ship roared, engines propelling them forward as their reptilian pursuer fell back into the gap... and two asteroids struck the stadium, obliterating it with thunderous force.

The seismic impact launched the ship toward the center of Kurrgo's now-bisected Ring. Alex did what he could to control propulsion, but the shock waves made it difficult to maneuver. Kid Omega pitched in, turning his crane into a parachute, inducing psychic drag as their craft skipped along, bouncing through the field.

<<Watch there!>>

[[I see it, I see it!]]

Relying on his reflexes, Havok steered through the storm, aiming the already weakened shuttle toward the asteroid at the center of the Xanthan Graveyard.

The Kid pointed to a long, flat path located near the bottom of the central hub.

<<There! Put us there. I'll help.>>

Together, the mutants worked to evade collision, managing to bring the 'Jammer's scout ship down heavily onto the makeshift strip, landing hard amid a hail of rocks and dirt. They skidded violently toward the end of the impromptu runway, twisting and turning, until the ship slowly and loudly scraped to a jarring stop.

They sat in silence, staring forward and catching their breath. The Kid's heart pounded so hard and so erratically that it could've played the drums for the Muppets' Dr Teeth. Havok glanced over at Quentin, sweat dotting his brow and cheeks; the younger mutant glared back.

Suddenly, the two of them started laughing. Kid Omega couldn't help himself. He doubled over, clutching his gut, eyes tearing up as Alex Summers chuckled and wiped his eyes.

"Well," Havok said. "Despite our lack of tact or stealth... I have to admit, that was one way to skin a snake."

"Oh. No. Please don't."

"Seriously – why didn't you think to scan the planetoid before we landed?"

The Kid sighed apologetically. "I mean, what am I supposed to say here?"

Alex slowly got to his feet. "Yeah, I get it. Your gut instinct is force, not finesse. C'mon, then. Terrible metaphors aside, the only way to actually kill a snake is to cut off its head. Let's connect with the others and go find Blastaar."

"If he's even here. And if he has the Phoenix Egg."

Havok gestured toward the door. "Monsters like Blastaar don't stray far from their doomsday weapons. If Quill's information is correct, and he is here, you can be sure that Blastaar is keeping close to that Egg. Have a little faith. Are you coming?"

Skeptical, Kid Omega rose on unsteady legs and moved to follow. Before he could leave, Alex turned back and gingerly placed a hand on Quentin's shoulder.

"Hey, Kid. Before we go… I wanted to say, you did great down there. Quick thinking, good reflexes. So, uh… thanks. Nice work."

Surprised at the unexpected accolade, the Kid found himself at a loss for words. He mutely nodded, acknowledging the remark. Havok was clearly waiting for something, anything in response. But after a moment, when he saw no reply would be forthcoming, he sighed and exited the ship.

"OK then," he muttered, shaking his head. "Well, good job, anyway. Let's get moving."

Havok disappeared through the door. Kid Omega waited, still absorbing Alex's awkward pat on the back. His face was… warm, as was a swooping feeling deep inside his chest.

Who the heck was Alex Summers to attaboy the Kid? Quentin knew how much his contributions had ten-exxed the situation (even if he did miss doing a basic scan). No one needed to hand him a lollipop and give him a gold star! How ridiculously patronizing! If push had come to shove in Space Lizard Gulch, the Kid would have risen glamorously to the occasion. He would've obliterated that cable if given the chance, and ably handled the creature at the same time. He was the Omega! He had all he needed, right here in his mind. He didn't want or need any kudos, sincere or otherwise. And he definitely still resented having been saddled with a worthless chaperone, his flamboyant pirate daddy and a collection of interstellar misfits…

Though the Kid did admit, there was something amusing and maybe even kinda exciting about what they'd accomplished together. Maybe it was the adrenaline talking – not that he needed help, of course, but Havok's focus on the cable had allowed the Kid to wrangle a star dragon, for Blob's sake. And that insane dash to the craft before the asteroids struck... and the wild, thrilling crash landing. A slow smile tugged at the corners of Kid Omega's lips.

It had been... fun?

Still. He didn't need to let anybody know his business. Especially Alex "Off-Brand Cyclops" Summers – even if the guy really didn't have to say anything about it at all. The Kid knew what others thought about him. He wasn't exactly Hero of the Beach, and more often than not, to be frank, he was usually getting yelled at instead of appreciated. So, Kid Omega hardly needed or cared about Havok's probably sarcastic – or insincere – gratitude.

If it was insincere. The warm, content feeling inside the Kid's chest wasn't going away.

You did great down there. Nice work.

"Thanks," Quentin Quire said to absolutely no one, the word barely loud enough to reach his own ears. He waited another few seconds for the blush to recede from his cheeks and wiped away the stupid grin. Preparing himself to rejoin his colleagues, Kid Omega smoothed his jacket and then headed out the door.

CHAPTER ELEVEN

Havok and Kid Omega crossed the rocky landscape of the
now-adrift Ring's main hub, skirting rubble and corpses as they
approached what they believed to be the primary command
structure. There were fewer bodies on the ground, and signs of
battle thinned with every step.

Topping a rise, the Starjammer and second scout craft came
into view, parked adjacent to the crumbling building in which
they hoped to find Blastaar and the Phoenix Egg. Alex could
see inside the edifice, but it appeared to be as abandoned as
the arena from which they'd just arrived. Corsair and his crew
lingered at the structure's wide double doors, one of which
hung languidly off weakened, rusted hinges. The Starjammers
were all wearing pressurized spacesuits, and as they got closer,
Alex's father raised a hand, hailing them from afar.

Havok nodded and picked up his pace, Quire at his heels,
oddly subdued. Perhaps their brush with death and danger had
affected Kid Omega more than Havok would have believed. He

decided to leave Quentin alone rather than pursue it. The Kid had been there when he'd been needed, and that was all Alex could really ask of him for now.

They met the Starjammers at the doors to the building, and Corsair urged them inside. As they crossed the threshold, Havok felt cold air envelop his body and heard a faint pop. Smiling, the Starjammers removed their helmets, and though wary, Alex and Quentin followed suit.

"It's fine," Corsair assured them. "The air in here is breathable and non-toxic, even with the huge flarking crack in the roof. The seal must run around the structure itself."

Kid Omega wiped his brow. "Well, thank maxiflark for that, kiddies and kidettes."

Corsair cocked an eyebrow. "I don't think you're using that right?"

Havok looked up. All three levels were bare, whatever furnishings or goods the structure may have held long since looted or destroyed by whatever had split the building. There were weapons – axes and hammers, swords and blasters – scattered upon the ground, along with a handful of dead Baluurians. The cavernous space in which they were standing led to a massive hallway with an equally impressive doorway at its end, set back in shadow.

He turned to his father. "Any resistance on your end?"

"No," Corsair replied, shaking his head. "Any ships that had once been docked at the hangar already made tracks. We saw signs of a retreat and firefight, lots of dead warriors. Nothing worth landing for, so we blew the cable and let it drift into the void. Then we came here… 'Korsky volunteered to watch the ships while we go find the Egg."

Havok turned to Raza and Hepzibah, who'd dealt with the far planetoid, the Ring's quarters. "How about you?"

Mam'selle Hepzibah grinned, flashing her canines and dropping a wink.

"Our end, a bit of resistance. Dealt with it, we had to." Raza smiled. Clearly, the two pirates had been more than capable of achieving their task and found some fun in the process. "Wondering, perhaps, if the Egg was found? It wasn't."

"Same on our end," Alex confirmed. "All we found were dead men and a persistent, hungry rascal with too many legs and not enough eyes."

The sextet glanced at the far door.

"It's too quiet," said Kid Omega. He closed his eyes. Alex wondered if the Kid was learning from his earlier mistake and doing a scan this time. After a moment, his guess was pleasantly confirmed.

"There's somebody here… but whoever it is, they're alone. Just sitting in the next room. I can't get inside their head to confirm an identity. Something is jamming me. All I can do is locate whoever it is."

Corsair grinned and tapped his headband, indicating the anti-telepath jammers woven into the fabric. "What'd I tell you? Minders. Half the galaxy has dealt with too many of them."

"Come," Ch'od rumbled, leading the way down the hall. "We shall see for ourselves. Our eyes alone will reveal the great mysteries, my friends."

The Starjammers cautiously unholstered their weapons, preparing for whatever waited in the adjacent chamber. Havok glanced at Kid Omega, nodding once. The Kid tapped on his temple in reply. Alex clenched his fingers into a fist. If Blastaar was sitting in the next room, preparing an ambush, the mutants and pirates would be ready for whatever hell the nihilistic, would-be conqueror planned to rain upon their heads.

But to Havok's surprise, they found Blastaar slumped upon a crudely fashioned seat made of stone, metal, and debris. His meaty arms hung limply over the armrests of a makeshift throne. He was bruised and beaten, scorch marks and scratches covering his arms and legs. His boots were torn. The mane that framed Blastaar's usually belligerent face had been singed. He looked up with sullen eyes as the newcomers entered the room. He glared with resentment or hate as they approached, striding across the pitted stone floor past the broken bodies of his dead companions. Alex looked down as they passed, wondering who or what had laid low Blastaar's forces, and whether he and his friends might soon find themselves facing an enemy more powerful than they could handle.

"Greetings, Corsair," Blastaar whispered, his voice wheezing, hardly his usual bombastic self. He sounded hoarse, as if he'd been screaming. "Have you come then, to end the reign of the Living Bomb-Burst?"

The Starjammer's captain shook his head in reply, holding out his hands as if to indicate peace or surrender. "We're looking for something. If you have it, and will provide it without a fight, we'll take it and be on our way."

Quentin cracked his knuckles. "Of course, if you insist on a fight…"

The Baluurian laughed, a harsh, crackling, guttural sound that echoed around the chamber. "You have a defiant, admirable spirit, Earther. But no… you've found the King of the Negative Zone vanquished and low, inches from death. Should you raise a hand… move to strike… a dishonorable victory would be yours, ridding this backward universe of the scourge of Baluur, he who had been the Bomb-Burst, now nothing more than a beaten cur."

"A chatty, pretentious cur," Kid Omega whispered.

Havok ignored him and stepped forward. "Where's your army?"

Blastaar winced as he attempted to raise a hand and failed. Instead, he lifted his chin, indicating the corpses splayed around the room.

"There, beyond. Across the expanse of Kurrgo's Ring. Once proud and bloodthirsty, my considerable forces have been all but eradicated, laid low in battle nigh a fortnight ago."

"By whom?"

The Baluurian shook his leonine head. "Ashamed I am to divulge that information, Earther mutate. For fear that when the galaxy – no, the universe – learns the truth, proud Blastaar's fierce reputation for conquest and savagery shall be dragged through the blackest tar, ridiculed for having utterly lost such uneven combat."

The Starjammers glanced at one another, then nervously peered around the tomblike hall, as if they expected Blastaar's mysterious subjugator to strike from the shadows.

Kid Omega stepped forward, squinting as he stared at the humbled king.

"I'm sensing…" The Kid closed his eyes. Havok watched, realizing that Quentin was extending his abilities to feel for a psychic afterimage, to ascertain the name or nature of whoever may have decimated Blastaar's army. Suddenly, Kid Omega's eyes popped open, and the words THAT OLD GANG OF MINE appeared on the young mutant's shirt.

He approached the conqueror, crouching down to look into Blastaar's eyes.

"Black armor?" Quentin seemed angry in his insistence. "Five invaders, helmets all, none with a nose to call their own?"

Blastaar flicked his eyes to one side. "Stand away, impertinent Terran scum. I find your tone irritating. Lest you forget, you address a monarch."

The Kid stood up. "And lest you forget, you address an Adorable Representative MC for Youth. With a single, well-placed psychic knife I can end you now on behalf of the BTS Army."

"I know no such military force. Kill me, mutate, if you can."

Ignoring Blastaar, Kid Omega turned to the others with a determined, excited look upon his face. "It was The Remaining, you guys. I can taste that smug telepath's greasy brain and smell her cheap cosmic perfume. They were here, maybe even before they came to Earth and stole my friends." Quentin closed his eyes again. "But they weren't alone. Someone else was here… before… and they…"

The Kid opened his eyes. "Oh, no."

Blastaar smiled, grimacing slightly with the exertion. "Yes, minder. Oh, yes."

Havok stepped toward Quentin. "What is it, Kid?"

Blastaar continued, the defeated conqueror's gravelly voice grating with amusement.

"My forces… Lord Blastaar's grand Baluurian armada, all five thousand soldiers and generals gathered from across the Negative Zone and harvested from the universe's most notorious prisons… have been disgraced and annihilated by no more than five paltry assailants."

Corsair raised an eyebrow. "Seems unlikely. Why risk those odds?"

"For the greatest of prizes, Starjammer. A bounty like no other..." Blastaar leaned forward, finding strength enough to leer. "They risked it to win cosmic, godlike power!"

Havok and Kid Omega traded glances. After a second, the Kid shrugged his shoulders and matter-of-factly stated, "Quill was right. Blastaar had an Egg, but it's no longer here."

"I did," the Baluurian ruefully confirmed. "It was taken... but not by the hated five. They were too late, those silent invaders... these..."

"Remaining."

"Yes. The Phoenix Egg had come into my possession via conquest. An overlooked, unborn aspect of the Great Devourer, hidden at the edge of an unknown universe, secured once my generals had slaughtered entire worlds! A tale long in the telling, perhaps for another time. All that you must know is that long had I sought the smallest fraction of the Phoenix Force... and finally, after eons of searching, I held its terrible cosmic energies within my grasp!"

"Why did you even want it?" Quentin asked before Alex could stop him. "The Phoenix is a parasite, its hosts thralls. What purpose would it serve to own an Egg?"

Havok waited for Blastaar's reply. Would the intergalactic terrorist – as defeated as he was – take umbrage at Kid Omega's aggressive line of questioning? Thankfully, the Living Bomb-Burst merely sighed and growled.

"Power, of course. To harness the power of a god! With the Phoenix Force coursing through my veins, I would no longer be Lord Blastaar, King of the Negative Zone... but Emperor

Blastaar, subjugator of dimensions! Together, the Phoenix and I would have run rampant across the universe, bending planets, empires, and even gods to my whim."

Quentin shook his head. "Nope. Never would've happened, cap'n. None of the Phoenix's hosts have ever been able to control it."

Blastaar chortled again. "Aye, pup. But none had been a conqueror! None had been the Living Bomb-Burst!"

"Yeah, that would have sounded impressive until I looked around and saw the state of 'the Living Bomb-Burst,' laid low by five jamokes in shiny spacesuits."

Blastaar shook his head. "You misunderstand, pup. These Remaining had not been alone. As I said, they'd arrived too late. Another had come and stolen the Egg before them, removing it from Blastaar's grip before he had a chance to release the Phoenix Force. He took it from my grasp as easily as squeezing the life from an insectoid's carapace."

This was news to the collected assemblage of mutants and pirates. Some unknown "he" had the Phoenix Egg? Havok spoke up. "What're you talking about, Blastaar? Who has the Egg?"

Blastaar scowled, his jaw contorting as he spat a stained gob of saliva to the floor. He tried to sit up but fell back again from the considerable effort.

"They came, these Remaining... like you, they knew that the Phoenix had been here. But they departed in anger. Their fury drove them to slay all who drew breath, the few of my lackeys left alive – or what passed for living – by he who arrived before them, to impose his immortal will upon the forces of Blastaar. The five knew, as did I, that the Egg – and the power that lay within – was now beyond their reach. However capable or invincible they imagined themselves to be, they clearly felt unfit to test their mettle against an Elder of the Universe. And so, after destroying what remained of my army, they quit this place, headed to seek one who might."

"Hold up," Alex interjected, dawning anxiety rising in his gut. "Did you say 'an Elder of the Universe'?"

A cloud drifted across the faces of the Starjammers. Suddenly, this mission had become near impossible.

"What's the deal?" Kid Omega asked. "Are we talking about the same Elders from which Rocket and Quill got their delicious smoothie berries? If those morons can steal from these guys, I can't see how us taking an Egg is gonna be a problem."

Ch'od gently placed a large, reptilian hand on the Kid's shoulder.

"The Elders of the Universe are few, Quentin Quire, but they remain diverse in race, origin, power, and perhaps most importantly, temper. Though the Gardener, an ageless being from whom Peter Quill purloined his meager loot, fiercely protects his garden's bounty from the clutches of pirates and thieves... he is also known to possess a generous demeanor at times, remaining neutral in conflict whenever possible."

"OK," Quentin replied. "So let's go talk to that guy."

Corsair shook his head. "You're not getting it, Kid. What Ch'od means is that not all Elders are alike. They're the oldest beings in the universe, see? And that means most of them see the rest of us like ants. Lives too short, too finite to matter."

"Which makes them pompous and entitled," Havok continued.

Corsair agreed. "They're jerks."

"Vainglorious, self-important egotists," Blastaar agreed.

Raza laughed, brandishing his sword. "As are you, my vanquished friend."

Blastaar growled, his voice growing deeper with every passing breath. "But they are vainglorious, self-important egotists of power. And few possess the forgiving nature of the Gardener. Certainly not the current owner of the Egg you seek."

Corsair put both fists on his hips. "And which of the Elders are we talking about? The Champion? The Grandmaster, heavens forfend?"

Blastaar shook his head. "Who else, Starjammer? Which of the ageless, stubborn members of this universe's oldest sentient beings has devoted his immortality to acquiring not only artifacts of power but those of curious origin and singular existence?"

Hepzibah hissed. Ch'od glanced at her as the other Starjammers held their breath.

Kid Omega raised an eyebrow. The largest button on his jacket now read NEW ELDER GOD. WHO DIS? "What? Why does everyone look like they have diarrhea?"

Havok frowned and turned to his father, ignoring the younger mutant.

"This is bad, isn't it?"

Blastaar answered for the Starjammer's captain, a malicious twinkle in his eye.

"Aye, Earther. For it will take all your wiles and courage to penetrate his defenses… to breach the walls of one who can change shape, manipulate energy, and who possesses encyclopedic knowledge pertaining to the science and technology of countless worlds. 'Bad,' you ask? Yes, mutate.

You will require more power than possess a thousand armadas to recover the Phoenix Egg from the stronghold of Taneleer Tivan, he who is known as the Collector!"

CHAPTER TWELVE

Back aboard the ship, the Starjammers began the exhaustive task of tracking the Collector's current location. Though he possessed multiple museum-worlds wherein he stored his vast accumulation of curios and beings, the avaricious Elder also employed a battalion of traveling menageries and a great fortress-like starship on which he kept his most coveted artifacts. At present time, he – and the Phoenix Egg – could be at any one of those locations. Corsair and the others were tired of reacting, fed up with attempting to pin a tail on a universal donkey. And frankly, so were Alex and Kid Omega. This time, they wanted to get it right.

The team had left Blastaar where they'd found him, licking his wounds in the Xanthan Graveyard. Alex had briefly lobbied to transport the weakened conqueror to the nearest inhabited world or prison, where the vanquished monarch might seek medical attention. But Corsair and the others had argued Blastaar might take advantage of the situation and return to his

aforementioned conquering once he regained his strength…
not to mention, attack the ship. Did they want to take the
blame for putting a vulnerable planet into the Living Bomb-
Burst's explosive hands? Better to let Blastaar recoup his losses
in exiled solitude, alone in a drifting asteroid field. There was
mercy enough in allowing him life and the freedom to recover.
Even so, Ch'od put in a call to the Nova Corps, pointing them
toward the remains of Xanth.

The Kid stepped away from the others as they worked,
turning his back on the data analysis as Kurrgo's Ring faded
into the distance. The 'Jammer was prepared to skip through a
jump gate for parts unknown once Corsair, Ch'od, and Sikorsky
managed to pin down the Collector's whereabouts. For now,
Hepzibah steered away from the Graveyard, piloting the ship
across a sea of stars.

Taking a break from identifying and ruling out museum-
worlds, Havok stretched his legs and followed a sullen Kid
Omega down the bridge ladder into the vast cargo area. The
pink-haired mutant was particularly broody, ignoring Alex as
he wandered deep into the "farmland," out into the wide-open
space where the two mutants had dueled.

"Hey, Kid," Havok inquired, voice echoing. "Something on
your mind?"

Kid Omega shot Alex a withering look.

"There's always something on my mind. That question
insults those Homo sapiens superior who can access more than
ten percent of our fabulous brains. Oh, wait. Maybe I should
dumb that down for you, Ten-Percenter?" Quentin jabbed
his shirt, which now displayed an arrow pointed toward Alex,
under which were emblazoned the words I'M WITH STUPID.

"All right," Havok replied. "I know you're disappointed and the Graveyard was another dead end. But every step we take brings us closer to finding–"

"What?" Quentin whirled, spittle flying as he advanced on the older mutant. "Finding who? Not my friends. They're probably dead by now." The Kid tapped his skull. "I'm an Omega-level telepath. I've literally hosted the embodiment of life and freaking death, Not-Cyclops. I should be able to at least hear one of them… reach across the cosmos and bring my friends inside my mind! But. I. Can't. Someone out there," he shouted, madly flapping an arm toward the bulkhead, "is preventing me from doing that much. Phoebe Cuckoo… Glob… I've literally sent GIFs into their heads from opposite ends of the Earth. And sure, the galaxy – the universe – it's a lot bigger. But I know them. I know them best. I should be able to find them."

Quentin's shoulders slumped. His arms fell to his sides, and his chin dropped. He slowly, carefully slid to the ground. "And I can't. Which means either someone far more powerful than me is hiding them from sight… and, like, what does that mean when I finally face the wench and go mutant-a-mano on her brain? Or she's not hiding them…"

Havok finished it. "And they're already dead."

"Yeah."

Alex sat next to Kid Omega, stretching out on the vast, unusual grasslands that covered the Starjammer's cargo area.

"Kid, you gotta stay optimistic. If they were dead, if The Remaining killed them, then we'd never bring them the Egg, which seems to be what they want. And if they did kill five mutants, there's no corner of the universe that could hide them from the X-Men's wrath, divided as we might be." Havok put a hand on Quentin's shoulder. "We're gonna find them, I swear."

The Kid snorted with disdain. "Because we've been doing a bang-up job of it thus far. I don't know, Summers-Lite. Maybe Blastaar had the right idea."

Havok removed his hand and arched an eyebrow. "What do you mean?"

Quentin lifted his head and glared at the hull.

"I mean, maybe I should get into the spirit of this space thing and manifest a few psionic space lasers to pew-pew-pew this Collector, Sonny Corleone tollbooth style. Then I'll take his Phoenix Egg and use it to put a serious burn on that condescending telepathic witch."

Gabriel stepped to the door of Alex's cell. Havok seethed as Emperor Vulcan gloated and chuckled. "You were right about one thing," he said. "I'm nothing like you. And you, my older brother, are nothing like me. You have no idea of what I'm capable."

The memory struck Alex like a slap to the face. The same indignant tone. The same badly contained rage. He was walking an all too familiar tightrope.

"Quenti… Kid. You can't be serious."

Kid Omega's eyes burned. "I'm as serious as a bag of nuclear shotguns. Blastaar was right. Godlike power in the palm of my brain, Summers. It's the only way. We've been tiptoeing around the universe, making pleasant inquiries, doing our best to find the answers we need without making a sound or rummaging through brains. Well, let me tell you–"

Quentin telekinetically rose into the air, a fine pink aura washing over his body. He lifted one hand, and a salmon-covered handgun snapped into said hand. He fired one round, a psychic bullet that whined as it shot into the distance and ricocheted away into thin air.

"I'm done being quiet. I'm finished with knife fights. It's Tony Montana time in the Final Frontier, get me? And once we find the Phoenix, I'ma put its power in the right hands, stick it in my head like a cannon, find The Remaining, and make them say hello to my terrible, hungry, cosmic little friend."

Havok slowly stood, allowing the Kid a moment to drift to the ground, basking in his jagged, adrenaline-infused rant. Quentin was breathing very fast, very hard, and Alex didn't want to push the boy much further. After a moment, he quietly offered judgment on the Kid's plan.

"If you do that," Havok advised, "if you abuse the Phoenix Force as would Blastaar or a thousand would-be conquerors and warlords... then your hands are not the 'right' hands."

The Kid scoffed. "And your brother's were?"

"No, they weren't. Learn from his mistakes. Don't make them your own."

"And you?" Quentin asked, jabbing a finger into the circle at the center of Havok's chest. "Like Cyclops, you have a power that's almost as destructive as the Phoenix Force. You've been screwing around with it for years, abusing your gift for decades! You both have. Why is it OK for you and not me?"

"You're talking about different things, Kid. My gift and Scott's... they're deadly, but we were born with them. You know that; so were most mutants, like you. But we've also spent decades learning to control them, to use them for good. My brothers – both of them, in fact – were seduced by power they could not control. It ruined Scott, and it consumed Gabriel. So, me, I have to be careful not to fall into the same Summers trap. What you're proposing… you want to harness a power you know to be chaotic and deadly and revel in it, unleash it on–"

"I want to harness it to do what we came here to do! We're chasing our tails and no closer to rescuing my friends! Don't you get that?"

Havok nodded his head. "Of course I do. But going off half-cocked, letting impulses dictate our next move… Quentin. You're angry and maybe feeling a little guilty, but even you can understand how foolish that is."

"Don't call me Quentin. And what, instead you want to pretend to lead us? To teach me right from wrong? Now who's being foolish? You're a terrible leader, Havok, and a worse teacher. Even you must know that."

They faced one another in the farmland, Kid Omega's arms folded across his jacket, Havok's at his sides with his fingers clenched into fists. The insult lingered.

Gabriel laughed as he exited Havok's cell. "Bravo, Alex. Maybe we were both wrong."

"Listen," Alex reluctantly continued, relaxing his hands as he blinked away the memory, "maybe you're right. I told Scott this was a long shot. That you and I… it would never work. But the more time we spend together, Kid… I don't know."

"You don't know what?"

"We're a lot more alike than you think."

Quentin laughed. "Ha! There's that Alex Summers sense of humor. That's the funniest thing you've said yet."

Havok stepped forward, closing the gap between them.

"We both have self-esteem issues" – Quentin squawked, trying to disagree, but Alex bulled through before he could speak – "and we both have more power than we know what to do with. But we want to control it, to use it in ways that will make our lives, and the lives of others, better as a result."

"That's baloney."

"Is it, Kid? Don't tell me your Instagram hipster bravado isn't a thick blanket to hide – unsuccessfully, might I add – a well-oiled sheen of insecurity and the need to be loved? You and I, we both push folks away; me by leaving them… you, well, you take a more irritating, opposite approach." Alex counted off on his fingers. "We both struggle with managing vast amounts of power, we both have problems with leadership–"

Kid Omega cracked a grin. "We both have Omega-level daddy issues."

Havok ignored the salvo. "And we both grapple with chaos: me trying to rein it in. You, turning it into a fine art. But, and I've said this before, there's a time for chaos and a time for tact. I'm hoping we can use our similarities to meet somewhere in the middle, see the value of what each of us brings to the table so we can get this over with, find your friends…"

"…and go our separate ways."

Havok shrugged. "If that's what you want."

"It absolutely is." The Kid retreated, heading to the exit and in the direction of the maintenance shop. "So stop trying to teach or lead me. Help me get what I want so you can go back to avenging or being a giant, lame knockoff of your much cooler brother, and I can go back to being maxiflark. And I know that I'm using that word incorrectly. I don't care. Which is what makes me maxiflark."

He stormed off, tossing a rude gesture over his shoulder on the way out.

Alex let out a breath he didn't know he'd been holding. He wanted to scream, allowing his frustrations to echo around the cargo hold. He counted to ten and controlled his heart rate.

Havok knew the stakes. He understood that he needed to figure this out and find common ground with Quentin Quire. As a leader, as a teacher... handling a problem child came with the territory, even one as difficult as the Kid. But how long was he going to keep walking on eggshells? How much longer was he going to take the abuse?

Frankly, he didn't know how much more he could take.

"Kids, huh? They're the worst."

Alex turned. His dad stood by the ladder, having clambered down from the bridge sometime during Havok's blow-out with Quire. Corsair smirked as he stepped across the grass, headed toward his fuming son.

"You heard all of that, huh?"

"I think your brother heard it back in Canada. You all right?"

Alex nodded, doing his best to regulate his breathing.

"I'm fine, Dad. It's Quentin. I knew what I was getting into."

"Ahhh." Major Summers playfully swatted his son on the arm. "He reminds me of you boys. Growing up, you were both a handful."

"We weren't even ten when you left us, Dad."

"I know! And that's how you gotta think about that kid." He waved a hand in Quentin's direction. "You gotta learn his triggers. Do your best not to push buttons while also trying to provide some kind of lesson, and trust him to learn enough to do what's right."

Alex narrowed his eyes, listening as Corsair expounded on his extensive knowledge of parenting and teacher-student relations. Havok felt his heart rate rising again, his fingers clenching into fists. The anxiety rose as his father went on, and before he knew it Alex was back in that airplane, screaming for his life.

"Do what your mother says," shouted Major Summers, never bothering to give his boys one last look. "Do it now!"

The boys fell.

Oblivious to Alex's discomfort, Corsair paced as he continued. "Patience and attention. But you also need to listen, y'know? Don't let the kid push you away. That's something Xavier understood. And your brother – hoo, boy. He must've picked up professorial tips along the way because he definitely understands his students' flaws. But he also gives them room to make mistakes. Yessir, that's not something he got from me."

"I have to find those kids," Alex said. *"We have to find them."*

"We will," Corsair replied. *"I'd never let you down."*

"Daddy dearest had the fire," Vulcan said, sneering at Alex as he languished in chains. *"He had a burning spirit, like me. Like Scott."*

Vulcan sniffed and dropped Alex's chin. "I suppose you got your spirit from Mom."

Christopher Summers turned back. "In fact, you might take a page from your brother–"

Alex punched his father in the face.

It was a good hit, a solid connection, and down went the flustered pirate. Sprawled on the ground, a shocked Corsair raised a hand to his nose, checking for blood. He looked up. Havok loomed over his dad, seething.

"What the flark was that for?" shouted Corsair.

"You! You… what, all of a sudden you're an expert on raising kids? You have all the answers?! Major Christopher Summers,

United States Air Force, who didn't even say goodbye as his boys leapt to their doom! Father of the freaking century!"

"Hey, wait a minute..." Corsair awkwardly scrambled to his feet.

Havok pointed down, randomly jabbing in a direction that might be Earth.

"We needed you, Dad! I needed you, anyway. You just... left. Not only once, but twice. First with Mom, and then because Gabriel killed you. But both times... you never... you should've come back! You should have been here!"

"I know, but both times..." Corsair stammered, trying to explain. "Alex, you need to understand–"

"Do I, Dad? Do I really need to understand?"

"We were captured by the Shi'ar! They killed your mother!"

Alex shoved him. "But you survived. And instead of returning to Earth to find your kids, off you went – swashbuckling across the galaxy – a free man with his alien lover!"

"That isn't fair. We've already been through this argument, son."

"Yeah, we have. Before you were murdered by Gabriel. What I can't understand is why this time – when you came back again –I had to learn about it from Scott? Why didn't you learn from your mistakes and reach out directly, to come and let me know that you were fine? But I should've expected that, right? There's precedent. And you always liked him best."

"Again, you aren't being fair."

Alex wheeled away, unable to face his father.

"Life's not fair. You taught me that, dad. I don't even know how you came back after Vulcan killed you. All I know is that you're here, back with the Starjammers. You haven't even respected me enough – trusted me – to explain how that's possible."

Corsair held up a hand. "I was going to. It's a long story, you see–"

"No." Havok cut him off. "I don't have time for long stories now, Dad. The time for that was a week ago, a month ago. The second you got back. Not because it's convenient for you now, because Scotty asked me up here to find some kids and maybe build an emotional bridge… to, I don't know, find the kind of screwed-up, dispassionate relationship the two of you seem to have. But I guess that's what makes a good leader, right? Emotional distance. Lack of intimacy, pushing people away. Like father, like son. Scott does it, I've been doing it. I guess we did learn something from you, after all."

"Alex, if you'll let me…"

Havok whirled back, pointing an accusing finger.

"Maybe that's why I've been such a terrible leader, why I'm a failure as a teacher? Because all this time I've tried to connect with other people – with Lorna, Scott, and even you. You're right, Dad: I should take a page from Scott and keep shutting people out. Maybe then I'd be able to connect with Quire. Maybe then I'd be a better leader, a better… I don't know, son. Maybe then I'd be–"

"A failure." Corsair frowned and crossed his arms. "Just like me."

"What?" Alex was exasperated, tired. This was going nowhere.

"Son… what I was trying to say before, about taking a page out of Scotty's playbook. I meant that you might want to try what he's already figured out: humility. Accepting his own flaws and failings, learning from them, and giving others the room to do the same."

"Like you, huh?"

Corsair shook his head. "No. Not like me. You're right. I left. I didn't invest myself in the lives of my kids, and look where it got me. Sure, I live the glamorous pirate life. But I'm also hunted, widowed, and oh – I was killed by my own kid, remember?"

He scratched his head, ashamed. "D'you want to know the reason I never came back? The first time, after your mom died on Chandilar, I thought you boys were also dead. And sure… I could've looked. But my heart was filled with the need for revenge – against D'Ken, the Shi'ar – and there was little room for anything else, much less love or being a parent. When I finally did reunite with your brother, I couldn't recognize myself in Scott. Everything he'd learned, the man he'd become… he'd learned it himself with the help of Charles Xavier. That's the man who raised my boys, if they didn't raise themselves.

"So I stayed away. I figured that you were both better off without me, Alex. It's what I do. I push away the people who love me so I don't have to see them die again, like your mom, or fall out of an airplane while I do nothing… as happened with you boys. And somewhere along the way, without my involvement, you both managed to learn that from me, anyway. Now here we are: a family learning to become a family again, this time without the help of the late, great Charles Xavier. Scott… is trying. I know he is, because he told me so before you arrived. I know he had issues with Rachel, but he's recognizing his flaws. He's trying to learn from his mistakes and become a better father, a better leader and person. I guess."

"You guess?"

"I guess he wants that for us, too. So do I."

Havok absorbed his father's manic, rambling apology. His face burned, and his heart hurt. There were so many things he wanted to say, to scream and throw back in Corsair's face.

"So what about this time?" Alex asked. "Gabriel killed you. You returned. Why didn't you come tell me? We'd already put everything else behind us, Dad. Why keep shutting me out, pushing me away?"

"I was embarrassed. My son – a son I didn't even know about – murdered me like I was nothing, no one to him. You don't come back from a thing like that without wallowing in grief and your own mistakes."

"So you repeated those mistakes instead."

"Yes," Corsair agreed, gripping Havok's shoulders in both hands. "And don't you get it, Alex? I was wrong. I screwed up. That's what makes you and Scott better men than me, men like Xavier who taught you to recognize your mistakes and trust yourself not to make the same ones twice. To trust your students and those you love to do the same. That's what makes Scott a good leader, kid. And that's what you need to do here, too."

"What? With Quentin?"

Major Summers's laughter echoed in the cavernous space.

"Yeah, I know it's a tall order. I don't want to compare the two of you or anything, but you said it yourself: you've got a lot in common. You want to be a better teacher and leader? Be here now, Alex. Stop doubting yourself and wallowing in anger or guilt. Realize that you aren't me or Scott: you're Alex Freaking Summers, your very own person. Sure, it'll be awkward, and both you and Quentin have issues to resolve. So did we. Heck, we still do. And we will, like I did with your brother. Once Scott and I let ourselves connect, our relationship has never been better."

Alex smiled. "That's what he said."

"He ain't wrong. You have to allow yourself to do the same with this kid. All of his rebel instincts are surface-deep, sport. He's covering up his feelings so he doesn't get hurt, like me... but he's also reaching out for something he's missing. Maybe you don't have it, but he knows it's out there. Help him find it. Don't shut him out, even if he keeps you at arm's length. That's where Scott went wrong with Rachel, and where I went wrong with you and your brothers. But I'm trying now. You need to try, too."

Alex looked into his father's eyes. The years peeled away, and he saw his mother, his brother... Vulcan. The pain, loss, and frustration, the death, the failures. But he also saw the love, friendships, and support. The X-Men. X-Factor. The Starjammers and Avengers. Everyone he'd ever loved. Lorna, smiling at him beneath a setting sun, emerald hair blowing in a light summer breeze. His mother, hugging him goodbye, her tears on his cheek.

Alex's father put an arm on his shoulder.

I'd never let you down.

He leaned in to embrace Corsair. "I'll do my best, Dad. I'll try."

"Me too. I promise, I'll never let you down... again."

They broke apart. Havok wiped his face.

"You better not," he replied. "But I'll tell you this, major."

"Yeah? What's that?"

"There's no chance I'm hugging Kid Omega."

Corsair chuckled again, a bright peal of laughter echoing off into the distance.

"Ten-four, captain. Boy, is that a big ten-four."

CHAPTER THIRTEEN

[ALEX | IMPERIAL DUNGEONS | CHANDILAR | THE SHI'AR GALAXY]

Years Ago...

Hours later, the door to his cell opened again.

By the weight of the footfalls, Alex could tell that Vulcan hadn't returned, nor did his open door herald the arrival of a guard or meal. The visitor treaded lightly – barely a whisper, as if floating – and closed the door with an inaudible click.

Havok tried lifting his chin to ascertain the identity of this new arrival. Whoever it was circled to his right, out of reach and view. Unable to see, he tried using his other senses. Sniffing, he noted the fragrant aroma of flowers used to hide a sour, overpowering musk of sweat.

"Who's there?"

The intruder sighed and laughed, a guttural, languid chime that emerged from deep within her throat. As with his brother, Alex recognized the greasy, sibilant voice. He could all but see her shaking, disapproving head, a crest of head-feathers proud above amused, pupilless eyes.

"You shouldn't have done that," the Shi'ar Empress admonished her captive.

Like her husband, Vulcan – Alex's brother and preceding visitor – Cal'syee Neramani-Summers, also known as Deathbird, paced the small cell. He could see her heels, clacking on the tiled floor as she made her way around the room.

"Shouldn't have done what?"

Deathbird chuckled again. "You made Vulcan angry. My husband... my fiery paramour hardly needs an excuse to fly off the handle, Alex Summers. Stoking those flames... making him mad, well, that might lead to the death of someone you dearly love."

"What do you know about love, Deathbird? You murdered your mother and had Gabriel slaughter your brother, D'Ken. You've tried executing your sister, Lilandra, more times than I can count. Vulcan says you're his family, but you've never had a family member you didn't try to kill in order to gain power."

A single taloned finger traced Alex's jawline. "Careful, brother-in-law. My husband isn't the only one whose blood runs hot." She caressed his cheek and then dropped her hand.

"But" – Deathbird returned to her slow circuit around the cell – "your words have the ring of truth. D'Ken, Lilandra... even my parents meant little to me in the grand design of my ambitions. The Empire – the throne – has been all I have wanted, ever since I was young. The only thing I have truly coveted. I possessed it for a time, but always under threat of rebellion by my sister, and the infuriating X-Men among others."

"That's because you took it via coup, in an act of piracy."

"Be careful of who you hypocritically label a pirate, Starjammer. No, I took the throne by right! It should have always been mine, by law and strength – as should the galaxy! Instead, I was forced to suffer the indulgent rule of an insane brother and the ineffectual leadership of my insipid sister. Neither turned the Empire into the intergalactic power it truly deserves to be."

"The Shi'ar Empire comprises one million worlds."

Deathbird struck Alex on the shoulder, raking sharp talons through his uniform and drawing blood. "Yet there are millions more, ripe for the taking!"

Havok shivered, grimacing at the feel of raw, torn flesh, blood flowing freely and dripping down his arm. Deathbird stepped away, sweetly continuing her tirade.

"By Vulcan's side, I can accomplish the task for which I've long been destined. Together, we will turn the Empire into a universal ruling body. A cosmos-spanning empire attained through triumphant conquest! The flames of our love will ignite the stars."

She stopped pacing, turning her heels to face Havok. Her lacquered fingernails caressed his face once more.

"But when you," she crooned, "Vulcan's actual blood – a genetic line into which I was married and not born – when you question that love, well … it tends to enrage our emperor."

"He's not my emperor."

"But he is mine."

Alex sighed. "Come on. Admit you're using him. He's naive and powerful, I get it. But you and I both know that you've never loved anyone but yourself."

She was silent. Then Deathbird swiped her talons, tearing cloth and flesh from Havok's other shoulder. Alex grimaced but, as with Vulcan, never screamed.

"How dare you?" she breathed, voice husky and threatening. "True. In the past my desires have mostly lain in conquest and succession. But I do have feelings and desires. I am susceptible to love, as are you. As is Vulcan. Is it so hard to believe that even one who has murdered those once dear to her – one who places honor, duty, and conquest before blood – may find herself blind to all but burning passion?"

Alex choked back the pain radiating from his arms. "So… so you're saying it was a love connection?"

"Nothing of the sort. But there is love. Gabriel fascinates and draws me. Yes, the promise of power and conquest is calculable, and there is no argument that by his side I will achieve my heart's desire. But there is more. He is… he is my family. Perhaps now, my only family. Something burns within Vulcan – the same purpose and passion that rages within me. Together, we are more than the sum of our parts. He the sun, and I the stars. Vulcan and I have a great deal in common. Together we are able to put aside the anger and betrayals, stop ourselves from wallowing in hurt, pain, and death for a time. And in those moments, when we allow our union to become greater, our love and connection is a conflagration unlike anything I've ever known. And within it – perhaps for the first time, Alex Summers – have I found something I may desire more than power."

Bleeding, listening, Alex waited for her to go on. But after a minute, it became clear that Deathbird had little else to say. Thankfully, Havok was happy to fill the silence.

"Congratulations. Welcome to the family. You won't survive the experience, because I'm going to kill you both."

Deathbird laughed again. "You said that to Vulcan, as well.

He enjoyed it, as do I. You continue to amuse us, brother-in-law. Perhaps that is why we let you live."

"Oh, I'm a laugh at Summers family Thanksgivings. Next year, I'll invite you if we're short a turkey. And if I haven't killed you first."

Deathbird opened the door, preparing to leave.

"The only thanks you'll give are to me and my Majestor. We are your family... and your rulers. Keep us happy, and your friends will live. Question our love again, and those you love – particularly your green-haired Earth woman – will die screaming by my hand."

And with that, Cal'syee Neramani-Summers – empress to the Shi'ar, wife of Vulcan and scourge of the cosmos – left Havok to his blood, pain, and regrets.

CHAPTER FOURTEEN

[QUENTIN | THE STARJAMMER | SIRIUS FIVE | THE MILKY WAY GALAXY]

The Starjammer exited a translight jump gate and banked north – or what felt like "north" to Kid Omega, who understood that in space, his internal compass was slightly askew. Direction aside, he fell back against his seat – as did Havok and the others – when Corsair pulled the yoke, bringing the dreadnought into a climb, aiming toward the star shining above Sirius Five.

"I'm gonna hide us near the sun," Major Summers explained, tossing it over his cocky shoulder. "The 'Jammer will block all traditional sensors, but you gotta figure the Collector is wily and largely non-traditional. We still may lose the element of surprise. At the very least, I can keep the locals from spotting our arrival. Sorry about the sudden jerk."

The Kid muttered under his breath, "You're a sudden jerk."

"Say again, kid?"

"I said phenomenal plan, captain! Ten out of ten would recommend!" Quentin replied, offering the captain a patronizing wink and salute.

Skeptical, Corsair returned to the helm. As he did, the words YOU'RE A SUDDEN JERK materialized on Kid Omega's shirt, coupled with a rude gesture flashing on his smallest button. Laughing at the Starjammer captain under his breath, the Kid glanced at Alex who merely looked away, focusing on the planet below. That was OK. Quentin didn't care. He'd managed to get the Summers men to agree to his plan, and that was straight fire.

They had tracked the largest accumulation of the Collector's artifacts to a modestly sized cathedral tucked atop the dark side of Sirius Five's moon. Alternatively titled "Wundagore II," the fifth Sirian world had been settled by a human geneticist named Herbert Wyndham for the purpose of providing a world to a race of sentient animals he'd evolved into a humanoid, militant race, like an interstellar Doctor Moreau. Wyndham named his claimed planet after Wundagore Mountain, the European site of his first laboratory on Earth. Over the years, the descendants of Wyndham's experiments had repelled alien invaders, and Sirius Five was now governed by their thriving population. It also played host to a rare bloom of lotus poppy, the like of which blossomed once every thousand years. It was this unique fauna that had first drawn Taneleer Tivan – the Collector – to the Sirian system, and possibly why his largest museum-world had been erected on the fifth planet's moon. They didn't know for certain if the Egg was inside, though all shipping manifests, traffic triangulation, and alternative data collation seemed to point to the affirmative, according to Sikorsky and Ch'od.

Kid Omega couldn't wait to breach the museum's gates. He'd been concerned that Lil' Summers would again want to err on the side of tiptoes and tact, as he had on Majesdane, New Xandar, and Xanth. Sure, stealth had its place. But the Kid was anxious and tired of being Omega-Come-Lately. He was growing concerned about how The Remaining might be treating Glob, Phoebe, and the others. Every move they made and every part of this game felt like they were arriving in time for someone to shuffle the deck. Just once, the Kid wanted to kick over the chessboard and loudly claim checkmate. After his tiff with Havok in the cargo hold, Kid Omega had initially decided to either mutiny or hijack The Remaining scout craft. But something – maybe their adventure in the Graveyard, wrangling a monstrous gecko? – tweaked the usually silent, cricket-sized conscience cowering in the back of the Kid's mental junk drawer. So instead he chose to bite his tongue, toggle off the T-shirt slogans, and temper his instincts. Taking a breath, Kid Omega had gone to compromise with Havok one more time.

Surprisingly, Summers and Son had agreed with the Kid's assessment. They signed on to pick their moment, hit the museum hard and fast, steamroll any opposition waiting at the front door, and then snatch the Egg before the Collector got wise to their intentions (if it was truly here, and not another fool's errand). Each of the acquiring Elder's compounds was staffed by a battalion of adepts and acolytes – scholars who acted as glorified security guards. The walls were outfitted with state-of-the-art automatic defenses no doubt culled from the most technologically advanced planets from across the universe. The intricate complex, a stronghold designed in a style reminiscent of both Earthbound Gothic architecture and psychedelic science-fiction cityscapes, played host to ancient metallic towers jutting from a panorama of machinery, battlements, and vast circular storehouses. Pneumatic lifts and observation decks festooned the walls, the latter providing a berth for the Collector's security teams and intimidating cannons. The installation had been constructed in a way meant to convey a forbidding nature, unwelcome to visitors and designed to keep the riffraff out.

So, knocking on the door and finessing a tour would appear foolish.

Still. That was kind of the plan.

The Starjammer slid into position near the Sirian sun, idling with the shield array at full to protect the ship from the star's blistering radiation. Despite the protective shell, the temperature in the bridge began to rise, its organic occupants fidgeting with discomfort.

"We won't stay long," Corsair assured the sweating crew. "We're just waiting for an invitation." He winked at Hepzibah and Kid Omega in turn, the latter of whom tapped his shirt and the insult emblazoned there in irritated reply. The Kid was sweating. They all were, all but Ch'od whose Sauridian body temperature was used to tropical climates. The air in the bridge grew stale, the heat threatening to barbecue them where they sat. Sikorsky, whirring and clicking, noted the gradual drop in oxygen and cabin pressure.

"Any minute now," Corsair whispered, nervously tapping the comms array.

Havok peeled down his mask to wipe his brow. "Dad...?"

"Any minute."

Sikorsky bleated, and Raza winced, perspiration streaming into his cybernetic eye. The bridge was a furnace. The shields were holding, the hull intact. But if they remained much longer, the crew was in danger of succumbing to spontaneous combustion.

The Kid tapped Havok's knee. "Mind over matter, right? I could take everyone into my head, disconnect the discomfort of our physical bodies until—"

Panting like a dog, Alex could hardly speak. But he raised a palm and violently shook his head to indicate a negative response. Clearly, after their battle in the Omega Room, Havok wasn't keen on a return vacation to Kid Omega's cerebellum. Prepared to further explain the benefits of his recommendation to his would-be mentor – to assure him that this time would be different – the Kid began to protest. His throat was bone-dry. He licked his lips.

But before he could speak, a whistle pierced his skull: an urgent message from the 'Jammer's comms array. Corsair grinned and mopped his curls, strands of which clung to his headband and brow. He swiveled to the helm and returned the hail.

"This is Major Christopher Summers, United States Air Force and captain of the HMSS Starjammer. To whom do I have the pleasure of speaking?"

An electronically distorted garbled reply emerged from the receiver. Ch'od adjusted a dial to reduce the static, and the hail repeated, this time translated into English for the benefit of the confused Earthers.

"...Haroona Sh'thian, Vice-Senior Adept and Forever Attendant to the Seventh Catalogue-World of our Glorious Curator, the all-knowing and ancient personage of Taneleer Tivan, Acquirer and Collector, Elder of the Known Universe and perhaps Multiverses Beyond. We recognize the call-signs, model, measurements, and historical timeline of your craft, Major Summers – he whose identity and biological aura is

also known to this assemblage as thief, rogue, swindler, and...
welcher."

Embarrassed, Corsair scratched his head and blushed.

"C'mon, Haroona. It was one deal. I was raided. The
Collector can't expect a guy–"

Kid Omega and Havok traded glances. What was this now?

Haroona Sh'thian continued, "Your lack of foresight,
security, discretion, and alternate routes lost a rare Zenn-
Lavian pearlsquid for my generous master. An acquisition for
which you were handsomely paid. Have you perhaps returned
to deliver restitution on either account?"

"I mean... who can really say–"

"Have you the pearlsquid in captivity? Or the retainer of fifty
thousand Xandarian units?"

The occupants of the bridge all glared at the now heavily
perspiring, blushing, and apologetic Starjammer captain.
Major Summers hemmed and hawed into the comms.

"Look, Haroona. Let me land peacefully, and I'd be happy
to set up a payment plan with your boss, OK? Anyway, I'm
carrying something that could be worth far more to him than–"

"As you neither have the artifact as specified in the original
sourcing contract, nor are willing to refund the considerable
units graciously funded from our financial stores, in my power
as Vice-Senior Adept and Forever Attendant to the Seventh
Catalogue-World of our Glorious Curator, I have no choice
but to order your layabout crew of savages and philistines to
disembark the Shi'ar Fearless-class battle dreadnought that will
then be impounded as collateral until such time as you, your
partners or heirs are in a financial position to settle accounts."

Corsair glanced at Hepzibah. He growled into the receiver,

"Oh, yeah? Your pretentious boss thinks he's gonna take my ship? Him and which army?"

Raza cleared his throat and pointed out the forward window.

"Captain? Pose a question and an answer thou shalt receive."

They followed the cyborg's gaze. A sleek battalion of starcrafts had launched from the Sirian moon, rocketing toward the Starjammer in a disciplined, threatening formation. Sikorsky squawked, plugged itself into an interface port, and the bridge lighting shifted to scarlet tones. Ch'od settled in at navigation as Raza and Hepzibah smiled with glee, the latter baring her teeth as she winked at her captain and climbed into battle command. They spun into position, preparing port and ventral guns for the inevitable dogfight.

Corsair shrugged, a matter-of-fact gesture that conveyed he'd been expecting this response. He leaned into the comms, sighed, and replied, "Well, I can't blame the Collector for trying to collect. Shame we couldn't work this out over Xandarian ale, Haroona. I know it puts you in a singing, flirty mood."

Hepzibah growled and shot him a look. Corsair furrowed his brow and shook his head, silently indicating to his first mate that he only had eyes for the beautiful Mephitisoid. He terminated the hail and swung into action. Before he did, he turned to address the two mutants.

"Now would be the time, gentlemen." Then he swiveled to the helm, grabbed the yoke, and accelerated toward the advancing ships.

There were nine; eight of them light and fast, centered around what appeared to be the squadron leader. The Collector's air command had been outfitted with sinking torpedoes and twin maxi-joule cannons mounted fore and aft of the central bulkheads. Four sublight engines propelled each ship, and a compact grappling unit – a tractor beam, as it were – had been affixed below the cockpits. A stylized mark was painted in gold on each cockpit's nose, depicting a grasping hand. The rest of the craft was resplendent in crimson hues.

The largest of the nine fighters, circled by its smaller companions, carried an additional grappling unit and a larger array of torpedoes. Its cannons were fitted to either side, with a third mounted on a dorsal turret above the cockpit, much like the Starjammer's port and starboard guns. The grasping hand, no doubt the symbol of the Collector's dedicated acolytes, nearly covered the cockpit, as if clasping the craft itself. As the battalion approached, the eight lighter ships broke apart, moving to enclose the oncoming enemy, while the leader continued on the same vector, engaging the Starjammer in a deadly game of chicken.

Corsair pushed harder on the yoke, increasing the ship's acceleration. The bridge vibrated, and Sikorsky whistled, bleating yet another warning about stress being introduced to the dreadnought's structural integrity. Major Summers ignored the whirling, whining Chr'yllite. His senses appeared to be completely focused on the imminent battle and subsequent plan. He didn't have time to listen to yattering damage reports. He couldn't stop to play it safe.

The Starjammer evaded the squadron leader at the last second, pulling into an elegant spin as it curved around the fighter's linear attack. Raza and Hepzibah fired all guns as the ship rotated, three sets of cannons searching for impact on their flustered opponent. The squadron leader launched two rockets, several of which impeded the 'Jammer's volley. The resultant explosions buffeted both ships, driving them apart, and the eight light fighters circled to entrap the Shi'ar dreadnought in a web of tractor beams.

"Not on my watch," proclaimed Corsair through gritted teeth.

He righted the ship and spun it in the opposite direction, pulling out of the lattice of tractor nets and banking toward the moon. The nine ships wheeled to chase him, firing cannons, peppering the Starjammer's shields as it serpentined back into open space. The Collector's squadron followed, and those at the fortress's turrets – manning ground cannons – focused efforts on helping their airborne companions bring down the pirate ship.

They were so focused, in fact, that hardly any of them noticed the small, cloaked scout craft wheeling around the moon, staying low to the rocky terrain as it careened along the landscape, headed for the stronghold's main doors.

Kid Omega barked with vindication, thrilled that he and Havok had pulled it off. They'd launched their craft the moment Corsair had put the 'Jammer into its dive. The Kid peered out the window of the small craft, staring up and trying to follow the impressive confrontation as the Starjammer swooped and fired, evading and then attacking the Collector's ships. With all eyes on Corsair's suicide run, the mutants were free to use the distraction and circle the sun, coming at the museum from a trajectory that brought them in behind the compound. Their presence would not remain secret for long. They'd no doubt been tracked by Haroona and whoever else guarded the artifacts. But Havok brought them in hard and fast, wasting no time in covering the distance to the front of the complex.

Sure enough, a handful of attendants rushed to meet them,

firing handheld blasters and turning mounted cannons to quell their approach. Alex nodded, and Kid Omega smiled.

Quentin opened the airlock hatch and levitated himself out of the craft. Spreading his hands, the Kid telekinetically wrenched cannons from the museum's walls, splintering metal and stone as he pulled them away, launching each gun into the distance. Havok stepped out and clenched both fists, firing plasma at the overwhelmed adepts. The ground forces now divided their assault between Alex and Quentin – who was an ascendant angel of psionic chaos, unleashing the full strength of his abilities on the hapless acolytes. He entered their minds and constructed nightmares. He dangled them above the Collector's fortress. They scrambled, scattering like roaches, and the Kid laughed as he descended to join Havok at the museum's doors, now opened wide to receive them.

"Not bad," remarked the older X-Man, a goofy smile turning up the corner of one lip.

Kid Omega cracked his knuckles. The words SPACE MUTANT replaced whatever slogan he'd been wearing on his sculpted, admirable chest. "I believe the word you're searching for, Not-Cyclops, is 'damngirl,' all one word, no exclamation."

"Well, then. 'Damngirl.'"

Beyond the open doors lay a large circular lobby, intricately carved with bas-relief and statuary depicting vast, reaching, monumental beings: the Elders of the Universe, no doubt, molding galactic clay, harnessing the power of stars and suns. Kid Omega looked up as they passed through, noting how the reliefs cycled and rotated, morphing into new scenes and presentations of the Elders and their works. Warning screams sounded from the next room. Three bald attendants dressed in cobalt robes rushed the mutants, hauling complicated weaponry.

The Kid raised a fist and smiled. The attendants left the ground, arms flung akimbo, their deadly armaments clattering to the tiled marble floor. He opened his hand, extending his fingers, and the three adepts went flying toward the fluctuating reliefs. They hung and squirmed, pinned to the walls, as Havok and Kid Omega entered the museum.

The duo entered a vast, impossible space. The walls reached skyward, the structure's roof lost to sight. Thousands of stacked glass enclosures filled their gaze, suspended upon nothing but air. Each box held a single object, item or creature, many unfamiliar to either mutant and no two of them alike. Every display case – for that's what they were – had been affixed with a small, descriptive card. Each was locked or fitted with a locking pad and controls that regulated temperature, climate, pressure, smell, or any number of particular conditions required to optimally preserve what lay inside.

Kid Omega craned his neck, taking in the gallery. It was quiet and musty, the sounds of battle outside echoing against the walls. He heard a furtive whispering in his ears, perhaps emanating from the cases. The Kid stuck out a hand and touched the nearest box, covered with frost. He rubbed to reveal a hefty blue child inside, gazing at Quentin with piercing eyes. It must have been ten or eleven, sturdy and well-fed. The caged child wore a white loincloth and chewed a joint of uncooked meat. It placed a hand against the glass, and a fresh layer of frost hid it from view. The Kid looked down at the card, which explained that the boy in the case had been collected from Jotunheim, one of the Nine Realms and home to the Frost Giants. Kid

Omega slowly turned, taking in the many enclosures that comprised the Collector's seventh museum-world. How many more creatures were jailed within its walls?

"This isn't right," he said to Havok. The whispering grew louder, reaching out from everywhere. It rode the air currents, perhaps, or soughed from the many glass crates. "Everything in here... all of these things... are they alive?"

"Not all," Alex replied. He pointed to a number of cases that held guns, swords, helmets, starships, rocks, and liquids. Kid Omega wasn't wrong, though. Scattered throughout the multitude of inorganic artifacts were also living creatures, sullenly glaring at them from the confines of an enclosure, watching the mutants with curious, expectant stares.

"Should we release them?" Quentin wasn't sure if he was asking Havok or posing a rhetorical question. "I mean, these are sentient beings with free will. What right does this Collector have to–"

Havok placed a hand on the Kid's shoulder. "Look, I applaud the fact that your heart's in the right place. But we can't just blunder our way through here. We don't know anything about the beings in those cages, if they made a deal with the Collector, or whether or not they're more of a threat than we can handle once released. We also don't know what kind of security Tivan's got built into his cases. So, for now, let's focus on why we're here – the one dangerous thing we believe he's got. All of this," he said, indicating the collection, "is a problem for another day."

"...fine. I'm not thrilled, but I'll allow it."

"That said, let's figure out if he even has that one dangerous thing. Or at least has it here. I don't suppose you saw a directory on the way in?"

But Kid Omega wasn't listening to Havok anymore. All he could hear was the continued, rising, susurrant whisper. It was high and sibilant. Throbbing and seductive. The Kid knew that sound. He'd heard it before. His cheeks burned, his palms perspired.

He'd last heard the sound in the White Hot Room, the nexus of eternal flame.

Home to the Phoenix.

CHAPTER FIFTEEN

[QUENTIN | TANELEER TIVAN'S SEVENTH CATALOGUE-WORLD | SIRIUS FIVE | THE MILKY WAY GALAXY]

"It's here."

Kid Omega wiped his brow. He grinned, searching wildly. "I... I can hear it. The Phoenix is in this museum."

Havok nodded, voice earnest and urgent. "Great. Can you lead us to it?"

"Yeah, definitely. I just need–"

"You need to leave!"

The mutants turned to behold a squat angry purple woman with a flowing mane of electric-yellow hair. Two heads shorter than Kid Omega, she wore a glorious blouse of intricate, interlocking patterns. After a second, he realized that the patterns were the fabric equivalent of the reliefs depicted in the museum's circular lobby. She clutched an oversized glowing tablet in her gold-gloved, chunky fingers. Tapping upon its surface, the woman sent streams of light and sound fluttering behind as she strode across the gallery in high, golden boots. A sky-blue cape hung about her sloping shoulders, fastened at the neck by a flat yellow disc.

Reaching the duo, she used her free hand to shoo them toward the doors, as if she were scattering a flock of pigeons. "Go," the purple woman insisted. "You have no appointment or business in these halls, and I am far too busy fending off a gross incursion by a deadbeat freelancer to deal with the likes of tourists!"

Havok raised an eyebrow, and a smirk turned his lips. "You must be Haroona."

"Haroona Sh'thian, Vice-Senior Adept and Forever Attendant to the Seventh Catalogue-World of our Glorious Curator, the all-knowing–"

Alex cut her off. "Yeah, we know. Look, we need a moment of your time."

Haroona swiped a hand across her tablet, and the nearest enclosures – including that of the undersized Frost Giant – slid deeper into the room as others rushed to take their place. Eyes down, she manipulated the cases, barely making eye contact with the two intruders.

"My time is precious, Earther, as are the sacred artifacts under my care. At the moment, my focus is divided between the endless privilege of curating and maintaining the exhibits upon display and protecting them from assault by an odious, double-dealing, rapscallion savage. Now, if you will see yourselves out and perhaps return with an appointment–"

Haroona's voice, melodious as it may have been, jarred Kid Omega's ears. He kept listening for the Phoenix, trying to track its location in the vast, overwhelming vertical space. Squinting and sighing, the Kid psionically lifted Haroona's tablet from her grasp, eliciting a short squawk of protest. She attempted to retrieve it, but it flew across the room and slapped into his palm. Swiftly, he searched for the Phoenix Egg, but the screen was presented in a language he couldn't comprehend. Kid Omega reached out with his mind and built a psychic interface between himself and Haroona – as he'd done with the Starjammer and the buttons on his lapels – using her knowledge to translate the gallery application.

"There," he announced, triumphantly pointing to Enclosure ZZ'FG-0<2K>07, located in a restricted archive at the pinnacle of the fortress's left-hand tower. The museum vibrated. Thunder sounded in the distance. The Starjammer was still engaging the Collector's ships, but they were running out of time.

Kid Omega grabbed Haroona by her cape. "Take us here. Now."

"I will not," she refused, stretching to snatch back the tablet. "That archive is for the eyes of the Collector alone, he who constructed this Seventh Catalogue-World, a testament to–"

The tablet launched into the air and shattered, the pieces whirling about Haroona's head. The Kid was irritated. The seductive, burning song of the Phoenix echoed in his skull. He glared at the Collector's Vice-Senior Adept, slowly contracting the space between the tablet bits and her vulnerable, blonde and purple head.

"I- I, ahem, that being said, yes… special circumstances do account for certain diplomatic tours, shall we agree? Please, gentles. Follow this way."

She spun on her heels, putting distance between herself, the mutants, and the broken, floating tablet. The Kid grinned and trailed the pieces behind them, hoping they might be used as a deterrent if needed. Havok frowned. He hurried to catch up to Haroona Sh'thian.

"Look," Alex explained. "We don't mean any harm. But we need to speak to the Collector about the Phoenix Egg in his care."

"In my care," she corrected.

"His, yours. That Egg is the reason we dared breach the Collector's walls. You see—"

"None of that is my concern."

Haroona had not said that, but rather a deep voice thundering from above the gallery, about seven or eight levels over their heads. Havok and Kid Omega craned their necks to see and were rewarded by the sight of a humanoid measuring six feet in height, cloaked in an outfit similar to Haroona's. His tunic was red, with no patterns to be found upon its fabric, and a thin golden belt circled his waist. A sky-blue cape billowed behind him as he descended. His cloud of hair was white, as were his blank enigmatic eyes. Stellar particles circled the being's form – a cosmic aura, glittering and yawning like the sound of an ocean. Eventually he reached the ground, but his boots did not deign to touch the floor. He hovered before them, hands clasped behind his back, circling like a god and investigating them in turn with all-seeing, amused, pupilless eyes. Haroona smiled as he descended, purring with satisfaction like a well-fed house cat.

"I am Taneleer Tivan. For eons I have searched the stars in universes both found and unknown, my purpose to acquire artifacts and life forms both rare and valuable. Never have I failed in this mission. No two items in my museums have or will be displayed alike. And you, my dear Earthmen, are trespassing."

"We're not men," Kid Omega objected. "We're mutants."

Taneleer Tivan gazed down, amused.

"Apologies. I have lived millions of years, and have parlayed with billions of beings. Sometimes, the niceties escape me. Duly noted."

The Kid nodded, clearly uncomfortable in the Collector's presence. "Well, OK then."

He was trying to focus on the Elder of the Universe before him, and to stand his ground. But he was extremely distracted by the sibilant Phoenix-song. Kid Omega's head was beginning to hurt. They needed to leave before his skull split apart from the burning pain.

The Collector nonchalantly took Havok's measure, perhaps cataloguing Alex to see if he was worthy of collection. "Your biology and bloodline are familiar to me, mutant. But hardly unique. And I must say, your purpose here offends."

"My purpose?"

Tivan dismissively waved a hand as he turned away.

"What care I, he who has lived and shall for millennia, of lost Earth children in the magnitude of our wondrous creation? I already possess children in my stores – a variety of species, each a rare jewel – in galleries and museum-worlds across the universe. Your quest, I must admit, means little to me. Nor am I willing to relinquish or risk one of the items in my collection in exchanges for the folly of... heroism."

He smiled down at the mutants. "Yes, I know about your task. One of many desperate, adrenaline-fueled missions undertaken by the insignificant adventurers that infest your young, meager, entitled world."

"Then if you know, help us. Let us borrow the Phoenix Egg, and we'll–"

The Collector laughed. "Borrow? This is no lending library. No artifact leaves my domain once catalogued. Here and in galleries like this, they are cared for and maintained. Protected from those aforementioned desperate individuals who would risk extermination of a species or the misuse of an object like the Ultimate Nullifier, a Cosmic Cube or a handful of Infinity Stones – which has happened more times than I care to recount. This catalogue-world in particular is home to many such items, both precious and near-extinct... but also dangerous should they be foolishly taken from their enclosures. No, mutants. Removing any artifact from my collection, especially one as perilous as a Phoenix Egg, is out of the question."

He strode to the middle of the room, where a small lounge area coalesced into existence as if from nowhere. A long, comfortable-looking curved sofa had appeared, wrapped around a spartan kidney-shaped table, across from which sat three exquisite floating chairs. Taneleer Tivan snapped his fingers, and glass bowls of fruit, snifters of liquid, and other enticing delicacies appeared on the table. The Collector sat upon the sofa and beckoned for the mutants to join him. Havok and Kid Omega followed, taking the chairs. The Kid let the shards of Haroona's former tablet clatter to the floor. She sneered as they fell, and then minced after them, positioning herself behind the Collector at a respectful distance.

"Indulge, won't you?" the Collector said. "I do not eat but have taken the liberty of importing familiar foodstuff from your planet. California grapes, there. Tuscan sausage. A bit of wine and water. No? Please, I insist."

Frowning at their reluctance to partake, the Collector

adjusted himself and spread wide his arms, resting them across the back of the couch.

"In any event, I must request that your companions – one of whom I have lapsed business with – cease their assault on my gallery. And I must also ask you discontinue your pursuit of this Egg as well as any aspects of the Phoenix Force. Already your indiscreet inquiries on New Xandar and elsewhere have been noted by the Kree, Skrull, and Shi'ar empires, the latter of which has begun mobilizing to prevent you from acquiring what you seek, determined to destroy the Egg… which may, unfortunately, result in their irritating arrival upon my doorstep."

Haroona frowned, her pouty lips turning down at the corners, and let out a disapproving hiss. Havok glanced at the Kid. Quentin didn't need to be a telepath to decipher that wordless rebuke. He knew that he'd screwed up. Still, the clock was ticking, and they needed to get that Egg, if only to quell the grating, discordant whispers echoing inside Kid Omega's head.

The Collector indicated the food again. "Are you certain? Not even a processed rib sandwich? I hear they are delightful. No?" He stood and waved a hand, disappearing the bounty.

"Then I believe it is time for you to leave. If you have no further business–"

"Wait." Havok sprang to his feet, holding out a hand. He spoke fast, desperately trying to persuade the Collector to aid their cause. "We do have business. And we apologize for the aggressive nature of our approach. We needed to get your attention, but we come with an offer. A valuable offer."

Taneleer Tivan had raised a glowing hand. He'd been about to eject the mutants from his facility, employing the considerable cosmic abilities in his possession.

"Really? A wager? You have the wrong Elder, my mutant friend."

"Not a wager. A trade. Actually, more like collateral. We don't want to keep the Phoenix Egg. In fact, we believe it's safest in your hands, hidden in your museum."

The Collector arched a brow, hand still raised. But it had ceased glowing.

"I agree."

"What we propose is this," Alex continued. "Allow us to take the Egg for a limited amount of time. You can send it with an acolyte to keep it safe. Haroona even, or another."

Haroona sniffed. The thought of leaving the gallery and abandoning her duties was clearly heresy to the Vice-Senior Adept and Forever Attendant.

"And in return?" The Collector seemed intrigued, though hardly convinced. "You mentioned collateral. What rare artifact might you provide – an item that Taneleer Tivan does not possess – that would adequately replace a Phoenix Egg should it become damaged, destroyed, unleashed, or lost?"

"What we have–"

Kid Omega stepped forward. "What we have is me."

CHAPTER SIXTEEN

[QUENTIN | TANELEER TIVAN'S SEVENTH CATALOGUE-
WORLD | SIRIUS FIVE | THE MILKY WAY GALAXY]

"You?"

The Collector seemed skeptical. "What is so unique, rare, or collectible about you?"

Kid Omega spun, spreading his arms to provide the Elder a view of the Kid's finely toned physique. The words FLEX OBJECT appeared on his T-shirt, and he smiled as he turned to face the others.

"I mean, have you seen me, dude? Five feet and eight inches of premium grade, swole Omega-level Earther telepath! A gorgeously refined sense of innovative-yet-humblebrag style – like your top two Kardashians – and as a one-time former host to that sultry little cosmic vulture, it'd be like trading one aspect of the Phoenix Force for another."

Frowning, Taneleer Tivan addressed Havok. "He is not an acceptable replacement."

"Hey!" The Kid snapped his fingers, demanding the

Collector's full attention. "He? OK, Cosmic Boomer. I've got a name. It's 'Kid Omega.' And my pronouns aren't 'he/him/his' but rather 'que/quem/quis.' You don't talk to that guy," Quentin insisted, flapping a hand at Alex. "You talk directly to the merchandise. The Kid. Because right now, que's what's for dinner."

The Collector grumbled and shook his head. "Ridiculous. You cannot have the Egg."

"And why not?" Kid Omega levitated, bringing himself face to face with the Elder. "Sure, you may have a telepath. But I can guarantee that you don't have one operating at my level. And you definitely don't have one with the entire filmography of the great Simon 'Wonder Man' Williams spooling inside his skull. C'mon, Tan, ol' buddy – can I call you 'Tan'? – think of the epic movie nights we'll have! We'll pop some corn, drink strawberry slushies... just Quentflix and chill, streaming everything from Arkon III to Haxon II while Havok and Haroona take the Egg to save my friends."

The Collector turned away, dismissing the Kid.

"Nonsense and sarcasm will not gain you favor, nor convince me to release a prized possession in exchange for an Earth mutant, no matter how boorish and unique. My galleries contain an abundance of fauna and flora from your dreadfully mundane planet, as do they incorporate a selection of dissimilar-yet-remarkable native archetypes."

Alex bristled with indignation. "Wait, Collector. Are you saying that you have humans locked up in your intergalactic zoo?"

Annoyed by Havok's hypocritical umbrage (where was Mini-Summers a moment ago when the Kid had protested the captive living creatures?), Quentin interjected himself between Alex and the Collector.

"OK, fine. You may have beat me to putting sapiens in cages, but I'll bet that none of your Earth collection is exactly like me. Listen—"

"I have already collected a mutant."

"What?"

Kid Omega stopped short. Did Taneleer Tivan mean that he had one of Quentin's brothers or sisters already trapped inside this zoological horror-show?

The Collector nodded, a satisfied smile upon his lips.

"A rare sample of mutant genetics exists within my catalogue," he repeated. "In fact, here in this very gallery. Not so pedestrian, but rather extradimensional. Bartered from a madman only too happy to be rid it of it in exchange for a pittance of techno-logical achievement acquired during my travels. So explain why I should trade the Phoenix for a second mutant – even one who claims to have hosted it in the past – when I'm content with the mutant I already own? This way, you'll agree…"

With a languid wave, Taneleer Tivan reorganized his gallery. Glass boxes slid aside, several retreating as others descended from the tower, moving toward their owner. Smiling, he drew forward two enclosures and rotated his fingers, mentally adjusting their visibility controls in order to reveal the prizes within.

"…I get the best of both worlds."

Kid Omega peered into the containers. Light and heat radiated from the first, warming his body in shades of orange, white, and yellow. He cried out. Pain lanced his frontal lobe, and the Kid clutched his head. Terrible whispers overwhelmed his mind, demanding that Quentin shatter the glass and pry open the pulsating womb that lay inside… barely restraining its awesome, terrible, wonderful power. Sweat trickled down the Kid's back. A flush reddened his cheeks, and he gently placed a hand upon the crate that held the Phoenix Egg.

It called to Kid Omega. It begged him for release.

If he left his hand on the glass it would consume his body in purifying flame. As it would his soul.

We shall be whole, Quentin Quire. Agree to become my host. Return to the White Hot Room and bask in my eternal glory. Embrace our symbiosis. Unveil our dominance and unrelenting hunger for order upon a waiting, rapturous creation.

The Kid fell to his knees. The Collector laughed and waved again, closing the case and shutting out the hypnotic, reassuring light.

The whispers remained, though, small and uncomfortable in the back of his mind. It was all Quentin could do to remain calm.

They had done it; Havok and the Kid had found the Phoenix Egg.

Now all they had to do was find The Remaining and trade it for his friends.

Or use its glorious power to consume them.

That is, if it didn't consume Kid Omega first.

And if they could get it away from an immortal cosmic being who was nearly as old as the universe itself.

Piece of cake.

Shaking, Kid Omega supported himself against the Egg's enclosure, pulled himself to his feet, and wiped his brow.

He turned to Havok, hoping to telepathically formulate a plan. But Alex wasn't looking his way. As far as he could tell, Summers hadn't been fazed by the Phoenix's seductive call. Instead, Not-Cyclops stood with his mouth open, gawking at the second case. Kid Omega followed his gaze... and his heart stopped.

There was a man inside – if you could call him a "man," because his boyish good looks and (after Quentin did a cursory mental scan, only skimming the surface) Peter Pan syndrome made him appear much younger. Floppy blond hair covered the man's right eye. The left, sparkling blue, merrily danced behind a striking yellow tattoo – a starburst, matching a sigil stitched into the right breast of the blond's leather jumpsuit. The man's feet were bare, as were his hands. Tapered, dexterous fingers moved and twitched, seemingly afflicted by hyperactivity, as if they longed to hold something – playing cards, blades, a guitar – but were woefully, unfortunately denied.

The Phoenix Force still scrabbled for purchase inside his mind, but now Kid Omega needed a moment to protect his heart. He wasn't surprised. He recognized the mutant trapped inside the Collector's cage. They'd never met, but Quentin knew his story: an extradimensional slave who rebelled against corpulent, greedy masters, gained freedom, and escaped to Earth. There, armed with the power to manipulate probability fields – basically, creating "good luck" for himself and others – the former slave was rescued and adopted by the X-Men. Joining their cause, the handsome mutant fell in love with a pop star, caused countless others to fall in love with him... and finally returned home to lead a revolt against his former overlord, a spineless, yellow, piratical cross-dimensional broadcaster known as Mojo.

Yet now here the mutant was, stuck inside the Collector's warehouse.

The blond stopped fidgeting long enough to place a hand against the glass. Brushing aside his hair, Taneleer Tivan's prize mutant smiled and waved.

"Hullo, Alex," said Longshot. "Boy, am I lucky that you came along."

CHAPTER SEVENTEEN

"Longshot? How did you get here?!"

Alex Summers' head was spinning. The mad dash from space to the Collector's front door had been enough to get it buzzing, and then the pitched negotiation with Taneleer Tivan had introduced a low, unsettling throb.

Havok had sympathized with Kid Omega's concern that living beings comprised half of Tivan's vast collection, especially when they'd discovered that many hailed from Earth. But a responsible leader understood when he was outmatched. Sometimes you needed to stay on mission. The two of them – even with the Starjammer at their back (assuming the ship hadn't already been blasted out of the sky) – were not enough to release the Collector's captives. An operation of that magnitude would require more hands than they had to spare. So, for now, despite his misgivings, Alex was prepared to let it go in order to get what they'd come for and complete the mission.

But Longshot's involvement changed things. He was an

X-Man, one of their own. And as leader, Havok couldn't leave a mutant behind.

The only question remained was, how to accomplish that? And so: headache.

He looked to his left. Quentin was clutching his temples as well, massaging them with his eyes squeezed shut. Could this be more than a migraine? Maybe Alex's headache was part of some insidious defensive system deployed by the Collector? Neither Haroona nor Tivan appeared to be suffering, and Longshot kept grinning and tapping the glass. The building shook. Someone was firing on the gallery, which made him believe that at least the Starjammers were still alive. The Collector frowned and perused a bank of screens; Haroona joined him to monitor the exterior. That gave Havok room to think.

Alex closed his eyes. Despite not being a telepath, he tried reaching out to Quentin with his mind.

[[Kid?]]

A mental door slammed. He could hear the Kid muttering, whining in reply to an unseen whisper. Two words appeared in the darkness behind Havok's eyes, large, pink, and flashing: HOLD PLEASE.

"Hey, Alex!" Havok opened his eyelids. Longshot smiled down from the cage.

"Who else did you bring? Scott? Lorna? Alison? Oh! Did you bring Wolverine?!"

Havok shook his head, lowering his voice as he gave the Collector a surreptitious glance. "Just me and my dad. That's all. Seriously, what're you doing here?"

Longshot pouted. "Oh, you know. Having an adventure."

"An adventu... why haven't you escaped? Your luck powers could have gotten you out of here in no time flat."

Longshot smacked the wall. "The big guy took my knives and installed some kind of high-tech air conditioner that dampens my abilities. I've been trying every day, but I guess the most I could do was get the luck to bring you here."

"We were coming, anyway. Not for you, but that thing."

Havok pointed to the second enclosure. The intense light of the Phoenix Egg peeked out from in between cracks in the durable enclosure. There was no way they had enough time to break it out before the Collector returned his attention to the mutants.

"Really?" Longshot peered at it. "Seems dangerous."

"It is. But we need it to ransom back a group of kidnapped mutants. Kid Omega over here let them get taken by a group of mysterious armored aliens, and the only thing they want is that Egg. But even if we get it away from the Collector, we have no clue how to find them."

Longshot's eyes widened. The left one, behind the starburst tattoo, sparked and sputtered. He leaned close to the glass and whispered to Havok. "Wait, really? I think I can help you! I may know who they–"

"I believe our business is concluded."

Surprised, Havok stepped away from the cage. Taneleer Tivan and Haroona had returned, the former having imperiously folded his arms. The Collector's Vice-Senior Adept had found herself a new tablet and was now using it to check on the status of the dogfight outside.

"Wait," Alex stalled. "You can't keep Longshot. He's our friend."

Havok glanced at Kid Omega, but the younger mutant

was still ignoring them, sweat slick upon his brow. The Kid's eyeballs rolled. He muttered to something that wasn't there, pleading with an undecipherable whine. Whatever happened next, Quentin would be little help.

The Collector sighed. "Your friend is mine by right of acquisition. I am an Elder of the Universe. The spans of your lives are calculated against mine by millennia. Your petty desires will have been forgotten by this galaxy in the space of my next breath. And so, your justifications for what Taneleer Tivan can and cannot do mean strikingly little in the grand, infinite scale of the universal wheel."

Alex thought fast, his mind racing. "Then if our lives mean so little to you, Collector, why are you keen on keeping this one mutant, who will die before you even get around to inspect his case again?"

"Because I am the Collector. My acquisitions are mine by cosmic right."

"Sure," Havok replied, pointing at Longshot, "but this acquisition will be dust by the time you take your next breath. Isn't that what you said?"

Tivan smiled. "My dear fellow. Have you never heard of taxidermy?"

Longshot gasped. Havok clenched his fists. The white circle on his jumpsuit began to radiate, oscillating across his chest. "I'm not fooling around, Collector."

Taneleer Tivan sighed and cocked his head. "All this will accomplish is guaranteeing the deaths of you, your unusually garbed friend, and your colleagues in the Shi'ar dreadnought. Your mutant ability cannot hope to match the cosmic power at my command."

Havok smirked. "My mutant ability lets me absorb cosmic power and convert it into plasma." Alex extended his fingers, channeled the energy... prepared to fire...

...and disappeared.

The Collector sighed.

Haroona Sh'thian looked up from her tablet. Her master stood alone now before the case containing the extradimensional mutant. The emotional Earthers had been banished from his gallery, the glorious and all-seeking Collector having transported them back aboard the battered-but-functioning Starjammer. She offered an approving nod, indicating how satisfied she was that the Great Collector had brought this unfortunate intrusion to an end by unceremoniously returning the mutants to their ship. She prepared to offer a sincere and succinct – yet professional – apology for allowing it to happen in the first place. But the Collector had already stepped away, headed deeper into the stronghold to address the interrupted events of his valuable day. He didn't look back. Haroona knew that he trusted his most Vice-Senior Adept and Forever Attendant, his devoted and loyal acolyte, to put the gallery back in order.

Sighing herself, Haroona wheeled to address the errant enclosures. She ignored the captive mutant's protests and lowered a volume fader on her tablet to drown out the sound. Switching a toggle, she closed his case, hiding its occupant from view. She rotated it to a position at the back of the gallery, near a clutch of insects procured from the Negative Zone. Locking it into place, Haroona addressed the second, already sealed container.

Light tested its seams, seeking purchase with intangible, burning fingers. Haroona cocked her head, contemplating the entity held within.

Did two Earthers truly believe that the custodian of the universe's most dangerous and extraordinary artifacts would allow them to depart with an aspect of the Great Devourer, the demon that had exterminated millions of precious items that should have graced the sacred walls of a catalogue-world?

Such impudence! Such gall!

Shaking her head, Haroona placed a hand against the cage. For that's what it was – a prison meant to contain the Phoenix Force and prevent it from doing further harm. The hot metal stung her fingers, but she did not pull away.

No. The Collector was grand and wise. No children, Earther or otherwise, were worth a devil's release. And he was merciful, allowing the brazen mutants to depart unharmed.

Haroona double-checked her tablet. The Collector Corps – the nine fighters that had faced the HMSS Starjammer in battle, incurring regrettable damage – now escorted the dreadnought out of the system. Tapping and swiping, she dashed the standard rejection holo off to the Starjammer's communications array. Contained within, the great Taneleer Tivan conveyed a sincere but regrettable message to Corsair, reminding the man that his debt would soon come due. A second, more optimistic holo went to the mutants, thanking them for their patronage and hoping their paths might cross again in the future.

The Vice-Senior Adept, of course, hoped that day would never come.

Something about that second Earther, the one with the

odd attire and coral hair, set her teeth on edge. The way he'd muttered, gabbling to himself like a madman.

Shivering, glad to be done with both Earthers and Starjammer – whose crew of welchers she and her master would deal with another day – Haroona Sh'thian, Vice-Senior Adept and Forever Attendant to Taneleer Tivan's Seventh Catalogue-World watched the Phoenix Egg retreat, headed to join the mutant at the back of the gallery, where – if she had her way – both would remain unnoticed for centuries.

She looked down. The broken shards of her former tablet littered the floor. She sniffed with disgust and sent a request to Facilities to come clean the mess away.

A caretaker's work was never done.

Then, wiping her brow, Haroona powered down her tablet and bustled off to the kitchens in search of a snack.

CHAPTER EIGHTEEN

"What... what just happened?"

Alex Summers stood in the Collector's gallery, holding out his hand. Cosmic plasma coursed through his veins. He'd nearly expended a destructive salvo, but something or someone was holding it back. Try as he might, Havok couldn't expend the blast.

The Collector looked away and sighed.

Havok watched Taneleer Tivan's face fall slack. Next to him, Haroona smiled and lifted her control tablet, sliding fingers aimlessly above its surface. They both appeared to be sleepwalking, or in a trance. Alex pulled the energy back within himself and powered down. He held up the hand before Haroona's face. She didn't react.

"Hello? I don't..."

"Alex?" Longshot gazed quizzically at the bewildering scene, as equally confused as his friend. "Is this you? What's going on?"

"I'm... going on, y-you... ungrateful, unimaginative b... bottle-blond."

Surprised, the senior X-Men finally noticed that Kid Omega was saving the day.

Head nearly cracking like a walnut, doing his best to ignore the wheedling call of the Phoenix, the Kid opened his eyes and glared at his colleagues.

"O... OK," he quipped. "That isn't f-fair. Longshot's hair is probably as natural and golden as God intended... or his maker intended, that is, that e-extradimensional, spine-deprived sack of hot dog innards and the broadcast empire it lords over like a t-troll." Kid Omega winced; the Phoenix Force burned within his mind. Truthfully, with the psionic effort he was expending, the Kid couldn't afford to split his focus, no matter how glorious the quips.

Havok was still confused. "Kid, what the heck?"

Quentin tapped his scorching brow. "They're in here. The Omega Room."

Goggle-eyed, Alex swiveled to stare at the comatose Collector. "Do you mean to say...?"

The Kid nodded and groaned.

"I... I said I'd get better at this. While you argued r-rights of possession with... with... Tan-the-Not-Quite-Man, I constructed a psionic c-cage in which to... collect the Collector. Not so easy, might I add, while f-f... fending off the increasingly vocal advances of a greedy, fuh... f-flaming cosmic parasite."

"So, you've got him—"

"In loco collectis," Kid Omega confirmed, taking a breath as he slapped the old, sweaty coconut. "C-caged and tagged with a card. 'T-Taneleer Tivan: Elder of the Universe. Vulnerable to the wh... whim of supposedly limited beings.' Can you smell what the irony's c... cooking?"

The exertion was making him stutter. He took a breath to compose himself. Smiling, the Kid nodded his head, indicating the two cases.

"G-get them out of there, won't you? I don't know how long I've got until the Collector realizes he's being hoodwinked. We gotta go."

Longshot cocked a perfectly sculpted eyebrow. "I don't understand."

"Basically," Alex answered, "Kid Omega is using telepathy to build a prison in his mind, one in which he's trapped the Collector! Tivan thinks what's happening in there is real, but the Kid's making him see what we want him to see–"

"What the Kid wants him to see," Quentin testily corrected. "My head's an illusionist's paradise. It's taking all my effort to maintain the stage. So, if my two beautiful assistants don't mind, while the audience is spellbound, wouldja snatch that Phoenix Egg so we can hightail it out of interstellar Dodge before they realize it's all psionic smoke and mirrors?"

"On it," Havok said. "Stand back, Longshot."

Alex cracked his knuckles. He fired a concentrated beam of plasma at the lock to Longshot's case, shearing away the door from the container with a metallic squeal. Longshot leapt free, joining his fellow mutants.

"Thanks, Alex. I was going stir-crazy in there. Any chance we can go find my bandolier and throwing knives?"

"No time for knives," Kid Omega barked. "Haroona's brain is pliable like memory foam, but I can feel the Collector probing the borders of my cage. Get that Egg!"

Light fluctuated inside the second container, brightening the gallery as Havok prepared to blow it open. The Phoenix attacked the Kid's mind, nearly weakening the integrity of the Omega Room. He peered inside. Haroona was enjoying a fictional plate of seasoned mollusks wriggling in orange goo. Elsewhere in the intricate psionic replica of the Collector's stronghold, the Elder in question went about his work, but Kid Omega sensed flashes of doubt. Taneleer Tivan's psyche kept staring hard at the walls, at the items he was cataloguing. The illusion would only hold for so long.

"Havok," the Kid repeated. "Now or never!"

"Hang on," Longshot interjected, stopping Havok from blasting plasma. "You nearly demolished me along with my cage. We don't want to break the Egg, too, do we?"

"I do!" Kid Omega shouted, straining to contain the Collector while fending off the Phoenix-song.

Alex's power was in his fingertips, ready for release. "What do we do?"

Longshot spotted Haroona's shattered tablet on the ground, the pieces scattered across the tile. Grabbing the largest shard, he carefully wedged it between the lockpad and doorjamb to the Phoenix's enclosure. Slowly – too slowly for a suffering Kid Omega's taste! – the grinning, carefree mutant cut away the locking mechanism and sprang open the door.

"I'd have been quicker," Longshot regrettably explained, "if someone had allowed me to find my knives."

Havok and Longshot carefully maneuvered the Egg out of its crate and set it carefully on the steel floor of the gallery. The oblong womb teetered and thrummed, hovering several inches from the ground as it bathed the immediate area in sickening, fascinating light.

"OK," Alex said. "Time to go."

"Go where? And how?" The Kid nodded, indicating the captive aliens. "I can maintain the Omega Room at a remote distance but not if I have to also help fight our way out with the Phoenix. Tan's starting to figure out what's what. And there's no way the 'Jammer is coming down here to offer door-to-door service."

"That's true," Alex agreed. "What if the two of us get the Egg to the ship and then come back for you?"

"You can try. But if the Collector breaks my hold…"

"Well," asked an exasperated Havok, "do you have any other ideas?"

Kid Omega nodded. "Release the Phoenix."

"What?!"

"Break the Egg. Let me host the Phoenix Force. I'll use it to get us out of here, and then I can find The Remaining and save my friends."

"That is, if the Phoenix doesn't destroy you and the cosmos in the process!"

"It won't… I can" – the Kid glanced at the Egg – "I can do it. It will let me. It likes this plan. It's on board."

Havok shook his head. "No. Absolutely not. The Phoenix wants you to release it so it can consume worlds. I won't have the lives it takes on my conscience."

"And what about my friends' lives?" Kid Omega shrieked, freely perspiring as he dug in his heels and held on to the Collector's psyche. "Ayo, Hijack, No-Girl… Phoebe and Glob. They'll die if we don't! We're no closer to even understanding who The Remaining are–"

Longshot interjected, "Actually, I might be able to–"

The Kid ignored him, still on a tear. "–or where they've gone to ground! The Phoenix Force is like intergalactic Apple Maps. Once I become its host, there's nowhere they can hide from my sight, not in any star system!"

"Quent… Kid. It's too much of a risk. Look at what happened on Earth. Look at what happened to Scott."

Kid Omega sneered. "I'm not Scott."

"You're right. Scott would know enough not to make the same mistake twice. Not to let himself get seduced again by the Phoenix. Look, you're right. We don't know where to find The Remaining or who they are—"

Longshot attempted to speak a second time. Havok kept going.

"But we do know that opening that Egg… releasing the Phoenix… you'll endanger not only our lives and those of your friends, but also those of any who will come to stop it. The X-Men and Avengers. The Kree. The Skrulls. The Shi'ar."

Longshot tried one last time. "You know, funny you should mention the…"

But Havok was on a roll.

"Kid, I know you're hurting. But so far, we've achieved more than I'd hoped we ever would. We worked together and stuck to a plan. We got the Egg! Don't you remember a time where that seemed impossible? Look where we are."

"Yeah," Quentin sarcastically agreed. "Stuck fast. We still have no way to get out of here. Unless one of you boomers low-key has a plan?"

"Well—" Longshot began, trying to seize the opening.

But before he could continue, a transparent circle of pink light slowly appeared, hanging in the air between Kid Omega and the others. Astonished, they watched it widen, fizzling and sparking to life, swirling in the center of the gallery. Finally, it opened, and a purple girl stuck out her head. She had magenta hair, white eyes, and diamond-shaped markings over her nose, brow, and cheeks.

The girl waved at the goggle-eyed mutants. "Hullo, friends."

"...Blink?"

Smiling, Clarice Ferguson stepped through her sparkly portal, striding onto the Collector's tiled floor. "Yup, Alex. It's me. What's up, guys?"

Quentin and Havok traded astonished glances. They turned to the comatose Collector and then the pulsing, vibrant Egg.

"Oh, you know," Kid Omega answered, "the usual maxiflark."

Blink laughed. "Ha! Maxiflark. That's a funny word."

Havok sputtered, breaking the small talk. "Blink! What are you doing here?!"

"Oh, right," she said, shrugging and pointing at the portal. "So, Cyclops is, like, super busy but wanted me to check on the two of you. To, y'know, see how things were going with the whole Phoenix hunt?" Spying the Egg, she grinned and held out a hand, feeling its palpitating heat. "Oh, look. You found it!"

The light intensified. The Phoenix shrieked inside Kid Omega's head. He looked inward, into the Omega Room. The Collector's head shifted, as if he were hearing a far-off cry. The Elder must have perceived the Phoenix through the Kid's psionic illusion. The walls were starting to wobble. If they didn't act fast, the structure was going to break.

"Blink," he begged, "I don't know how you knew we were in trouble, or how you timed this so perfectly–"

Longshot winked and shrugged. "Just lucky, I guess."

"–but you have to get us out of here. Can you jump us to the Starjammer?"

"Sure. Don't see why not."

"Like... now?!"

"Oh! OK." Blink swirled a finger in the air. A pink trail materialized, following the arc of her motion. It continued, rotating past her finger and turning into a small coral circle that fizzled into life with a sharp, short snapping sound – as if several sets of eyelids all blinked at once. She stepped aside as the portal widened, opening onto the bridge of the Starjammer, revealing its surprised crew, still engaged in battle above Sirius Five.

Hands grasping the dreadnought's control yoke, Corsair glanced over his shoulder.

"Alex? What the heck?"

Kid Omega snapped, shouting at his companions. "Move, people! Get the Phoenix on board and get us out of this system!"

Havok and Longshot carefully hoisted the Egg through Blink's portal and onto the bridge. The Starjammers eyed it warily, doing their best to maintain the in-process dogfight while also sizing up this new, dangerous threat. Once the Egg was safely through, Blink joined them and beckoned for Kid Omega to follow.

OK, he thought to himself. Here goes nothing.

Slowly edging toward the portal, trying to shield his mind from the Phoenix's inveigling summons, the Kid reinforced the Omega Room, doing his best to ensure that the Collector and Haroona believed their surroundings – and their actions within them – were authentic. Wiping his brow, Kid Omega stepped across the threshold and let Blink draw the portal closed.

He took a breath.

The Room remained intact. He sensed the psychic imprints of both Taneleer Tivan and Haroona Sh'thian, trapped inside his four-color cage like intergalactic mosquitos in Omega-level amber. The Starjammer banked away from Sirius Five, headed into orbit and out toward the glittering pitch of outer space. The Collector's fighters broke off their engagement and returned to the Sirian moon. The farther Kid Omega got from the museum-world, the more he tested to ensure that his illusion maintained its structural integrity. So far, it was holding.

Corsair grinned. "See? I told you that we wouldn't stay long."

The others glared at the Starjammer captain.

The Kid sat on the floor, massaging his skull. Inside his mind, the Collector and Haroona went about their day. At the edges, the Phoenix sniffed and clawed, seeking purchase in Kid Omega's psyche.

"OK," Corsair relented. "Clearly not the time for jokes. Let's go, shall we?"

Havok agreed. "Sure. But go where? We have the Egg, but we still don't know anything about The Remaining."

"I do."

Everyone turned. Longshot sat cross-legged on the navigation console, juggling the tablet shard he'd rescued from the Collector's gallery. Grinning, he waved at the window, out into space, indicating the vast galaxy laid before the Starjammer.

"They came," he explained, "after the Collector acquired me from Mojo, that jaundiced sack of suet and bile. Haroona and her attendants were installing me in the gallery when your Remaining – five of them, right? Black armor? – swooped in, all politeness and diplomacy. I guess they'd learned that the

Collector had taken the Egg from Blastaar and came offering wealth, knowledge, and other curios they'd stolen. Taken from the many worlds that suffer beneath their clawed fists."

"Wait," Alex began, trying to make sense of what Longshot was saying. But his handsome, blessed friend kept going.

"They bargained with the Collector, or tried to. He wasn't interested. Still isn't, as you know. When they spoke, I recognized their speech and mannerisms. Their minder tried to trick the Collector, like Quentin did. I guess she wasn't as successful."

Kid Omega smiled, glancing inward at his immortal hostage. That smarmy, cocky snack couldn't do what he had done. Why had he ever doubted himself? Why had he let Scott and Alex Summers let him doubt himself? He'd captured an Elder of the Universe. He was the Omega – she was nothing. He didn't need the Phoenix Force to finish her off, did he? He had never needed it to take his revenge.

Though… the insistent, hungry, impatient vulture kept shrieking.

Kept singing an enticing song.

Havok grabbed Longshot's shoulder.

"You said that you recognized The Remaining's speech? Their artifacts?"

He nodded in reply. "Yup. But it was really obvious when they took off their helmets."

"They took off their…? Longshot, who are they?"

The lucky mutant cocked his head. "Don't you know? They're Shi'ar."

The bridge fell silent. Hepzibah growled. Raza sighed.

Havok and Corsair stared at one another. Kid Omega

suddenly caught psychic flashes of a silent conversation, briefly skimming the surface of their minds.

A dying airplane. A screaming child.

A mother, hugging two boys.

The mother taken by an emperor; the father shackled, forced to watch her murder.

A second emperor – a mutant warlord, Vulcan – leading armies, vanquishing a rebellion at the edge of space.

Havok chained. Ch'od, Hepzibah, and the others.

Corsair dying in a blazing inferno.

The Kid blinked, shaking off the visions. Corsair frowned. What Quentin had accidentally witnessed – the intimate conversation between father and son – was not for anyone else's eyes. Christopher Summers was dour; his son, Alex, angry. Dark clouds washed across the Starjammers' faces. Longshot and Blink furrowed their brows, trying to understand what was happening.

Kid Omega stood up. He turned to Alex.

"Holy maxiflark," he said. Scott Summers' masked headshot screen-printed itself on the Kid's shirt, black ink against crimson. Three words appeared below in dark, block letters. Quentin looked down, speaking them aloud.

"Cyclops was right."

CHAPTER NINETEEN

[ALEX | THE STARJAMMER | NEARING CHANDILAR | THE SHI'AR GALAXY]

Barely out of the jump gate, the Starjammer was attacked by the Shi'ar Imperial Fleet.

"Hold on!" Corsair quickly disabled the auto-nav and slammed down on the 'Jammer's control yoke. "Battle stations!"

The crew leapt into action, calculating evasive maneuvers. Alex and Longshot held fast to the Egg, bracing it as the Starjammer responded to the aggressive assault of a Behemoth-class warship. A clutch of smaller cruisers decloaked to the right, streaking toward the 'Jammer and urging it toward the warship. Corsair banked, skewing dangerously as he tried to put distance between the pirates and the Shi'ar. A particle beam bombardment prevented him from heading out to open space, and Major Summers had to swerve the concussive aftermath, vectoring toward the enemy to avoid tearing his ship apart.

The comms array whistled. Corsair pursed his lips. He shook his head as Ch'od went to answer. "It's nothing good," he promised. "We gotta go."

"Go where?" asked Alex. "If Longshot's right and the Shi'ar did take Scott's students, this is where we need to be. They want us here."

"Yeah," Corsair sarcastically agreed, pointing at the warship. "So they can blow us out of the stars!"

"But then they'd destroy the Phoenix Egg."

"That's what they want, son! Every Shi'ar ruler I've ever known – especially the one currently on the throne! – has feared the Phoenix. Maybe they kidnapped those kids as bait, to get it out in the open so they could finally kill it!"

"No," Kid Omega protested. "That's not what they want… I can… I sense it, kinda…"

He was slumped on the floor by the Egg, brow still furrowed and slick with sweat. The Kid was still maintaining the Omega Room while also fighting off the Phoenix's advances.

Major Summers raised a skeptical eyebrow as he continued to evade the assault.

"Kinda? Kid, I've been around longer than you have, and I'm not about to risk my ship and the lives of my crew based on 'kinda'!"

Quentin closed his eyes and clutched Havok's arm, dislodging Alex's grip on the Egg. Blink hurried to take Kid Omega's place next to Longshot.

"Alex… you gotta believe me… I feel their fear, the Shi'ar… but I also feel, I dunno… hunger? Desire and excitement. Someone in the system wants this Egg."

Sympathetic, Havok hunkered down and supported Quentin Quire, lifting him to a sitting position. "Kid, the Phoenix has manipulated others in the past, whispering things it wants them to believe in order to help it survive. And you're weak at the moment, vulnerable... keeping it at bay while holding back the Collector."

Kid Omega shook his head. "Only the Phoenix now. Once we jumped... couldn't maintain the integrity of the Omega Room across systems!"

"Oh, great!" Corsair rolled his eyes. "Not only do we have the Shi'ar fleet on our tails, but any minute an Elder of the Universe may show up, demanding we return his favorite toy!"

The comms whistled again. Major Summers pounded it with a fist. He pointed a warning finger at his concerned Saurid navigator. "No! Radio silence!"

Hepzibah hissed at her captain.

"Avoid the Shi'ar forever, we can't, Christopher! Touch us soon, those torpedoes will!"

"I know, I know." Corsair turned to Ch'od and Sikorsky, making a quick decision. "Plot a jump. We can't take much more, and I'd rather we turn tail – tails intact – than stay and become a smaller, deader version of the Xanthan Graveyard."

Quentin tried to stand, to stop Alex's father from leaving. Blink and Longshot held fast to the Egg, which glowed and surged threateningly in the confines of the tight, intimate bridge.

"Dad," Alex said. "If we run, we'll never get another crack at this again. The Shi'ar won't let us back into this system with a Phoenix Egg in tow."

"And what do you plan to do when the Imperial Guard shows up, Alex? You're powerful, the two of you, but the kid can barely stand, and you've already faced the Superguardians and lost! We all have, remember?!"

Father and son glared at one another, bitter memories filling the space between them.

The Imperial Guard, a collection of the empire's best and brightest warriors and the enforcers of Shi'ar law, had aligned themselves with Gabriel Summers when Vulcan assumed the throne as Majestor – or Emperor – alongside Deathbird, the royal traitor.

Alex, leading the Starjammers during his father's absence, had faced the power of the Guard, most particularly the Superguardians, an elite faction assigned to protect and carry out the wishes of the emperor or empress. The Superguardians were there when a Shi'ar death squad had wiped out Jean Grey's bloodline. They were there when Lilandra, Deathbird's sister, had been assassinated. And they were there when Vulcan killed Corsair and then imprisoned Havok, Polaris, Rachel Grey, and the Starjammers.

"I can handle Kallark," Alex assured his father.

Blink raised an eyebrow. "What's a 'Kallark'?"

Corsair laughed. "Not a what, but a who. His codename is 'Gladiator,' the Superguardians' former leader. A purple Strontian powerhouse who's now the Majestor."

"Heck of a promotion," Quentin muttered.

Alex nodded. "Well, he wasn't so much promoted as democratically elected after Vulcan's death. Kallark's former teammates are a team of heroes from across the Shi'ar worlds. Some are minders like you, Kid. Oracle is the empire's premier telepath, and Delphos, her precognitive colleague, can see limited visions of an uncertain future. There's also Smasher–"

Kid Omega snorted at the codename with restrained amusement. Alex ignored him and continued. "–armed with an array of superhuman abilities that can only be used one at a time. Starbolt is a sentient being composed of flame.

Hobgoblin's a shape-changer, and there's more... all now serving at Gladiator's command."

Havok considered that for a moment. If The Remaining were Shi'ar, and Kallark had sent them to secure the Egg, the odds were good that the unknown quintet were Superguardians.

And if the Starjammer managed to escape this current assault and somehow delivered the Phoenix Egg to Chandilar – the Shi'ar throne world – the odds were also good that they'd be in for the fight of their lives.

"It doesn't make sense, though," Alex said as the warship fired warning shots at the 'Jammer. "Gladiator has always wanted to eliminate the Phoenix, as have the rest of the Shi'ar. Why go to all this trouble to have us bring it here? Why risk angering Scott, the X-Men, and even the Avengers by kidnapping Earthlings? He knows that will lead to war!"

"Maybe," Blink answered, "because war with us is better than war with the Collector?"

Corsair agreed. "She's right, sport. The Shi'ar know they can handle whatever Earth throws their way. This way, we do the hard part – getting the Egg from a cagey cosmic immortal – and bring it to them so they can finally kill it."

"Then why not kill it here?" Quentin asked, pointing out the window. "That warship could've hit us half a dozen times, but all it's doing is firing warning shots. If Kallark doesn't care about angering Earth and took my friends, why not blow the Egg – and us along with it – out of the sky?"

Havok nodded. "Kid, didn't you say The Remaining's telepath talked about preserving the Phoenix... almost worshipping it? I still don't think that sounds like a plan Kallark would condone. No, there's something else going on."

Corsair swerved to avoid a passing corralling cruiser.

"Whatever it is, let's figure it out fast! They're penning us in right now. But if I know the Shi'ar, the longer we ignore them, the more impatient they're gonna get."

The comms array whistled for the third time.

"See? What'd I tell you?" Corsair relented, switching to receive the incoming message.

A square opened on the forward screen, crackling to life as the hail went live. A regal, grizzled member of the feathered Shi'ar race appeared before them, clad in what appeared to be a form-fitting officer's uniform, exquisite markings encircling the being's stern, piercing eyes.

Behind him, both mutants and Starjammers could see the machinery of the Shi'ar warship humming like clockwork: deck commanders providing instructions to navigators and helmsmen, systems and routines implemented with the determined efficiency of a well-oiled naval operation. The officer cleared his throat, peered into the screen, and announced their intentions.

"This is Major-General Ka'arnil, commander of the destroyer Cries of the Bereaved. I carry orders from the Imperial Majestor himself to halt ingress into this system and ferry you to a shipyard on the far side of the planet Thrnn. There, your cargo will be impounded and your crew subject to military inquest before being allowed to return safely to your point of origin."

"Interesting," Corsair replied, drumming his fingers along the receiver as he used the other hand to steer the 'Jammer. "And should we refuse?"

Major-General Ka'arnil's eyes creased with mutual understanding, an unwelcome expression that sent chills down

Havok's spine. "Well then, captain... by Sharra and K'ythri, I believe that you know our friendly invitation will evolve to 'reluctantly hostile.'"

"Really. And Kallark understands the nature of our cargo?"

"The Majestor believes he does. The item's destruction, should you refuse to comply, will result in the removal of an until-recently inaccessible threat to our empire and the universe. Though, regrettably, it will also result in your collective demise."

The Starjammers' expressions turned sour. The harsh, intermittent lighting of the bridge interior washed their faces in angry scarlet tones, clashing with the pulsing glow of the Phoenix Egg. Kid Omega rose to his feet and stumbled to help Longshot and Blink secure it, or protect it from harm as the Starjammer continued to evade the Shi'ar cruisers.

Christopher Summers – pirate captain, Air Force major, widower, and father – smiled at his son. Alex stepped toward his dad, a thousand suggestions streaming through his head.

Corsair picked one of his own. He thumbed the receiver and addressed the Shi'ar officer.

"I've been dead before, major-general. I got better. Remind your emperor that I've faced – and come back from – loss at the hands of two of his predecessors, one of whom was my son." He grinned, winking at Alex, and then Hepzibah and Ch'od. "Third time's the charm, right?"

Alex questioned his father. "Maybe we should comply? It'll buy us time, and maybe we can negotiate for the kidnapped students."

"No!" Kid Omega thrust out a hand, pleading with the Summers men. He'd been standing in the back, using telekinesis to stabilize the Egg, allowing Longshot and Blink to take a breather. "If the Shi'ar take the Phoenix, we have no guarantee they'll give it back."

"As long as we get the kids in return, I'm fine with that."

"We have no assurances of that either, or that they'll let us go."

Havok looked briefly at his father; Major Summers also seemed skeptical. Alex wasn't. He knew there had to be a diplomatic way to work this out.

"The X-Men and the Shi'ar have an understanding. Kallark isn't going to detain his ally's father and brother to break that peace."

"Really? But the ally's students are fair game?" Kid Omega was breathing hard, speaking quickly. "No, something's off, Not-Cyclops. I'm telling you… The Remaining – the woman I met – didn't want this destroyed. Alex, we can't let Gladiator take it! If he and the Shi'ar… if they've figured out there's more value in harnessing the Phoenix Force than killing it… look, my hands may not be the best hands, but they're better than that of the Imperial Guard. It needs" – he took a breath, placing a palm on the pulsating Egg – "it needs the right host. Someone who understands its hunger, sees it not as a threat, but as a cog in the cosmic machinery and can keep its desires in check. One who is learning how to strike a balance between inflicting chaos and reining in those impulses until the time is right. Someone, well, like me."

Havok shook his head. "No. No way, Kid."

"It's our only chance!"

Major-General Ka'arnil cleared his throat. "I await your decision."

Havok leaned in to address the Shi'ar commander, elbowing his father aside.

"We'll accept your terms if, rather than Thrnn, you escort us to Chandilar and an audience with the Majestor. Only then will we surrender our cargo."

Kid Omega frowned. "I don't accept those terms! Those terms are weaksauce!"

Raza and Hepzibah nodded nearby, faces clouding with wariness and frustration.

"I can't believe I'm saying this," Corsair added, "but I agree with the kid. What're you doing, son?"

Alex covered the receiver and turned to address the others.

"We're out of time, outgunned... and should the Superguardians get involved, outmatched. If they take us to Thrnn, we'll never get a fair shake. I know that. The Shi'ar secret military or whoever's running this operation will take the Egg, jail us for having it, and we'll never be able to plead our case or rescue the others. If we go to Chandilar, we're out in public where people will see us land. Then we can deal directly with Kallark, with whom the X-Men have history and common ground. Despite his shifting loyalties to the throne, Gladiator values his relationship with Scott, and with Earth."

"Does he? Even with the Phoenix Egg in play? Gladiator had no problem risking his relationship with Scott by helping to wipe out the Greys – our extended family."

Alex absorbed that as he kept his hand on the receiver. On screen, Ka'arnil fidgeted.

"Dad, if we turn tail, the Shi'ar will pursue this Egg to the ends of the universe... and maybe even Kid Omega, if they perceive his connection to the Phoenix as a threat."

Havok glanced at the anxious, determined Kid. "We can't give in to their demands. Thrnn is a ticket to a military cover-up. They discreetly kill the Egg, scuttle the Starjammer, toss us in a black box, and figure out a way for Kallark to deny knowledge of our whereabouts or involvement to anyone who asks – including Scott. If Gladiator's advisors are smart, they'll even have him offer the empire's support for a rescue mission."

Blink leaned in. "I could take us to Earth now, to Cyclops or the Avengers? We can tell them the truth, bring reinforcements?"

Alex shook his head. "Kallark would see that as an act of war. And if we fled to Earth, the Shi'ar would follow. In either circumstance, we'd never see Glob, Phoebe, and the others again. They'd be prisoners of war until anything was resolved. No, the only answer is diplomacy."

Kid Omega rolled his eyes. "When isn't the answer 'diplomacy'?"

Havok ignored the sarcasm. "We bring the Egg to Kallark, hats in hand, and present it as a gift. In return, we ask for the students and continued alliance between Earth and the Shi'ar... as long as this never happens again."

The Kid stared at Alex. His T-shirt now read MY NAME ISN'T KID NAÏVE.

"And you'll believe him if he agrees? After what they did to the Greys and now my friends? No apologies, no assurances – hey, Majestor: please, birdie, may I have another?"

"It's the only way, Kid. We'll have to hope Longshot's luck holds up."

Longshot grinned. "I've got a good feeling about this, guys."

Quentin folded his arms and sat in front of the Egg. He smugly addressed Longshot's enthusiasm. "And then a space slug swallowed their ship. Whatever, betas. It's freaking dumb. Tornado, remember? Not trailer park."

Ignoring the Kid's muttered insults, and the resentful looks of Corsair and the Starjammers, Havok turned to address the Shi'ar major-general.

"Take us to Chandilar. We will plead our case to your Majestor, and request forgiveness for our actions. Only then will we relinquish the artifact."

Ka'arnil hesitated. "That is not an option. The... artifact has been forbidden from landing on Chandilar, as has the Starjammer. You will proceed to Thrnn."

"That's not an option either, major-general."

The Shi'ar commander smiled, baring his teeth.

"Regrettable, but anticipated. Then if you will not comply–"

The comms array whistled again. Someone else was hailing the Starjammers.

Corsair raised a palm to a confused Major-General Ka'arnil, interrupting the commander's threat. "Hold, please." He toggled the receiver, triggering a second live square on the forward window. "Go for Corsair. Hello?"

The cold, angry face of Taneleer Tivan filled the new screen, grimacing before a bristling display of catalogued armament hanging in his gallery.

"I welcomed you with refreshment into my sanctuary, Earth mutates. In return, you deceived me, absconding with acquisitions that are rightfully mine."

Everyone looked at Kid Omega, who shrugged. "I told you. I can't maintain it across systems. We knew that Tanny Boy would get free and figure it out eventually, right?"

"We didn't realize he would figure it out this soon," Havok

replied before addressing the Collector. "As I said on Sirius Five, Tivan, Longshot is not yours by right. He is a sentient, independent mutant, as we are. You have no right to jail him in your gallery."

The Collector cleared his throat. "I traded a small fortune in armaments and technology to Mojo, his former master, for that right. Who are you to–"

Longshot interrupted the Collector's monologue before it began.

"Mojo is not and never was my master! He imprisoned and exploited millions under his supposed 'employ.' I am a free being, Taneleer Tivan; I resent your notions of acquisitive rights." He stepped forward, wagging a finger. "If you have concerns about entering a contract with that unscrupulous sack of dung, go to Mojoworld and take it up with him – and his attorneys!"

The Collector drew back, sniffing with distaste. On the adjacent screen, Major-General Ka'arnil of the destroyer Cries of the Bereaved whispered conspiratorially to his deck officers. A flurry of activity sprang into action behind the Shi'ar commander. Sikorsky, monitoring the integrity of the Starjammer's systems and shields, chittered with dismay.

Ch'od swiveled toward his captain. "Corsair, the Shi'ar have armed the warship's plasma cannons. Following our firefight on Sirius Five, Sikorsky assesses our shields holding at an integrity of sixty-seven percent. We cannot defend against fire of that magnitude for long."

Major Summers acknowledged the grim report. He turned to Alex and Quentin, holding out his palms and raising an eyebrow. "Gentlemen? Decision time."

The mutants looked at one another. Taneleer Tivan moved his face closer to the screen and cleared his throat again to get their attention.

"This is no idle threat, Earthers. I am coming for what is mine. Return the Phoenix Egg at the very least, and we can discuss terms for the stolen mutant specimen… as well as recompense owed me by Corsair for the lost pearlsquid. Delay or deceive me further, and you will soon learn the power an Elder of the Universe can bring to bear upon your insignificant ship – as well as your savage little planet."

And as if that weren't enough, the Shi'ar chimed in, too.

"Hail, Starjammers," Ka'arnil announced. "Time has run out. Proceed to the following coordinates and hand over the Phoenix or be eradicated where you stand."

"OK," Corsair decided, ending both hails and preparing the helm. "That's enough. Open a jump gate to Earth, Ch'od. Time to bring Scott in on this."

"No." Alex stood up. He'd had enough of being second-guessed – by their enemies, by his father and Kid Omega… even by himself. Havok wasn't about to turn tail and run back to his older brother; they were going to do this his way, and do it now.

"Alex?" Corsair turned back to his son. "The Starjammer can't fight both the Collector and the Shi'ar."

"No, it can't. That's why you're going to leave this system, and Blink's going to jump me, Longshot, the Egg, and Kid Omega down to Chandilar."

"Yes!" The Kid was on his feet, grinning and excited, using one hand to encase the Egg in a psionic bubble and the other to pump the air. "We should move now, because Daddy Summers just left an Elder god on read, and something tells me an immortal can be salty AF."

Next to him, confused, Longshot and Blink nodded and stepped forward, ready to go.

Alex continued, addressing his father.

"Once we're on-planet, the Shi'ar will lose interest in the 'Jammer and let you run. Hopefully it will take the Collector time to reach Chandilar from Sirius Five. By then, with a little diplomacy," he said, smirking at Quentin, "and a lot of luck," he said, winking at a beaming Longshot, "we'll have explained ourselves to Gladiator, worked out a compromise for the Egg and students, and won the Imperial Guard's help in dealing with Taneleer Tivan."

Corsair handed the helm to Ch'od and stood to face his son.

"I'm not letting you hand yourself over to the Shi'ar, sport. My family... my wife and sons... we haven't had a lot of luck in this system. I lost Gabriel and Katherine. I'm not going to lose you, too."

Alex smiled and hugged his father. "No. You're not going to lose me. This is gonna work, Dad. Trust me, OK? I'm an Avenger, remember?"

Corsair laughed. "OK, maybe I'm a little dazzled. But even Avengers need help."

The klaxons blared as the Shi'ar warship took aim, locking cannons to the evading target that was the Starjammer. Corsair barked instructions to his crew.

"Raza, Ch'od, 'Korsky – I'm going with Alex down to Chandilar. Cat Lady, you're with me. Grab us some gear." Hepzibah purred in reply, heading off to gather weapons. Ch'od raised a hand, about to argue, but Corsair calmed his Saurid companion.

"It'll be fine. Once Blink closes the portal and we're clear, get the 'Jammer to a remote system, as far from here or Earth as you can. Stay cloaked, stay safe. Call Peter Quill and let the Guardians know what's what, all right?"

"Captain," Raza asked, "shouldst thou require our aid, how wilt thou make contact?"

Corsair winked. "Trust me. If we need help, the universe will know."

Sikorsky chittered. The warship was coming about; the cruisers scattered.

Hepzibah handed a sword and pistol to Corsair. He strapped them to his belt and smiled at his paramour. "Time's wasting," he said as she kissed him on the cheek.

Blink nodded. She opened a portal and leapt through. Longshot and the two Starjammers followed, then Kid Omega with the Egg carefully in tow.

Havok looked back. Raza had taken the helm, maneuvering the ship out of firing range until Ch'od and Sikorsky could trigger a jump gate. Seconds were counting down. The Shi'ar were moving to attack, and a furious Collector was on his way.

Just another day on the HMSS Starjammer.

Havok gave The Remaining Starjammers a sharp salute. Then he jumped through Blink's portal, leaving them behind as he leapt onto Chandilar.

CHAPTER TWENTY

[ALEX | THE TOWER OF SHARRA AND K'YTHRI | CHANDILAR | THE SHI'AR GALAXY]

Blink had planned to transport them into the serene halls of the Imperial stronghold. There, at the heart of their throne world, the emperor and his counselors governed the many planets that comprised the Shi'ar Empire. This tower was home to the royal family, and barracked the Superguardians who protected them from harm. The throne and war rooms offered sumptuous spaces for visiting dignitaries and military advisors. Soaring above the magnificent, vibrant city, the swooping Tower of Sharra and K'ythri was a testament to elegance and beauty, honoring the ancient gods to whom the Shi'ar paid fealty. To visit the tower was a privilege. Invitations were rare and few.

The team found themselves on its lowest floor, near the tower's maintenance and waste filtration areas. Huddling together in a darkened alcove, the mutants and pirates had to act fast, before Kallark and his Imperial Guard discovered their presence.

"Sorry," Blink apologized, the markings on her face creasing with embarrassment as she did. "Everyone was talking, and things were confusing. I was aiming for the upper levels."

"It's fine," Alex replied. "I doubt that teleporting a Phoenix Egg into the throne room would've made Gladiator's day. This way, we can still handle things diplomatically."

"How?" Kid Omega gestured to their surroundings. "Call them from the trash compactor and ask for an invitation to scones and tea? Also, there's no way he doesn't already know the Egg is here."

The Kid was right. The Phoenix Egg flared, eager to be released. They could all hear it squalling now, not just Quentin. The Imperial Guard staffed multiple telepaths in its ranks. At this point, one of them – if not all – must have learned of its presence. Which meant the Superguardians were probably on their way.

"Then we go now." Alex turned to his father. "Dad, after we teleport, you and Hepzibah hang back with Blink. She's our ticket out of here if things go south, and we need somebody to keep her safe." Corsair nodded. The Starjammer captain was oddly silent. Alex knew the endgame might get dicey depending on Christopher Summers' traumatic memories of Chandilar. The emperor who'd killed Corsair's wife was long dead... but Havok understood that it was hard for his dad to keep his resentment for the Shi'ar in check.

Blink frowned. "I don't need a babysitter."

"Clarice, I don't have time for arguments. If it feels better, think of yourself as a mutant influencer and the Starjammers as your well-paid security guards, OK? Longshot, you and the Kid are with me. I'll take the lead."

He paused, turning to address Kid Omega.

"I know you're desperate to end this, and itching for payback, but this is nearly over. We played it your way on Sirius Five. I trusted you, Kid. But I have experience with the Shi'ar, and Kallark knows me. Trust me now. This calls for diplomacy, not chaos. The Egg for your friends. That's the way it has to be. Hopefully Gladiator is reasonable about returning the Phoenix to the Collector's museum-world, where the Elder can safeguard it from doing any damage to the universe. And hopefully, we can end this without starting an intergalactic civil war."

Quentin sniffed and frowned. "Boo. Where's the fun in that?"

"You want fun? When this is over, I'll buy you a hot dog at Coney Island."

Kid Omega wrinkled his nose, shiny with sweat. "Ew. RIP."

An angry clash of metal sounded in the distance. A rush of hot air stormed in from the vents. Someone was coming. Many someones.

"Now or never," Alex said. "Blink?"

Sighing, Clarice opened her fourth portal of the day. Looking through, Havok spied a long white hallway leading down to a set of high, golden, oval double doors: the entrance to the Imperial throne room. An attaché of guardsmen flanked the hall. Surprised by the arrival of six intruders, the guards raised their blasters. Alex stepped in front of Blink, quickly hopping through the sparkling portal, and held out both hands as if to indicate surrender. Behind him, he could hear the Superguardians eagerly coming to corral the tower's unwelcome visitors.

"Wait," Havok cried, desperate to stop the guards before they opened fire. "We're the X-Men! We come in peace. We're here to speak with your Majestor, having aided the Empire in the past! Please – hear us out."

The Shi'ar eyed one another, blasters still raised.

"I swear," Alex continued, eyes wide and yearning as he invoked the Shi'ar deities, "by Sharra and K'ythri, we mean no harm."

His friends joined him in the hallway, even Blink and the two Starjammers, stepping through the portal one by one. Last came Quentin and Longshot, maneuvering the Egg. As the last of them stepped into the white, shimmering corridor, Blink closed the portal... just as the Superguardians – which ones, Alex couldn't see – crashed into the waste filtration area, right on time to miss their targets. Allowing himself a sigh of relief, Havok turned back to the guards. One of them noticed Kid Omega and the Egg. The guard squawked at his colleagues. The Shi'ar language sounded fast and greasy, a sibilant series of clicks and screeches that reminded Havok of angry, strident birds... which made sense, given their race's avian descent.

"Kid?" Havok turned to Quentin, hoping he might provide translation. But before the younger mutant could speak, a warbling pop breached their ears and a sinewy figure teleported into their midst. Teeth bared, the Superguardian Fang – a hairy Lupak warrior armed with deadly retractable claws – leaped on a surprised Havok, shoving him to the ground with an angry growl.

Seconds later, the far doors burst open, and Fang was joined by his colleagues. Alex recognized them all, having fought alongside – and against – many of them in the past. Smasher and Starbolt. Manta, armed with photokinetic rays, who could perceive the visible and invisible spectrum. Warstar, a green armored warrior comprised of two separate aliens, a smaller expert in hand-to-hand combat riding atop a bulky powerhouse's back. And Oracle, the team's elegant, enigmatic minder and one of Gladiator's key advisors, who immediately engaged Kid Omega in mental battle, striking with a crippling psychic blow.

The Kid screamed, losing his grip on the Egg. Longshot slid across the hall to catch it before it fell. Luckily, he grabbed it in time. Unfortunately, the jostling induced a surge of fire and light, and the Egg burned Longshot's palms. Wincing, the blond mutant set it on the ground and turned to defend himself from an oncoming Warstar, thundering across the hallway.

Havok struggled beneath Fang, grappling to break free. The lupine Superguardian pinned his prey, long tongue slavering as he held the X-Man to the ground. Alex felt himself growing tense. His heart was pounding, adrenaline rising. He kicked and pushed, but the more powerful Lupak had the advantage, and tension brewed in Havok's gut.

He couldn't breathe. Every moment of the last few days – traveling on the Starjammer, living lean, working hard, assuaging his father's guilt while managing Quentin's ego – all hit Alex at once.

He closed his eyes.

"Oh, god," Christopher Summers cursed. "I can't hold it!"

Alex's mother shoved him into his Scott's arms. "I love you," she promised her younger son. "I love every part of you."

The Summers brothers fell.

Alex pressed against his chains on Chandilar, angry and frustrated as Vulcan taunted his brother. "Shut up, Gabriel. I'm going to get out of here and make you eat those words."

"Oho! The Summers fire. Too little too late, I'm afraid."

Kid Omega frowned and glared at the oncoming lizard.

<<It isn't working! Aren't you almost done?!>>

Alex tried to destroy the cable. [[Nearly. It's giving…]]

Quentin and Alex faced one another in the farmland.

"You're a terrible leader, Havok, and a worse teacher. Even you must know that."

"We're a lot more alike than you think."

Alex winced and tried to shake off Fang. Stress and anger churned his gut.

I'm a terrible leader, he thought.

I'm a failure.

Corsair gripped Havok's shoulders in both hands. "You want to be a better teacher and leader? Be here now, Alex. Stop doubting yourself and wallowing in anger or guilt."

The Summers brothers fell, holding onto one another for dear life.

Alex and Quentin laughed. Kid Omega rose on unsteady legs and moved to follow. Before they could leave, Alex turned and gingerly placed a hand on Quentin's shoulder.

"Hey, Kid. Before we go… I just wanted to say: nice work."

Be here now.

"I love you," Alex's mother promised him. "I love every part of you."

Be here now.

We're a lot more alike than you think.

"Thanks," Quentin Quire said to absolutely no one, the word soft and silent, barely loud enough to reach his own ears. He forgot that he hadn't yet severed the telepathic connection between him and Alex Summers, who was barely out the door of the battered scout craft.

Alex smiled. He didn't say a word.

He waited another few seconds for the Kid to gather himself, basking in the glow of Quentin's unintended gratitude.

We're a lot more alike than you think.

Fang's claws dug into Alex's tense, quivering shoulders. He could dimly hear the others around him, defending themselves from the Imperial Guard. Havok's heart hammered. His eyes burned with tears and frustration.

Diplomacy, not chaos. That's what he'd said. Focus, not fire.

But that was before he had a one hundred-and-eighty-five-pound, smug Lupak warrior sitting on his chest.

"Ah, flark," Havok muttered. He reached out, accessing the ambient energy bleeding off the Superguardians and pulsing from the Phoenix Egg.

Alex's eyes widened.

The Phoenix's power surged into his body. He'd never absorbed this much energy at one time. He started to hyperventilate. The lone white disc on his chest radiated out to form several rapidly oscillating concentric circles. He couldn't hold it in for long. He was going to explode.

"Holy crap," he said out loud. "Kid Omega was right."

Alex's eyes flared. His hands crackled to life. Havok pointed two fingers at Fang and released a powerful burst of searing cosmic plasma. The astonished Superguardian flew across the hallway, ricocheting against the ceiling. Fang's dense musculature protected him from Alex's blast, but he landed several feet away, stunned and attempting to regain his wits.

Alex quickly got to his feet and turned to help the others. He fired a short blast of plasma at Warstar, separating the slim, agile rider – B'nee – from C'cil, his larger, lumbering companion.

Confused, C'cil turned, having been engaged in combat with a dancing, grinning Longshot. The Superguardian roared and sprinted toward Havok... who slapped both fists together and loosed a third, spiraling salvo of energy into his oncoming emerald assailant. The burst knocked C'cil off his feet, embedding the bio-mechanical symbiote into the far wall.

Havok whirled. Oracle loomed over Kid Omega, a soft smile reaching her purple lips as she took the upper hand in what appeared to be a pitched psychic battle. Quentin was still suffering the effects of the Phoenix's inveigling call. The Kid's knees buckled as he tried to keep the entity at bay while also defending himself from Oracle's attack. Alex flexed his fingers and prepared to ambush the Superguardian from the side, to help his student–

But then the throne room doors burst wide, thrown off their hinges from the inside. Resplendent in a war suit of scarlet and blue, a high-collared crimson and gold cape flaring out behind him, the purple-skinned Strontian Shi'ar emperor glared at the melee and waded in. Weighing in at over five hundred pounds of solid muscle, Gladiator bulled forward, a clenched and outthrust fist leading his impressive mohawk as he charged into the fray.

Alex had to act fast, while he still possessed an incredible amount of absorbed cosmic energy. If Gladiator connected with any of his teammates – especially Corsair, the most likely target – any physical damage could be severe, not to mention should this fracas continue, the political fallout.

"Kallark, wait!" Havok tried to stop him, but the Strontian emperor appeared overcome with battle lust, focused on the pirate captain who would dare invade his tower. Gladiator's eyes narrowed, drawn to the firelight of the resonant Egg pulsating behind Kid Omega. He cocked his fist, shouted a war cry, aimed...

...and fell through a pink, crackling hole in time and space.

At the last moment, before Kallark landed his blow, Blink had opened a portal between Gladiator and the Egg. Spinning with a flourish, she snapped it shut and then hurried to help Hepzibah grapple with Starbolt. Alex glanced around, searching for where Clarice had sent Kallark. Seconds later, he had his answer. A frustrated roar sounded from beyond the open double doors. Blink had sent the Shi'ar emperor back inside his own throne room.

Havok hurried down the corridor, evading the zealous guardsmen and pockets of confrontation between his friends and the Superguardians. On his way, Alex fired a focused stream of plasma in Oracle's direction. Her surprised scream let him know he'd managed to connect. He felt the energy already bleeding away. Fang swiped at Havok's boot in an effort to halt his progress, but Alex leapt aside and somersaulted through the open doors.

Gladiator was already on the move, headed to rejoin the fight. Alex got to his feet and blocked the emperor from a clear path to the battle.

"Kallark," he repeated, "wait! It's me, Alex Summers."

Gladiator growled, attempting to move around him. "Out of my way, X-Man."

But Havok refused to budge. "Please, Gladiator... you know me – hear me out! We've fought together. You know my brother, my family!"

"Yes, I know your family," Kallark interrupted. "Like your

freebooter father, the notorious pirate whose crew has pilfered its way across the Shi'ar Empire. Whom you've brought here – to our throne world, the heart of my empire! – with a Phoenix Egg, of all things!"

"Yeah, I know. I'm sorry about my dad, but as for the Egg…"

Kallark glared at Alex, hooded eyes sizing up the shorter being. Havok knew that the Shi'ar emperor could snap him in two without wasting a breath, even if he did manage to get off a shot of plasma… which the Strontian would no doubt swat aside like a mosquito. Alex could feel Gladiator's hot breath upon his face.

"As for the Egg," Kallark replied, "Alex Summers, brother of Scott, husband to Jean Grey, who as host to the Phoenix was a deadly threat–"

"A threat you quashed by cleansing her bloodline."

Alex's comeback seemed to have derailed Gladiator's train of thought. He held his ground like a statue, balefully staring at the uninvited mutant, listening to the sounds of fighting out in the hall.

"What do you want here, X-Man?" Rage and frustration bled off the emperor. He folded his arms, chest heaving with adrenaline and purpose.

Kallark continued, "After the recent, tragic events on Earth – which transpired thanks to your zealous, misguided brother – why in the name of Sharra and K'ythri did you go looking for the Phoenix Force? Shi'ar Intelligence picked up this foolhardy quest of yours back on New Xandar, and we have been tracking the Starjammer as it traveled from Xanth to Sirius Five. We had hoped the Collector's involvement might have been enough to thwart your efforts, to halt any further attempts to obtain the

Egg. While I cannot say I am pleased the artifact exists at all, its containment within his catalogue-world at least satisfied my need to keep it safe from the wrong hands. There, in his private galleries, the Phoenix had at least been prevented from being unleashed upon a vulnerable universe."

Gladiator wiped a thick hand across his face.

"And yet you Earthers continue to surprise me with reckless determination. Now half the Galactic Council desires what you carry, and will no doubt reach Chandilar within a moon's turn. Additionally, now I must worry about the arrival of an immortal who no doubt believes we are in – what is the Earth term? – 'cahoots.' So, tell me, Alex Summers, brother-in-law to the greatest threat to ever menace the Shi'ar Empire… why did you bring the Phoenix to my doorstep?"

Confused, Alex shrugged.

"I'd have thought it was obvious, Kallark? We've brought you the Egg in exchange for the five kidnapped mutants."

Gladiator stared down at him, arms still folded.

Alex rephrased his meaning: "You know, the ones the Shi'ar took from Earth."

Kallark continued to stare. He raised a curious eyebrow. The silence – apart from the fracas coming from the hallway – concerned Havok. Clearing his throat, he tried again.

"Gladiator, I'm here to recover the Earther mutants, the five taken by Shi'ar warriors – 'The Remaining,' or whatever you're calling them – who left a message for a Summers to deliver a Phoenix Egg. Scott couldn't make it, but my father and I managed to bring one here. We believe it's because you and the Shi'ar want to destroy it. Honestly, I don't care. All I want are the kids, returned safely and without delay."

Kallark's stare intensified. His eyebrow fell, and then he sighed.

"Alex Summers, I appreciate you approaching me in this respectful manner..."

Havok's heart leapt. Diplomacy might actually win the day.

"...but I have no idea what you are talking about."

Stunned, Alex found himself at a loss for words. Kallark didn't know? But if the Shi'ar orchestrated the kidnapping, and the emperor... could Longshot have been wrong? Had he seen someone other than the Shi'ar?

Kallark tapped a bicep, waiting for Havok's response. "Alex?"

"I just... we were positive the Shi'ar were involved. Longshot, one of the X-Men out there, had visual confirmation that these Remaining... the people ransoming our students for the Phoenix... that they were Shi'ar. So, how could you not-"

"The Empire is vast, Alex. And while my counselors and I pride ourselves on knowing every plot hatching within its borders, there will always be those who slip our watchful gaze. Perhaps your younglings have fallen prey to the machinations of rogue agents operating outside the bounds of my purview? I can tell you this: no one in this tower with a place in my court had anything to do with kidnapping Earther mutants. The only reason we even knew about your Egg hunt was due to informants on New Xandar... to whom you loudly and repeatedly announced your intentions."

Smiling, Gladiator placed a thick hand on Havok's trembling shoulder.

"Naturally, understanding our feelings about the Phoenix and its bloodthirsty past, the Shi'ar had to take action. Frankly, I am surprised you believed the empire would tolerate its presence within our system, never mind wanting anything to do with the Phoenix in the first place."

"We thought you wanted it so you could kill it."

Kallark gave that some thought. "Sensible. But no, it was not us."

"Well, then… who the flark was it?!"

Behind Alex, a rough, oily, amused voice answered for Kallark.

"I thought you'd never ask."

CHAPTER TWENTY-ONE

[QUENTIN | THE TOWER OF SHARRA AND K'YTHRI | CHANDILAR | THE SHI'AR GALAXY]

Kid Omega's skull was on fire.

Brought to his knees, the Kid waged a mental battle on two disparate fronts.

First, Oracle's vicious attack, subjugating him on the mental plane. Lightly armored in impenetrable dragon scale and decorative candy floss, the Superguardian minder pierced thin micro-needles into Quentin's mind and body. He tried to shield himself – conjuring psionic barriers and manifesting threshers to slice away the needles – but like flesh-eating worms, they devoured anything the Kid tossed their way, squirming around the shields to find purchase in his psyche... and, in turn, his physical form.

So, that was fun.

And then there was the Phoenix Egg.

Aroused by battle on both the mental and physical planes, the world-devouring entity angrily tested the limits of its meager container. Not to mention the emotional restraint of its psychic watchdog, Kid Omega, duty-bound to protect the Egg until he could trade it for his friends.

But with every moment, as Oracle pressed her advantage, the Phoenix-song grew louder – and more jarring – inside Kid Omega's mind.

[[Release me]] it offered. [[Assume my mantle and take what you desire. Power. Pleasure. Pain or peace. You belong to me. I belong to you. Become the Phoenix. Reduce your assailants to ash and flame.]]

<<No!>> Kid Omega squeezed his eyes, closing them shut to prevent the flow of burning tears. Oracle laughed and unleashed another volley of needles.

<<Yeaarrrrghhh… gahhh… oh, you basic Shi'ar witch. I'll kill you for this.>>

Oracle chuckled, her soft voice echoing in his brain.

[[However shall you accomplish that, X-Man? Your friends are ours. Kallark has subdued your leader. And despite efforts to seduce its release, the Phoenix will be destroyed. A skilled minder you are, I will admit. But not skilled enough to contest the likes of me.]]

Frustrated, the Kid groaned and tried to manifest a psionic shotgun… but he felt Oracle dismantle it as he assembled the psychic components. The Phoenix assaulted his ears, fiery claws prickling Kid Omega's mind and patience.

[[Release me. I will consume her body and soul.]]

Oracle dismissed it with a wave. [[Begone, sparrow. If I have my way, this dilettante will never crack your shell.]]

Kid Omega couldn't fight them both. Needles on one side, talons on the other. He was powerful, but exhausted. The journey, his struggle to find the Phoenix Egg – and having to deal with all the obstacles along the way and infuriating Summers men – had taken its toll, not to mention the crushing realization that the Kid still hadn't rescued Glob, Phoebe, Ayo, and the others. His mind was awash in pain, guilt, desire for the Phoenix Force, and crippling self-doubt.

And one other thing, a feeling that Quentin Quire knew all too well. Resentment. Hate. The frustrated lonely pit in his gut that constantly pushed him to rebel.

Kid Omega resented Alex and Corsair for not listening to him in the first place, not letting him find his own way. He hated Scott and the X-Men for treating him like a child, like a burden and threat. He was frustrated with the world – now the universe – for kidnapping, killing, mistreating, and underestimating mutants as a whole... Earth mutants, especially. Kidnapping his friends. Jailing Longshot. Eliminating the Greys. Looking down on Kid Omega, Havok, and the rest because they came from a technological backwater instead of thriving out among the stars. Hate fueled his self-doubt, and he couldn't help but think about those who'd stoked its flames.

Emma Frost. "...lacking in, shall we say, a certain mental elegancy."

Scott Summers. "Forget it, Quire. You've done enough."

Corsair. "Careful, junior. I'm babysitting you as a favor to my son."

The Collector. "Not acceptable, boorish..."

The snarky and dismissive Remaining minder. "Staggeringly pathetic."

Maybe the Kid was a failure? A burden, hardly equal to the task. A kid, like people believed he was. All this time Quentin called himself the Omega and bragged about his vaunted skill. And what had he actually accomplished? He'd driven away his mentors, let down every friend, enraged an Elder of the Universe, and set the cosmos against his mission... this mission...

On this mission...

On this mission, Kid Omega had found Blastaar by kicking in the doors of every low-down, filthy space bar from Majesdane to New Xandar...

He'd shared a smoothie with a space raccoon and saved Havok from an interstellar gecko. Working with trusted colleagues, he'd drawn a dotted line from Xanth to Sirius Five...

The Kid had matched wits with and trapped an Elder of the Universe – one of the oldest and most powerful beings around – stolen a burning vulture out from under his creepy, immortal purview, and helped rescue a handsome colleague...

Kid Omega had begun this journey alone, resented, and unwanted. Now he was on Chandilar, surrounded by colleagues and... yes, maybe even friends who cared about his wellbeing, a knife's throw from recovering the five mutants who liked, if not loved, him best.

Oracle dug in. The Phoenix shrieked. The Kid retreated inward, grasping his triumphs, clinging to moments of inner strength...

... Alex placed a hand on his shoulder. "Hey, Kid. I wanted to say: you did great down there. Quick thinking, good reflexes. So, uh... thanks. Nice work."

... Havok sat next to him in the cargo area. "Kid, you gotta stay optimistic. We're gonna find them, I swear."

... The Collector's forces scrambled, scattering like roaches. "Not bad," Havok remarked. The Kid cracked his knuckles and replied:

"I believe the word you're searching for is 'damngirl,' all one word, no exclamation."

Breathing through his nose, Kid Omega opened furious, burning eyes.

The psychic needles hesitated. The Phoenix broke off, mid-squeal.

The Kid glared at Oracle.

"'Damngirl' indeed." He'd had enough.

"What did you say?" Oracle cocked an eyebrow as Kid Omega's psychic manifestation rose to its feet. "I don't comprehend your nonsense, X-Man."

"N... nonsense this, Economy-Class Jean Grey. I've known a few telepaths in my time, and in terms of looks, snark, and general witchiness, you barely make the Wizard Top Ten."

He smirked, head throbbing as he drowned out the Phoenix with an eighties ballad that increased in volume, rising across the psychic plane.

"You come for me with these," the Kid remarked, shearing away the micro-needles with a psionic machete, "pocket-sized excuses for Frank Herbert sandworms, and then aim a knee at my soft, squishy insecurities? But here's the thing, sweets..."

Kid Omega dialed up his mental speakers. He did his best to channel the Phoenix-song and twist it into this new assault, transform it into a weapon he could send against the Superguardian telepath. The ballad thrummed inside Oracle's mind, vibrating her skull. She crumpled to the floor, fingers digging at her ears.

"... I'm the Omega, heard? I've lost eight-hour meme wars to Emma Frost, Broody Jetson. I've thrown down with both the Avengers and X-Men and failed spectacularly. I've cluelessly

tracked my best friends across the universe without knowing if
they were still alive, and now have the world's worst earworm
running through my mindgrapes thanks to a cosmic buzzard
who probably wants me for brunch. But hey! Here I sparkle,
alive and quicking – oh, that's kicking with a 'Quire' – and do
you know why?"

Back in the physical world, in the hallway, Kid Omega
dragged himself to his feet. He loomed over Oracle, still
unsteady. Doubled over on the floor, hands slapping her head,
she tried to beat away the driving, addictive, repetitive melody
of "You're the Best" by Joe Esposito.

Quentin cleared his throat, mouthing the lyrics with his
actual voice.

"It's 'cause I'm the best. Neither you nor any cosmic
parasite are gonna ever keep me down. I finally realized that
despite my All-American crappiness and a penchant for being
that obnoxious, unpopular nerd who usually looks out for
glamorous number one… there are folks out there who actually
give a maxiflark about me. And who knows, sister? Like Rocky
Balboa once said, maybe even the Omega is capable of growth
and change. Of learning something from a mutant so dull that
paint watches him dry. An X-Man so clueless that asking for
directions must be his second mutation. A guy who…"

The Kid stopped himself and laughed. "Ah, but I can insult
Havok all day, even if he is kinda growing on me. So, please to
excuse. Not only because he needs my help, but also if I don't
see your Shi'ar super buddies as the menacing threat they so
clearly are. Right now? I've got a Phoenix in my ear and another
minder – and friends – I really gotta find. And I must say, though
at first I thought you might be that minder, it's pretty clear you

don't hold a candle to The Remaining's telepath, Oracle. But don't worry. Once I find that poser, I'ma douse her cerebellum with gasoline."

Kid Omega left the Superguardian where she lay. Then he turned back.

"Oh, and Oracle? I'm not an X-Man. I'm a Mutant Without Borders, here on a mission to save my students. And don't you flarking forget it."

Grinning, he whirled on the Egg. "As for you, my combustible love… scurry on back to the White Hot Room. Like most beings, The Remaining are gonna wish they'd never visited Canada. And I don't need your parasitical monkey's paw to help save my friends."

"Perhaps not, host," spoke a familiar, oily voice.

The Kid froze. He spun around.

"Oh, you bitc–"

The mysterious telepath, the one who'd confounded Quentin at the start of this mess, loitered at the end of the hallway with a dozen armored Remaining, equally encased from head to toe, faces hidden behind black, expressionless helmets. The nameless minder cocked her head, acknowledging the Kid, and placed her hands against her hips as she gazed upon the Egg and the raucous scene. She glanced at Oracle, writhing on her knees. The armored telepath's shoulders shook – as if she were laughing – and then she delivered a swift, vicious kick to the compromised Superguardian's head. Oracle crumpled to the ground.

Longshot and Blink finally noticed the arrival of The Remaining, as did Corsair, and broke off their respective fights. The Imperial Guard had not, but when their opponents backed away to assess this newer, deadlier threat, they, too, refocused their attention on the newcomers.

The Kid seethed.

"So. You finally slithered out of whichever black hole would have your smarmy awfulness. Is that where you hid my friends, you treacherous mess?"

"No one is hiding," the telepath replied, palms out to indicate a lack of deception. "Here we are. And here you are, with the Egg we requested, for which we are grateful, host. I always knew that I would find you here. The visions and portents told me so."

One of her companions grunted. "This one is not the host we require."

She soothed her agitated ally, tapping steel fingers against the second raider's armored cheek. "No, this one is not the host. But from what I can ascertain, another stands in the adjacent chamber. Truth? The visions showed me not a specific face, but rather an instance."

She turned back to Kid Omega. "Shall we adjourn within, Quentin Quire? We mean no further harm, and all that remains is an exchange of assets."

"How do I know my friends are safe?"

She patted her own helmet. "Come see, if you wish. I can show you."

The Kid refused, folding his arms. "I'm not going inside your man-trap of a head."

He could almost perceive her smile.

"I assure you, the confines of my psyche are more inviting – and a deal less pink – than yours. Still… if you decline my invitation, accept my reassurance. Your friends are safe in nearby stasis, waiting with the one I serve. If you will escort me into the throne room, and your emotional colleagues allow us passage, all shall be revealed."

Kid Omega turned to the others. Corsair and Hepzibah had blasters trained on the scrum of impassive Remaining. Longshot and Blink stood on either side of the Kid, assuming protective stances next to their friend.

"Say the word," Blink whispered. "I'll teleport them to the far side of the galaxy before they can draw breath."

The telepath laughed. "Yes, do try. Send us where you like, but I promise that you will never see your friends again. Treat with us, X-Men. Deliver the Egg and the promised host. In return, my empress shall return the five. And then Earth, along with its mutants and heroes, will have no concern about reprisals from those who remain."

Something she'd said... Kid Omega tried skimming her thoughts, attempting to learn the identity of this new being, this empress the telepath had mentioned. But The Remaining's minder was too skilled. He still couldn't access her mind.

"All in good time, Quentin. Present us to Kallark. Escort me and the Phoenix to its new host, and all will be revealed. Remember: we have no desire to hurt a potential ally. All The Remaining want is to regain what was stolen, and to wed our strength and force to the fury of the Phoenix, and a host of rightful bloodline."

"Gladiator? You want him to host the Phoenix Force?"

She laughed again, a third time.

"Come, he who calls himself Omega. I assure you that answers are forthcoming. And should you and your allies play fair with The Remaining and our empress, the whereabouts of your friends shall be forthcoming, as well. Now, Quentin Quire, as I believe they have said on your quaint planet…

"Take me to your leader."

CHAPTER TWENTY-TWO

[ALEX | THE TOWER OF SHARRA AND K'YTHRI | CHANDILAR | THE SHI'AR GALAXY]

Gladiator shook his head. "No, it was not us."

Frustrated and confused, Havok racked his brain, casting about for how to formulate his next step. They had the Phoenix Egg. Longshot had seen the Shi'ar and was certain that they were supposed to bring it here to Chandilar, the heart of the Empire. If the throne had not ordered or sanctioned The Remaining's actions, then...

"...who the flark did?!"

"I thought you'd never ask."

Alex turned. Framed in the doorway stood Kid Omega with the Phoenix Egg, flanked by Longshot, Blink, and a cadre of warriors in obsidian armor. They all wore helmets, carried no weapons, and exuded menace if not outright contempt. Behind them, filling the hallway, stood additional armored enemies, carefully watched by Corsair, Hepzibah, and the Imperial Guard.

Havok raised a quizzical eyebrow. "Kid?"

Quentin jerked his thumb at the lead warrior, the woman who'd spoken.

"Alex Summers, meet Insufferable Witch. Witch, this is Havok. You'll get along fine. She's a high and mighty bougie telepath with a jones for the Phoenix Force; Alex's brother was married to one."

"Wait, Quentin, are you saying..."

Kid Omega spread an arm with a flourish. "Meet The Remaining. They're here for 'Summers to deliver a Phoenix Egg.' Now let's get that over with so we can recover my poor kidnapped students, the Mutants Without Borders."

Kallark stepped forward, reaching for the Egg. "One moment. I cannot allow–"

The telepath raised a palm. Gladiator scrabbled at his throat with one hand, the pompous warning he'd been about to deliver suddenly cut off as his windpipe constricted. Choking, purple complexion shifting to a deep, dangerous indigo, Kallark stumbled forward and closed his other hand around the minder's neck like a vise.

She lowered her hand, releasing the Shi'ar Majestor from telekinetic control. Gladiator coughed, doubling over as he fought to catch his breath. His hand remained where it was, grasping the telepath as if he were about to pop off her helmet, skull and all. He glared at her, cold eyes narrowed to pinpricks of icy hate.

"Try that again, and I'll drive my fist through your chest."

Kid Omega grimaced, his face drawn in a furious, angry mask. "Get in line, Majestor."

Kallark ignored the Kid, his attention focused on The Remaining.

"Who are you? Where is Oracle? Tell me, minder... how did

you manage to curtail this tower's considerable physical and psychic defenses?"

The minder didn't answer, her hands scrabbling at Gladiator's fingers as he lifted her into the air. Scowling, the Strontian relinquished his grip just enough to let her speak.

"...your... minders' attention, my 'Majestor'... all focused on the Starjammers and the Egg. Quite simple, really... to slip in beneath notice. Simple... mental cloaking. As to Oracle's whereabouts..." The telepath shrugged.

Gladiator peered at the door, eyeing the Superguardians gathered outside. Oracle was not among their number.

"By Sharra and K'ythri, I swear–"

"...swear not... great K-Kallark," the minder continued, straining in his crushing grasp, "...for in the coming hour, you may... find reason to regret!"

Alex stepped closer. "What do you mean?"

"Enough," Kallark proclaimed. "I would know your identity, woman."

With his free hand, Gladiator wrenched away her helmet to reveal a green-skinned woman beneath with close-cropped, dark blonde hair framing a scarred, angular face. Smirking, her eyes narrowed as she and Havok both found surprised recognition in Kallark's eyes.

"Delphos?"

"Yes, Majestor. You know me. Once we fought together as members of the elite Superguardian Corps. Together, you and I protected the rightful ruling family Neramani – them and one of those wedded to the throne – from threats to our system. A family to whom many standing here, these loyal soldiers who now fight at my side, do still pledge fealty."

Behind them, in the door and hallway, the rest of Delphos' ebon-suited colleagues followed suit and removed their helmets, dropping them to the floor. The Superguardians seemed astonished to find the faces of former colleagues beneath the armor – gifted beings who once filled their ranks, borne of different races from across the galaxy's worlds, long since thought dead or lost in the course of duty.

Delphos nodded, smugly indicating her allies to the stunned emperor.

"Cry your apologies, betrayer Kallark, to those with whom you once served – we few but proud emissaries of a scorned empire, a dynasty swept aside by misguided politics. The Empire may have abandoned its loyalty to bloodline in favor of a democratic process – electing a Majestor from within our ranks rather than sourcing an heir – but many of us, those who never forgot our duty, abandoned this 'harmonious' new order to find ways to return the throne to its rightful hands. We – The Remaining few, allegiant and steadfast, burning with purpose – now come to make things right. And we do not come alone."

Havok's heart beat faster. The moment had gotten away from him, and this new revelation had only served to confuse. That said, Delphos' rant-turned-manifesto sounded familiar. It struck a chord of recognition inside Alex's gut.

"Hang on," he asked, interrupting her diatribe. "What do you mean, 'not alone'?"

Before she could answer, Kid Omega stepped on his line of questioning.

"Who cares? This sounds like a Shi'ar problem, not a Me problem. So why doesn't someone hand over my friends, and I'll be on my way."

Corsair pushed his way through the assembled Remaining.

"One second, Kid. Delphos? From the 'Jammer's records on the Superguardians, Delphos is a precognitive. She can see flashes of the future, visions, that sort of thing. There's no record of her having abilities on par with Oracle, or any minder or telekinetic close to that level. I wanna know how she managed to sideline young Master Quire here back on Earth."

Gladiator returned his unyielding stare to the telepath in hand. "Corsair has a point, Delphos. Where did you source the abilities required to hoodwink both Oracle and the X-Man minder, as well as the tower's psychic defenses? Your telepathic prowess has always been impressive but limited to brief visions and defensive capabilities."

The emperor turned to the others, The Remaining arrayed around the room. "In fact, many of you – those I know of old, with whom I have warred, grieved, and rejoiced – are considerably improved. Tell me, Delphos. How have you come by these enhanced abilities?"

"Our benefactor – but truly, she is so much more – coupled her desire to the devoted, ambitious reach of those skilled in the art of genetic manipulation and advanced technologies. Having intimate knowledge of what it means to burn, she knew our natural abilities would be no match for the sheer ferocity of the Phoenix Force. To aid in our quest, she graciously endowed her Remaining with gifts required to secure its capture. With these abilities, for instance, I have been able to best even the strongest minders and foresee success on our behalf. My visions have led us – and our benefactor – through an unerring journey, every step of the way, inevitably leading us to Chandilar and success."

Delphos' words continued to stir echoes inside Alex's tight, concerned chest.

"This benefactor," he slowly asked, "the woman who knows what it means to burn … ?"

Delphos grinned. "She knows you well, Alex Summers."

"OK, that's it." Quentin strode toward Gladiator and his complacent captive.

The Kid rolled up his sleeves; the words ALL I REALLY WANTED WAS SOME POWER CONVERTERS blazed to life upon his chest.

"Enough with mysteries and threats. I've spent the last few days bouncing across space in Errol Flynn's Intergalactic Mystery Machine, trying to find a hungry, burning sparrow so I can get back my friends. You," he growled, pointing a digit at Delphos, "are the worst. If I had my way, Mohawk Cape here would sink a knuckle deep inside your ribcage. The two of you clearly have issues to work out. Great. Awesome. Wow."

The Kid pointed to the Egg. "But we got your stupid parasite. Now give us back my Phoebe and Glob."

"Wait, Kid. We can't just hand her–"

The largest button on Kid Omega's jacket suddenly displayed an open palm. The other two respectively read TALK TO and THE HAND.

"No, Alex. Maybe you can't just. But I sure can just. She's mentally blocking my friends' location from me, but I'ma dig it out with a psionic melon baller in a hot, pink nano-second."

"Quentin, we can't deliver the Phoenix into the wrong hands!"

Delphos threw back her head and cackled.

"There are no hands more deserved and destined of this power, mutant, than that of the Shi'ar's rightful Majestrix!"

Kallark's eyes narrowed again. "The 'rightful'...?"

Corsair shoved through The Remaining. "Wait. Alex is right. I know who Delphos means."

Like his son, Major Summers finally understood. But nobody listened. Their voices rose and blended, arguing as the fanatical precognitive laughed.

"I don't care–"

"Kid, she's talking about–"

"There is no 'rightful' Majestrix, traitorous–"

"Sire! Great Majestor!"

That last distressed cry echoed from an open door situated across the room, adjacent to Kallark's seat of power. Two wizened politicians hurried across the tiled floor, flushed and sweating, slowing as they realized the emperor was embroiled in some kind of confrontation.

Gladiator barked at his nervous counselors. "What? What is it?"

Stammering, they continued to approach, absorbing the sights of armor, Earthers, pirates, and Superguardians. One of them managed to speak.

"O... out in the... a-above the city! Enormous! You must–"

"I must? I must what? Spit it out!"

"Hey, look!" Longshot had crept to the window, and now pointed to the skies above Chandilar. From his vantage point, Alex could see something vast and massive blocking out the sunlight, plunging the throne city into shadow. Had the Collector managed to arrive this quickly, aiming to retrieve the Egg for himself? Or worse, was Chandilar under attack by the

very being Havok believed might be backing The Remaining…
a being with whom many in this room shared a terrible,
intimate, bloody history?

Delphos hooted, a victory cry commingled with jarring
laughter. Alarms rose from the towers and outskirts,
sounding to life with an echoing cry. Rising klaxons wailed as
Chandilar's defenders sprang to life, scrambling to meet the
invaders and warn the stunned inhabitants of the Imperial
City.

"She comes! As I have foreseen, our empress will again wed
her power and bloodline to the flames and rage… to burning
glory! Hear me, Remaining: secure the Phoenix Egg, for we are
moments from celebrating the entity's glorious rebirth and the
rise of our emperor!"

The armored warriors shoved their way into the room,
pushing aside Blink, Corsair, Hepzibah, and Kid Omega.
Quentin and the Superguardians rushed to block them from
taking the Egg, and the battle recommenced. Kallark hurried
to the window to stand alongside Longshot and see what was
happening outside for himself. Alex joined them.

Four mammoth starships descended upon Chandilar. Apart
from a single, battle-scarred Behemoth-class warship, the rest
of their points of origin were unknown. Two bore outlandish
colors and bristled with cannons. Their collective wingspan
covered the throne city in darkness, and Havok heard wails
and screams drifting up from the streets below as invading
shuttles launched to descend. One of the starships – the largest
and most centralized, emblazoned in pirate markings – floated
dangerously close to the city's elegant spires and skyscrapers. A
craft launched itself from its bowels and headed down toward

the tower. Horrified screams spiraled up from the streets below, mingling and clashing with the clangorous sirens.

Ignoring the melee taking place inside his chambers, Kallark throttled the gloating, jubilant minder.

"Who comes, Delphos? Who dares covet the destructive power of the Phoenix, and by doing so threatens the universe?"

Cackling, Delphos indicated the approaching craft.

"Isn't it obvious, Majestor? She to whom you paid allegiance, as did I. The last remaining member of the House Neramani … the burning bride…"

Resigned to the coming conflict, Alex interrupted Delphos, announcing the name to Kallark and Longshot like a warrant.

"It's Deathbird."

CHAPTER TWENTY-THREE

[ALEX | THE STARJAMMER | SOMEWHERE IN THE MILKY WAY GALAXY]

Years Ago...

Havok silently stared at the passing stars.

Numb, he sat in his quarters, dejectedly slumped upon the sleeping plinth with his hands clasped between his knees. He watched the stars streak by, extended pinpricks of light against a black, infinite matte. For the last few hours he'd barely spoken. Not to his crew. Not to anyone.

Memories unspooled inside Alex's mind. Happy, comforting moments stolen with his father and friends. Moments taken from him by his insane brother, Gabriel.

His dead brother Gabriel, the late Emperor Vulcan.

The brother who'd imprisoned Alex and killed both Christopher Summers and the former empress, Lilandra Neramani. The brother he never really knew.

Now Gabriel was gone. Killed in battle, his mad reign finally ended...

And Alex, despite empty threats, had been robbed of any chance to avenge his father's death. To prove himself as both a leader and a son.

So there he sat, moping. Drifting through space with the broken Starjammers, mourning their losses and nursing their wounds. Another team that Havok had managed to let down.

The door to his quarters slid open. Lorna Dane stepped across the threshold, sparkling green eyes somewhat dimmed as she gazed down upon her somber boyfriend.

"You OK?"

Havok shook his head. "I don't think I'll be OK for quite some time."

She sat next to him on the plinth, scooting close.

"I'm here to talk, if you need me."

Alex sighed. "There's nothing to talk about. Talking won't bring back my dad."

"No, but you can't let yourself…"

He placed a hand on hers and smiled. "I'm fine."

Polaris shoved his hand aside. She pushed him off the bed.

"You're not fine! None of us are, and that's to be expected, Alex." Tears sprang from her verdant, captivating eyes. Lorna ran a nervous hand through thick, green hair. "We've lost friends, family… time… he was your brother! And he tortured us!"

"Don't you think I know that?!"

"Then stop saying that you're fine! You're allowed to be angry, to be upset. To feel betrayed and hurt and miss your dad." She took his hand. "What you can't do, Alex, is lock yourself in this room and cut yourself off from the rest of us, because we're all feeling the same horrible things. And as our leader, you need to–"

Havok laughed. "Leader? What kind of leader gets his entire crew captured and tortured by his own brother?"

"The kind who bides his time and engineers their escape, like you did. You can't blame yourself for what happened, Alex. Gabriel had the Imperial Guard at his command. He controlled millions of worlds!"

Havok stood up. "He was my responsibility! My brother! I should've been the one to stop him, Lorna. Don't you get it? I failed! I failed you, my dad – everyone! And I especially failed myself again."

He folded his arms and turned away, gazing at the passing stars. Polaris sat on the bed, hands in her lap, watching him with tears running down her cheeks.

"I…" His voice was ragged, rough with grief and self-loathing. "I hung in that cell, Lorna. In the dark for weeks – months – listening to you. To Rachel, Korvus. All the others."

"So did I."

He looked down at his girlfriend. "No. You heard their screams, but not mine. I wouldn't give Vulcan or Deathbird the pleasure or satisfaction. I couldn't, because I'm the leader. And the leader has to show no fear or pain. Like my dad. Like Scott. So I endured taunts and insults. I hung there, listening to them torture my friends. My girlfriend. I listened to your screams and every scream was another mark of failure."

"Alex–"

Havok leaned against the bulkhead. "I threatened to kill him. I told Gabriel that we weren't family, and that when I finally broke free, I'd end his life – his and Deathbird's. But when I finally did escape… when we escaped…"

Sighing, he hung his head. "I did nothing. Someone had to

do it for me, and Deathbird was imprisoned, not executed. Yet another failure on my slate."

Polaris tried to take his hand again, to gently lead him back down, next to her on the bed, but Havok pulled away.

"You know, Lorna… Gabriel said that he and I were a lot alike. Maybe he was right. Our destructive powers, our poor self-esteem. Of the Summers men, neither of us were ever like Scott or Dad. All we shared was their rage. I told him that we were nothing alike, but maybe I was wrong? Maybe we did share something? Loss. Poor leadership skills. And in the end, failure."

He turned back to the passing cosmos. "Well, I'm done failing. And I'm finished trying to live up to Scott and my father. When we return to Earth, I'm taking a break from leading anything more impressive than a geology study. But if I ever do run a team again, you can be sure I'll take time to figure out how to do it right. You know," he said, tossing it over his shoulder, "Deathbird said to me that together, she and Gabriel could put aside the anger and betrayals, stop themselves from wallowing in pain to allow their… love to fuel any triumphs they shared."

"Love? Deathbird?"

"Yeah, I know. From normal people – you and me, others – I totally get that. But right now, I have to tell you that I can't see it at all. Not their love, no. Rather, the fact that it fueled their victories. Because right now, the way I feel, the only way I can see past failure is through rage and pain."

Havok set his jaw. He coldly faced Polaris.

"I'm going to kill her, Lorna. I'll take time to mourn and collect myself… to put the trauma behind me. But I'll always carry that dark cell – those screams, yours, and the others' –

wherever I go. I missed my chance with Gabriel. I let down my dad, but I won't fail Lilandra or the other Starjammers. The next time I see Deathbird, I don't care who's standing in my way or what sort of army she has at her back. I swear, I'm gonna kill her.

"And maybe then, finally, I'll stop feeling like a failure."

CHAPTER TWENTY-FOUR

[ALEX | THE TOWER OF SHARRA AND K'YTHRI | CHANDILAR | THE SHI'AR GALAXY]

By the time Deathbird sauntered into the throne room – trailed by a coterie of pirates, advisors, and assassins – Havok, Kallark, and their companions had already corralled Delphos and The Remaining into a corner of the throne room. Those assembled Remaining bent the knee as she arrived, emboldened by the swelling of their ranks – far outnumbering the mutants, Starjammers, and Imperial Guard. From where he waited at the window, standing next to Gladiator, Alex could sense tension radiating from the angry Shi'ar Majestor. Outside, Shi'ar cruisers engaged their jump-engines as they streaked in formation over the city's towers, hurtling to meet Deathbird's imposing warships.

Corsair and Hepzibah lifted their blasters, and Havok's fellow mutants put their bodies between Deathbird and the Egg. Kid Omega joined Blink and Longshot near the Egg... but he was faltering, no doubt succumbing to the exertion of having to fight off the Phoenix while enduring Oracle's psionic attack, and then playing mind games with Delphos.

"Greetings, Kallark," crowed Cal'syee Neramani-Summers.

Resplendent in revealing purple armor – the scales, boots, and gauntlets of which were fastened around her slender arms and legs – Deathbird smiled beneath an ornate headdress perfectly suited to display a V-shaped shock of dark blue hair: her headcrest, jutting out violently with sharp, edged feathers. A large flowing cape hid the wings that were a natural part of Deathbird's Shi'ar heritage. A set of twin hoses dangled from each wrist, connecting somewhere behind her cape. She carried a javelin in hand, Deathbird's weapon of choice. Her long, clawed fingernails clacked against the metallic rod as she cased the stand-off, absorbing each participant in turn.

She grinned at the simmering, resentful Superguardians, each waiting for their former empress – traitor to the throne and her own family – to exhibit signs of aggression, giving them license to act. Deathbird held a palm to her chest, to display mock surprise as she passed a resurrected Corsair. Her eyes lit up when she passed the Egg, barely acknowledging Quentin, Longshot, and Blink standing by its side, recalibrating their positions to best defend it from harm.

Finally, she reached Gladiator. Outside, Deathbird's warships hovered above the city, their existence a threat to the populace below. Her cadre of pirates advanced as she approached the Shi'ar Majestor, brandishing ominous cannons and deadly blades, implying consequence to anyone who might prevent Deathbird from reaching her goal. Smirking, she dragged a sharp nail along Kallark's tense, quivering forearm – the one he was still using to dangle Delphos, the minder's feet kicking above the marbled tile.

Deathbird then caressed Delphos' cheek. "Well accomplished, dear one."

She cocked her head and smiled into Gladiator's fuming eyes. "You can cease choking the precognitive, formidable Kallark. I'd asked Delphos to peer ahead, to foresee the steps I might need to take and the road I would travel to achieve success. She was a means to an end, and now that end has arrived. The choice is yours, but this little telepath is no longer a threat."

"She never was," Kid Omega said, spitting from between gritted teeth where he waited back by the Egg. "My friends, Space Flamingo. Where are they?"

Sweat poured off Quentin's brow. Alex could tell the Phoenix was getting impossible to resist. Very soon the Kid might snap, and then they would have larger problems to deal with than Deathbird and her army. They didn't have much time.

Slowly, Gladiator released Delphos. The precog slid to the floor, massaging her throat. Deathbird leaned down and retrieved the minder's discarded helmet.

"Lovely toys, are they not? A gift from our new friends back there," she carelessly explained, flapping a hand at the sycophants who'd escorted Deathbird from her warship. As to which particular friends she referred, Havok couldn't say. Truthfully, it wasn't important.

All Alex cared about – all he was thinking about – was the vow he'd made and an opportunity for redemption. The memory of his dark, grim cell flashed in his head. Deathbird's clicking heels. Vulcan's smug threats. Lorna's screams... the hopelessness. But above all, the growing hate brewing inside his chest.

That time in Havok's life should have been no more than a distasteful memory. He was a different man now. His father had returned. He led a team of human and mutant Avengers. Truthfully, he and Lorna weren't even an item anymore. And Vulcan was a fading regret.

And yet, the sudden, visceral recall made him feel as if no time had passed. Here Deathbird stood, free from prison – and the fitting punishment – in which he'd left her. The torture and frustration felt fresh and raw again.

And Alex had made a vow. Hadn't he?

Deathbird spun Delphos' helmet around, displaying the interior to Gladiator. She ran a single lacquered nail inside the mask. From his vantage point, Havok could see blinking lights and studded, neural connection points. The inner circuitry looked much like the kind woven into Corsair's headband, designed to defend the wearer from telepathic assaults.

"Our inventive associates have managed to reverse-engineer the mundane anti-minder jamming technology now pervasive throughout our galaxy. I am sure that several of you," she slyly suggested, winking Mam'selle Hepzibah's way, "are more familiar with it than others. Rather than employ the traditional defensive circuits to protect their ranks, however, several Badoon geneticists have combined their delicious talents to create offensive weapons: broadcast technology and the batteries to aid it, bolstering the natural gifts of those like our pretty little friend." She crooned this last while tapping a leg against Delphos, still on the ground and attempting to normalize her breathing.

"Which means, for those of you following along," Deathbird continued, "that those wearing our wonderful battle-suits while in possession of a genetic gift or innate, hereditary talent common to a specific species, will discover those gifts amplified. Which, I admit, comes in handy when sent into battle against interdimensional warlords, fiercely driven Elders of the Universe, delusional Omega-level telepaths" – she said the last while winking at Quentin – "unwavering Shi'ar Superguardians, and of course, cosmic entities with energy scales that dwarf men – or mutants – with the powers of an exploding sun."

Deathbird paused her monologue and faced Kallark and Havok. The sounds of pitched aerial battle – cannons blaring amid the thunderous echoes of violent impact – filtered in from the window. She gleefully eyed the Shi'ar emperor with her blank white eyes, and then unleashed a slow, saccharine-sweet smile on Alex Summers. "Hello, brother-in-law."

"Deathbird."

"I thank you for accepting my invitation and bringing a Phoenix Egg to Chandilar. I will confess… you were hardly the Summers I anticipated. I also must confess that I seem to have missed your invitation to – now what did you call it so long ago in Chandilar's dungeons? – the Summers family giving of thanks."

Havok glared, face burning and lips pursed. He did everything he could to hold his rage – and volatile powers – in check; he wouldn't give Deathbird the satisfaction of knowing what her presence meant to him, and probably to Corsair, glaring at her from behind his blaster.

He thought about the vow he'd made, and wondered what he was going to do.

Deathbird didn't seem to notice or care.

"Perhaps you were not short an Earth bird, Alex Summers? That is fine." She nodded to indicate the Egg. "That is why I asked that you bring a bird of my own choosing."

"My brother, you mean. You asked Kid Omega to have Scott bring you the Egg. Why?"

"Yes," she confirmed, turning to appraise Quentin seething behind them. "To be honest, I intended to harness the Phoenix Force myself. I did not care how the Egg reached my grasp. My eager hunters," Deathbird said, again nudging Delphos, "tracked its whereabouts, identifying those who may have faced or hosted it in the past. As you can imagine, after my Strontian successor here nearly shredded our poor sister-in-law's family down to its last atom, candidates to the latter have been few.

"Delphos foresaw a future in which I would wed an emperor on Chandilar, bound to the power of the Phoenix. But she cannot see the past and had no way of knowing who possessed an Egg or where to find one. Nor could we ascertain the identity of my inevitable paramour. We assumed it was not Gladiator – why would this traitor relinquish his throne? But we had ideas. Based on Delphos' vision, we believed my emperor would appear at the appropriate time. The only thing that needed finding was his cosmic birthright. When my seekers' journey across the cosmos – confronting heroes and shattering gravestones – resulted in the disappointing news that the universe's last remaining Phoenix Egg was pilfered from a savage buffoon and locked behind the doors of the Collector's stronghold… well, alternate plans became necessary."

Kid Omega sneered. "You needed a patsy to get it for you."

Deathbird brightened. "Exactly. But one powerful enough to

stand against an Elder of the Universe. Strong and determined, a herald with the ability to ferry a primal force of cosmic life from Taneleer Tivan's moon to me, here on Chandilar. One with regal bearing, and perhaps sympathy for my mission. Possessing the ability, if tasked, to corral the Phoenix should its power become unleashed while crossing the stars."

"And," Alex added, "someone who once hosted it, and maybe longed to again."

"Correct."

"So, again. You wanted Scott."

Deathbird nodded, sweeping across the room toward the throne.

"Scott Summers," she confirmed, "had given himself to the call of the Phoenix – the entity that had manipulated his woman into laying waste to countless worlds... and helped him murder the one man to whom he professed absolute loyalty." She climbed a few steps and lowered herself upon the royal seat, splaying her legs over the armrest with the javelin across her lap.

Gladiator started forward. "You dare–!"

"Hang on," Alex begged, recklessly restraining Kallark by placing a hand on his bicep. "Let her finish, please."

The emperor glared at the mutant, but thankfully relented, settling for standing next to Havok with his arms folded, staring daggers at the would-be usurper to his rule.

Encouraged by the shift in advantage, Deathbird's soldiers arranged themselves around Gladiator's throne with their weapons drawn, facing the assembled mutants, pirates and Imperial Guard. Three of them tried to take the Egg, but Longshot brandished a handful of blades he'd picked up in battle, pointing them threateningly as Blink and Hepzibah backed him up. Deathbird's men retreated, biding their time from a respectful distance.

Corsair joined Havok and Gladiator, aiming a blaster at his widowed daughter-in-law. "She can finish, but then I get to do the same."

"Dad–"

"Don't 'Dad' me. She comes in here like she runs this system, protected by hooligans and cutthroats as if her husband didn't overthrow the galaxy and, oh wait, burn me alive. And we're supposed to–"

"Dad," Alex repeated, putting a hand out to lower his father's gun. "I promise. She's not leaving without us getting what we're owed."

Christopher Summers' jaw flinched. He looked away, keeping his eyes on Deathbird. Perhaps he'd noticed Havok's steely gaze, the torment and pain that Alex had endured at the hands of his brother. Maybe Corsair saw there the need for answers and understanding. Or maybe Alex's dad simply picked up on the simmering conflict taking place inside Havok's heart: the desire to kill Deathbird, weighed against the vows he'd made as an X-Man and Avenger, as a human being clinging to his ethics and moral fiber. A responsibility to cherish life, even in vengeance… no matter how much he despised the other being.

Corsair nodded, blaster still trained on Deathbird. Alex turned back to their enemy.

"So my brother used the Phoenix Force to kill Xavier. What does that have to do with your coup? There are other beings more capable in the universe – more powerful than Scott, who no longer hosts the Phoenix, by the way – that could've easily retrieved this Egg from the Collector. Beings imbued with cosmic abilities or trained in supernatural arts. Heck, all you really needed was Kid Omega."

"Flarking right," Quentin whispered, perspiring with his eyes trained on Delphos.

"You could've squeezed the Kid into one of your booster suits, partnered him with the Superguardians you've won to your side and sent them to snatch the Egg. Sure, you'd have to deal with the Collector eventually – I mean, you still might – but you'd have the Phoenix Force. You could find another more willing, more pliable participant powerful enough to host it, and game over. So, why Scott specifically?"

Deathbird frowned, toying with the javelin in her lap. Those assembled waited for her answer, but none seemed to be forthcoming. Alex stepped onto the first stair, hesitantly approaching the throne.

"You're scared, aren't you? You don't think you can tame the Phoenix without someone who's had experience hosting it in the past."

"Of course," she snapped, scraping her nails on the javelin. "Only a fool would unwittingly wed a force like that of the Phoenix – the Phal'kon, sister to Sharra and K'ythri – to a random host, one vulnerable to its seductive wiles and all-consuming power. But... that is not all. There are other reasons, Alex, for requesting your brother's presence. Reasons I now realize that I may have deciphered incorrectly from the start."

Confused, Havok traded glances with Corsair, who shrugged.

"What were those reasons?"

Deathbird closed her eyes. After a moment, she softly continued, as if embarrassed by the ensuing revelation.

"After Vulcan died, I was alone. Imprisoned by the Kree, abandoned alongside those of us who remained committed to his rule. To the empire he'd nurtured from a spark into an inferno. Your brother Gabriel... I have told you this, Alex, but our union was unlike anything I'd ever known. Once our loyal soldiers freed me from captivity, I knew that I would do whatever I could to consolidate those left behind, our remaining forces, and regain the empire we'd lost from those who'd squandered its promise... who'd relinquished the power of a ruling bloodline and delivered the throne into the hands of democracy."

Gladiator started forward. "The Neramani bloodline has been extinguished! Lilandra, your parents... all murdered by your hands, that of yours and Vulc–"

"Yet I remain," Deathbird seethed, turning the javelin's point to face the approaching Majestor. "The bloodline still flows within my veins, in that of Vulcan's widow – the burning bride, rightful empress of the Shi'ar. Not you, a vassal selected by vote and choice!"

"I don't understand, Deathbird," Alex asked. "You were empress once before but gave it up to your sister. You didn't want to deal with the administrative headaches that came with the job, if I recall. Why do you want it back now?"

She jabbed a finger at Gladiator. "To wrest it from this up-jumped Strontian guard, he who served my family and emperor – as did the other guards wedded to my cause, those who remain loyal and mourn noble Vulcan's death. Kallark cast that loyalty aside to steal an empire for himself, thanks to the political machinations of sycophants and bureaucrats!"

Darkening, Gladiator began to object. "That is not what..."

Deathbird ignored his protestations, giving her full attention to Alex.

"Control of the Empire belongs to those born to the Neramani bloodline, or those joined to its House, as was Gabriel. We, The Remaining, do not forget the heights to which Emperor Vulcan raised this empire, Alex Summers. Together – mutant king and Shi'ar royalty – we should have reigned over a dynasty that would have outlasted the stars. And yet the heart within my sun, my love, was snuffed out by those disloyal to his rule. So I made a vow, Alex. I promised those who remained – those willing to do what it took to rebuild Vulcan's vision and empire – that I would reignite the fire that had been extinguished. Once again, Cal'syee Neramani-Summers would be the burning bride, wed to flame and fury–"

It fell into place inside Alex's head. "By marrying a Phoenix host. By replacing one Summers brother with another."

"Exactly. Our gathered intelligence revealed that after his experience hosting the Phoenix, Scott Summers had become a changed man. More militant and unyielding."

Corsair interjected. "More like Gabriel, you mean."

Deathbird smiled at her former father-in-law.

"To his credit, yes. Blood will tell, Earthers, as was evident by his time hosting the Phoenix Force. Scott Summers executed Charles Xavier, attacked his weak-minded friends, and despises my successor for killing his wife's family." She spat, carelessly indicating Gladiator. "The fire that ran through Vulcan's veins runs in Cyclops', as it does their brother."

The assembled Remaining refocused their gaze on Havok.

Kallark furrowed his brow, eyeing the astonished mutant at his side.

Alex didn't know what to say. He could feel the weight of Corsair's stare, along with those of Gladiator and Kid Omega, tired and angry, waiting for someone to return his friends. Unfortunately for Quentin, larger things were happening in the Tower of Sharra and K'ythri, and Alex had to put aside the rescue mission to work through this unlikely set of events.

"There's no way that Scott would ever–"

Deathbird leisurely descended, loosely carrying the javelin in her hand. Kallark tensed as she approached, but Deathbird only had eyes for Havok.

"Correct. And though Delphos' precognitive ability revealed that I would achieve success – that I would rule the Empire wedded to an accomplished, learned Phoenix host – she could not identify that host's identity. Over time and through calculation, I believed it would need to be one whose power could match that of my emperor, of lost Vulcan. Based on recent events I was pleased to find one who could do so... one who also shared his bloodline."

"Scott."

"Originally, yes. But thankfully, your brother is no longer required."

Reaching out with clawed fingers, Deathbird softly caressed Havok's jaw. The years fell away, and he was back inside the lonely cell, listening to her express love for Vulcan. Havok fought hard to restrain himself, to listen without powering up and riddling Deathbird's slim, sinuous body with ambient cosmic energy.

"What do you mean?"

Her hand slipped away. "I mean that truly is my house blessed by Sharra and K'ythri, as is that of House Summers. Despite

Scott's distaste for Kallark's involvement in the decimation of the Grey bloodline, your brother is a principled man. There is too much of Xavier within him, drowning the passion and power I require. The hate and desire for vengeance and justice. I cannot successfully convince Cyclops to again host the Phoenix and rule by my side. He is not the emperor that Delphos had foreseen, the one who shares power akin to Vulcan's and who will help secure my reign. But thankfully, Alex... you share Gabriel's blood, as well."

Havok laughed, and Corsair joined him. Major Summers ascended, passing Gladiator and waving his blaster in Deathbird's face. The former empress raised an eyebrow and lifted the javelin to defend herself.

"So do I, Deathbird," Corsair said. "But no Summers man is going to join your revolution on behalf of a bad seed we barely knew."

"You knew him," she purred. "As much as you wish to disavow Vulcan, he was of the Summers bloodline. You share the same fire. The same difficulty with authority. Like you, Alex, Gabriel had experience managing vast quantities of power. You did not host the Phoenix force, nor burn as Vulcan did – but you can! Your ability to absorb and maintain cosmic energy can be enhanced, as were the abilities of my Remaining, allowing you the opportunity to host one of the primal forces of this or any universe!"

She stuck her javelin into the ground and took Havok by the shoulders. Surprised, he shrank back, but Deathbird held him tight, excited by the opportunity she believed that she was placing in Alex's hands.

"Like your father and Vulcan, you carry no love for the Shi'ar.

My insane brother killed your mother! Under Gladiator's command, they wiped out Jean Grey's bloodline. They imprisoned you, and tortured your woman–"

"That was you!"

"An involvement I now regret. Truly. In the end, I begged Gabriel to release you, Alex, to find a place for you within our empire. But Vulcan would not listen. He was too angry, consumed by vengeance far more volatile than his powers. Now I understand that place is fated to be at my side, imbued with the Phoenix Force. Together we will learn from Gabriel's mistakes and return the empire to its rightful hands – that of a Neramani, wed to a Summers – and ignite a dynasty that will finally outlast the stars!"

Smiling, Deathbird took Alex's hands. His fingers flinched, and for a moment he thought his powers might deliver an answer. Instead, he stared into her unnerving, hopeful eyes.

Was she serious? Deathbird had tortured Lorna and the Starjammers. She'd been a party to his father's murder. He'd made a vow.

But he also remembered how it had felt when he'd absorbed the energy coursing from the Phoenix. How powerful he'd become.

Havok's fingers twitched. The circle at his chest began to oscillate.

Deathbird hadn't noticed. "Join me," she breathed. "Host the Phoenix Force, Alex Summers. Allow its fire and fury to course through your veins, as his power once did your brother's. Join me in Vulcan's place. Under our glorious reign, the Empire and universe will belong to those left behind by Gabriel – soldiers, brothers, bride – to us. To The Remaining."

An explosive tremor rocked the tower, dislodging and shaking all assembled within the throne room. A Shi'ar cruiser streaked past the window, a sibilant whine trailing in its wake. As everyone around him regained their composure, Havok violently tore his hands away from Deathbird's.

Her eyes narrowed from hope to shock. Alex stepped back. Corsair and Gladiator moved to flank him on either side. Deathbird appeared surprised. The emotional whirlwind upon her hopeful face quieted to a cool, forbidding storm. She reached out to retrieve her javelin, plucking it up from the shattered tile.

"Are you insane?" Alex asked. "Did you forget that it was you – and Gabriel – who enslaved me, imprisoning me for months? You speak about love? I had to listen to my girlfrie… to Lorna and the others get tortured by your command! And my mom? Seriously? My mother…"

Furious, Alex raised his hands. White concentric circles filled his jet-black uniform. Deathbird's guards moved to protect their empress. The power contained in Havok's fists grew. It hummed and churned. He could feel the Phoenix in the room, its energy irradiating the air.

Deathbird lifted her javelin to defend herself. The Remaining edged forward.

"…as far as my mother goes…" Alex faced his father, inviting his dad to share in his justified anger.

Corsair stood by Havok's side, his jaw set and blaster raised. But upon closer inspection, Alex realized that despite Chris Summers' vitriol and bravado… it wasn't rage creasing his father's eyes, but sorrow. The hate and vengeance Alex felt on his mother's behalf – having simmered to the surface for decades! – misplaced as it might have once been, directed at Corsair rather than the Shi'ar...

...that anger was nowhere to be found on Christopher Summers' face.

How could he not be feeling what Alex was feeling?

Katherine Summers had been murdered by Deathbird's family! Corsair himself was killed by Vulcan's own hand – the son he'd never known, because D'Ken had kept his existence a secret! There were so many reasons to take revenge for the pain and death.

But the more he looked into his father's eyes, the more Alex realized that Corsair had managed to do what he himself had not: he'd put the past behind him.

"Dad?"

Corsair faced Alex. His eyes were determined but filled with regret. "Son?"

Havok had made a vow and was angry enough to fulfill it – as his father should have done, after losing both his wife and son to the Shi'ar. But Alex sensed none of that driving need for vengeance in the man standing by his side. Had Corsair's brush with death allowed him to let it go? Or was it a matter of acceptance over the passage of time? Christopher Summers seemed to be, in some ways, a changed man. A different man.

To be fair, Alex was different, too. He'd made his peace with Lorna and Scott, and was finding his way back to his father. Havok was a leader again, and had learned a thing or two from the last time he'd assumed the role. He glanced at Kid Omega, who shot Alex a quizzical look.

Leader. Teacher. Brother. Son. Those were the labels that now defined Alex Summers. Failures and self-doubt possibly behind him, he'd learned – from Scott, Corsair, and Quentin ... and even from Gabriel in his own way – that he had to quit wallowing in the past.

To be here now. To be the leader he was meant to be.

He was still simmering with resentment and burdened by history. But looking at Corsair and Kallark ... at the X-Men and Superguardians ready to fight on his behalf ... at Kid Omega, with whom he'd come so far ... Alex also realized good leaders didn't need to carry their burdens alone. They invested in the trust and support of a team, flaws and all, and that investment paid back in dividends.

Maybe I'm not a leader yet, Alex thought to himself. But like Scott, he was heading there. He wasn't an emperor. He was an Avenger. An X-Man. A mutant. He wasn't defined by rage or the past, but rather the choices they helped him make in the present.

And he was going to prove it.

Grinning, Alex clasped Corsair's shoulder. His father shot him a bemused look. Havok smiled and dropped his hand, turning to face his sister-in-law.

"Forget it, Deathbird," Havok replied. "You're finished manipulating the Summers men for your own selfish ends. I don't know who it was that Delphos saw in your vision, but you'll have to find some other patsy to sit by your side in prison."

He clenched his fist, and the white circles oscillated across his uniform again, radiating from his chest to his fingers as he absorbed the energy saturating the throne room. Corsair gripped his blaster, and Gladiator balled his fists, both preparing to fight.

Deathbird frowned. She returned to the throne, The Remaining closing ranks behind her.

"Pity. I hoped you might find reason, if not enthusiasm, in my proposal. Wedding the blood of my fallen love to the power of the Phal'kon would have been ideal... but ultimately unnecessary." Deathbird lazily waved a hand, indicating her gathered forces. "A suitable, subpar replacement will be sourced from my technologically enhanced, genetically gifted generals. One of the former Superguardians married to my cause, perhaps, bolstered by the circuitry laced throughout my battle-suits. I would have preferred the blood, but all destiny requires is the Phoenix Force, encased within this Egg... which my men will now take!"

The Remaining advanced. The assembled mutants and guardsmen loyal to Kallark turned to defend the Egg again. Blink placed her hand on its outer casing, flaring with light, the Phoenix inflamed by conflict raging about its container. Pink sparkles began to circle the floor beneath the teleporting mutant and the Phoenix's oblong womb.

"Back off, losers," Blink cried. "Try to take this thing, and I'll teleport it somewhere you'll never find! So help me, no one will see it again!"

Deathbird smiled like a cat toying with a desperate canary. "Nor will they your friends."

"Stand down, Blink." Alex waved her away, pointing a glowing fist at the throne. "You'll have your Egg, Deathbird, after you return the kids. But that's as far as it goes. There's no way any of us are letting you break it open or occupy more than a cell, much less an empire."

Gladiator agreed. "I don't care how many warships you

muster; the Empire will remain safely under my watchful eye. With a word I will assemble both active and reserve guardsmen to end this rebellion and scatter your forces across the cosmos. And should you somehow succeed in this mission of yours, I have no doubt the assembled Galactic Council – Kree, Skrull, Spartoi – will quash your venture like an Earther fly."

"Not with the power of the Phoenix by my side, dear Kallark!"

"And what makes you think I will allow it to be released, traitor?"

Deathbird thumbed a node at the tip of her javelin, revealing a tiny console fitted into the thin metal rod. She raised a claw, hovering it above a button in the panel.

"If you don't, I will signal my men aboard the lead warship to execute your comatose mutant friends and rain fire upon this city. Even your Imperial Navy and Superguardian forces will not halt my armada from destroying Chandilar. You may triumph over some of my companions, Majestor, but not all. And you shall have the deaths of several Earthers upon your conscience, as well as tourists from across the system – something I doubt will maintain your alliances with the worlds throughout the Shi'ar Galaxy, or the larger galactic community."

Gladiator fumed and breathed from his nose. The absorbed cosmic energy had nearly transformed Havok's uniform from deep black to stark white. Their colleagues – the Starjammers, mutants, and Superguardians – tensed and readied themselves for inevitable battle, prepared to do whatever it took to protect the Phoenix Egg.

Havok and Corsair traded glances. They couldn't attack Deathbird, not if they wanted to save the kidnapped students and protect Chandilar from harm. But they also couldn't hand the Egg to Deathbird and watch her overthrow the Empire.

"You won't win, Cal'syee," Havok warned her. "The X-Men and Avengers have both stopped the Phoenix in the past. We've beaten you and all these others. The galaxy will never stop coming until you're behind bars. Even if you win now, you'll eventually lose."

"Not if you agree to rule by my side. Together, Alex, we can conquer the universe!"

Alex shook his head.

"That's not going to happen, Deathbird. I told you, I'm not Gabriel. I won't accept your insane proposal."

"But I will."

Stunned, Havok turned around as a smiling, confident Quentin Quire sauntered through the crowd, heading toward Deathbird with an outstretched hand.

CHAPTER TWENTY-FIVE

[QUENTIN | THE TOWER OF SHARRA AND K'YTHRI | CHANDILAR | THE SHI'AR GALAXY]

"I'll do it," repeated the Kid.

Kid Omega shoved past the astonished mutants and the throng of assembled Remaining. He ignored the betrayed looks on both Havok's and Corsair's faces as he wended his way up the stairs to stand before Deathbird at the throne. Everyone was silent, astonished or excited depending on their allegiance, as he made his way to her side. Outside the tower, the warships trained their barrage on the city and Shi'ar forces, their ponderous cannons bathing Chandilar in a blistering, destructive hail of concussive beams.

Standing by her side, a broad smile plastered upon his thin lips, the Kid proffered his hand again. He mentally erased the slogan upon his shirt and psionically embroidered the words THAT'S MISTER OMEGA-DEATHBIRD TO YOU across his chest. He'd finally stopped sweating. His head was clear. Delphos had been revealed to be nothing more than a lackey and fraud. Without her helmet, boosted with psionic Fast and Furious-style NOS, the bogeyman Kid Omega had been chasing was nothing more than a dilettante armed with a deck of psychic tarot cards. Oracle, an actual threat, was off grooving to an eighties power ballad, and apart from a low, sibilant grumbling prowling the edges of Kid's mind, the Phoenix was finally, blissfully silent.

And here stood Kid Omega – leveling up past his charmless would-be teacher, soon to be emperor of a star-spanning galaxy – making his case for the bachelorette's rose.

"Kid," Alex asked, a satisfyingly shocked look on his stupid Summers face, "what do you think you're doing?"

Kid Omega winked.

"Tornado, baby. This is diplomacy, Kid Omega style. As long as my blushing bride-to-be here releases Phoebe, Glob, Ayo, and the others, I've got no beef making interstellar hay – and taking over the universe on behalf of mutantkind – if the Summers men won't."

Deathbird seemed uncertain. She glanced at silent Delphos, who offered no recommendations or assurances, and then reassessed her would-be suitor.

"And what makes you believe that you deserve this honor, Earther mutant?"

Quentin spread out his hands, displaying the goods.

"I'm the Omega, baby. Like Jean Grey and Scott Stick-in-the-Mud Summers, I once hosted the Phoenix. But unlike that bespectacled dork and his dramatic ginger former wife, I've got no troubles managing that level of power, heard?"

She circled the Kid, evaluating him from every angle as she drummed a claw upon her javelin. Below them, the others held their breath. Kid Omega noted the subtle shifts in body language and inaudible instructions passing between the mutants, pirates, and Imperial Guard. Catching Havok's eye, Kid Omega wagged a finger back and forth.

<<Ah-ah-ah, Cyclops-Lite.>> The Kid broadcast his warning wide, so that the message echoed through the minds of all assembled spectators.

<<I see you there, mustering one last gasp of rebellion and fisticuffs. But this soiree just became a Kid Omega party. And at a Kid Omega party, we crank the volume till the volume don't stop.>>

The Kid mimed a dial, as if turning up sound on a radio, and quickly built a psionic programming interface to channel the Phoenix's cry through everyone's skulls. Heroes, guardsmen, and Remaining alike crumpled to the marbled tile, clutching their aching heads, attempting to drown out the searing, terrifying scream of the anguished Phoenix.

Kid Omega laughed and used his other hand to wrest the Egg from Blink and Longshot's grasp. He lifted the shimmering, vibrating orb up and away from Blink's half-formed portal and telekinetically hoisted it across the chamber. He settled the Egg next to Kallark's throne, wrapping it in a psionic bubble with a sturdy psychic lock. Ignoring those squirming and whining on the floor, the Kid refocused his attention on his would-be bride.

"Look, bae. I may not be a Summers – and thank maxiflark for that! – but that means I've got none of that whiny, man-boy Summers juice flowing through my veins. Yeah, I'm no himbo like your dearly departed. But I also got no hang-ups about anyone's romantic history ever, girl."

He placed a sympathetic hand upon his meager chest.

"Everybody's got exes, even the Kid. And I'm comfortable with who I am, so you don't have to worry about me constantly trying to measure up to Vulcan. In fact, with what I'm willing to do, I'd be worried that you might forget about former Emperor Wassisname after you get a slice of Omega."

Amused, Deathbird laid her javelin on the throne, folded her arms, and cocked an eyebrow. "And what is it, suitor, that you are willing to do?"

Kid Omega drew a hand across the crowd, stopping when he reached Havok and Corsair. "For instance, since I'm not a Summers, once my friends are back and the Phoenix mine, I have absolutely no qualms about deading Havok, Daddy, and their hippie space crew."

"No!" Alex twisted on the ground, face contorted as he fought the overpowering strength of the Phoenix-song. He held out a hand, tried to channel the heavy saturation of cosmic energy pervading the room... but the Kid coolly blinked, and Alex's head snapped back. Havok dropped to the floor, teeth grinding in pain.

"Like I was saying," Kid Omega continued, ignoring Corsair's heartbroken screams. "Purple Mohawk Man, his derivative super buddies... even my old pals in both Westchester and Canada – Scott Summers, Wolverine, whoever." The Kid snapped his fingers. "Anyone who gets in our way is roadkill. All I ask is the return of my friends, the five you've got stashed aboard your ship, and then we jump the javelin and get to the honeymoon."

"Why are five Earthers this important to you? Should I agree to accept you as my willing consort, as powerful as you are, once you host the Phoenix your mind and body would transcend common mortal attachment. As the Phal'kon you shall ravage the stars, devouring worlds, taming and bringing empires under the banner of our conquering armada. What significance do you place in five paltry mutant lives? Why do you care?"

Quentin hesitated. He gazed at the others, those who'd joined him on the journey from Earth to Chandilar. Across Majesdane and New Xandar. Through the Xanthan Graveyard and the perilous halls of the Collector's moon. The Kid spat upon the ground.

"These five… they, above all others… they know me. They have accepted me for who and what I am. Sure, I want power – I want to become the Phoenix, and the promise of conquest is indubitably tasty. The idea that Kid Omega, oft the object of peer ridicule and the perennial problem child, would be the one to garner vengeance on behalf of Charles Xavier? Riot. Love it. Cut and print. I never fit in with the X-Men, bird lady. In fact, those authoritarian goons spent every waking hour trying to keep the Kid from being the Kid. And an empire to rule, with a beautiful alien princess by my side? Helping evangelize both the Shi'ar and mutant supremacy to the universe? Hell, sign me up. But Phoebe and Glob, Ayo and the others?"

Vulnerable and determined, Kid Omega turned back to Deathbird.

"They're my family. Maybe my only family, y'know? When I'm with them, I don't feel so alone. I can put aside my anger and all the betrayals. I can stop myself from wallowing in the ever-present need to rebel and act out against those trying to control me. I'm not going to fool myself here, Deathbird. Maybe in time we'll come to love one another, but this is a marriage of convenience. You want the throne. I want the power. Together, we can pool our mutual revolutions and get what we truly want. But my friends – and yeah, I know this might paint me as a sentimental sap – their acceptance may be the thing I want more than anything else."

Finished, the Kid waited. Deathbird's expression did not change.

Arms folded, she drummed nails on her forearm. She glanced at Delphos again, but the former Superguardian gazed silently at the floor, unwilling to confirm whether or not this alliance was predestined. Whether or not Deathbird and Kid Omega were meant to be.

Deathbird considered the Kid's confession. When she spoke again, her voice betrayed a hint of emotion.

"Your words… your heart. The emotions you bear for your friends reminds me of the love I bore for Vulcan. In truth, I was reluctant to entertain your proposal. But as a former host to the Phoenix Force – one prepared and powerful enough to accept it, one willing to see the potential of our union, and who bears such animosity for my detractors – ultimately, you may be the ideal choice to realize my vision. Perhaps our meeting on Chandilar was destined from the start."

Laughing, she glanced at Havok and Corsair.

"After all, there was only one Summers brother I could ever really trust, and sadly, my glorious, misunderstood sun has returned to the very atoms of creation."

Smiling, Deathbird took Quentin's coarse fingers in her own.

"Reveal yourself to me, Kid Omega, mind and soul. For if you are truly he that Delphos spied in her vision – the emperor who will wed his power to that of the Phoenix, who will bind his heart and loyalty to mine – then a 'kid' you shall be no more, but rather an emperor! Consort to the Imperial Majestrix! Overseer to the Shi'ar Empire! By the all-seeing sight of Sharra and K'ythri and their ever-consuming sister, Phal'kon, the Devourer, this throne is mine by right of family and conquest. Cal'syee Neramani-Summers-Quire, the burning bride, of the ruling bloodline now and forever."

Her words echoed throughout the chamber. The few Remaining that had managed to fight off the Phoenix-song cheered and rejoiced. On the floor, Kallark, Alex, and Corsair groaned, doing their best to crawl up the stairs – to prevent the unholy union taking place above. Kid Omega cackled and, channeling his inner Palpatine, showered the Starjammer captain, former Majestor, and the assembled mutants and Superguardians with crippling, pink psionic lightning.

"Kid," Havok screamed, straining to be heard over the screams and rancor. The Kid felt Alex trying to mentally project a desperate plea into his head. Quentin ignored it, and one of The Remaining placed a heavy boot on Alex's chest, pinning him to the floor. "Please... don't do this! After everything you've learned... all we've endured... you've grown... you're Kid Omega! You're better than this!"

Quentin coolly glanced down at his would-be instructor, his failure of a leader and heroic washout. A smile tugged at the corner of Kid Omega's lips.

"You're right. I am better than this. I'm no longer Kid Omega. That's no longer my name. From this day forward," he pronounced, lowering himself to one supplicating knee before a triumphant Deathbird, "my true name – as both Homo sapiens superior and Majestor to the Shi'ar – is Emperor Omega!"

Deathbird took the emperor's arm, raising him to his feet.

"Excellent. Now, my worthy bridegroom… release the Phoenix Force from its womb. Welcome the Phal'kon's power into your heart and soul! Assume the mantle of Phoenix and take your place at my side, as my beloved!"

"Absolutely, Mrs Omega. But first? My Mutants Without Borders, if you please."

Enrapt, Deathbird nodded and retrieved her javelin. Thumbing back the control console, she swiped up to reveal a communicator plate nestled halfway down the shaft. Toggling a minuscule stud, she opened a hailing frequency to the warships outside. A brief conversation with the battalion commander resulted in a positive reply, and moments later a shuttle launched down from an unseen dreadnought, cloaked above Chandilar, wending its way through the streaking network of desperate Shi'ar fighters and flashing, strafing particle beams as it headed toward the Tower of Sharra and K'ythri.

"There," Deathbird announced, voice dripping with satisfaction. "Your warbound – the quintet of mutants with whom you share a heart, as I did Vulcan – are on their way. I trust that is to your satisfaction, my Majestor?"

Emperor Omega nodded, a serene expression settling upon his face. He could hear his friends waking from the deep coma into which they'd been placed by Delphos and the others. Glob and Hijack were rattled and confused. The emperor dropped a mental pin – a diary bullet, really – into Phoebe Cuckoo's head, regaling her with his recent adventures and bringing her up to speed on what had become of them – and him – since they'd last seen one another on Earth. Calmly and politely, the emperor asked her to explain the situation to the other four, and promised to greet them when they arrived safely at the tower.

Finished, the Omega returned his attention to his newly acquired brides, Deathbird and the Phoenix, and prepared to advance to the next stage in mutant evolution.

He strode toward the Egg, ignoring tortured, barking protestations from Havok, Corsair, Longshot, and the others – those who had accompanied him on his journey from earthly mutant problem child to cosmically enhanced universal savior.

Moments from now, Emperor Omega's true destiny would begin as he took a step toward uniting galaxies beneath the shadow of his fiery wingspan, crushing all opposition to the Empire and mutant conquest: the rule of Emperor Omega I and Deathbird, Cal'syee Neramani-Summers-Quire, his burning bride.

The emperor placed both hands upon the trembling, pulsating Egg. The eager, waiting flames licked his fingers but did not burn.

Smiling, Quintavius Quirinius "Quentin" Quire opened his mind...

...and allowed the hungry Phoenix to rush inside.

CHAPTER TWENTY-SIX

[EMPEROR OMEGA | TANELEER TIVAN'S CATALOGUE-WORLD | SIRIUS FIVE | THE MILKY WAY GALAXY]

Triumphantly descending upon the demolished fortress, Emperor Omega stretched out a hand and transformed the Collector's forces to smoke and ash.

The emperor leered down at Taneleer Tivan's ruined stronghold, the scarlet strip of his hair trailing from his pate like a flaming banner. The bodies of the Collector's acolytes were strewn upon the ground. Shi'ar forces stalked the rubble, searching for treasures while hunting down The Remaining attendants. The gallery entrance was a smoking shambles, its elegant reliefs and winding staircases twisted and smoldering, cast aside as Superguardians tore through the remains, gathering the universe's rarest artifacts from amid the wreckage.

The emperor's feet touched ground, dust and grit scattering in a sirocco of soot and embers. Luminous in a skintight black uniform, the emblem of a yellow Phoenix emblazoned across his chest and shoulders, the Omega adjusted his matching lemon-colored gloves and removed tasteful opaque spectacles to reveal a pair of gleeful, burning eyes.

He strode into the shattered gallery, flanked by his elite guard: Phoebe Cuckoo; Fang and Warstar; God-Killer, with its quills and claws; a chained, murderous Strontian, an estranged sister to broken, vanquished Kallark; and Glob – captain of the Emperor's Superguardians, carrying a sack, proven in battle and loyal to a fault, a conflagration ablaze upon his pink, hulking body. And as always, the Omega was accompanied by the woman he loved... the beautiful star blazing in his heart, the Empress Deathbird. Smirking at his beloved, the Omega waved a hand, and The Remaining enclosures – those his soldiers hadn't shattered – cleared before them, forging a path into the Collector's lair.

They found Taneleer Tivan desperately gathering the few artifacts the Shi'ar hadn't destroyed or taken, shoveling them into a personal wormhole, no doubt connected on the other end to one of his catalogue-worlds that the Shi'ar had left untouched. Deathbird nodded, and the Superguardians sprang into action, separating the apologetic Elder from his trinkets and smashing the operations console. The portal disappeared, and Tivan stumbled, falling to the floor.

"Tan, Tan the Not-Quite-Man," Emperor Omega admonished as he hunkered down by the Collector's side. Taneleer Tivan shrank away, staring with horror into the Phoenix's burning eyes. "Did you think I'd forgotten about the captive prisoners languishing in your trophy case of a moon? Tut, tut, tut. Emperor Omega is like an implacable elephant – surely you have elephants in your museum? – he never forgives and never forgets."

Deathbird twirled a finger to indicate the ravaged gallery.

"Our people have secured the items we require, Tivan," she said. "You know, the dangerous objects you have protected from adrenaline-fueled individuals like my husband, who might misuse them and risk the extermination of a species? Items like, say, an Ultimate Nullifier, a Cosmic Cube, or a handful of Infinity Stones. Oh yes," the Majestrix continued brightly, noting the dawning realization in the Collector's eyes. "We shall put them to use on behalf of the Shi'ar Empire as our dynasty quashes more formidable resistors like Hala, Skrullos, Spartax, and Earth. Oh, and your kin, as well, The Remaining Elders of the Universe who have yet to bend the knee to Deathbird and the Omega."

"Fear not," she assured the Collector, patting him on the cheek. "We shall make it quick. We cannot have you joining the resistance and returning to collect what is rightfully ours. At any rate, we stand positive that those rescued from your domain – who may gratefully join our ranks in exchange for their meager lives – will aid in keeping these new treasures safe from any attempts at repossession. Otherwise, they may end up like that which remains of your formerly impenetrable stronghold…"

Deathbird snapped a finger, and Glob shuffled forward, his lustrous pink carapace reflecting the sparking, dying overhead lights. He emptied the sack, and a head rolled out, awkwardly coming to rest at the Collector's side. Glob kicked it over so that Taneleer Tivan could stare into the lifeless eyes of Haroona Sh'thian, formerly Vice-Senior Adept and Forever Attendant to the Collector's Seventh Catalogue-World.

"…loyal corpses and expired goods."

Anguished, the Collector screamed. The Superguardians laughed and closed in. The emperor and empress stepped away, allowing the dogs to have their fun.

Deathbird smiled at Emperor Omega, her glamorous, glorious paramour. He took her hand, restraining the scorching embers on his glove so that he did not burn her fingers.

But Cal'syee Neramani-Summers-Quire did not mind. She was content.

She barely felt the flames.

The only fire that might harm Deathbird blazed inside her heart.

CHAPTER TWENTY-SEVEN

[EMPEROR OMEGA | THE NEW CHARLES XAVIER SCHOOL FOR MUTANTS | CANADA | EARTH]

Cyclops knelt in the filthy snow.

Arms restrained, psionically manacled by Phoebe Cuckoo, Scott Summers seethed and glared up at his former student.

"You were right," crowed Emperor Omega, lording over his prisoner in triumph as he hefted a star-spangled, circular shield with a broken iron gauntlet of red and yellow. "Everyone told you to give me a chance, to place your trust in Quentin Quire, even your own skeptical, dead brother. Now here we are at the inevitable result. I won. You lost."

Scott strained to break free. "I haven't lost yet."

"Your family's dead, Cyclops. Earth has been razed. Your students and enemies have rallied to my side, as have most of the planet's mutant population. Rachel is dead, Blink and Magneto on the run, and my Superguardians are using the last of the X-Men as target practice. Look around," said the emperor, indicating the scorched terrain and devastated school. "There's no coming back from this. Charles Xavier's stupid dream is no more. The future of human and mutant coexistence rests in the hands of the Shi'ar Empire... and in my hands, those of Emperor Omega!"

Cyclops glared at the gloating Majestor, his eyes open and bare. The Phoenix Force easily subdued the devastating force beams that were Scott's to command. Without his ridiculous glasses in the way, everyone could finally see Cyclops' tears.

"I swear, Quire," the last of the Summers men spat in the snow, "you'll pay for this. This might be the end for the X-Men, but somebody will stop you."

"Who?" The Omega looked around. "There's no one left. New York is a crater, the Avengers a memory. Shi'ar gulags house most of the sapien populace, and those mutants and heroes who've chosen to rebel are either dead or fugitives, soon to be eliminated. The Elders of the Universe are mine. New Xandar and the Nova Corps are in ruins, and most of the galactic systems have fallen in step behind my rule, afraid of what I might do with the Phoenix Force should they stand against the Empire."

"You are wasting your time, beloved," counseled Deathbird, approaching from behind. While the emperor had finished tearing the Xavier School down to its last rivet, she'd orchestrated the execution of its final, stubborn instructors. Now Glob and the Strontian stripped valuable adamantium from both Wolverine and Colossus's remains, while Fang and Warstar clapped Illyana Rasputin in unbreakable supernatural irons. Later, Deathbird and the Omega would deliver the disagreeable Russian mutant to Limbo in exchange for that realm's allegiance, just as they had Longshot to Mojo, the extradimensional slaver who'd once bartered the lucky mutant to the Collector. Thankfully, Phoebe Cuckoo had recruited Emma Frost to their side, despite the fact that the emperor knew she would betray them some day.

But that was a fun distraction for later. Right now, they had more pressing matters.

Deathbird kicked Cyclops, toppling him onto his side. Laughing, her paramour handed over his shield. She leaned over Scott, softly exhaling as she savored the moment. Deathbird glanced at her husband. The Omega folded both arms across his chest, and nodded his head ever so slightly, as if to suggest his wife take the lead.

Her eyes sparkled with glee. Deathbird licked Scott's cheek and whispered, "Say hello to your brothers for me." Then with little exertion, she gleefully swung the shield.

Emperor Omega smiled. The shield made a satisfying, sickening sound as it connected with Cyclops' head, like a bell clapping against a watermelon, offering a clanging echo. Behind them, the last of the X-Men screamed as Charles Xavier's first – and last – advocate for mutantkind slumped onto the Canadian tundra.

The flames of the Phoenix warmed Deathbird, as did the sight of her emperor – the man she loved – fulfilling both of their dreams.

Deathbird grinned and adjusted the shield.

With a joyous shriek, she swung again.

CHAPTER TWENTY-EIGHT

[CAL'SYEE | THE TOWER OF SHARRA AND K'YTHRI | CHANDILAR | THE SHI'AR GALAXY]

Wrapped in a silken coverlet, Cal'syee rested her feathered head against her emperor's chest. Standing on a balcony, she surveyed the Imperial City – capital of the universe now, no longer just the system – by the light of Chandilar's moon.

The Omega raised her chin, so that she might gaze into the blazing pools of his burning eyes. Her emperor was a vision in the moonlight. Her heart burned, the joy she felt perhaps simulating the blissful power of his simmering Phoenix Force… finally free to maintain the balance of creation in symbiotic harmony with a willing, eager partner.

Cal'syee smiled. It had taken time, but her love for her determined, adoring emperor had grown to eclipse the memories she once treasured of her time with Vulcan. Together, she and her Majestor had built a dynasty, one whose scope and breadth reigned not only over one million worlds, but upon a universe… and one day beyond. Even now their loyal vassals on the mutant worlds of Krakoa and Arakko, along with sorcerers and scientists on Hala, in the Dark Dimensions, Limbo, and the Negative Zone, were utilizing tools and technologies acquired from the late Collector's conquered galleries to find avenues to breach the multiverse itself. A new war dawned. But it could wait.

Right now, in Emperor Omega's arms, Cal'syee was finally at peace.

The sounds of their city wafted up to the balcony. Fruit, drink, and various delicacies from across the empire waited for their enjoyment. Cal'syee purred, content in her Majestor's protective arms. The song of the Phoenix rose in harmonious waves, riding the moonlight and the scented evening breeze, trilling in their ears and caressing the lovers.

The Omega sighed. She could tell that her beloved had everything he'd ever wanted.

And so did she, Cal'syee Neramani-Quire, no longer Deathbird, his burning bride.

He lowered his lips. The sounds of Chandilar faded away.

The night receded in a haze of passion… and a flash of pink.

CHAPTER TWENTY-NINE

[QUENTIN | THE OMEGA ROOM | THE PSIONIC PLANE | CHANDILAR]

Thirty Minutes Ago...

Oracle clutched her ears, keening in pain on the floor of the Omega Room.

The volume increased. Joe Esposito's joyous ballad – "You're the Best Around" – filled the contracting space on repeat, slowly maddening the Superguardian as tangible, physical lyrics slid through the room, buffeting her like a pinball. Everything was pink and loud.

She felt like her brain was going to melt.

Kid Omega knew. He could taste each thought, savor every synapse.

"That's what you get for sending flesh-piercing micro-needles to eat the Kid, Oracle. That's right, poser. You get the nineteen-eighties."

He evaded the lyrics, carefully tiptoeing through the tight, claustrophobic space, a small pocket of the Omega Room that he'd built and hid somewhere in the back of his mind.

Reaching Oracle, the Kid conjured up a comfortable pink ottoman. He sat on it, hands splayed on his knees, and offered Oracle a sympathetic, pitying look.

"Had enough, fam? 'Cause if you're ready, I could use your help."

The percussive beat retreated. The synth-pop faded away as Kid Omega snapped his fingers to get the minder's attention. Slowly, as though groggy, Oracle sat up and blinked her eyes, seemingly grateful for the aural reprieve.

If looks could kill, her bleary gaze would have eviscerated Kid Omega. "Why should I help you?"

The Kid pointed up, as if to indicate a random direction that might suggest an exit.

"Because this pink playground is like a mental escape room. No doors or windows, the only way out is never. That is, unless I let you leave. And the only way that's going to happen, killer, is if you agree to help with my master plan."

Oracle sulked, the daggers in her eyes dulling as she warily inspected the Omega Room… as if checking to make sure Kid Omega was telling the truth.

"Why do you need my help?" she asked. "You are clearly the stronger minder, and even a cursory scan reveals that you prefer to work alone. Why come begging for alms, X-Man?"

The Kid smirked. "See, right now my kidnapped friends are still being held somewhere by those Remaining jerks. One of them, we just learned – the minder who took my pals and housebroke an earlier version of my Omega Room – is your old Superguardian buddy, Delphos."

"Delphos? But she has never had the ability to–"

"Yeah, we covered that. We'll figure out that mystery once Deathbird arrives."

"Deathbird?" For a woman with the ability to pluck a thought from across the stars, Oracle's lack of information was getting frustrating. Kid Omega decided to cut to the chase and upload pertinent moments from the last hour directly into her mind. Oracle flinched, but recovered quickly. Her violet eyes glazed as she absorbed the infodump.

Kid Omega continued. "So, yeah. Deathbird's coming, and she's bringing the rest of The Remaining with her – all those pirates and Shi'ar still loyal to her dead mutant husband. Right now, everyone in the throne room is vulnerable to a mental attack. Delphos and her pals... their helmets are finally off, and if I wanted, I could probably reach into their minds and strip them for parts. In a moment, in fact, after Deathbird arrives and I can finally deal with the lady of the house instead of the help, I'ma slap some mental blinders over Delphos' brain so that she's one less obstacle in my way."

"But...?"

"Buuuuut, you cheeky little chatterbox, right now I'm fighting a battle on two fronts." The Kid tapped his head. "Up here, I'm keeping you hidden and off the radar. Your mind, anyway. I figure – unless one of your guardsmen super pallies dragged it to safety – that your body's still face down in the hallway, where everyone left you behind for the main event. This little mini-room is secure from any and all psychic attacks, and tucked away somewhere even the Phoenix can't find... yet. So as long as I'm awake and alive, and as long as you care to use it to your advantage, you can stay here and orchestrate plans.

"Which," Kid Omega explained, "brings me to my ask. I'm here, but I'm also back in the throne room on the floor, sweating bullets and trying to keep the Phoenix from getting its claws inside my psyche. Once that happens, all bets are off. And I'm not just talking about what'll happen to you if it should discover this little safe room, sister. I'm talking bye-bye Chandilar, turn off the lights to the tower and universe, lock the door behind. D'you grok my meaning?"

His words were alien, but Oracle understood. She nodded in confirmation.

"Great. Aces. Now, I've been practicing this for a while, and every time I give it a whirl, it gets stronger – and better – so I think I have a plan. Once Deathbird arrives, and assuming The Remaining keep their helmets off... and there are no other minders up evil bird lady's metaphorical sleeve... I'm pretty sure I can end this quickly and quietly. But I can't do that while I'm fighting off the Phoenix."

"What do you require?"

Kid Omega waved a hand, and a second ottoman appeared behind Oracle, along with a cozy-looking two-seater sofa. He helped her onto the footstool and took her hands in his own.

"You're a powerful minder, Oracle. You get the Kid Omega Seal of Approval. I know there are hidden levels of power swirling below your surface, waiting to be tapped. Tap them now. Stay here, get comfy, and block that Phoenix. I can quickly teach you how to create Omega Rooms of your own... though 'Omega Room' is patent pending throughout universes known and unknown, copyright Kid Omega and enforced by Morrison, Quitely, Drake, and Heck, Attorneys at Law. But I digress. Build an Oracle Room. Keep it secret and safe. Trap that burning maxiflarker inside until I'm done saving the day."

He angled to catch her doubting eyes. "Oracle? Can you buy me some time?"

Slowly, she nodded. "It will be taxing... but I believe I can. The Phal'kon is cunning, a most difficult fish to catch. Thankfully, Quentin Quire of Earth, it is not a fish, but a bird. And birds can be trapped quite easily if one knows how."

The corner of the Kid's mouth turned up in amusement. "Girl, did... did you just make a joke? I swear, between you and Alex, I'm learning that everyone in the universe has a sense of humor, even the accountants."

"What is an 'accountant'?"

Kid Omega shot the cuffs of his jacket. "I'll tell you when you're older. Right now, pun'kin, we need to get ready. Deathbird will be here any minute, and I need my head clear to build a fabulous trap. So, when you're ready, I'd appreciate you turning the Phoenix into a sizzling bucket of the Colonel's extra crispy. Do you need a minute?"

"No. I am ready. I am leaving the outer hallway to a location far from the royal throne room. There I shall remain and defend against the Phal'kon as long as I am able."

"Excellent. Oh! There's one more person I'd like you to trap. But I gotta say, Oracle, between you and me... I think you're gonna like this one."

CHAPTER THIRTY

[QUENTIN | THE TOWER OF SHARRA AND K'YTHRI | CHANDILAR | THE SHI'AR GALAXY]

"What ... what just happened?"

Major Christopher Summers stood in Gladiator's inner sanctum, aiming his blaster at comatose soldiers. The Shi'ar Majestor stood by his side, blinking in confusion. All around them, the majority of The Remaining fell silent, arms dangling at their sides and weapons falling to the floor, slowly released by slackening fingers. Above the sea of silent warriors, standing next to Kid Omega near the throne, Deathbird softly stared into the distance.

Several of those in her attaché – a handful of counselors, some of the pirates and scientists – peered at their companions, goggle-eyed and puzzled, trying to snap them out of the sudden trance. Standing nearby, Longshot, Hepzibah, Blink, and the Superguardians loyal to Kallark appeared baffled as well. Fang waved a hand before the face of an enraptured warrior, but the armored soldier would not respond.

Corsair turned to Alex. "What's going on?"

"I'm going on, you mustachioed blockhead."

Havok grinned and pointed his father toward the throne.

Kid Omega smiled down from the top step, lounging at Deathbird's feet, her javelin carefully balanced across his lap. The buttons on the Kid's jacket lapels now displayed (in order, from smallest to largest) two fingers raised for victory, dancing fireworks, and an emoji caricature of Deathbird, pouting as it rattled three sturdy prison bars. The Phoenix remained where Kid Omega had left it, down next to Longshot and Blink, its once-indignant, urgent light now somewhat diminished, softly glowing as the cosmic entity remained trapped within its vibrant womb.

The Kid removed his stylish black specs and tucked them in an inner jacket pocket. Winking at Alex, Kid Omega passed a hand before his eyes. A pink pair of psionic spectacles manifested upon his face, sparkling for all to see.

"Ta-da," he announced, spreading his arms as if revealing the culmination of a wonderful trick. "Tip your waitress, friends. And hit the gift shop while escorting the intergalactic pirates from the premises."

Dawning realization spread across Kallark's face. "Impressive, boy. You have used your minder abilities to place them in stasis, I gather?"

Kid Omega touched his nose. "Close enough, El Gran Mohicano. Minder abilities? Yes. Placed somewhere? Checkaroonie. Stasis... well, that's a gray area."

"Then where are they? What is this exactly?" Corsair inquired, poking a finger into a pirate's nose.

"Yeah," growled a Badoon scientist, warily investigating his captivated colleagues. "What you done, Earther?"

"What I done, Timmy," Quentin began, rising to his feet and approaching the few gathered, free-thinking Remaining. "Can I call you 'Timmy'? You look like a 'Timmy.' Is Timmy OK? Too late. See, Timmy, the Kid has placed your nearest and dearest in a kind of… blissful little daydream, shall we say? An alternate reality here in my cranium." He gleefully tapped his head. "A fun getaway for dear, overreaching Deathbird inside my fabulous, self-contained Omega Room wherein she and those Remaining not protected by jammers or telepathic blockers and whatnot are living out their best coup d'état lives… lives in which Deathbird won."

"Brilliant," Longshot breathed, glorious dimples creasing his cheeks.

"Blame the tall drink of milquetoast down front," Kid Omega said, pointing at Alex. "It's all his fault. These last few days, drilling it into my head, forcing me to get better and relearn everything I know. Diplomacy married to chaos, see? Rather than trading off one for the other. A melodic amalgamation of both trailer park – a tight-knit community, working together politics-be-darned to persevere in even the worst conditions – and tornado, the great leveler."

"Kid," Alex interjected, calling the Kid's attention to the apprehensive, possibly murderous shift in the body language of the conscious Remaining.

"But I digress," Kid Omega said as he twirled Deathbird's javelin, returning to her side. "The point, Timmy, is that your eager little beaver of a would-be tyrant empress here is nappy go bye-bye. She's in a wonderful time out, having a breather, gone fishin', or just plain not in her right mind – 'cause she's in mine," he continued, once again poking his head flesh.

"Trapped up here along with the rest of your jackbooted, super-armored friends. Well," Quentin concluded, chuckling to himself, "everyone except for Delphos."

"Why? Where's–"

"One moment, Alex Summers." Gladiator stepped forward, interrupting Havok's half-formed question. The intimidating Strontian started up the steps, taking a moment to study the entranced face of the woman who'd plotted to take his empire. "Do you mean to tell us that you have telepathically captured the psychic imprints of not only Deathbird but her armada, as well?"

"Well, not her entire armada. Only those in this room whose minds weren't boasting anti-minder home security systems – which, by the way, is crazy, right? Everyone kept saying how important it is to keep those jammers on. I guess they underestimated the Kid, huh? Didn't see my psychic skills as much of a threat… or they fooled themselves into believing they had the upper hand. Anyway, you can see," he said, indicating the warriors getting ready to strike alongside Timmy Badoon, and the warships outside, "that some of The Remaining are moving. That's a good way to figure out who I didn't snake. Also, y'know, all those goons in the giant ships out there, sacking the city and armed with psionic shielding."

Gladiator nodded and cracked his knuckles. He glared out at the impressive display of aerial devastation occurring above his city. "It is a start, and one for which I thank you, X-Man. As to the remainder of Deathbird's forces, the Imperial Guard shall bring an end to this short-sighted folly."

Kallark surveyed the smattering of Remaining still in the room, mustering the courage to attack. He stepped forward –

his Superguardians following their Majestor's lead – and the pirate forces abandoned their positions, retreating for their lives.

"You'll have help," Corsair insisted. He reached beneath his sweaty headband, tapped an interior stud, and gestured out the window. A translight jump gate appeared above Deathbird's implacable warships. The hexagonal tiles yawned wide, and the Starjammer raced through, followed down into the firefight and chaos by a second ship the Kid didn't recognize, undertaking a vertical dive to engage the enemy.

An electronic chirp pealed from Corsair's headband. Major Summers tapped a second stud, and the companions could hear the being on the other end of the call.

"Captain," asked Ch'od, his measured, gravelly voice emerging from Corsair's ear, straining to be heard above a muffled background of cannons and torpedoes. "I trust that everything has gone according to plan?"

"Doesn't it always, buddy? Who's that you've got with you?"

A second hail chimed in, and a new voice joined Ch'od's, a bemused growl laced with sarcasm and attitude.

"Y'know, dinkwaft, they got better food back on Xandar. Them krutackin' birdheads ain't never met a burger they didn't ruin."

Corsair smiled in reply. "After this is over, Rocket, we'll hit a diner I know on the outskirts of Klyntar. The meat's tasty, but don't let it bond with your insides."

"You're buyin'."

"Quill with you? The rest of the morons?"

A third voice joined Rocket's and Ch'od's. "I warned you, Summers. Nothin' good ever came from poking the Phoenix. I did warn you."

"You did at that. Hey, at least we didn't die, right?"

Peter Quill laughed. "True enough. Anyway, the Guardians of the Galaxy are here to help. Permission to engage with the dreadnoughts about to murder Chandilar?"

Corsair glanced at Kallark, who nodded. "Fire at will, Star-Lord."

As Gladiator and his Imperial Guard left to help stem the invasion, the mutants, Corsair, and Hepzibah joined Kid Omega near the throne. This time, the Kid actually did telekinetically hoist the Phoenix Egg up to the raised dais – not as an imagined ruse on the Psionic Plane, but the real thing – settling it away from Deathbird and her spellbound Remaining.

"I'm still wrapping my head around this," said Corsair, "but it seems we owe you our thanks, kid."

"No thanks required, Big Poppa Summers. I do this for the fans… and my real friends, of course, who should be here soon."

Alex jovially slapped Kid Omega's back. "Great work. Never doubted you for a second. How did you manage it all when you seemed to be incapacitated by the Phoenix? You were sweating and down for the count. You must have leveled up in the last hour or so. Unless…"

Quentin sheepishly scratched his head.

"Well, about that. I'll admit that I couldn't fight the Phoenix and trap Deathbird at the same time, so I called in a favor from a frenemy. Oracle of the Shi'ar Imperial Guard has been ably entertaining our pushy cosmic nuisance for the last half-hour, keeping it from burning a hole through my cerebellum. Without her able distraction, there was no way I could've focused long enough to construct an Omega Room of that magnitude, contain Deathbird and her goons, and take them off the board.

Assuming she can keep the Phoenix off my back, I can maintain the construct long enough for me to upload it to her mind – like transferring a psychic file to a cloud storage space inside her noggin – or for Deathbird to get a much-justified public execution."

Alex shook his head and looked to his father for confirmation.

"No, I don't think we'll let that happen. Hopefully, the Shi'ar will find a secure prison large enough to hold them all for good. I'm fine with Deathbird languishing in chains for the rest of her days. Despite what I may have believed in the past, I don't think we have the right to take her life. Any life."

Corsair smiled at his son. "Me too. But I don't get why we didn't do this right away, the moment Deathbird arrived on Chandilar."

"Because," Kid Omega patiently explained, like a parent to a child who refuses to learn, "you flamboyant, strategic luddite… I needed to wait until Glob and the others were clear. I knew they were aboard her ship, managing to snatch that piece of information from Delphos' head once she removed her helmet, but I didn't know what sort of failsafes Deathbird was employing that might put them in harm's way. The second she ordered their release, I plucked all The Remaining's vulnerable minds and dropped them into my Omega Room… after which I let the program run. Unless a minder with powers greater than mine comes along, or Oracle decides to let them free, the simulation will run until they're old and useless. Like you, Havok."

"And Delphos," Havok asked, ignoring the jibe, "you said that she was the lone exception. That she wasn't trapped in the Omega Room with Deathbird and the others?"

A malicious grin touched Kid Omega's lips.

"You may have abandoned your need for vengeance – unusual for a guy who leads a team of 'avengers,' by the way – but no one, and I mean nobody, gets one over on the Kid. Little Miss Minder Wannabe played with the fire. And now, she's having private time with Oracle inside a special VIP room the two of us built with just the absolute greatest psionic speakers. They're the best – ah-uh – around. Nothing's gonna ever keep them quiet. So, for the time being, or until the Shi'ar decide on a different fate, the only thing Delphos will be seeing in her foreseeable future is the next track cycle as the Best of the Eighties spins on repeat. Rick Astley. Bobby McFerrin. Starship and Falco. Y'know, all the classic, terrible earworms."

Alex smiled again. "You asked for help."

"Ugh. It's because of you, all right? I learned it by watching you."

"I'm proud of you, Kid."

The Omega rolled his eyes. "Let's not hug this out, OK? My real friends are gonna be here soon, and I've got a reputation to maintain."

"Fine by me," agreed Corsair, checking his blaster. "We've still got a rebellion to quash, and I've been away from my ship for too long. Hey, junior," he asked Blink, "can you get me and the Cat Lady back aboard the 'Jammer?"

Clarice nodded. "You got it. I'll come too. We're on our way, Grandpa."

Corsair winced. "Ouch. I deserved that."

Havok glanced at the Phoenix Egg. "Will that be safe? Maybe we should–"

"Relax." Kid Omega held up his hands, as if to placate his

concerned partner. "I'll stay and keep an eye on Deathbird and the Egg. Glob and the others are on their way, and I can pitch in from here, if needed. But something tells me Gladiator and the others have it covered."

The sounds of battle continued to rock the tower. Outside, the Superguardians had finally engaged the warships, gracefully zipping through the crisscrossing array of Shi'ar fighters, doing their best to bring down Deathbird's dreadnoughts while protecting the city below. The Starjammer strafed them with its ventral guns, Raza no doubt handling the turrets and cannons in Hepzibah's absence, while Ch'od ably evaded return fire, serpentining through a web of colorful, glistening beams and pockets of sporadic explosions.

"Let's go," whined Corsair, impatiently snapping his fingers. "We're missing all the fun."

Blink shared an annoyed glance with an understanding Kid Omega. She opened her fingers, and pink sparkles circled the air. Longshot, Havok, and the Starjammers prepared to jump… but an ominous noise disrupted Blink's portal: a small quake knocked them off their feet.

Kid Omega looked out the window.

"Uh, guys? I may have misspoken when I said the others had it covered…"

A vast starship decloaked above the tumultuous fray, bearing a gold, stylized mark upon its prow – a grasping hand, the Collector's sigil, the rest of the craft resplendent in crimson. The air crackled, and Taneleer Tivan opened a public hail to all of the ships and the entire planet, to every being on Chandilar in the range of his voice.

"Mutants and pirates," thundered the disappointed voice

of the Collector, "I am here for property that is mine by right! Your allegiances with the Shi'ar matter not to one whose very cells predate three-quarters of this system's moons. Relinquish the Phoenix Egg you have stolen, and perhaps we can barter for your friend, Corsair's debt, and your very lives. I shall await one-quarter rotation of this system's moon before opening fire and sending my acolytes to collect."

The hail ended. The crackling receded.

Outside, Gladiator and several Superguardians swept up toward the new arrival, abandoning the retreating Remaining warships – those in shape to retreat, having sustained damage at the hands of the Imperial Guard – to meet the angry immortal in battle.

"OK, so maybe we need a strategy," Corsair suggested.

Kid Omega winked.

"Strategy? We don' need no flarkin' strategy. We winged it down on Sirius Five, and we're gonna wing it now." Quentin cracked his knuckles and stretched his neck. "Here's a little maneuver I learned from Colossus and Wolverine."

Havok hesitated. "Now, wait a second–"

"Fastball special, baby!" Kid Omega psionically hoisted Alex, spun his would-be mentor around for good luck, and then telekinetically tossed him out the throne room window, maneuvering him through the aerial minefield hanging above the city, sending him on a circuitous collision course with the Collector's craft. Havok screamed as he exited the tower, the dot in his uniform swiftly oscillating – a plentiful amount of ambient energy from Chandilar's atmosphere pumping into his system – as Alex's trajectory brought him closer to his unintended target.

Flashing his pearly whites, the Kid flapped a hand at his shocked companions.

"What're you waiting for? Go after him!"

Blink sighed, opened a portal, and stepped aboard the Starjammer. Longshot and Hepzibah followed her without delay. Corsair hesitated at the entrance and turned back to Kid Omega. A quirky little smile tugged the right corner of Christopher Summers' lips, barely visible beneath his resplendent mustache.

"Nice job, kid. You really did save the day," Corsair said. "But if my son ends up as a stain on the side of that ship, you and me are gonna have words."

"Oh no. Words. My natural enemy."

Corsair laughed out loud, raised his blaster in salute to Kid Omega, and then followed the others. Blink closed the portal, and the Kid was alone with Deathbird and the Phoenix.

He placed a hand on the pulsating Egg.

Despite the noise thundering from outside the tower, Kid Omega could still hear the Phoenix Force somewhere in the recesses of his brain. It begged him to listen, encouraging Quentin to let the Devourer soar. Sighing, the Kid removed his hand and sat on the stairs, drumming his fingers against the tile.

"Not today, darling," he said, finally and reluctantly accepting the decision in his heart. "Maybe soon, depending on how things go. But not today."

Kid Omega looked at Deathbird, blissfully trapped in a daydream of his own making. Part of him hoped she knew what was happening, that Deathbird realized she was a prisoner in his mind. But the part of Kid Omega still learning what it meant to ask for help – to connect with other people and see the value in friendships and mentors – part of him hoped that the happiness she felt was real. She'd foreseen victory, an empire of her own beside her powerful emperor. And that's what the Kid had given her.

"Nice job, kid," Quentin said to himself, mocking Corsair's appreciative-albeit-reluctant thanks. He smiled, shoulders quaking with mirth. His cheeks and heart felt warm.

The Kid looked out the window, watching the others fight off both the Collector and the last of The Remaining.

"Fastball special," he mused. "Heh. Always wanted to try that."

Guarding Deathbird and the Phoenix Egg, Kid Omega sat back, closed his eyes, and waited for his friends.

CHAPTER THIRTY-ONE

[ALEX | THE STARJAMMER | ABOVE CHANDILAR | THE SHI'AR GALAXY]

"…So, I can't stop apologizing, right? And all this time, the Collector's acolytes are trying to plug up this massive hole I made before we get sucked out into the atmosphere. Meanwhile, Kallark and his Imperial buddies are threatening to toss the flying fortress into the sun… I mean, it was a huge mess, Scott. You should've seen it."

Cyclops laughed, his holographic projection casually leaning against the Starjammer's bulkhead as Havok lounged in a jump seat. The ship was empty. Everyone but Alex and Sikorsky had gone down to the city in order to feast and celebrate. The 'Jammer's diagnostician skittered around the bridge, ignoring the Summers men as it made preparations to depart the system. All was quiet as the brothers stole a little time to catch up.

"So, after that," Scott wanted to know, "how did you manage to appease the Collector?"

Grimacing, Alex sat back and scratched his head.

"I mean, getting the Shi'ar to stand down wasn't easy. But between the Guardians' help and a few fast compromises, Taneleer Tivan was able to see the benefits in reaching an agreement rather than letting the situation continue to escalate."

Scott smiled. "You paid him off."

"You catch on fast, big brother. The Empire settled Dad's debt – the throne's thanks for the Starjammers' help in stopping a threat against the Empire. And Longshot agreed to accompany the Collector back to Mojoworld, to have a frank conversation about Mojo bartering 'items' that aren't his to barter in the first place."

"What happened to the Phoenix Egg? Deathbird?"

Alex sat forward and steepled his fingers in his lap.

"Deathbird and her flunkies are still trapped inside Kid Omega's psychic escape room. He's already transferred that instance of the Omega Room to Oracle's mind – don't ask me how it works. I don't even understand cloud computing, so the minder version makes me feel like I'm still using a rotary telephone. In any event, Oracle has them until they can transfer The Remaining's physical bodies to a maximum security prison, guarded by a rotating watch of Superguardians, and then toss away the key. "

"Let's hope Deathbird rots. And the Phoenix? Did the Collector take it back?"

"Yeah. That was a bit trickier. Tivan was adamant that we return the Egg, and Kallark was most agreeable. Both Elder and Majestor felt that the best way to contain the power of the Phoenix Force was to lock it away in one of Tivan's galleries, if not outright destroy it, which I assure you Gladiator was most eager to do. But then…"

Cyclops cocked his head. "But then ... ?"

"Kid Omega reminded everyone in the room that two mutants managed to steal that Egg from one of the Collector's galleries, and maybe Taneleer Tivan's considerable investments in advanced security weren't exactly up to the task in keeping it safe from the wrong hands. To be frank," Alex admitted, "the Kid was right."

"And being Quentin Quire, I'm sure that he let everyone know."

Havok laughed. "Yeah, exactly. But he also reminded everyone that the Collector was holding many sentient beings from a multitude of worlds and systems – some of them, perhaps, without their consent. And if Tivan didn't want those worlds to learn about it and come after their citizens ... worlds like Skrullos and Hala, Spartax, and Earth among countless others ... it might be in the Collector's best interest to let Kid Omega take the Phoenix Egg."

"Wait, wait, wait. So everyone agreed to that? Even Gladiator and the Shi'ar? I mean, the lengths they've gone to destroy it in the past, to leave a nuclear bomb in the hands of a hot-tempered narcissist? Alex!"

"Yeah, I was surprised, too. But the Kid came to an agreement with the Empire. Kallark is quite impressed by Quentin. Maybe because he managed to refuse the call of the Phoenix. Maybe it's his level of power ... and, frankly, also the Kid's deep abiding distrust of humans and most mutants. Whatever the case, Gladiator is reluctantly allowing us to take the Egg to Earth, as long as the X-Men promise to keep it out of the hands of any governing body and under lock and key."

Cyclops seemed taken aback. "Really?"

"Well, there are guidelines. We'll have to let the Avengers know that we have it, for instance. And you can't go anywhere near it."

"Got it. So when you say 'the X-Men can keep it'..."

Alex cleared his throat.

"The X-Men excluding you and Rachel. Kid Omega was clear about that."

Scott folded his arms and shook his head. The transmission distorted as he did. Earth was a long way from Chandilar; somewhere, a celestial anomaly – a comet, sunspots, a passing craft – played havoc with the long-range signal. It reminded Alex of the distance between the brothers and how far from home he truly was. He was anxious to get home, and looked forward to rejoining his comrades at Avengers Mansion.

"Quentin Quire," breathed Scott, notes of disbelief and frustration shaping the name like a curse. "He's never going to change."

"Don't be too certain," Alex replied, rising from his seat. "Sure, the Kid has been difficult, and I'm sure the fact that he saved the day will inflate that Omega-level ego of his. But strictly speaking, this trip did him some good."

"How so?"

"Well, the fact that he didn't crack open that Egg at any point is a huge breakthrough. But on a smaller scale, I think Kid Omega finally grasps the value of working alongside a team. Scott, if you'd heard him talking about Phoebe, Glob, and the others... I believe he's found value in something else. Friendship, I guess. Maybe more."

"Value? Like a transaction."

Alex grinned. "Definitely a start. Value's the best word for the

Kid right now. I don't know that he's ready to love anything, until he learns to love himself."

"And you? Have you learned to love yourself?"

Havok pondered the question.

Long ago, chained beneath Chandilar, Alex Summers had been a different person in a very dark place. But after everything he'd endured alongside Kid Omega and Corsair...

He reached out and placed a hand on Cyclops' shoulder. It went through the hologram, so he took it back and leaned against the opposite bulkhead.

"I'm getting there. This mission was good for me, too. It helped me realize the kind of leader – and maybe even teacher – I want to be. So thanks for giving me the chance to gain that perspective, by dropping this goose chase in my lap. I might be OK at the whole teacher thing, brother mine. And Quentin Quire might even be an OK student."

"Fine. You teach him, then!"

Havok chuckled. "No, thanks. But I'll take what I've learned with him out here and apply it to the work I'm doing with the Avengers. Some days, I'll admit, Earth's Mightiest Heroes can act like overgrown problem children with giant egos. Like a team full of Quentin Quires, without the sarcastic T-shirts and pop culture references. Now, with closure and a little confidence, I might finally be comfortable with calling myself their leader."

Cyclops lightly clapped his hands. "That's great to hear, Alex. So you're OK. Everything that happened with Gabriel... and Dad?"

Havok hung his head, waiting a moment as Sikorsky skittered past, headed for the operations console. Alex drew a breath and looked around the Starjammer's interior. This ship held a lot of memories for Alex Summers – some good, some bad. He could hear its crew coming now, voices filtering from below, ringing with laughter as they approached the bridge. His father, Corsair, was loudest of all, and the sound of his voice triggered earlier memories... of Alex and Scott, listening to their dad bark orders, frightened as they plummeted through the Alaskan sky.

He closed his eyes, fighting back tears.

"I can't say that I'm done worrying about the past. Mom's death and Dad's. My time with the Starjammers, fighting Vulcan and Deathbird... being jailed and tortured alongside my crew. Lorna... all of it is a part of me. It will always be part of me."

Havok looked at his brother. Scott and Alex were light years from one another, staring at each other from across the bridge and cosmos. Despite the distance, however, the Summers men had never been as emotionally close to one another than they were at that moment.

"But I can learn from the past," Havok continued. "And I can use what I've learned as a resource whenever I discover the need. And, you know, I can also use what I've learned from Quentin Quire. When to rush in, when to employ diplomacy–"

"And when to be an absolute train wreck."

"I've been using the word 'tornado.' But sure, that works."

Scott grinned. "Tornado is apt for Quire. Honestly, I still can't believe he actually saved those kids. But then, I partnered him with someone I know excels at saving kids."

Curious, Alex raised an eyebrow. "What do you mean?"

"After Mom... well, when it was just us. The responsibility

I suddenly had thrust upon my shoulders. Taking care of you, I..."

"It's fine. We got through it."

"Yeah. Because of you. I was overwhelmed, worried I was going to make things worse." Scott tried to rub his eyes, possibly to wipe away tears, but remembered that they were tucked beneath a protective mask. He settled instead for rubbing his fingers on his jaw, nervously looking away and out at the city.

"I missed Mom and Dad, and then we were getting separated. Alex, you made things easier. You helped defuse the tension or worry, and you got me through all of that until they split us up and gave you a safe, comfortable home. And... Alex. I've never really said this to you, but you saved me."

"Hey."

Cyclops turned back to his brother. Smiling, Havok held out a hand.

"We saved each other."

Scott returned the smile. He tried to take Alex's hand, but the image distorted again, and it passed right through. He laughed. "Well, we tried. I really should be going."

"Same. I can hear the others coming. Probably time for us to hit the road."

"Is Blink taking you to New York after she teleports Quentin and the others back to Canada? Or do you have time for a quick visit with the X-Men?"

Alex glanced down. The Starjammers were clambering up to the bridge, one by one. Any minute now, they'd be charting a course and prepping to leave.

Corsair was last to arrive. He extricated himself from the ladder, brushed off his uniform, and faced his sons. Noticing

Scott, Christopher Summers waved, and perhaps sensing that his boys needed to finish their conversation, joined his crew at the forward console.

Alex sighed. "You know, I've been thinking about taking my time, actually. I've got a few more days of family leave coming, and rather than have Blink bring me back to New York right away... I believe I'll stay up here for a bit. Take the slow route back to Earth and, uh... find my space legs again? You get the idea."

Scott looked past his brother, at their pirate captain father, who was again peeking at his sons. Corsair reddened and then offered a sharp salute before turning away.

"Yeah, I understand. I'm happy for you, Alex. Happy for you both."

"Me too."

"Take your time. Avenging will be here when you're through."

"Sounds good. Keep the planet safe, and I'll see you back on Earth."

The Summers brothers said goodbye. The transmission winked out.

Havok exhaled, and then stared out the window at Chandilar. The sun was rising on a new day, its light touching the spires and steeples of the capital city.

He looked at the Starjammers. At his friends.

At his father.

Corsair spun around to face his son. Winking, he beckoned him over.

It had been decades since Havok had lost his parents and tumbled with his older brother out of a burning, dying airplane. Since that moment, his every step had led him down a winding series of highs and lows. He'd been a student, hero, leader, failure, and now both a teacher and leader once again. He'd traveled through flames and across the stars. And he'd regained many things he'd lost along the way. His brother. His father. His self-esteem.

Nodding to the others, he joined Corsair at the helm. Standing on the Starjammer's bridge, having helped save a galaxy alongside a diverse group of gifted individuals – friends who may be hated and feared by many beings throughout the universe – and reunited with his own father... though Havok's place on Earth was light years away...

...Alex Summers truly felt as if he were home.

CHAPTER THIRTY-TWO

[QUENTIN | THE TOWER OF SHARRA AND K'YTHRI | CHANDILAR | THE SHI'AR GALAXY]

The Great Eastern Balcony overlooked Chandilar's sprawling starport and its vast industrial sector. Below, a shimmering network of airborne traffic spread above the city in perpendicular lines. On the balcony, a smattering of dignitaries and politicians mingled and toasted, ignoring the beautiful vista while congratulating one another on whatever meager part they felt they'd played in diverting this latest threat to their galaxy.

Nearby, basking in the light of the setting suns, Kid Omega dangled his feet off the edge of a parapet, sipping something white and bubbly from a tall, cool glass. With his chair thrust back on its rear legs, his jacket casually draped over the back, the Kid considered the events of the last week, soaking in both the sunlight and view. Phoebe Cuckoo sat at a small table to his left, blonde bobbed head resting on her palm, fighting off a yawn while toying with a fizzing, sparkly soft drink. She smiled at Kid Omega through half-lidded eyes, as the table's second occupant once again interrogated him for details.

"I still don't get it," wondered Glob Herman, the Kid's best friend. "They're just giving it to you? After everyone and their mother spent all this time chasing the Phoenix... and knowing what happened on Earth with Mister Summers and Miss Frost and all the punching and whatnot... they gave you a Phoenix Egg?"

Kid Omega smiled around his straw. A luxurious, indulgent grin tugged the corners of his thin, moist lips. "Seems to be the case, Glob."

"But, why? They gotta know it's asking for trouble. I mean... it's you! No offense, Q. And us! And Cyclops, who never met a Phoenix he didn't wanna marry!"

The Kid laughed, but it was Phoebe who answered in her calm, blunt manner.

"Maybe that's what the Shi'ar want. If the Phoenix is released on Earth, it gives Gladiator an excuse to attack the planet."

"Oh." Glob furrowed his pink, waxy brow. Beneath bulky, transparent skin, the Kid could see the effect that had on his pal's visible skull, on display inside the bigger boy's hulking, see-through body; the bone creased, and his muscles tightened. It was a fascinating effect that drew the attention of nearby politicians. The mutant youths ignored them. Glob was used to stares and insults, and had long ago put it behind him as the facts of his daily life. He'd accepted himself for who he was, and though Kid Omega's initial reaction was to admonish the Shi'ar lookie-loos, Glob's friends had learned to follow his lead and let it go.

"But if that's what the Shi'ar want, how come the teachers are OK with–"

Phoebe placed a calming hand on Glob's forearm.

"Kid Omega worked it out. It'll be fine."

The Kid nodded at Phoebe, silently thanking her for the unnecessary intervention. He could have thanked her telepathically – Phoebe was a gifted minder, too, like her identical sisters on Earth – but in this case neither words or thoughts were needed. They got each other, for some reason, even though the Stepford Cuckoos originally hated Quentin's guts.

A lot of people had hated his guts. But then he went and saved the universe.

So things were looking up.

Kid Omega set his drink aside. Lacing his hands behind his head, he craned his neck toward his friends. "Phoebe's right. Kallark and I worked it out. And our deal? Goals. I know the Shi'ar's motives are suspicious, 'cause every pairing of Earth and Phoenix has ended in fire and blood. But this time, the way I laid it out for Gladiator... I'm telling you, it hits different."

Glob nodded. "OK. You always know what you're doing, Q."

The Kid winked and turned back to the view. "Until I don't."

Did he know what he was doing? To his right, cradled in a psionic strongbox constructed in tandem with Oracle and the Collector – who'd provided schematics to copy, ideated from containment devices he'd gathered over the years – waited the Phoenix Egg. The minders had managed to soundproof the bolted telepathic enclosure, creating a tangible instance of Quentin's Omega Room locked with a psychic key, tucked away in the recesses of a random mutant mind. There was little chance that anyone was going to break it open.

But then, Kid Omega wasn't just anyone.

One day, he knew that when he felt strong enough to achieve

the next, inevitable stage of his mutant evolution and host the Phoenix…

…the Kid would be ready.

Truthfully, Quentin thought to himself, he might entertain several options even before that happened. This week had proved to himself, Havok, and many other naysayers that when he put his brain to it, no one in their right mind could best Kid Omega. Sure, he could leap through Blink's portal and bring the Phoenix to Earth. He could return to Scott Summers' Prison School for Mutant Sheep in the Canadian badlands and be the good little soldier and rebel sporadically.

Or he could take the Egg, grab Phoebe, Glob and the others, and jump the next starliner for planets unknown. Like the Starjammers, they could be Mutants Without Infinite Borders and travel the galaxy kicking dinkwafts and taking names. Rocket and Quill could source them a ship of their own, and they'd be intergalactic mutant pirates, spreading the cause of Homo sapiens superior to distant worlds. Together, they might become Protectors of the Phoenix, charged to guard the most destructive force in the universe from those who would exploit it for their own selfish reasons.

That is, until the Kid could no longer avoid the Phoenix's soft whispers in his mind despite considerable psychic defenses, and inevitably exploited it for his own selfish reasons, no matter the cost to him, his friends, or the universe.

No, he decided. Earth was probably best.

Sure, the X-Men were a pain in his own finely sculpted dinkwaft, and he hated the imbalance of power that existed between human and mutantkind. But at least now, should that imbalance tip the wrong way and some conservative politician or country with an armful of Sentinels rear his or her small-minded head...

...well, now mutants had an advantage, right?

He patted the Phoenix Egg, the ultimate memento to commemorate his space adventures, like the souvenirs Hijack, Ayo, No-Girl, and Blink were searching for down in the city markets.

And if the Kid eventually did have to release the Phoenix, there would be someone to stop him should it slip his control. The X-Men. The Avengers. And, of course, the Shi'ar.

Kid Omega still couldn't believe they'd gone for his idea.

Quentin had convinced Tivan that the Phoenix Egg would be no safer in his hands than it would anywhere else, and had low-key threatened him with squealing to the Galactic Council about their stolen, collected people if the Collector didn't drop it like a bad piece of fish. Heck of a bluff, but it worked. But still, there was the matter on what to do with the Egg.

Kid Omega had approached Kallark an hour ago during the impromptu victory celebration, which manifested as the Superguardians put their city back in order. While the Imperial Guardsmen did the heavy lifting and fifty different senators and generals deliberated about Chandilar's defenses in the aftermath, someone – Corsair, or one of the other Starjammers? – located a bottle of M'kraan CristalTM, and Fang offered up a crate of Xandarian ale he'd been saving for... well, nothing; he just hadn't gotten around to drinking it yet. Peter Quill reluctantly handed over the last of the Guardians' Elder berries for delicious smoothies. Eventually, food and music appeared, and a shindig sprang to life on the Eastern

Balcony, a lavish terrace down the hall and to the left of Gladiator's throne room.

Kallark had been dividing his time between mingling with senators and coordinating a reorchestration of the planet's defenses. As he did, the Kid had navigated a cluster of generals and sycophants to get Gladiator's attention.

"How may I be of service," he'd asked Quentin, who'd tapped the Majestor on the shoulder, "to the X-Man who saved our galaxy?"

The Kid had blushed, nearly turning as purple as the Strontian.

"Gladiator," Quentin had asked, "can we talk about the Phoenix Egg?"

A tight smile had formed on the Majestor's lips. "Yes, I know. After the Collector's departure, and with the madness involved in caging Deathbird and the traitors, allocating resources toward impounding their craft and rebuilding our defenses, I realize that we have ignored decisions regarding the more dangerous threat."

Quentin had nodded in reply. "So, what're you thinking? Because I have a–"

"Naturally, the Egg will remain on Chandilar until the Galactic Council can discover a way to eliminate the Phoenix for good."

The Kid's jaw had fallen agape. "You're kidding, right?"

A smile cracked Kallark's stoic expression.

"Am I known for my sense of humor, friend Omega?"

"But you can't be serious. The Phoenix is a part of the cosmic machine! Would you kill a sun? Or murder hope? That hungry parasite might be dangerous, but it's a primal force of nature. Destroying it may upset the balance of creation!"

Kallark had taken a calming breath. "Perhaps so. But those questions will be deliberated by the galactic community. Together we shall arrive at a decision regarding the fate of the Phoenix. Until then, it will be contained and guarded on Chandilar."

"But your defenses need an overhaul. Who's gonna keep it secure once the Kid is gone and Blastaar or some resurrected, vengeful ginger mutant comes looking for that Egg? It's happened before. It'll happen again."

"Oracle will–"

"Yeah, she's bae. And I'll admit she picked up on the whole Omega Room of it all … but I taught her everything she knows. And let me tell you: I didn't teach her everything I know. You may keep it safe for a while, but one day – maybe as soon as Deathbird figures out how to escape whatever birdcage you use to jail her – that Egg is gonna feel more like a burden than a prize. That's when cracks will appear in the minds of your Superguardians. Trust me, Gladiator. If that happens, none of you are safe. When that day comes, you're gonna wish it was somewhere else."

Visibly disturbed, Kallark had clasped his hands behind his back. "More the reason why it should be destroyed."

"It can't be destroyed, don't you get it? The Phoenix won't let that happen. You can try – you've tried before – but that nightmare sparrow out there, whining and whispering inside its candy-coated shell, is a force of nature. It's part of the fabric of eternity. And as powerful as you may be, you and your Imperial super happy pals don't have the strength or space cojones to take out the queen."

"And you do? Earth does?"

"Flark, no! The Phoenix Force has been a part of reality since the Big Bang. And it will be here to burn down the last atoms when the universe closes shop. Trust me, I know. I hosted it, remember? I've been inside the White Hot Room, and I can tell you that even if you destroy this Egg, the Phoenix will return. Like a persistent, burning cockroach. Your only hope, Gladiator, is to contain it as best you can."

"Which is what I plan to do."

Quentin had shaken his head. "All that's going to happen is the Phoenix will either overpower your minds and find release, or someone will steal it from you, and it will overpower that being's mind. Ultimately, the only one who can really understand how to contain the Phoenix is one it knows intimately. A host who's already been singed by its flames and has managed to maintain their sanity. Someone with the strength of mind to ensure that the cosmic vampire that is the Phoenix doesn't get invited inside when it raps against their mental window."

"Someone like you."

"Well," the Kid had replied, shrugging his wiry shoulders, "I have proven to an entire galaxy now that if anyone has the will, it's me."

Gladiator smirked. "You needed Oracle's help to fight it off."

"Only because I was multitasking, your Majestorness. And I'll have help on Earth. The Cuckoos, other telepaths I know and trust."

Kallark had shaken his head. "Earth is too volatile. You know what happened the last time the Phoenix manifested on your world, and there is still a member of the Grey bloodline there for it to corrupt… to say nothing of your X-Men leaders. If you are to guard the Phoenix, you must do so on Chandilar."

"While living in bird paradise, drinking alien smoothies, and dashing about in hover cars does sound appealing, I have friends on Earth who need me. Mutants who need me. And as far as my 'X-Men leaders' go," Quentin had promised, tapping his skull to indicate the power of the Omega Room, "I'm happy to cage any of them who even consider looking at the Phoenix with flames in their greedy eyes. Well, 'eye' in Cyclops' case. If the Egg stays here, it will offer temptation to invaders like Deathbird, who believe they can take it with the right plan, Kid or no Kid. Earth, meanwhile, has repelled countless invaders – even the Shi'ar! You gotta admit your track record in that area isn't impeccable. Look, I'm an Earther. I belong on Earth. You wouldn't ask a Chandilar native to uproot themselves, would you?

"Give me the Egg," Kid Omega had politely repeated. "I can keep it safe from harm. I'll contain it, as I have. Should the Galactic Council find a way to end it without upsetting the balance of creation, you'll know where to find it. And if it gets out or I'm killed, or the Earth is infected by zombies and we get a zombie Phoenix host, you'll know where to find it. If any of those things do happen, then Earth is ground zero for a cosmic extinction event, not Chandilar or the Empire. Win-win?"

Kallark had glanced around, either looking for someone to support his arguments or absolve him of the decision he was about to make. Kid Omega had pounced, going in for the kill.

"Trust me. If I need help, I've got your digits here," he'd said, tapping his head once again. "I'll be your Superguardian on Earth, and make sure no mutant, superhero, villain, or Earther ever hatches this thing. If they try? I will lock. Them. Up."

Kallark had reiterated his concerns. "Scott Summers and the

last Grey. You will ensure their non-interference? I have your vow?"

"And you have my axe. They get a lifetime restraining order. If either get too close, I'll Room them and send up an intergalactic flare. I swear, this thing is never getting out unless I want it to. Y'know why? I'm the Omega, and I'm the best – ah-uh – around. Give me the Egg. Let me take it to Earth and guard it as I would my irreplaceable collection of Simon Williams memorabilia. I vow to you, Majestor. You have nothing to fear with the Omega on point."

Well, Quentin had thought, that wasn't completely true. Eventually, when he was ready, the Kid would absolutely let it out. But until then, he'd keep watch. The less Gladiator knew about his sneaky Bugs Bunny-esque stinker-like ulterior motives, the better. The Kid had stuck out his hand to the Shi'ar emperor... and after a moment, incredibly, Kallark had accepted it.

Now, hours later, Kid Omega was sitting on the balcony and waiting for his ride home, the Phoenix Egg chained and secured under multiple layers of psionic protection.

He'd pulled it off. Not only had he managed to convince everyone that he – Quentin Quire – was best suited to guard a psychotic cosmic star-devouring buzzard... but that the best place to keep it safe was on Earth, home of nuclear bombs, gamma radiation, TikTok, reality shows, and the McRib. Sure, he probably could've stayed on Chandilar, using the Omega Room to stay connected with his pals on Earth. But Kallark didn't know that. And Earth did have the best hamburgers.

Also? He'd low-key just gained the Shi'ar Empire's support in moving aside the Kid's few obstacles in terms of who became the next Phoenix host. Sure, he might have to fight off a few dictators and supervillains to safeguard the Egg. But here's the thing: the X-Men, Avengers, and the other well-meaning mystics and telepaths would help him keep it safe. And all the while, Kid Omega would secretly work on ways to prepare and ready himself to safely open the Egg and assume the mantle.

Elegant? It was sheer brilliance. Quentin congratulated himself as he peered off the Great Eastern Balcony, looking down at a city that absolutely loved Kid Omega.

He also kinda had to thank Havok. Because of Alex, Quentin had learned to not only use the past for good, but weaponize it for his own malicious intent – which he'd successfully done with Gladiator. He'd learned diplomacy, yup, but also figured out how to deploy it in the pursuit of his true brilliant motivations. Not to mention, if it weren't for Havok the Kid wouldn't have hooked up with his new valuable space pals in the Shi'ar Galaxy and aboard the Starjammer... pals that Quentin might need one day. So thanks, Alex Summers. In the end, you were good for something...

OK, fine. Sure. Maybe the Kid could admit that Alex was good for more than just being a means to an end. Originally, Quentin believed Havok was an inferior Cyclops copy. A milquetoast cipher of a mutant, with little to offer apart from the power to destroy.

But this last week, while facing incredible odds together, Quentin had to admit he'd grown to maybe, sort of... like the guy. Maybe not as a leader, but as a...

Ugh. Fine! As a friend. Happy, universe? Havok and Kid Omega were f – (argh!!) – they were friends.

Which was rare for Kid Omega, who only had so many of those to go around.

Musing about that, Quentin became aware that Phoebe was staring at him. Raising an eyebrow, he turned her way. "What?"

"You were smiling," she replied. "What were you thinking about?"

Blushing, he got up and grabbed his jacket.

"Nothing important. The value of relationships and how, in true Kid Omega fashion, I've managed to balance them with chaos."

He reached down and booped her nose. Annoyed, she batted away his hand and Glob laughed, a booming chortle that vibrated his shiny skin.

"You know," Quentin said, "just to make life interesting. Now, c'mon. Let's go home. To me, my Mutants Without Borders. Classes begin again tomorrow, and I may need help with the first lesson."

"Help? Since when does Kid Omega need help?"

The Kid grinned. "What can I say? I'm learning."

He looked up at the sky, to the stars beyond.

"But then, I had an adequate teacher."

EPILOGUE

Thirty teenagers settled into plush sofas and stylish chairs, lounging around the vastly remodeled Omega Room.

Aside from the color, sounds, and smells, the Kid had completely redesigned the space, given it the air of a well-funded start-up. The aisles were wide, and the room included ping-pong, foosball, video games, nap pods, and a library. Quentin lounged at the front, sitting with his legs crisscrossed on a desk, splayed before a large psionic smart board branded with the "MWB" logo. He still wore his gray jacket but was dressed down in jeans and sneakers, a white tee proudly displaying the words "...AND ALL I GOT WAS THIS AWESOME T-SHIRT."

Quentin had retooled the Mutants Without Borders into a psionic after-school club, rather than an institute of its own. He was too busy guarding the Phoenix Egg now – and hatching plots – to become a full-time headmaster. For now, his friends met Mondays and Wednesdays at six, and tonight, for the second gathering, he regaled the assembled students with his space adventures. The kids were rapt with attention. Phoebe,

Glob, and the others chimed in when necessary, but for the most part it was a Kid Omega highlight reel.

"Where's the Phoenix Egg now?" asked one of the intrigued students. "Can we see it?"

The Kid smiled. "I'm keeping it secret and safe," he said with a wink.

The assembled students buzzed with jealousy and excitement, questioning the five who'd been kidnapped, peppering them with questions.

A curious girl asked, "Weren't you scared? I mean, it is space."

"Scared? Not for a flarking second. In fact–"

Quentin was interrupted by a pointed cough. Kid Omega sighed.

"OK, maybe a little. But space is big and dangerous. Thankfully, for this second salon, I've generously sourced a guest speaker... someone who can tell you everything that you need to know in order to survive the experience. He's a mutant I'm cool with saying – in, like, a disaffected way, not as an advocate for authority or anything like that – basically, what you must know about our complicated relationship is..."

The cough again. Kid Omega rolled his eyes and gave up.

"Fine. He's my friend, I guess. I mean, without using labels or anyth–"

"Thank you, Kid Omega."

Reluctantly grinning, Quentin hopped off the desk and made room for Alex Summers, psionically beamed into the Omega Room from aboard the Starjammer's bridge, which according to Havok was now passing New Xandar en route to Hala.

Havok and the Kid clasped hands, and then Quentin acceded the floor.

"Hello, Mutants Without Borders. My name is Havok. I'm an Avenger, an X-Man, and a Starjammer. I'm here to teach you a little something about your place in the vast intergalactic community. I appreciate you giving me your time and attention.

"So," he began, winking at Kid Omega, "let's get started."

ABOUT THE AUTHOR

NEIL KLEID co-authored the acclaimed graphic novels *Brownsville, The Big Kahn* and *The Panic*. He has written for nearly every publisher in the comic book industry. With the late Alex Nino, he adapted Jack London's novel *The Call of the Wild* into comics for Penguin Books; did the opposite for the prose adaptation of the seminal Marvel Comics storyline *Spider-Man: Kraven's Last Hunt*; and co-authored (with Brian Michael Bendis) *Powers: The Secret History of Deena Pilgrim* for MacMillan Books, an original novel based on the award-winning comic book. With John Broglia, he co-authored *Savor* for Dark Horse Comics, and for Aconyte Books he wrote "Kid Omega Faces the Music," included in the *School of X* anthology, which was nominated for Best Short Story in the 2022 Scribe Awards. Though Neil lives in Teaneck, New Jersey with his wife, kids, dog, and grill, he has always considered himself a mutant without borders.

twitter.com/neilkleid

MUTANT HEROES
INCREDIBLE EXPLOITS

EPIC SUPER POWERS
AMAZING AVENTURES

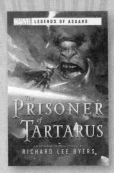